DAVE HUNT

HARVEST HOUSE PUBLISHERS
Eugene, Oregon 97402

The author's free monthly newsletter
may be received by request. Write to:

Dave Hunt
P.O. Box 7019
Bend, OR 97708

SANCTUARY OF THE CHOSEN

Published by Harvest House Publishers
Eugene, Oregon 97402

Library of Congress Cataloging-in-Publication Data

Hunt, Dave.
Sanctuary of the chosen / Dave Hunt.
Sequel to: The Archon conspiracy.
ISBN 0-89081-852-5
I. Title
PS3558.U46765S26 1992 91-120-82
813′.54—dc20 CIP
r91

Printed in the United States of America.

To my wife, Ruth,
who is my editor, faithful critic, and best friend,
and who tirelessly and efficiently accomplishes
a thousand other tasks so that I can write.

1

Betrayed!

LEIPZIG, EAST GERMANY—
late April, 1964

From the depths of Ari's hypnotic slumber the harsh ringing of the phone sounded, distant and muffled. Still it continued, with unrelenting insistence, growing nearer and louder. The dissonant, repetitive jangling seemed at first to be a part of the peculiarly familiar nightmare. As always, he was being pursued. Spectral figures, armed men in dark suits—one of whom he instinctively recognized but could never identify—leaped incessantly into the path of his flight from the shadowy recesses of his brain until at last he was surrounded with nowhere to turn.

From somewhere an alarm began clanging. As it continued and grew louder, the specters multiplied to become a demonlike horde with hideous, menacing expressions and powerful arms reaching out to seize him. There was the disturbing certainty that he'd been through all of this before—a certainty which made the experience as much one of bewilderment as of terror. Why must he relive it again and again? The answer to that haunting question always eluded him.

Now, in horrifying slow motion, like a panic-stricken diver, with lungs bursting, straining to reach the surface, Ari fought his way back to a groggy semiconsciousness. *The phone*...! At last the realization broke through that the jarring noise was coming from a familiar source. Groping for the instrument beside his bed, he knocked it to the floor, groped again, then finally got a grip on the receiver. Tonight, of all nights, when he needed sleep so desperately!

"Hello...?"

"I must speak to Fritz."

"Fritz...?"

"I'm calling from Berlin for Fritz! It's urgent!"

"There's no *Fritz* here. What number...?"

There was an abrupt click and the line went dead. Ari slammed the receiver down in disgust and turned on a light to glance at his wristwatch: 10:04 P.M. Two hours of sleep... so far. Somehow he must make up for the almost total lack of rest during the past forty-eight hours. There couldn't be any more interruptions. He reached over to take the receiver off—then froze.

"Fritz?" The name triggered an instinctive reaction that propelled him out of bed. For a brief moment he stood uncertainly. His stance bespoke the instant and cat-like wariness of the hunter—or the hunted. Trying to collect his thoughts, Ari ran his fingers through the thick, unruly black hair that hung disheveled over the wide expanse of his forehead. The tightness here and there in his pajamas betrayed the broad shoulders, thick chest and powerful thighs on a 5′10″ frame that gave him more the appearance of an NFL halfback than of a German intellectual.

"For Fritz... from Berlin!" he muttered aloud, his memory suddenly jolted. No, it couldn't be... but it *had* to be. No wonder the voice had sounded tense. It wasn't a wrong number! How long ago had they planned this warning—hoping never to use it? Two years?

In rapid procession the vivid pictures flashed before him. A peaceful, almost too orderly, student protest at Leipzig's university that had spilled out into the city streets. Jubilant that they had at last found the courage to *do* something, the marchers, nearly 500 strong and their ranks gradually swelling, were shouting loudly in unison, "Truth and honesty—free elections... truth and honesty—free elections...." How naive they'd been!

He'd been right in the front, one of the half-dozen determined organizers, an 18 year-old idealist who had become the sworn enemy of the Marxism he'd been raised on and had once believed in. Handpicked by the East German regime at the age of ten, Ari had been taken from his tiny village school and transported each day with a dozen other exceptionally bright students to a special science academy in the nearby town of Wittenberg, where he had spent seven years prior to entering university. That was how he'd seen with his own eyes, and tasted the delicacies of, the luxurious lifestyle of Party, leaders and how his disillusionment had begun.

At first, overwhelmed by the great honor and flattered by the heady promises that made him so *special*, Ari had succumbed to the seductive elitism which the program bred. Eventually, however, he had come to see—and to despise—the detestable favoritism that spawned the shameful corruption he experienced everywhere at the upper levels in the East German regime. It did not take him long to realize that such corruption was the inevitable result of totalitarian Marxism.

Nor did it take long for Ari to realize that one could fall from the regime's good graces very abruptly and for the most mysterious reasons. The East German Ministry for State Security had its informants everywhere. The secret tentacles of the Stasi reached even into the school classrooms and the home itself, where students and family members spied upon one another. Survival depended upon never saying anything the least bit derogatory about the government—and being careful not to praise it too highly as well—even to friends and family. The despicable system deliberately destroyed normal trust and made close and confidential relationships priceless—and rare.

With the passing years Ari's hatred for all things Marxist had become a passion. The protest at Leipzig University had been the culmination of a frustration and anger that had boiled within until it had to find release. He'd known it would cost him everything. He'd reached the breaking point, however, where he was willing to pay that price. It had been his moment of madness.

Now, in that brief hesitancy of indecision, standing beside the bed, he saw it all again—the horror he had relived countless times. Suddenly the police! Hundreds of them, charging head-on, hit the front of that peaceful march like vultures attacking and tearing dead meat apart. Cold, derisive faces leered from behind heavy, full-face Plexiglas visors. Long clubs were swinging, splitting heads with a sharp cracking sound that was still nauseous to remember. Out of the corner of his eye he saw it coming and ducked—a reflex action from his years of training and competition in the martial arts. He grabbed the baton and jammed it into the startled officer's midsection. With a grunt of satisfaction he saw the man's eyes bulge out and glaze over as he dropped to the pavement.

Something had snapped inside of him at the terrible sight of police beating unarmed students and the sudden, swelling sound of screams of terror and pain. Baton now in hand, he had whirled to do battle with two policemen rushing upon him, when suddenly something totally unexpected occurred—something he could not explain. Someone with unusual strength, whom he hadn't seen, had grabbed his arm in a viselike grip and irresistibly propelled him through the blur of bloodied heads, flailing arms, and falling bodies. There the memory went blank, beginning again as he found himself running all alone down a side street, the burning odor of tear gas and the horrible sounds of mayhem fading behind him.

In the ensuing days and weeks a reign of terror settled upon the university. Even students with no tangible connection to the uprising disappeared, swallowed up by an evil system that had to make certain that such a demonstration never happened again. Ari waited apprehensively for the inevitable arrest. It didn't come. Had someone of influence, strategically placed, been protecting him? That seemed the only rational explanation. But who? And why? He finally decided he'd been chosen by fate to carry on this fight against corruption. That was when he had sworn with all the idealism and belligerence of youth that he would never rest until East Germany's Marxist regime had been destroyed—or it had destroyed him.

From that time on there was no turning back. Their country was called the German *Democratic* Republic, but the people had no voice. *One day they would!* That determination became his driving passion—to lead an uprising of students that would succeed in overthrowing the hated regime. This time they would lay a careful foundation and make no move until they were strong enough to prevail.

At 19 years of age, with four trusted friends assisting him, Ari had secretly begun to build an organization that eventually stretched across East Germany. Working cautiously, they had uncovered an astonishing number of closet dissidents impatient to vent their simmering rage. Here was an eager revolutionary army that only needed competent and inspiring leadership for its explosive energies to be molded into a cohesive and irresistible force.

Ari had carefully structured the organization so that no one except himself knew more than a small fraction of the picture. Tight controls prevailed at every level. There would be no false start, no move until the moment was ripe. The next time they marched there would be hundreds of thousands in the streets. Their oppressors would be overwhelmed with sheer numbers. So he had thought.

After two years of meticulous planning, a nationwide student demonstration tied to a massive workers' strike had been set for the following week. The intensified preparation had left little time for sleep. Ari had been working feverishly day and night. And now this shattering phone call on the very eve of success! The coded warning they'd agreed upon included several levels of alarm. The key word, *Fritz,* signaled the worst possible scenario—that they had been infiltrated and betrayed. No questions. No explanations. Underground—everyone—on the instant.

Ari's mind was racing now. *The Stasi is on to us! Arrest! Torture! Get out of here! Don't panic! Think, man, think!*

Turning off the light, Ari groped his way to the window. Cautiously drawing the faded drape aside just enough to peer out, he searched the dimly lit street six floors below. It was deserted as far as he could see in both directions. He would have to work in semidarkness. The dread Stasi could arrive at any moment. They must not suspect that he knew they were after him. *Make it look like I've left earlier—not like I've fled in panic. That might buy some time, confuse, throw them off the scent.*

He threw the drapes open wide to let in the muted light that came more from the full moon than from the street below. In the half-darkness he dressed quickly, then with trembling fingers gathered the incriminating papers he had been working on and stuffed them back into his briefcase. *It's got to look tidy... no sign of haste.* Quickly, yet precisely, making the bed, he remembered the Luger on the night stand next to the phone and tucked it into his belt. He would not go like a lamb to the slaughter.

Closing the textbooks on his desk, Ari stacked them neatly, and the school papers beside them. *I wasn't ready for that exam anyway.* The thought brought a momentary smile, then an overwhelming sadness, followed by anger. *Another month and I would have graduated... with highest honors.* It was an irony he couldn't ignore, though he was not one to boast of his talents.

The reasons for his modesty went beyond common sense and good taste. He had tried to keep a low profile in spite of his outstanding academic record.

Pretending a profound loyalty to the Communist Party, he had professed little ambition beyond one day becoming a subservient physicist who posed no threat to Party leaders and policies. Now they knew the truth. *We were so close!* He couldn't stay here hoping for the same luck he'd had last time. If they didn't already know that he was directing the conspiracy, they soon would have enough information to make that deduction. No one could stand up to their torture.

The phone began ringing again. He turned toward it, then stopped and shook his head. If he answered it and *they* were monitoring his line, they'd know he was here. He could only hope they hadn't caught the brief call that had awakened him. What if it were Hans, or Wolfgang, or Karl... wondering if he'd heard, wanting to discuss their escape? No, they knew better than that. It was every man for himself, scattering and hiding as best they could, with absolutely no contact between them. But suppose it was Berlin telling him there had been a mistake, that it was a false alarm? He wouldn't believe them. Not now.

Whoever was calling seemed certain that he was there. The persuasive ringing continued. Ari reached out his hand.

No! He dare not lift the receiver. But what if...? There were a thousand possibilities. It was more than curiosity that gripped him. The call was obviously urgent. It could be the difference between life and death... for him or someone else. No, it wasn't *obviously* anything.

Forcing himself with great effort to turn away, Ari went quickly back to the worn briefcase resting on the floor beside the small desk. With its precious burden that he carried everywhere, it had become a part of him. Now he hurriedly stuffed into it an extra shirt, a pair of sox, sweater, change of underwear... and a box of ammo for the Luger. Silence—except for the pounding of his heart. The phone had stopped ringing and he hadn't noticed when.

Getting into a warm jacket, he stumbled back to the window and peered out once again. Two cars were just rounding the corner to his left. In frozen fascination he watched as they pulled over to the curb six floors below and a half-dozen men in plain clothes hurried into the building. *The Stasi! I'm cut off from the stairs and elevator!*

In desperation he used up precious seconds for the last task. Feeling around inside the small closet, he lined up the two pairs of shoes he was leaving behind and pulled the suitcase and tennis racket out from under the clothes into plainer view, then hastily hung the crumpled shirts and pants that had been thrown over a chair. *Make it look like I've just gone for a day or two, like I'll be back any moment... so maybe they won't be scouring the country for me.*

He seemed to be detached from reality, observing himself almost clinically from a distance. Clutching the briefcase, a soft, billed cap on his head, he was in the bathroom now and couldn't remember how he'd gotten there. Through the surrealistic fog that seemed to envelop him, he heard the phone start up again—then loud pounding on the main door to the hallway, and the dread command, *"Polizei! Öffnen Sie die Tür!"*

Sweat oozed from under his cap. With a herculean act of the will Ari went through the motions that, thankfully, he had forced himself to rehearse several times, "just in case." The rush of cold air on his face as he opened the window sharpened his focus. Carefully he dropped the briefcase the few feet onto the steep slate roof to the rear of the apartment building. It tipped onto its side and slid briefly, with a loud, grating noise, until it was stopped by the low barrier he had placed there for that purpose. Hoisting himself quickly through the small opening, he slid down to crouch momentarily beside his precious burden. As he reached up to close the window behind him, he could still hear the pounding and yelling—then a loud splintering of wood and a crash as the dead bolt was ripped through the door jamb.

It had been raining, making the moss-covered roof treacherously slippery. One misstep and it would be his last. Thankfully, the full moon had come out again from behind the clouds and he could see well enough to slip and slide as though he were skiing at a steep angle across an icy slope, digging in the edges of his tennis shoes. At last a dangerous leap across open space landed him onto the flat roof of an adjoining apartment building, where he crouched out of sight to catch his breath and to peer back at the window he'd exited. It was still closed. They couldn't have seen him through the opaque glass without opening it. And who would ever imagine such an escape route? Even for most expert skiers it would seem like suicide to attempt it. The Stasi would never suspect he'd been there when they had arrived.

Running as swiftly and noiselessly as possible across the flat roof, Ari climbed onto a rusted metal fire escape. After a hurried descent of four floors it was an easy jump onto a rear garage—then a precarious drop to land on the crumbling narrow top of a high garden wall, where he teetered for a moment, arms flailing, before regaining his balance. Finally, clutching the briefcase tightly, he made the last plunge into the dark alley below. A short sprint to the left brought him to the broad avenue around the corner from the entrance to his apartment building. Peering out cautiously, he saw no one in either direction.

A quick glance at his watch told him he'd just make the next train if he hurried. Entering the avenue, he headed off at a fast run toward the railroad station about three miles away.

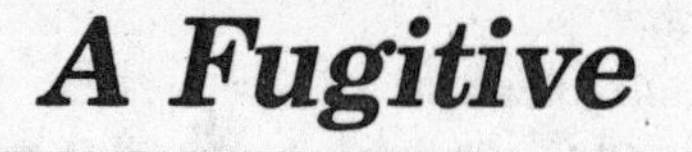

2

A Fugitive

After a brief burst of speed, Ari settled into a steady pace that he could maintain the entire distance. The only sound competing with the slap of his shoes on pavement was the eerie fluttering of the flags hanging from the dingy shop fronts. Plaster peeling from the once well-kept brick exteriors, and the gray metal storm shutters pulled down and locked tight over doors and windows, gave the impression of a city with a history of better days that had been lost even to memory.

The gaudy colors and frenetic motions of the flags snapping loudly in the stiff breeze marked the latest trade fair. These twice-a-year events, which were Leipzig's chief claim to fame, brought an influx of visitors, mostly from other Iron Curtain countries. They also brought an astonishing infusion of fancy foods, from caviar to strawberries, that appeared miraculously—and briefly—in restaurants to impress exhibitors from the West with the benefits of socialism available in this "workers' paradise." There was still a surprising number of Western intellectuals naive enough to be taken in by the transparent lie. Ari snorted contemptuously at the thought and slowed his pace to a normal walk until a passing car had overtaken him and sped out of sight. Then he broke into a steady run again.

Was this *really* happening? His legs told him yes, but his head seemed out of synch. It was hard to believe that he was fleeing for his life—that everything he had so passionately worked for over the past two years and had come so close to accomplishing was now in the process of disintegration. Faces flashed before him, the individual features of the inner circle of student leaders whom he'd known and loved so well and with whom he had worked, not only in Leipzig but at universities throughout East Germany. Each one a unique personality, so full of life. He had recruited and motivated and convinced them that they could win this fight for freedom—and now he felt responsible for their lives.

Who would be captured? Would anyone escape? Would he? They had all known the risks. For these young and zealous idealists, the dream of liberating their country had made their otherwise hopeless lives worth living. Were they now to rot in prison, or die? And all in vain?

The familiar faces flashing before him became twisted in pain. Interrogation. Torture. Death. A sob caught in his throat, and Ari quickly turned the sorrow into hatred. He had no illusions about his own fate if they caught him.

He would be accused of spying for the West and tortured until he "confessed," perhaps in a show trial. *They'll never take me alive. They'll never take me! Marxism has to be stamped out!*

As he settled into his stride, Ari remembered with anger the raising of the Berlin wall in 1961. In one incredible night that infamous structure had slashed its evil scar across the face of the city! He had been ashamed to be favored by a regime that had to imprison its citizens to keep them inside its borders. It had been the final straw for him and tens of thousands of others as well, and it had made his recruitment job that much easier.

The fragile spark of hope that had still been flickering throughout Eastern Europe had gone out. An unreasoning fear had swept across East Germany. In the succeeding years the fear had settled into a despondent resignation. Yet even now as he ran for his life, the determination was stronger than ever to help his countrymen somehow overthrow East Germany's oppressive regime—and perhaps even others in Eastern Europe. If *millions* would join together and refuse to move a finger until their demands were met, they could paralyze entire countries and win their freedom. That was the premise upon which he had formulated his plans, and even this present failure did not disprove it.

He turned the last corner. The railroad station could be seen half a mile in the distance. There was no escaping the responsibility he felt. He could never abandon his dream of seeing his homeland once again free.

This whole country is a prison! The thought brought a renewed surge of anger. Fleeing to the West, once the hope that kept life in the souls of so many, was no longer a viable option. It was not only the infamous Wall that prevented escape. Every inch of the nearly 900-mile East German border with the West had been sealed off completely by a heavily fortified wire mesh fence that was hung at head, chest and knee level with fragmentation mines that were connected to concealed trip wires. For hundreds of yards back from the fence the land had been laboriously cleared and meticulously mined. There were steel watchtowers mounted with machine guns and floodlights. Patrolling attack dogs were everywhere on the alert. The few tourist crossings were equipped with heat-sensing devices to detect persons hidden in vehicles or barges. As a result, a palpable hopelessness had settled like a choking fog over the country and people he loved.

Even if it had been possible for him personally, the moral duty he felt made any thought of escaping to the West completely out of the question. Yet how could he evade the omnipresent and omniscient secret police and remain inside East Germany? That was the challenge he faced. There was one possibility in Berlin—if only he could get there.

The station was now only 50 yards away. Clammy with sweat and gasping for breath, Ari slowed to a normal walk. Approaching the main entrance cautiously, he noticed with relief that there was no sign of police anywhere. The big clock over the door told him that he might have won a place on the Olympic team for those three miles. In seven minutes he'd be on the 10:49 P.M. train to Berlin. Warily he entered, wiping the sweat from his brow and neck.

The large and dimly lit waiting room with its few rows of worn-out, thinly upholstered chairs and wooden benches was almost empty, with only a scattering of somnambulant travelers on the softest seats here and there. Ari took in the scene with a glance. There was a nodding mother, her arms around two small sleeping children and her feet propped onto a stack of suitcases; a drunk stretched prone and snoring loudly; a middle-aged couple, overworked, underfed, wearing worried expressions, who clung to one another wordlessly.

Ari stiffened instinctively. Just inside the door to his right sat an unusually muscular man of medium height seemingly engrossed in a newspaper. His flattened nose looked as though it had been broken several times, leaving little doubt that he had spent considerable time competing in the boxing ring. On the other side of the vaulted room, next to the exit leading to the platform, a tall and younger man with the look of a finely conditioned athlete was also casually reading the evening propaganda sheets. Both men wore dark business suits. *Stasi!*

Ari stifled the impulse to turn and retrace his steps back out the front door. Where would he go? They had undoubtedly already seen him. Forcing himself to relax, he walked nonchalantly up to the one ticket window that was open and said in a loud voice, "One-way to *Fürstenwalde*, please." That was not where he wanted to go, but it would misinform his pursuers and the route would take him past his own village. Ticket purchased, he went through the exit, walked up a flight of stairs and across a set of tracks, then down another flight and onto the Berlin platform.

It was now five minutes until the next train. Ari walked slowly to his right until he had moved past the last of the few persons waiting for the express to Berlin. Sure enough, the two men in business suits, newspapers tucked under their arms, came out onto the platform almost immediately. With the burly one leading the way and the taller one a few paces behind, they began edging in his direction, like cats stalking a mouse.

Keeping the right side of his body away from the others on the platform, Ari pulled back his jacket, rested his hand on the Luger, released the safety, and waited. The men stopped about 20 feet from him, unfolded their newspapers and began to read once again. *They don't want to arrest me now, just follow me, hoping I'll lead them to others. Okay, we'll see where that game gets us.*

Ari engaged the safety again, took his hand from the loaded pistol, and let his coat fall forward to cover the weapon. When the train pulled up, he deliberately walked farther along the platform and entered the front door of the last car. The taller man followed him aboard, while the bruiser went on past and entered at the rear.

The car was empty except for an elderly couple sound asleep in the first row. Ari took a seat near the middle of the car. The man who had followed him aboard sat several seats in front of him, and Broken-nose seated himself a few rows behind. *They're so obvious, so overconfident, so used to having it all their way. Do they think I'm an idiot?*

The train started precisely on time and accelerated rapidly—the one public service that operated at something approaching proverbial German efficiency. Ari was thinking fast, going over the alternate possibilities, trying to formulate the best plan. Killing his two "shadows" and throwing their bodies off the train seemed the only plausible solution. Yet he couldn't just snuff out their lives. To do so would lower him to their level. Such an unconscionable act would cost him the moral basis for overthrowing their regime. Self-defense was one thing, but cold-blooded murder was out of the question. He knew he could never kill a man—unless it were the only way to save his own or someone else's life.

The conductor, a tall, portly man with a soiled uniform and friendly smile—out of character for any official, no matter how minor, in East Germany—came through to check tickets. That brief task finished, he sauntered back up the aisle, pausing to nod good-naturedly at the sleeping couple. With a wave of his arm he exited the car on his way toward the front of the train. He wouldn't return until after the next station.

Ari could not have the two Stasi agents get off the train with him and follow him to his home, but how could he prevent it? He had to somehow get off the train without their knowing it—or get them off ahead of time. Yes, that was it! In a sudden flash of inspiration, he knew what he would do.

This was an express that made few stops. His own village would be the second one. Ari looked at his watch. He had about six minutes.

Leaving the precious briefcase behind, he walked casually toward the rear of the car as though he were going to the toilet. Instead, he slipped quickly into the seat behind the burly agent. In one swift motion, he pulled the Luger from his belt and pressed the business end firmly against the Stasi's skull just behind his right ear.

"Get up! Now!" Ari whispered. "Walk to the front, hands by your side. Act normal. Try anything and you're dead!" Reluctantly the agent stood up. Ari patted him down quickly, keeping the Luger pressed against his skull. Pulling a snub-nosed 32-caliber revolver from its underarm holster, Ari tucked it into his own belt under his jacket. The man's pockets yielded a hand-held portable two-way radio, a wallet and a set of keys. Ari took the money, several thousand marks, and dropped everything else onto the seat, covering it with the man's newspaper. Then he shoved Broken-nose out into the aisle.

"Hands at your side! Eyes straight ahead! Go to your friend. I'm desperate. Give me an excuse and I'll kill you!"

The tall, athletic agent, now reading a paperback book, wasn't aware of what was happening until they were a few feet behind him. He whirled around in his seat, saw Ari's gun, hesitated, then raised his hands slowly. Ari shoved Broken-nose forward and motioned for his partner to get up and stand in the aisle just behind him. Swiftly removing the man's revolver, Ari shoved it into a pocket of his jacket. He went through the same routine, removing the money, dropping the wallet and two-way radio onto the seat and hurriedly covering it all with the newspaper.

The elderly couple was still snoring away, swaying with the erratic motion of the train.

"I'm a fugitive... no family, no future in this country... determined to escape," Ari told his captives in a low but earnest voice. "Follow orders—or you're dead. Through that door straight ahead!"

Grudgingly Broken-nose opened the forward door. Ari shoved the two men through, followed them into the narrow space, and shut the door behind them. The sound of the wheels racing along the track was now deafening and he had to yell to be heard.

"Open that door!" Ari pointed to the exit on the right side.

"We can't go out there!" objected the taller one, whose long nose, pointed chin and narrow eyes, Ari now noticed up close, made him look remarkably like a weasel.

"You'll never get away with this!" snarled the burly one. "They'll get you!"

Ari ignored them and glanced at his watch. "In about one minute," he yelled, "the train slows for an old bridge over a lake. It's only three meters to the water. There's a low railing you can jump over... but there's a support girder every 30 meters. You've got to go between them. Now open the door."

The men made no move. Instantly Ari hit Broken-nose on the side of his face with the Luger, spinning him around. Grabbing him from behind with his left arm around his neck, Ari once again shoved the point of the gun into the base of his skull just below the right ear and yelled at Weasel-face, "Open the door—*now*—or I'll kill you both and throw you out!"

The tall Stasi agent pulled the door toward him and stood in the opening, leaning against the steel wall just inside to keep his balance. Half obscured by clouds, the full moon gave barely enough light to dimly make out close objects as they flashed by. The train began to decelerate. Suddenly the steady, clattering hum of wheels on tracks took on a higher, more hollow pitch.

"We're over the lake!" yelled Ari. "There goes the first girder. When you see the next one jump fast, both of you! There it goes—jump!"

With a shove from Ari, they both went flying out into the night. He heard two almost simultaneous splashes. In relief, Ari leaned back against the opened door and wiped the sweat from his brow with the back of his hand. Eyes closed, heart pounding, he swallowed the rushing night air into his lungs in deep gulps.

The Stasis had landed somewhere near the middle of the small lake. The swim would be short, but the walk a long one. It would take them several hours to reach the closest village. By then, he hoped, he'd be safely in Berlin.

Slamming the outside door shut, Ari went back inside. The old couple was still snoring a duet. Quickly he gathered the objects he had taken from the two men, wrapped them in the newspapers, and threw them out the rear door. Returning hurriedly to his seat, he settled back to catch his breath and contemplate what lay before him.

There were some incriminating papers he had to retrieve—backup copies of what he carried in his briefcase. He'd hidden them at home several weeks earlier in the wall of his tiny bedroom. Among the documents were the detailed plans for the now aborted uprising and a complete list of names, addresses and phone numbers of all the key members of the conspiracy. The papers had to be destroyed. He could take no chances—had to do everything in his power to protect the others.

His parents wouldn't be happy to see him under these circumstances. He'd have to think of some plausible excuse for his sudden and hurried visit in the middle of the night. They must not suspect that he was a fugitive. When the police questioned them they had to be able to swear that they knew nothing of his plot or his flight. Otherwise it could mean prison and torture at the hands of Walter Ulbricht's secret police, a fate he wouldn't even wish upon his father.

His mother had often confided to him that the current gangsters were far worse than the Nazis they had replaced. The Nazis had concentrated mostly upon persecuting the Jews and certain other minorities, but the communist regime mistreated, imprisoned and tortured everyone. Under Hitler the country had prospered even while the rest of the world was in the Great Depression of the 1930s. Germans had never had it so good. Under Marxism, however, the Eastern half of Europe's most affluent and proudest nation had become impoverished, inefficient and incapable of competing with the West in anything except athletics. In order to deceive the world, vast sums that could not be afforded were poured into Olympic sports. Banned drugs were secretly used that enhanced performance over the short term but which would have devastating effects upon the athletes in later life. Rumors persisted about cancer and other ailments plaguing retired Olympic heroes and heroines.

Ari's father took a different view. His fanatical Nazism had metamorphosed with surprising ease into an equally rabid Marxism. For him, the regime could do no wrong, and he lost no opportunity to make his loyalty known. Yet his attempts to curry Party favor had thus far gained nothing for him, not even an easing of the harsh and menial tasks he performed at the collective farm.

"They'll promote me—you'll see!" his father had often told Ari's mother as he drowned his frustrations in alcohol. "Just one rotten Jew on the local committee stands in the way."

He'd turn me in! His only child! To make points with the Party! I know it! That distressing realization reawakened a pain long suppressed. *How can a father hate his own son?* It was a question that had tormented Ari for years, a question he had flung again and again into the silent void as he tossed and turned at night as a young boy not yet in his teens, while vivid scenes from that day's horror or some particularly ugly episode in the past flashed before him. A simple farmer with little education, his father resented Ari's intellect and the fact that he had been chosen for special favor by the Party—especially since it involved schooling that took him away from his farm chores for nine months of the year.

Ari's father was a large, powerfully built bully who could turn suddenly violent, especially when he was drunk. His frequent fits of rage had terrified Ari as a child. As far back as he could remember, he had been periodically beaten by his father for no apparent reason. His mother had often shared his fate for pleading on his behalf. Later, when Ari had taken up the martial arts, his fear had turned to contempt. On his fifteenth birthday, he had defended his mother and himself with a quickness and finesse for which his father's brute strength and barroom brawling tactics were no match. It had been a bloody beating, not because Ari savored revenge, but because his father wouldn't give up until he lay senseless on the floor. There had been no more physical abuse in the home—only looks that would kill—since that memorable day.

It would be after midnight when he got there. Perhaps he could slip in and out without being seen. It would have been easier if he and his parents hadn't been forced to move into that rabbit-warren of close-packed hovels when most of the farms had been collectivized in 1960. Their neighbors seemed to derive a perverted pleasure from spying on one another. Especially that obnoxious family of Jews with the sniveling son and sneaky daughter who always peered from behind their curtains and watched his every move! They had to be paid informants for the Stasi. Where else did they get the extra money that allowed them to have a TV, their own car, and other luxuries that no one else in the commune could afford?

Jews! How he loathed that Hebrew breed! Despising *Juden* was the one thing his father had taught him as a boy that he still retained as a personal conviction. He hadn't known many Jews, but those he had encountered were everything his father had warned him they were and everything that he despised.

Ari would have left home and never returned had it not been for his mother. He loved that good woman with a passion in spite of her foolish religious faith—praying to an imaginary deity who never heard her, "crossing" herself in a futile attempt to ward off evil, even imagining at times that a prayer had been answered. She was simple and kind, without guile, a relief of sorts in the complex world in which he moved.

"Believe in God, Ari, and the good Virgin," she had pleaded with him so often.

"You know I'm no atheist like the Marxists," he would protest. "Every atom has its design. And when you come to a living cell . . . and the human brain . . . of course there has to be some Intelligence that planned it all. Call it 'God' if you want...."

"But Ari," she would remind him, "you never pray...."

"That's *religion*, with its rituals and 'saints' invented by some power-hungry charlatans who pretend to speak for 'God' so they can control people. I hate to see you fall for that!"

"The Blessed Virgin has appeared all over the world," she would reply earnestly. "She promises to bring peace and take us to heaven. I couldn't go on if I didn't have faith."

"*Faith*!" he would shoot back, unable to hide his contempt. "Faith in a 'god' who allows disease, starvation, injustice—and Marxist devils to slaughter millions and make us all prisoners? We've got to change the world ourselves—no 'god' will help us!"

At her pained expression he would put an arm around her and tell her softly, "I'm sorry, mamma, but really... what evidence...?"

"*Evidence*? The Church says it's true. Someday you'll understand."

It always ended that way, with her "faith" unchanged and with him regretting he'd been so blunt. It pained Ari deeply to know that his skepticism caused her almost as much grief as his father's abuse. Ari was her only child and the one person she could look to for comfort. He gave it to her in every way he could, but he couldn't pretend to accept the fairy tales she swallowed.

How he longed to say goodbye to his mother and to assure her that he'd be okay. If she knew nothing, however, and hadn't even seen him, that might get her some leniency. As for his father, he had no more desire to see him than the devil himself.

3

"You're a Dirty, Stinking Jew!"

Ten minutes past the lake, after accelerating to top speed again, the express slowed and ground to its first stop. This station was always a busy one, as Ari well knew. He had moved to the seat next to the rear exit, from where he could observe the entire platform through the window and keep a wary eye on anyone entering his car. About two dozen passengers boarded the train, all of them in the forward cars, except for an affectionate young couple. Arms around each other, they awkwardly negotiated a few steps down the narrow aisle and seated themselves four rows from the front, where they cuddled and babbled intimately as though no one else existed in the entire world. *Nothing to fear from them.*

The train started with a lurch and Ari leaned back to relax. Eighteen more minutes at high speed and the express would stop at his own village. The police would almost certainly be watching the station. He wanted no more confrontation, which left him with only one alternative.

The conductor, now whistling his own off-key rendition of a nondescript tune, came through to check tickets again.

"I've got to transfer at Luckenwalde," said Ari casually. "How far...?"

"Three more stops... about an hour."

Ari leaned out into the aisle and motioned for the conductor to come closer. The man bent his huge frame down and Ari confided in a low voice, "Some 'bug' got me. Keeps me going to the W.C. If you come through and I'm not here, you'll know where I am."

"I won't go looking for you," came the easy response with a wink. He made his way slowly up the aisle and exited the car.

That was simple. He'll think I'm still aboard. Smiling with satisfaction, Ari leaned his head back on the seat, letting himself relax, but at the same time pondering alternate scenarios, trying desperately to keep himself awake. It would be a disaster to fall asleep and go on past his station, but it was a terrible fight just to keep his eyes open. If they once shut, he'd be gone.

The few minutes seemed like hours. At last the train began to slow. Ari was instantly on his feet. Taking his hefty briefcase, he went into the narrow exit area at the rear of the car, shut that door behind him and pulled the outside door open. About 50 yards before the train reached the station, he jumped out on the side away from the platform and disappeared into the woods. There he waited for a few moments, peering out from behind the trees down the tracks toward the station, making certain that no one had seen him. Then he turned and ran toward his parents' home.

The scattered clouds had thinned and at first only briefly and intermittently obscured the moon. Ari followed a faint but familiar path that avoided the roads. Traversing dampened fields and dripping forest, he savored familiar odors of dank earth and washed foliage that brought back childhood memories. He had taken this shortcut many times as a boy when ordered by his father to go to the village on errands. In daylight he could cover the distance at a steady run in about 20 minutes. But with the clouds once again growing thicker and the weight of the heavy briefcase impeding him it took almost double the normal time, costing him precious minutes that he could ill afford.

The long run was particularly exhausting because of the recent sleepless nights. Ari cursed the darkness each time he stumbled. As he approached the farm, however, picking his way cautiously along a narrow, wooded ravine that cut through the fields, he muttered a grateful thanks to the thickening clouds that obscured the full moon and covered his furtive movements.

At last he was close enough to make out, in the transient intervals of filtered moonlight, the dim outline of the dozen small houses that made up the commune. Huddled together in a semicircle, they faced the road about 100 feet beyond. All were dark except for his own house, where the kitchen light was burning. It was far too late for his parents still to be up. Were the loathsome secret police in there questioning them? Or had that job been finished and were the Stasis now hidden outside?

Where were the watchdogs that were always turned loose to roam the farm at night? Why weren't they yapping a wild, tail-wagging welcome for him? There was a soft, erratic breeze blowing past him toward the houses, carrying his scent. The dogs,whom he loved so well, should have come running to greet him. He had worried about that, wondering how he could quiet them quickly. Yet all was silent—too quiet. *If the police are hiding somewhere, watching for me, they would have had to order the dogs confined inside, or they would never stop barking. That had to be it!*

Ari knew every inch of the collective farm. Cautiously he circled to his left, following the shallow, tree-lined gully that skirted the cluster of farm buildings and marked the border between them and the surrounding acres of freshly plowed and planted soil. *Nothing.* At last he approached the narrow, graveled lane that led from his village to the next one a few kilometers away. He stood motionless for several minutes pressed against the trunk of a tall poplar tree, trying desperately to pierce the darkness along the road and through the trees toward the houses, every faculty straining to detect the slightest sound or faintest odor. Was that a whiff of tobacco exuding from someone's breath or clothing? It came and went so quickly on the light and shifting breeze that he couldn't be sure.

A twig snapped over to his right. Ari turned his head quickly and tried to pierce the impenetrable darkness. The noise had been so slight and fleeting. Perhaps his imagination was beginning to play tricks. Suddenly there was that faint and elusive odor of tobacco again. This time he was certain of it. *Someone's out there!* He could sense their presence now, but where?

More minutes passed in motionless alert as Ari pressed against the tree trunk, eyes and ears straining to locate his hidden stalkers. Did they know he was there? For a brief moment the clouds parted and his eyes caught the glint of moonlight on a windshield! A car hidden in the trees just to his right and only a few yards behind him! He had walked within a few feet without seeing it! Had they seen him?

Ari crouched low and waited for the clouds to part again, but the darkness only thickened. Suddenly a match was struck, briefly illuminating a man's face not more than 50 feet away! Ari heard the match blown out, saw the red glow of a cigarette, then smelled the burning tobacco. One enemy located. Where were the others?

The smoker was hiding on the edge of the narrow finger of fir and birch that extended up out of the gully that Ari had been following and onto a small promontory. It commanded a view of the country lane and each of the houses. Obviously they were not expecting him to come across the fields from the train station but to arrive in a car along the road. Cautiously Ari reentered the fringe of brush and trees and began moving in the direction of the red glow that appeared each time the smoker took a drag. How often he had crept among these very trees playing hide-and-seek as a boy, never dreaming he would return one day for this deadly game!

Thankfully there had been enough rain to soak the ground so that one could move across dead leaves without making a sound. Of course, if he could move noiselessly, so could *they*. Soon he was close enough to dimly glimpse his quarry on the slight rise silhouetted against the dark sky, where he paced impatiently back and forth, apparently not enjoying his duty. *Where are the others?*

"Hands up!" The deep voice, sounding as startled as Ari now felt, came from a few feet behind and to his right. "Alex! I've got him! Over here."

Raising his hands and turning slowly around, Ari saw a dark figure separate itself from the tree trunk it had seemed to be a part of when he had so carefully passed it moments before. Warily the man approached him. Ari could hear the crashing of underbrush as the smoker, now shining a flashlight, hurried toward them.

"Turn around!" The tone of voice had changed from surprise to fierce satisfaction. "Hands on top of your head!"

As Ari made as though he were obeying, the first beam of the flashlight came through the trees and hit his captor momentarily in the eyes. In that instant, in a smooth but swift motion that almost seemed to be part of his submissive turning around, Ari's leg lashed out. Just as his foot made contact with the weapon, he heard it go off and felt a searing pain on the side of his head. In another swift motion, as he whirled to face the second man, Ari's other foot nearly took his opponent's head off, sending him crashing into the tree he'd been hiding behind, where he slumped and lay still.

Ari was now on the ground, Luger in hand. Two shots from the man with the flashlight, now turned off, passed through the space he had just vacated. Ari answered with two shots of his own aimed at the fleeting pinpoints of fire that had come from his quarry's gun. The quick burst of gunfire echoed into the distance, then eerie silence. A heavy mist had settled in, and the accumulated moisture was beginning to fall from soaked leaves. The haphazard droplets provided the only sound as Ari lay in the mud and wet leaves, listening for any movement that would betray the presence of the rest of the team. Could there only have been two? His head was throbbing where the bullet had grazed him. Cautiously probing fingers came back wet with warm fluid. Thankfully the wound was scarcely bleeding. A close call!

Beyond the trees and barn Ari saw lights go on in several houses. Dogs barked briefly, were called hurriedly back inside, then silence again, punctuated by the now steady dripping. He waited, not moving a muscle, listening. One minute, two, three... five, ten. Precious time. One by one the lights went out. No one had come outside to investigate. They wouldn't dare.

Motionless, Ari continued to strain his eyes and ears, but still there was no movement he could detect either from the man he had shot at or from the one lying just behind him. *Alex, I've got him!* Those words, still ringing in his memory, seemed to indicate that these two had been stationed there alone.

Hugging the ground, Ari pulled himself in imperceptible increments back toward the motionless form. There was no sign of pulse or breathing. The man's head was at an impossible angle, his neck apparently broken. Still no sound from "Alex." Nothing except the light falling of rain and steady dripping. He had squandered far too much time already.

Jumping to his feet, Ari moved silently and swiftly from tree to tree. He almost stepped on the crumpled form before he saw it. A quick examination told him that this man also was dead. There was warm, sticky blood all over his head and face and jacket. With trembling fingers Ari felt through the dead man's pockets for car keys but found none. Rising slowly to his feet, he felt a sudden wave of nausea and had to grab a tree to steady himself. Never had he killed a fellow human being, nor been so close to death himself.

Half-dazed now, Ari made his way back to his other victim and went through his pockets. Still no keys. *They're in the car. Okay.* Hurrying out of the woods, he ran across the few yards of open terrain to the covering of the barn, then moved quickly along its exterior to the other end, where he peered cautiously around a corner at the houses. All was quiet, and dark, except for his own house. The kitchen light was still on. Were there more police inside? No, they would have come running at the sound of shots.

Noiselessly he approached the window and peered inside. Revulsion swept over him. There he sat, the tall, familiar hulk, hunched over the table, drinking the beer he loved too well and which they could ill afford. There were nearly a dozen empty bottles on the floor. His mother was standing nearby, tearful, unsure, emanating an air of hopelessness that infuriated Ari when he thought of all she had suffered. The words weren't audible, but it was obvious they were having a bitter quarrel. Had they even heard the shots?

Cautiously he circled the house, Luger in one hand, briefcase in the other, searching the darkness for any movement, ears straining to pick up any sound. Nothing. The only door into the tiny, poorly built dwelling opened onto a narrow pantry from where it led straight through the kitchen. There was no way he could slip in, recover the papers, and get away without being seen. Nor could he wait for them to go to bed. He shuffled his feet on the porch, coughed, then paused a moment before trying the door. It was locked. Knocking loudly, he heard his mother's footsteps approaching.

"Who is it?" she called in a tremulous voice.

"It's me."

There was a gasp of shocked disbelief and a moment's hesitation. Then the door was flung open. "Ari!"

He stepped quickly inside and closed the door behind him. His mother threw her arms around him, then drew back and touched his wound tenderly. "You're bleeding! What happened, love?"

"I'm okay. It's nothing. Just scratched myself on a dead branch coming through the woods from the station."

"Are you sure?" she asked tearfully. "It wasn't the police?"

"Police?" he asked, feigning surprise at such a question.

"They've been looking for you!"

"They have? Why?"

"You don't know?"

Ari shook his head. "They were *here*?"

"A couple hours ago," growled his father, who hadn't moved from his seat at the table where he'd been glaring in silence. "Got us out of bed. Tore your room apart. You've been shot, you liar! I wish they'd killed you!" His speech was slurred, but anger gave a convincing energy to the stinging words. He obviously still had his full wits.

"Did the police do that to you, Ari?" his mother asked again anxiously. She had gotten a clean cloth from a drawer, held it under the tap at the sink, and was now dabbing with it at his wound.

"I said it was a sharp branch." Ari pushed her gently away. "I'm okay. Look, I don't have much time."

"Less than you think," gloated his father. "I'm calling the police!"

"You want them to find you like this?" bluffed Ari contemptuously. "Look at you—slobbering drunk again!" There was no time to waste. He turned and started toward his bedroom.

"I'm not drunk. And I know *exactly* what I'm saying... *you Jew bastard*!"

Ari whirled around, stung by the ultimate insult, and started toward him. "What did you say old man? You dare to call me a *Jew*?"

Past all control, the words were flung out once more. "You're a dirty, stinking Jew!" He grabbed an empty bottle by the neck and raised it to defend himself as Ari advanced toward him.

"Stop! Ari! Franz!" Ari's mother threw herself between the two men as her husband lurched to his feet.

"No, he'll hear it—*now*. I told you it was a mistake keeping that *Jew baby*. But you just *had* to. Now look what you've got! We'll be in prison because of him... unless we turn him in."

"I promised. I gave my word. Please, Franz!"

"No! I'm not going to pretend any longer that this *filthy Jew* is my son. I'm calling the police!"

4

Into the Night

"Oh, my God!" Ari's mother fell to her knees in front of her husband, weeping uncontrollably now, clutching his legs. "Blessed Virgin, help me!" He shook her off and sank back into his chair at the table, staring at Ari with eyes that blazed hatred.

In stunned horror Ari recoiled at the scene before him. The stinging words had resurrected memories of childhood fears and uncertainties which now paraded before him in haunting progression. Even his name had made him wonder. "Ari" wasn't German; it was Jewish! Surely his father, who hated all things Jewish with a passion, would never have named him that. His mother had insisted that it had been her choice, but there were no relatives with that name.

Helping his mother to her feet, Ari held her hands and made her face him. "Look at me," he pleaded. "He's lying, isn't he? You told me I wasn't adopted... you swore that I wasn't!"

She turned away and pulled one hand loose to wipe at her eyes. "It's true," she mumbled almost inaudibly. "You're a Jew, Ari."

"Look at us, then look at you!" continued his father's taunting voice. "Did you never wonder? We're both very tall and blond. You're much shorter—with dark skin. You look like a Jew!" He spat out the last sentence contemptuously.

Ari was reeling like a boxer about to go down for the count. Yes, he had wondered—often. He clutched at his mother's arm and looked agonizingly into her face. "I've seen my birth certificate! It gives date and place—and says you're my mother."

She turned away again, unable to look at him. "I lied. It was easy. All the records of that hospital were burned in the war. They made new 'birth certificates.' I only had to sign a paper."

A low chuckle sounded from the now triumphant figure at the table. Slow of speech when sober, he became increasingly eloquent when drunk. "Everything you hate is what you *are*. I always said it was a pity that Hitler didn't kill them all—and you agreed! You wanted them *all* dead! Well, you're one of them!" An ugly laugh wobbled out of control.

Shattered and dazed, Ari took his mother by the arm and led her into the small alcove that had served as his bedroom. It had been thoroughly ransacked. Drawers were pulled out and emptied, the bed torn apart, mattress ripped open, but the hiding place was still intact. That piece of good fortune seemed meaningless now. *A Jew? It can't be!*

Hopelessly confused, Ari turned to the woman beside him again. She was weeping. "Tell me the truth," he demanded quietly.

"We had neighbors... where we used to live... far from here," she answered between sobs. "They were Jews. *Good* people. Schoolteachers. Intelligent. Very kind. I liked them. We were friends. It was 1944. Franz was on the Russian front. Jews were being 'relocated'... but we suspected the worst. They left their little Ariel—I shortened your name to Ari—with me... just before the Gestapo came for them. You were three months old. I promised to keep you until they came back... after the war. They never did. I couldn't have a baby—and now you were mine. It was two years before Franz came home. He didn't want to keep you, but I insisted. I'd made a promise—and I loved you, Ari. I always will!"

In silent pain they clung to each other. So she had lied all these years to protect him. He *had* been adopted. But he wasn't a Jew! He couldn't admit that. His real parents couldn't have been Jews. It had been a mistake. Hitler hadn't only killed Jews. He had killed lots of Germans, too. That's who his parents had been—German intellectuals who opposed Hitler just as he, their son, now sought to overthrow the present evil regime.

Glancing into the kitchen, Ari was alarmed to see that the pitiful drunk he was glad to know was not his real father had staggered to the phone, and was now talking to someone. Ari started toward him, but it was too late. The conversation was just ending with the ominous words, "He's here right now!"

Cursing himself for not paying closer attention, Ari went swiftly to work. While his mother watched in bewilderment, he pulled out a pocket knife and made four quick slits in the cheap wallpaper he had put up two summers ago and had "repaired" several times since. Prying a short length of board from the wall, Ari pulled out the papers hidden behind it, threw them onto the coals in the kitchen stove and crouched in front of it, fanning the flame and watching until every incriminating fragment was consumed.

"I've got to leave, mamma." He straightened up wearily and took both of her hands again. "Please don't worry. I'm going to be okay."

"If you're innocent, Ari... why not give yourself up?"

He looked at her lovingly. "That would only make it worse for both of us. Once they accuse you...."

"Why *you*, Ari?"

He ignored her question. "Listen! Don't defend me. Tell the truth—that you know nothing. Just stick to that!" He was terrified for her, for what might happen when the police came back. How could he leave her? But he must.

"You'll always be my mother," he said tenderly. She nodded, beginning to weep softly again. Ari put an arm around her frail shoulders, ignoring the man he'd called his father, pretending not to know about the phone call.

"They'll expect me to head for the railway station and Berlin," he told her confidentially, but just loud enough to reach other ears. "I'm going to fool them. I have a car, and I'm heading in the opposite direction, toward the Czech border."

"You can't get away, Ari!" she pleaded. "Wouldn't it be better—?"

"Don't worry. I know a place to hide for a few days. Then I'll slip into Czechoslovakia, then Yugoslavia—then into Austria. I've got a Western passport. I'll write."

The wretched figure slouched at the table had straightened up ever so slightly. The alcohol-dulled eyes had come to life and taken on a veiled cunning. He would tell the police everything. They would reward him for it. Certainly a promotion, maybe even a medal.

With a hurried kiss he bade her goodbye, then strode quickly toward the door, where he hesitated. "My parents... do you remember their names?"

She had followed and now caught up to him, clutching at an arm. Sadly she shook her head. "When they didn't come back, I blanked it all out. You were mine, and I didn't want to remember anything else. Don't leave me, Ari!"

"Were there other children?" he asked, stroking her hand gently and ignoring her plea.

She shook her head again. "They were young—you were their first. I remember that."

"They were dirty, stinking Jews! Just like you!" The pitiful creature at the table had lurched to his feet and was laughing at Ari now. "You won't get far you Jew!"

"Franz didn't know them!" she said defiantly. "They were *good* people, just like you, Ari. The children loved them. Everyone had flowers in those days, but no one could grow them like your mother. She had a special touch... in everything she did."

Ari pulled away from her, shoved the door open and ran into the night. *They were good people... the children loved them....*

As Ari reached the barn he heard that gloating voice yelling after him through the open door, "I called the police!" He was so eager to inflict pain that he couldn't keep the secret any longer. "*I called the police!*" he yelled again. "You won't get far. They'll get you... you... you *Jew*!" The words trailed off in a strangled spasm of coughing and laughter.

The moon was out now, for which Ari was thankful. He hoped that everyone in the commune was watching so they could all tell the Stasi. Running through the fringe of woods, he quickly found the hidden police car. Thankfully there were no markings on it and the keys were inside. It started immediately. He backed it out onto the country road and with a roar of the engine and high-pitched squeal of tires spinning in the gravel, he accelerated past the cluster of houses. He wanted everyone to see that he was heading in the direction away from the village and toward the south, just as he had pretended to confide to his mother. That monster back there would tell the police and throw them off his trail, momentarily gaining him precious time.

At the first crossroads Ari turned left, then left again at the next one, reversing his original direction. After winding through farmland and villages for several miles, he came at last to a major northbound highway that would take him to Berlin. He knew, however, that he dare not follow it for long.

The radio! Why hadn't he thought of it sooner! Turning the instrument on, he found it alive with frantic activity. The police had arrived at the farm shortly after his departure, had discovered the two bodies, knew the vehicle was missing, and were now putting out roadblocks to the south as fast as they could. They were searching for him with a vengeance, and would be especially vigilant at the Czech border. A general alarm had also been sounded to be on the lookout for him everywhere. He had to leave the car.

Leaving the main highway at a familiar junction, Ari angled west. With luck he'd reach the station at Juterbog, where all trains to Berlin stopped. It was now after 2:00 A.M. There was a mail train he had sometimes taken that left his village at 1:54 A.M., which would put it at this isolated station around 2:40 A.M. It would be tight, but maybe he could make it. He had to. The problem would be finding a place to leave the car where it wouldn't be found for a long time. In his search for a good hiding place, Ari turned off onto a smaller road that meandered through several tiny villages and would eventually lead directly to the station.

About five miles from his destination the terrain became rolling farmland interspersed with patches of woods. Two miles from the station the road began winding along a river. He thought of running the car into it, but the water wasn't deep enough to cover the vehicle. Valuable time was lost investigating dirt side roads that were little more than tire tracks leading into the woods. Unfortunately, in each case the tracks ended very quickly in fields. The car might remain hidden for days—or at dawn that very morning a farm worker driving a tractor through the woods to a field might discover it. He couldn't take the chance, but he was running out of time and had to catch this train. The next one wouldn't come for several hours.

Ari came to an abandoned farmhouse and was tempted to leave the car out of sight behind the barn. But as soon as he drove onto the property it was obvious that tire tracks across mud and weeds would be a dead giveaway. Backing out hurriedly, he continued his desperate search. Just before the road left the woods he followed one last set of tire tracks back through the trees. It, too, led to a large field that was under cultivation. This one, however, unlike most of the others he'd passed, had not yet been plowed, increasing the chance of early discovery.

He'd have to go back to a field he'd seen earlier that had just been planted and probably wouldn't be visited for some time. He should have left the car there instead of hoping for something better! A look at his watch told Ari that he'd never make it. Cursing his luck, he grabbed his briefcase and, abandoning the car, ran back through the woods to the paved road and along it as fast as he could toward the town about a mile away.

It seemed a fairly safe assumption that the police would not be watching this or any other train station so long as they thought he was in a car. At least the main pursuit was concentrated in the wrong direction in reliance upon information dutifully supplied. A father's betrayal of his only son would surely earn the goodwill of the Party. That piece of treachery must have brought great satisfaction and called for a few more beers, which he'd be sleeping off by now.

The painful thought reminded Ari of his *real* parents, martyrs of Hitler's cruelty. Their ashes or bones lay in some unmarked grave—unknown to the world and, more tragically, to him their only son. *But I'm not a Jew... it isn't true... it isn't true....* The refrain of denial kept cadence with Ari's flying feet as he pressed himself to the limit.

5

Enemy of The People

When at last, with chest heaving and legs about to give out, Ari reached the town and continued running at a slower pace through its deserted streets, uncertainty overwhelmed him once more. What if the police were watching this railway station after all? He'd heard the call on the radio for a general alarm nationwide and wasn't sure what that meant. When the manhunt failed to pick up his trail to the south, wouldn't they suspect he'd doubled back? Of course, they wouldn't expect him to head for Berlin. The infamous Wall made that city the least likely place for a possible escape to the West. However, there was no predicting where the police might be or what they might do, precisely because they couldn't be certain of his movements. More than likely they'd be watching all routes.

One thing was certain. He must not even think of leaving East Germany. In 1956 the Hungarians had relied on brave promises of support from the West, only to find themselves abandoned in their pitiful attempt to stand up to Soviet tanks. Nor would there be help from the West this time. If that shameful Wall was ever to be brought down—and with it the entire Iron Curtain—it would have to be done from inside.

Grandiose dream? Perhaps. Yet seemingly impossible aspirations had always been and always would be the propellant fueling every great advance in human history. He had talked with hundreds of people—enough to be confident that at least 95 percent of the university students and workers in Eastern Europe had the same passion to throw off their shackles. They only awaited effective leadership and the right opportunity.

He would lie low for a while. Disappear. Eventually they would believe he had escaped to the West. Then he would start again. He had a genius for organizing students, and he had painstakingly nurtured a network of key contacts throughout Eastern Europe, reaching even into the Soviet Union. Those names and addresses were the secret weapon he carried in the briefcase—a weapon for freedom that he was convinced would prove in the end to be more powerful than the most sophisticated military hardware. There would, unavoidably, be a cost in lives, but eventually oppressive regimes would collapse if only enough people stood against them. It was a dream worth living, or dying, for.

Legs trembling with fatigue, Ari paused to recover his breath in the shadows just around the corner of a tobacco shop that faced the train station. A look at his watch told him that he'd barely made it. He couldn't see into every part of the waiting room, but it appeared to be empty. Two women stood on the open platform. There was no sign of police.

Anxiously he glanced at his watch again and waited. The approaching train could just be heard in the distance when a small car drove up and slid to a halt in the tiny station parking lot. A well-dressed man of about 40 jumped out. Carrying an expensive briefcase, he ran into the waiting room, bought a ticket and hurried onto the platform. To all appearances a legitimate traveler and all the more convincing because he was alone.

The train pulled into the station, steel screaming against steel as the brakes were applied. Still there was no sign of the police. One minute went by. The two women on the platform boarded. An elderly and poorly dressed woman he hadn't seen exited the waiting room and boarded wearily. Two minutes. Another woman of about 50, bent under a heavy load wrapped in a huge cloth, shuffled past him and onto the platform, heaved her bundle up and climbed aboard. Still no sign of police. Three minutes. *Now!*

Ari heard the sledgehammer blows of his heart as he hurried across the street, hat pulled down and handkerchief pressed to his nose, and walked straight through the waiting room. The lone clerk on duty was dozing and didn't even open his eyes. Running along the platform, he jumped aboard the last car just as the brakeman signaled for the doors to shut and the train pulled away.

Ari went immediately into the small W.C. and locked the door. From his briefcase he pulled out a kit prepared for just such an emergency. Quickly he shaved off his beard and moustache, taking great care not to cut himself. The ugly wound that angled upward just above his right ear was starting to scab over, but still oozed some blood. There was nothing he could do to hide it.

He found the small tube of dye that would turn his black hair into a light brown and nervously skimmed the instructions. Unscrewing the lid, he hesitated for a moment, then screwed it back on. What if he botched the job? No, it was too risky. Cotton stuffed into his nose spread his nostrils and changed his voice. Adding a pair of thick glasses, he now resembled, except for the hair color, Heinrich Seibel, the person pictured in the false identification papers that had cost him 1,000 marks.

Entering the car, Ari took a seat in the rear where he could observe everything and make a hasty exit if necessary. The early run into Berlin was emptier than usual. There were only two other passengers in his coach.

Ari had just taken a magazine from his briefcase and pretended to be absorbed in reading it when the conductor came through to check tickets. "Sorry. I was late and didn't have time to get a Berlin ticket at the station." Ari kept his head averted so that his wound couldn't be seen.

"What if I don't have one? You can't count on that!" came the ill-tempered response. The conductor stirred angrily around in his bag, muttering about people who made his job unbearable. At last he found a Berlin ticket, punched it and gave it grudgingly to Ari, took his money and then complained again under his breath about having to make change.

That's what Marxism does—kills incentive! Ari turned his attention again to the magazine as the conductor headed doggedly back up the aisle. At least the grouch gave no indication of having been alerted to watch for a fugitive. Everything seemed normal. Of course the police could come aboard at any station down the line. What then? Should he rely on his phony papers, or try to escape? He'd have to decide that at the time. Somehow he would make it to that haven in Berlin.

Fragmented thoughts drifted in and out as Ari fought to stay awake. It was a battle that he no longer had the strength to win. The dull, monotonous hum of the train's engine and the rhythmic clickety-clack of the wheels on the tracks quickly dulled his fear of danger and rocked him to sleep.

How long he had slept he didn't know, when he suddenly jerked upright in his seat, heart pounding, awakened by some instinct that signaled danger. Something wasn't right. The train was grinding loudly to a halt, but the feel and sound were different, not like the usual approach to the many stations along the route to Berlin with which he was so familiar. Looking around he noticed that he was the only passenger left in his coach. A quick glance out the window revealed, in the first rosy light of dawn, only the desolate reaches of farmland and heath. A highway, no more than 50 feet away, ran alongside the railroad tracks.

What's going on? Now he could see the scarlet glare of emergency flares up ahead. A lone police car had pulled off the highway and was parked near the tracks, the rotating light on its roof flashing amber and red. Two men in plain clothes stood by the car, waiting as the train screeched to a stop. *Stasi!* Had they found the car he'd abandoned already? It couldn't be. Instinctively he made the critical decision. His false I.D. would probably pass inspection during any routine encounter with ordinary police. But the hated state security forces were far better trained. Under these circumstances they'd be especially thorough. Better not to risk it!

Ari jumped from his seat and ran to the back of the car. Opening the exit door away from the highway, he prepared to leap out and make his escape. Unfortunately, as he had already observed through the window on the other side of the train, nothing but newly ploughed fields met his gaze. No forest in sight. It was hopeless. They would see him immediately. There was only one thing to do—get back to his seat quickly, pretend to be asleep, and somehow bluff his way through, hoping he wouldn't have to shoot his way out of this one as well.

Just then to his right he caught sight of a ladder leading upward. On an impulse he stepped onto it, leaned out and silently closed the door. A few more moments and he was lying flat on top of the train, breathing in short, sharp gasps, clutching his briefcase, wondering if he'd made a mistake, and hoping.

Had the road and the parked cars been on a level with or above the train he would have been seen. But, luckily, the terrain at this point sloped down to the road, which was about 20 feet lower than the tracks. Footsteps crunched past in the gravel alongside the train. Voices yelled indistinct instructions.

The magazine! He'd left it on the seat! The conductor would remember. Ari pulled the Luger from his belt and waited for a head to appear above the top of the train. Minutes passed like hours. Nothing.

At last, with a welcome lurch, the train began to move forward. Ari lay still for a few more moments as it gathered speed, then he cautiously raised his head to peer around. He could see the police car still parked in the same place, the two men climbing back into it. Breathlessly he watched as they pulled out onto the highway and headed in the opposite direction. As the car faded into the distance he slid over to the ladder and made his precarious way back down. The train was nearing full speed when he reached the door, pulled it open with great effort against the wind and stepped inside.

Ari made his way quickly back to his seat and collapsed, trying desperately to control his pounding heart and gasping breath. Then he noticed something that made his heart start pounding again: The magazine was gone! What did that mean? Why hadn't the police looked on top of the train or at least searched for footprints in the adjoining field. The only footsteps he'd heard had been on the side of the train closest to the road. Something must have convinced them that he'd never been aboard. What luck!

After the train made a routine stop at the next station to let off and take on more passengers, the conductor came through once again to check tickets. Ari was still the only one in the last car.

"What was *that* all about?" he asked casually when he showed his ticket again. "Mechanical problems?"

"They were looking for some 'enemy of the people,'" came the matter-of-fact reply. His expression was wooden, but his eyes, looking into Ari's now, seemed to be saying something. "Some guy about your age and size—with a beard. I told them I hadn't seen anybody even close to their description."

"Really?" Ari responded warily. "They were looking for some fugitive?"

The conductor held Ari's eye for an uncomfortable moment. "They would have found him if I'd told the truth," he said quietly, "but I hate the Stasi." He reached under his coat and, without changing expression, pulled a familiar magazine from his back pocket and thrust it under Ari's nose. "You left this on the seat."

Too stunned to reply, Ari took the magazine. He felt the hair rising on the back of his neck. "Thank you . . . very much," he finally managed to stammer. "*Very* much!"

"And next time," grumbled the conductor, "don't be so forgetful. My job's bad enough without having to cover up for people like you!" He turned and shuffled back up the aisle toward the front of the train.

6

R. Harrison Dunn IV

A fine, powdery snow, unseasonably late, had covered the ground with a blanket an inch deep and was still falling when at last the train reached Berlin. It was nearly an hour's walk from the central station to Ari's destination—the apartment of an American friend. No buses served that area of the city, and Ari didn't dare take a cab. The driver might be questioned and remember him. The dry powder crunched under his feet and a bone-chilling wind seemed to go right through his pants and light jacket. The discomfort was hardly noticed, however, at the elation of knowing he had escaped and would soon be in a safe hiding place.

The streets were alive with the early morning press of workers hurrying to their jobs. They were reluctantly bundled up against the unusual storm in winter clothes that had already been put away for the season. Ari held his hand over his wound and turned his head away whenever he encountered anyone along the sidewalk. No one seemed to notice him as they scurried past, each preoccupied with his own thoughts.

After Ari had been walking briskly for about 40 minutes the number of pedestrians thinned out until the streets were almost empty. Only an occasional small East German car, spewing exhaust, chugged past, while the number of large foreign cars and chauffeur-driven limousines increased dramatically.

Ari had now entered one of the few once-affluent neighborhoods in East Berlin that had been somewhat restored since that city's destruction. Many of the solid old brick or stone mansions had become embassy residences, mostly of diplomats representing Eastern bloc countries. There were refurbished large apartments as well that only the privileged upper class in this "classless" Marxist society could afford. Those that were not occupied by top communist party officials were leased to a few wealthy Westerners who had business of some nature in East Berlin—among them Ari's American friend, Roger Dunn. His apartment would make an ideal place to hide, assuming that the oft-extended welcome was still in effect.

Roger was a tall, lanky Texan in his late twenties with crew-cut blond hair, a quick smile, ready laugh and an easy going disposition. A clever cover, Ari sometimes thought, to hide the computer-like mind that a glint in the steel-blue eyes only rarely betrayed. His father was an extremely wealthy cattle rancher whose sprawling acreage had turned out to be rich in oil. As a result of that added wealth, R. Harrison Dunn III now had his finger in a surprising number of domestic and international banks, as Roger had casually confided. A close friend of fellow Texan Lyndon B. Johnson since childhood, the elder Dunn had been appointed to a United Nations diplomatic post when the latter became President at John F. Kennedy's death. He was now involved in arms negotiations with the Soviets at Geneva.

It was from Roger that Ari had first learned that there was also corruption, even at the highest government levels, in the West. What a disillusionment it had been. Until that distressing revelation, he had imagined that Western democracies were immune to the viral dishonesty that was an endemic infection in Marxist regimes.

"L.B.J.," Roger had confided to Ari one day, "broke laws at every level in his climb to the presidency, including vote stealing in order to get into the Senate. He's a scoundrel. But he's done a lot of good, too. Don't get the wrong idea—Johnson's lily white compared with the monsters running communist countries. That kind of corruption isn't possible under our system. But there's still a lot of selfish abuse of power—from the White House on down."

"What about your father?" Ari had asked in surprise. "If he's Johnson's close friend... what about *him*?"

"Money is power," Roger had expounded dispassionately. "My dad controls billions and knows how to use that leverage on an international scale... including Eastern Europe and even the Soviet Union."

"Really? I don't understand that." Ari had been greatly perplexed. "Maybe I'm naive, but having lived all my life under Marxism I can't fathom why capitalists would invest a *pfennig* in communist countries!"

"The issue isn't so much Marxism against capitalism," Roger had explained patiently, "but the survival of the whole human race. Western capital has financed Marxist regimes for decades. The stakes are too high to quibble over fine ethical points. Almost anything goes, including... well, let's just leave it at that."

That was where the subject had been left, and Ari had never raised the issue since. As to where the young Texan himself fitted into the picture, and why he was living in East Berlin, discretion had always prevented Ari from asking. Maybe some day Roger would voluntarily tell him.

It was during his periodic visits to the University of East Berlin that Ari had met Roger. They had taken an immediate liking to each other. Roger had encouraged Ari to practice his English on him, and their relationship had grown into a solid friendship. The young American, who was fluent in German, Russian, French and several other languages, was a somewhat mysterious figure. There had never been any question of trust, however, because the mere fact that a person was an American was credential enough for any Eastern European.

Roger had a diplomatic passport and traveled back and forth to West Germany on errands which he never discussed. In fact, he spent most of his time in West Berlin, yet chose to live in the East "to get a closer view of communism," as he explained. There was no doubt that this unusually knowledgeable and sophisticated American, whom Ari suspected of having ties with the CIA, hated Marxism with a passion. In their long discussions on the subject, the handsome Texan often predicted an end to the Cold War and the collapse of international communism. But when Ari asked him what made him think so, he would only smile cryptically and say, "Believe me, it's just a matter of time."

Ari had been extremely careful about his contacts with Roger. They had met only at the university—always, seemingly, by chance, and only in confined public areas where it was a simple matter to know whether they were being observed. Ari had been confident that neither he nor Roger had been under surveillance. Nevertheless, as an extra precaution, he had never visited the American's apartment, in spite of the repeated invitations and assurances that he was more than welcome if he ever needed a place to stay. That time had now come. The police would never find him there!

When at last Ari turned onto Roger's street, it was a great relief to find it deserted. Arriving eagerly at the address he'd long ago memorized, Ari recognized it immediately from Roger's descriptions—an unusually large apartment with a black-streaked white marble facade and its own imposing entrance directly from the street.

It was 8:10 A.M. and Ari was famished. A quick bite of breakfast would help him sleep longer—something he desperately needed to do. Wearily he climbed the half-dozen stone steps onto the broad marbled porch. Set in the rich marble facade beside the huge, double door of solid dark mahogany was a lighted button. Over it, on a shiny brass plaque, was written, R. Harrison Dunn IV, Esquire. Feeling suddenly nervous about the reception he might receive, Ari pushed the button. Muted, musical chimes sounded within.

Almost immediately heavy footsteps could be heard approaching. The door opened and there was Roger, towering over him, with a scowl on his face, looking not at all friendly. "Who are you looking for?" he demanded in flawless German that bore no trace of any foreign accent, let alone his usual Texas drawl.

"Well, you told me to stop by sometime," said Ari, taken aback by the frigid reception. Then he realized that without his beard, and with muddy, crumpled clothes and dried blood on the side of his face, he probably looked like a drunken bum to his wealthy friend. "I guess you don't recognize me," he added uncertainly.

Roger had been looking at him closely and his stern expression now changed to a broad grin. "Ari! You son-of-a-gun," he exclaimed in English. "What a surprise! Come on in."

Ari glanced up and down the street. No one had followed him. He stepped quickly inside. "You told me so often to drop by," he began.

"You bet I did—and I meant it." There was no doubt about Roger's warm enthusiasm. "You just make yourself at home, now, you hear?" He led the way through a long entrance hall into a lavishly furnished living room that opened onto a dining area with a large kitchen beyond. "Why did you shave your beard? I thought it looked great."

"Just got tired of it," said Ari with a wry smile. "Besides, it gets itchy after a while."

"I suppose so," returned Roger, sounding unconvinced. "I've never had a beard."

"Boy, quite a place you've got here!" continued Ari, trying to change the subject. "I've heard about that famous 'Southern hospitality.' You're sure it's okay? I must look horrible...."

"Hey, you've come to the right place." Roger had been looking him over. "Been up all night crawlin' around in the brush and mud? Looks like you had a close call!"

"I ran into a branch. Didn't see it in the dark. Looks worse than it is."

Roger smiled skeptically. "Come on, Ari. We're friends. You can level with me. I've been around guns all my life. They almost had a funeral for you!"

Too exhausted to stand any longer, Ari sank into an overstuffed armchair. His jacket fell back, exposing the Luger stuck in his belt. Quickly he covered the weapon, then realized that Roger had already seen it. Ari sank back with a sheepish grin. "Yeah, you're right," he admitted. "Somebody almost got me."

Roger let out a low whistle. "So you're on the run. I think you'd better tell me...."

"Look, I didn't want to get you in trouble," began Ari apologetically, "but I didn't know where else to go."

"Don't worry. You're lucky you got here. I'll help you any way I can. Hide you...smuggle you out to the West...but I've got to know what we're dealing with."

"Forget the West. I'm staying here to bring down that Wall. You've told me it would happen."

"Just level with me," said Roger. His smile was warm, but the steel-blue eyes seemed to pierce into Ari's soul.

"You know how much I hate Marxism. We've talked about it a lot. What I never told you...well...I've been involved in...uh, revolutionary activities...."

Roger's eyes had relaxed and the smile broadened. "I've known that for a long time."

Ari's mouth dropped open. "You have? How?"

"I can't explain that right now."

"Well, then, the Stasi...maybe they knew all along, too."

"They didn't have a clue. Must have just got onto you."

"If you knew *all that*, then why ask me?"

"Just to make sure you'd tell the truth. If we're in this together, we've got to know we can trust each other." Roger was thinking. "I didn't see anyone. Nobody followed you?"

Ari shook his head. "I'm positive. But this place must be watched."

"They're not watching me." Roger's voice carried absolute conviction. "Now, let's get down to practical matters. You need some breakfast—and a bed. But first we've got to clean that wound. Looks nasty. Can't have an infection on our hands." He disappeared down a hallway that led off from the living room and returned in a few moments with a small bottle and some cotton.

"Mouthwash?" asked Ari in surprise, reading the label.

"It's all I've got—but it'll do the job. It's 37 percent alcohol." He soaked the cotton and scrubbed at the shallow gash mercilessly, making Ari grit his teeth with pain. "Sorry, but I've got to make sure it's clean. Can't take any chances."

"I'm sure there isn't a microbe left!" protested Ari.

"Okay. Now come into the kitchen. Sit yourself down at the table, there, while I get something for you. Then to bed."

Ari was too exhausted to do anything except mechanically obey. He could hardly keep his eyes open while Roger fixed some toast and coffee. With that in his stomach he followed his host, as though he were groping through a thick fog. Roger led the way across the plush wall-to-wall carpet through the well-furnished living room and down the hall into a spacious bedroom with its own private bath, two king-size beds with a folding partition between them, a desk and sofa. A large sliding glass door opening onto an interior garden.

"This is where my family stays when they visit." Roger's voice sounded miles away. "I'll put your briefcase here on the desk. Take either bed. I've got some things to do...probably get back here around three o'clock. If you wake up before then and want anything, just help yourself."

Too exhausted to do anything else, Ari pulled off his filthy clothes and collapsed into the nearest bed. A firm mattress, clean sheets and warm blankets—what a welcome contrast to what he might have been facing at this very moment. *Safe at last! They'll never find me here. Roger... bless him... maybe some day I can repay the favor....* He drifted off into a delicious unconsciousness.

— ✦ —

Without so much as a dream that he could remember, Ari awakened to hear rain beating on the window. A glance at his watch told him it was after four o'clock. *Seven hours. I could use a couple more, but I want to sleep tonight.* He lay there for a few more luxurious moments, drifting in and out of consciousness, thinking how lucky it was that he'd met Roger those many months ago.

At last Ari forced himself to get out of bed. There, hanging over the back of a chair, he saw his muddied and bloodied clothes now cleaned and pressed. What a friend Roger was—and what miracles could happen when money was no concern. He took a shower and dressed. There was the sound of movement at the other end of the apartment, and a tantalizing aroma was wafting into his room.

Ari came slowly down the hall and stood just inside the living room, watching Roger, who was stirring something on the stove and hadn't seen him yet. "What do I smell?" he asked.

"Oh, you're up!" responded Roger cheerfully. "You were really zonked when I came back about an hour ago. I bet you've never smelled anything like this. Wait 'till you taste it! I'm making enchiladas. A Mexican dish. You'll love it. If you're staying with a Texan, you have to eat like one."

"I'm hungry enough to eat the plates. And thanks for taking care of my clothes. How'd you do that?"

"No problem. Just threw them into the washer and drier. How about a beer?"

"No thanks. Never touch it. Reminds me of my old man. He's an alcoholic. Gets ugly when he drinks."

"Sorry about that. Say, I picked up a newspaper for you. It's over there on the sofa."

"Thanks." Ari turned and took a few steps toward the paper, then froze. His picture, about eight inches high, was on the front page. The headlines read: "CAPITALIST CONSPIRACY UNCOVERED!" The lead article was headed, in large, bold print: "**Manhunt Underway. Large Reward Offered.**"

Feeling suddenly light-headed, Ari picked up the paper, walked over to the kitchen table, pulled out a chair and sat down. As he read, the words seemed to blur on the page. Roger busied himself silently with his cooking until Ari finished the article and threw the paper on the table with a curse.

"It's a pretty wild tale," suggested Roger. "They make you sound like a one-man army. Any truth in it?"

"Some. They've done a lot of guessing. And I can't believe they haven't found the police car yet. They stopped a train I was on. . . ."

"Another train after the one you threw the two policemen from?"

"Yeah. And they weren't police. They were Stasi."

Roger stepped back from the stove and gave him an admiring look. "You must have nine lives. Lucky you got here. Sounds like an incredible ordeal."

"It was. I'm glad it's over."

"I'd like to hear about it . . . sometime when you feel like it."

"Yeah. Rather not talk about it now. Later, maybe. I sure appreciate you taking me in. I don't want to put you in danger."

"Don't mention it. I've got some ideas. We'll talk about them when we sit down to eat."

Roger went back to his frying pan. Ari sat in deep thought. How long could he stay? When would he dare to venture out into the streets and start his work again? It seemed more certain to him now than ever that Roger was connected, if not to the CIA, then to some center of international influence that gave him access to Western intelligence. Otherwise, how could he have known so much? Would he do more than hide Ari—perhaps use that power to help in other ways? Was that what he meant by "some ideas"?

The momentary silence was broken by the musical sound of chimes. *Someone's at the front door!* Instinctively Ari sprang to his feet, then sat back down in embarrassment. *You can't jump at every shadow.*

"Relax," said Roger. "It's probably the mailman with a package I'm expecting." Turning the heat down under the frying pan, he went down the entry hall and opened the door.

Ari could hear muffled voices in a brief exchange. Then he heard Roger exclaim angrily, "You can't do this! I'm an American citizen. I have diplomatic immunity!"

Ari shoved his chair back from the table and stood up uncertainly. What was happening? Should he run to the bedroom for his gun?

There were hurried footsteps coming toward him. Too late, Ari started across the living room toward the interior hallway. He was cut off by two men in business suits who burst into the room. The taller of the two had an ugly scar that angled across his face from chin to ear. His companion looked like a bulldog, from pug nose and barrel chest to bowed legs. They were pointing submachine guns. From somewhere Ari heard the chilling words, "You're under arrest!"

Roger was standing behind the intruders, mouth agape, and looking at Ari apologetically. "I'm sorry!" he kept repeating. "I'm sorry! I don't know how they found you!"

The pressures of the last 48 hours seemed to crush Ari at last. He stood stunned and motionless, unable to believe that after safely reaching this perfect haven it could all end like this.

"Hands behind you!"

Mechanically Ari obeyed. What was the point of trying to resist any longer? All his efforts to get here... and still they'd found him.

Keeping their weapons aimed at Ari, and an eye on Roger, the two men circled warily around on opposite sides out of range of Ari's lethal feet and came up behind him at last. Handcuffs were snapped on his wrists with speed and precision.

While Scarface stayed with him, the Bulldog ran down the hall and in almost no time returned. In despair Ari noted that he was carrying the briefcase with its priceless contents. Then, one on each side, they grabbed his arms in vise-like grips. "Get moving!" came the steel-cold order.

Almost before he realized it had happened, Ari had been hustled out the front door past Roger, who was still frozen in helpless astonishment.

Nightmare

As though it were happening to someone else, Ari felt himself propelled across the shiny marbled porch and down the front steps toward an unmarked car that was waiting at the curb. He was stunned by the apparent omniscience and omnipotence of the Stasi. They seemed to know everything about him. And why not? They were in complete control of the country, with every resource and advantage on their side. It was an unfair battle that only they could win. His dream of destroying Marxism had been just that—the grandiose fantasy of someone too young to know any better.

They'll drug and torture me...get me ready for a phony trial. Milk it for a trainload of propaganda. A public execution. An "example" for the "people" never to forget. Why did I let them take me? Better to die fighting than be captured like an animal. No, they knew exactly what they were doing. There was no way. I'll get my chance...a lucky break somewhere...sometime...soon!

He was shoved roughly into the back seat of the waiting car beside a slender, balding man in a tailored gray suit who sat with his back to him, staring out the window on the other side. There was something disturbingly familiar about him, something that triggered a fragmented memory. *When? Where?* The door slammed shut behind Ari, and the two men who had arrested him eased quickly into the front, Bulldog taking the wheel.

The car pulled away from the curb. Looking back, Ari saw Roger standing in the open doorway wearing the same bewildered expression. Was it an act? Had he told the Stasi where to find him? No, Ari couldn't believe that. Roger had been genuinely stunned. The Stasi probably watched that apartment day and night. He'd been a fool to come there—but how could he have known?

To Ari's astonishment, after a few blocks the driver made an abrupt right turn. Instead of heading toward the beige, concrete headquarters of the Ministry for State Security on Normannenstrasse, they were now going in the opposite direction.

"Where are you taking me?" Ari demanded.

"To the railway station," said Scarface.

"What? Why?"

"You're going to make a 'miraculous escape' into West Berlin."

Ari felt the handcuffs—apparently electronically controlled—fall from his wrists onto the seat behind him. The mysterious figure beside him hadn't moved. He was still looking out the window in silence, chin in hand, as though totally absorbed with the passing scenery.

"You have a great sense of humor," responded Ari acidly. What were they really planning to do? Never mind. With his hands now free—why had they done that?—he could put a quick choke-hold on the man in the back seat and threaten to break his neck unless they drove him where he wanted to go. But where could that be?

"I know exactly what you're thinking," said the man beside him. "Don't try it." That voice—so familiar, yet so elusive... and persuasive. Still he stared out the window.

What's happening? Scarface had started taking off his clothes. He glanced back at Ari. "Off with yours, too," he ordered as he struggled to get out of his pants. He held up the uniform of a police colonel and started to put it on. "Here's one for you," he said, throwing a plain uniform with no marking of rank on it and a pair of black shoes back onto the seat beside Ari. "Get into it."

"*A police uniform? What are you guys up to?*"

"That's your ticket to the West. Move!"

"You think I'm crazy? You're setting me up."

"Do what he says!" snapped the driver.

"I get caught in a police uniform trying to 'escape,'" objected Ari, "so you can shoot me on the spot. Makes better propaganda, doesn't it! I'm not *that* stupid!"

"Your cuffs are off," argued Scarface, who had just finished putting on the uniform. "The guns and 'arrest' were for the benefit of your friend. We're here to help you get to the West."

"I don't want to go to the West. I belong here. I haven't done anything wrong!"

"Nothing wrong? Stop bluffing!" growled the man beside him impatiently. He was obviously in charge. "You've plotted to overthrow the government... left a trail of mayhem... two dead agents and two others that nearly drowned...."

"Then why help me get to the West?"

"You don't have any choice, do you?" He turned to face Ari. It was the man of his nightmares! Or was it? Where had he seen him? In real life... or just a dream?

"I know you from somewhere," said Ari, feeling those eyes penetrate his soul as though his innermost thoughts were being uncovered. His head began to spin. Quickly he turned away, trying to shake the confusion. "Where have I seen you?" he persisted, now certain that he knew this man. That first demonstration... was he the one who'd grabbed his arm? An elusive memory taunted Ari from just out of reach. "At the demonstration in Leipzig! That's it!"

"I've been in contact for years," came the enigmatic response.

Ari took off his jacket and started to unbutton his shirt. There was no other choice. "Who are you?" he demanded.

"It's not for you to understand now—but you will. I'm a mentor...from a higher dimension of consciousness."

"And I'm the reincarnation of King Tut!" snapped Ari angrily. "You're CIA...right?"

"No. We've come to help you because we share your concern for saving this planet. The karma of the entire galaxy is at risk."

Karma...galaxy? What's their game? "So how do you plan to do this...and what do you want from me?" asked Ari, playing along with the game for the moment.

"No time to explain now. Get into that uniform—fast!"

Ari hurried to obey. Perhaps the uniform would come in handy when he made his escape. "What did you mean by 'a higher dimension of consciousness'?" he asked, pretending to take such nonsense seriously.

"Of course you don't believe me—yet."

"Well, I do and I don't," returned Ari quickly. Could this enigmatic figure beside him really read his mind, or was he just making good guesses?

"I already told you, I know what you're thinking," came the impatient reply. "This physical plane is only a small part of the universe, yet it holds you a prisoner and blinds you to the ten levels of consciousness beyond it. At your level, what I'm saying makes no sense...but one day you'll know."

There was a brief conversation between his captors. The language escaped Ari. He finished changing into the uniform. "Okay. Now what?"

"You're going with the colonel to check passports on the train from Moscow. It's due in the station in 20 minutes. Stay with him—and do exactly what he tells you. I'll be in touch with you later...."

"In the West?"

"In the West."

"That's who you are—West German Intelligence!"

"We've nothing to do with them," came the curt reply. "You'll get instructions...in Paris. Build your base from there. Same project, but worldwide."

The whole thing was insane. But playing along with them was the best option at the moment. The car pulled up in front of the station. "I've got to have my briefcase," Ari demanded.

"No. It doesn't go with the uniform. We've got one for you—with 50,000 West German marks in it. That will get you started."

The driver got out and went to the trunk. A moment later he opened Ari's door and shoved an official police briefcase onto his lap. "Put everything in there—and be quick."

Ari raised the lid. He couldn't believe his eyes. The money was there, in neat bundles of 100-mark notes. He covered the cash with the precious papers from his own briefcase, the Luger and ammunition, and the clothes and tennis shoes he'd just taken off.

"You'll use those names and addresses—most of them—one day in the West," said Hypnotic-eyes.

"Maybe. Anyway, I'm not leaving them here."

"Let's go," ordered the colonel. "On the double."

Ari climbed out of the car and hurried to follow Scarface, now dressed as a police colonel, into the station. He had no other choice—but what was he getting into? Was there a faction within the police that was working to overthrow the regime and wanted him safe in the West? Or was it a trick—perhaps something far more elaborate than he could even imagine?

"Stay beside me and do what I tell you," the colonel muttered softly. "Act like you know what you're doing—not like you're my *prisoner*!"

Still unable to believe what was happening, Ari followed Scarface through customs and passport control. Every officer along the way saluted his companion, and several greeted him by name.

Out on the platform half a dozen police were conversing together, smoking and laughing as they waited for the Moscow express. A captain stood nearby, who was apparently in charge. The colonel stopped with Ari about 30 feet away. "Wait here," he confided. "I'll be right back."

This is where I get shot! He's giving them instructions. It's a setup, just like I thought! They expect me to make a run for it. I won't. That would be insane.

The captain saluted the colonel smartly and the two of them withdrew a few paces, where they talked in subdued tones. Ari strained to hear but could only make out an occasional word. *I'm not going to run so they can shoot me in the back. They'll have to kill me in cold blood, face-to-face—and I don't think they'll do that here with all these people watching.*

When the colonel returned he was smiling. "The captain has a bunch of new recruits. I told him you were just as green as they are, but you've got unusual potential and I want to instruct you personally. We'll take the first two cars. It's a simple job. We move down the aisle together checking passports. The train is filled with Western tourists who've come either from Moscow or Warsaw. When we're done, I'll tell you what to do."

In a few minutes the train pulled into the station and Ari followed the colonel aboard. Moving slowly down the aisle of the first car and checking passports with the colonel at his side, Ari began to relax. Maybe it was really happening! The colonel wasn't going to shoot him in front of a hundred Westerners—and certainly not without some provocation, which Ari was determined he wouldn't be tricked into providing. In fact, as he saw how genially his mysterious companion dealt with each passenger, Ari's feelings began to undergo a surprising metamorphosis.

They finished their task without incident. All passports were in order and everyone was accounted for on the list of passengers they'd processed for these two cars. As they moved to the back door of the second car the colonel paused beside the W.C.

"Get in there and lock the door," he told Ari. "Change back into your own clothes. Stuff the uniform into the bottom of the trash bin. Don't come out for any reason until the train has crossed into West Berlin."

"How are you going to explain my absence to the captain when I don't come back with you?" asked Ari, reluctant to say goodbye. Could he really be concerned for the safety of this man who, less than an hour ago, had threatened him with a submachine gun?

"He's one of us," replied the colonel with a short laugh. "Now hurry! Get in there." He looked at his watch. "I've got to signal the train to move."

Ari stepped inside, locked the door and peered out the window. *One of us? So there is a rebel faction inside the police! If I'd only known that and worked with them, things might have been different. Why didn't they contact me sooner?*

He saw the colonel signal the brakeman, then walk toward the station. The captain was already herding his men through the door.

With a jolt the train started. It couldn't be true—but it was. In a few moments he would be a free man!

8

Le Professeur

PARIS, FRANCE—
Early May, 1989

From its watchful post on the centuries-darkened stone exterior high above the western entrance to the University of Paris, the weathered face of the ancient clock looked down solemnly on Place De La Sorbonne. Its corroded hands stood at 11:47 A.M. Already the sidewalk tables of the *brasseries, salons de thé* and *grillades* along the south side of the small square were crowded, though it was still too early for most of the business clientele. Students hunched over their drinks and conversed with great gusto in small groups, four or five around a tiny table made to accommodate two—saying very little about their studies, but contending earnestly and at times heatedly about politics and human rights, as though the fate of the world hinged upon their sagacious pronouncements.

One outdoor table at Brasserie L'Escholier, a restaurant which specialized in Carlsberg and Dortmonder beers, had been occupied since midmorning by two men in business suits. Muscular and tanned, they looked more like professional athletes than entrepreneurs. They exchanged little conversation. A certain restlessness and an occasional glance around the square as they thumbed disinterestedly through the morning edition of *Le Monde* suggested that they were waiting for someone. When the hands of the clock moved past twelve the two men seemed to grow increasingly alert and glanced more frequently over the tops of their papers toward the door below the ancient timepiece.

At about ten minutes past noon, after the flood of departing students had thinned, a lone figure exited the door and was greeted by the uniformed attendant standing outside with a hearty, "*Bon jour, Professeur.*" The professor responded with a nod and a brief smile, took a few steps to his right along the narrow Rue de La Sorbonne, then turned abruptly to angle across the square in the direction of Boulevard Saint Michel. One of the two occupants of the table stood to his feet and moved casually along parallel to the professor, while the other continued to peruse his newspaper for another few moments. At last he folded his well-thumbed copy of *Le Monde*, directed a few quiet words into his inside pocket, then joined the procession.

As for the man now being shadowed, the passage of years had added a quiet projection of mature wisdom that was befitting a professor at France's most prestigious university. Time had, of course, taken its inevitable toll. Although the unforgettable deep-set brown eyes still seemed to take in everything within sight in one sweeping glance, the once-thick, jet-black curly hair was now slightly thinned and streaked with gray. Yet his face seemed hardly to have aged—perhaps because it retained that same intense expression of one driven by a consuming cause with little time to waste on anything else.

Even the loose-fitting tweed jacket couldn't hide the fact that the man who wore it was in top physical condition. In every movement he seemed to exude the explosive energy of one 20 years his junior—as much an athlete in disguise as the two younger men who were now intent upon keeping him closely in view. Anyone who had known Ari at the time of his escape from East Berlin at age 20 would have had little trouble recognizing him now in spite of his new identity as Professor Hans Mueller, at 45 the well-liked and respected head of the department of political science at the Sorbonne.

Twenty-five years had passed since Ari had so mysteriously disappeared from East Germany. At that time very few who cared had suspected that he'd had the good fortune to escape. Most of those who had been close to him had been quickly swallowed up by the Stasi, never to be heard of again. It was quite naturally assumed that Ari had suffered the same fate. His foster mother, however, had never given up hope. Unfortunately, by the time Ari had felt it was safe to write to her, she was dead, the victim of a brain tumor that mercifully took her quickly. Her husband, consumed by guilt that his periodic fits of violent abuse had contributed to her untimely death, sought increasingly to drown his remorse in alcohol. Not long after her demise, that tragic figure succumbed to cirrhosis of the liver, still awaiting official recognition for the information he'd supplied that surely must have led to the arrest of that Jew-bastard-enemy-of-the-state.

Ari's letter to his foster mother, written in carefully guarded language, was eventually returned by the censors. They had opened and read it without understanding its significance. A subsequent letter mailed hopefully some months later was sent back unopened. Across the front were the words, in the handwritten scrawl of the village postmaster, "addressee deceased." He would never learn the circumstances of her death. The last days of the only "mother" he'd ever known would remain forever hidden behind the same sinister cloud of totalitarian oppression that obscured the fate of his real parents.

That impenetrable veil, woven by the great evil that had left Europe in ruins, allowed Ari to maintain in his own mind the hollow denial that he was not Jewish. After all, that accusation had only come from two uneducated people and was impossible to verify. Nor had he given the painful circumstantial evidence that his parents had been swallowed up in Hitler's holocaust more than a passing thought for years. The uncomfortable question of his true origin, uneasily laid to rest, had long since been submerged by the rising flood of swiftly moving events that demanded every waking thought.

The irreplaceable list of contacts Ari had brought out of the East in that official police briefcase—plus thousands of subsequently acquired ones throughout the Western world and Asia—had been meticulously screened and nurtured by an internationally dispersed staff that he had personally recruited and trained. The process had taken many years, but one of the greatest lessons he had learned from his earlier failures behind the Iron Curtain had been the absolute necessity of patience—and more patience. Revolutions couldn't be rushed; they had to ripen. And with the patience, his vision had grown so that now at last he was within a few months of pulling off on a worldwide scale what he had so narrowly missed accomplishing within the limited confines of East Germany.

Though founded by Robert de Sorbon in 1253, the institute that bore his name had its origins in the school that Charlemagne had opened for Alcuin in 780 A.D. That venerable institution became the University of Paris, to be eventually known as the Sorbonne. It was here, by the end of the 13th century, that most modern university customs, including the writing and defense of theses, the issuance of degrees, academic regalia and rituals such as commencement exercises, all had their origins. With its early history of radicalism and unrivaled reputation as the chief center of education for all of Europe as far back as 1116 A.D.—under that arch radical, Pierre Abélard—the Sorbonne was the ideal base of operations for Ari's worldwide student revolution.

In the classes he taught, Ari could openly advocate, should he care to, the overthrow of existing governments both in the East and West without so much as an eyebrow being raised. Publicly he aggressively promoted a position that was extreme enough to make him popular with students and faculty alike, but which did not betray his true ambitions and plans. Such public radicalism in his position as head of the Sorbonne's political science department was the ideal cover for the real revolution Ari was pursuing in secret. His fame as a brilliant debater and captivating public speaker had opened to him the doors of Europe's major universities on both sides of the Iron Curtain, providing Ari with university-sponsored travel and endless contacts throughout the world of academia.

Ari had remained an avowed enemy of religion, that great opiate of the people—the only tenet of Marxism to which he still subscribed. It was ironic that the university where he taught had in its early days been intimately linked with the theological school at the nearby Cathedral of Notre Dame—and theology was still a major factor in its huge Sciences des Religions department. Oddly enough, however, that department, in attempting to blend science and religion, had destroyed both and now sheltered more skeptics than believers. Ari relished pointing out such contradictions.

In 1431 A.D. the eminent theologians at the Sorbonne, by that time Europe's foremost center of theology and chief supporter of the papacy, played a major role in the Church's condemnation of Joan of Arc to the stake. Yet today, inside the cathedral of Notre Dame, one of the most popular statues, with a large number of candles always burning before it, is that of Sainte Jeanne D'Arc, now France's "national heroine." Nor had the Sorbonne itself escaped the plague of contradictions. Always a seething cauldron of revolution, the University of Paris had been shut down when the French Revolution abolished all French universities on September 15, 1793. As Ari often pointed out in his lectures, revolutions too often established worse systems than the ones they replaced, the Soviet Union being a prime example. He was determined that the uprising he would lead would not repeat such errors. That was reason enough for him to maintain total control and impenetrable secrecy.

Most university students, in Ari's estimation, had no sense of direction and little motivation for changing themselves, much less the world. He had proven that in 16 years of teaching. And the vast majority, unfortunately, no matter how sophisticated they considered themselves to be, would, in the final analysis, follow any leader who knew how to put the ring in their noses and lead them along. There was a dangerous minority who were simply rebels and would join any movement that opposed those in power—then turn against the new government they had helped to establish. Of course there were always a small number of "activists," some very sincere. Their activism, however, was confined to poorly planned, sporadic and ineffective protests—and scrawling graffiti, most of which was unintelligible and only alienated the general populace.

At that very moment the statue of Auguste Comte that dominated the small square was being sandblasted to remove spray-painted initials that probably belonged to some obscure extremist student group, but who would know? What a waste of effort on both sides, for as soon as it was taken off the graffiti would reappear. And why was the workman carrying right on during the noon break? He couldn't be a Frenchman! As Ari detoured around the statue, some of the wet, sandy spray blown by the breeze hit him in the face. He wiped it off in disgust and hurried on.

Auguste Comte—another contradiction! This founder of sociology, a term he invented, had been a complete failure in his personal life and business and in relationships with others. A suicidal megalomaniac, Comte couldn't even hold a job. Yet his theories heavily influenced 19th-century thought and were still being honored, studied and taught, not only at the Sorbonne but worldwide. Though an atheistic humanist, Comte had also fallen prey to religious delusions, founding the *Religion of Humanity* with its elaborate rituals, hymns, saints—even canonizing his favorite mistress, Clothilde de Vaux.

Human follies seemed endless. Was there any hope? *Leadership! That's what it boils down to. The rabble will follow anyone, anything, anywhere. We've got to destroy present leadership structures—not just in the East but in the West as well—before we can make a new world of freedom and justice!*

As he reached the sidewalk and turned to follow Boulevard Saint Michel toward the Seine, Ari's thoughts were interrupted by a voice in his ear and a hand on his arm. "Would you sign our petition, professor?" He paused and turned to smile at the speaker, whom he recognized as one of his most serious graduate students. The young Iranian,who had been hurrying to catch up with him as he crossed the square, thrust in front of Ari a large picture album and began to turn its pages, revealing photos of current public executions in Iran and apparent documentation of the most barbarous torture imaginable.

"These are just a few examples," the young man explained earnestly. "Look how the ruling Muslim elite treats not just dissidents but anyone at random! People are falsely accused, condemned in mock trials, tortured to death without a public hearing."

Another young Iranian student had moved onto the center of the sidewalk and was holding high a placard on which was scrawled in large letters, "*KHOMEINY EST MORT! MAIS LES CRIMES DE SON REGIME CONTINUENT A ETRE COMMIS.*"

"What you really want is not just my signature, but a contribution—right?" commented Ari dryly after glancing at the form.

"Yes, of course. We're trying to raise money to help these poor people."

Ari looked him squarely in the eye. "I don't doubt the atrocities, but how do I know this organization is legitimate?"

"You know me from class. I wouldn't be involved if. . . ."

"Maybe you're deceived, too." Ari signed the petition and handed the young man a ten-franc coin. "I want to have the full documentation on this organization—in writing—and an oral report to the Justice in Government class. If it's legitimate, then this information needs to be publicized widely and everyone ought to give to this cause. If it's not legitimate. . . ." He left that question hanging and turned to walk briskly along Boulevard Saint Michel, heading ever deeper into the Latin Quarter.

It was a day of rare and dazzling clarity without a trace of the choking smog that had been growing steadily worse in recent years. So often it settled in mercilessly for days at a time during the heat of summer. The sidewalks were crowded with both tourists and Parisians savoring the sun and the overpowering aroma of assorted spring blossoms wafting on the air. Ari glanced at his watch and quickened his pace as he hurried past Musée de Cluny with its visible ruins of Roman baths dating back to the third century. Crossing Boulevard Saint Germain, he turned right to Rue Saint Jacques, then left along that narrow street between the ancient churches of Saint Séverin and Saint Julien le Pauvre.

Saint this and *Saint* that. There was no way to escape the "Saints" in Paris. Their pervasive presence always reminded him of his East German mamma. She would have loved it here if she had only survived long enough and could have come to visit him. There was the Wall . . . but they might have let her out to save the money of supporting another old woman. She would have been happy surrounded by so many "Saints"—and absolutely ecstatic inside the cathedral of Notre Dame de Paris, dedicated to "Our Lady of Paris."

A momentary wave of nostalgia swept over Ari. He had a love for Germany and for that village—and even for that miserable farm—in spite of the painful memories. There was something about *home* and the presence of a woman.

His obsessive dedication to the liberation of communist countries, the growing worldwide organization he secretly directed, the continual travel, the clandestine meetings all over Europe—all of that on top of being a professor at the Sorbonne, and department chairman as well—had left no time for anything else.

Ari's daily experience had been devoid of all that was sentimental, intimate or tender—devoid until Nicole had entered his life six years earlier. She had exposed and then filled the aching vacuum he had refused to admit was there. For him the old adage had proved true: life had indeed begun at 40. Life and love as he'd never imagined it could be.

A pre-med major, Niki had been in only one of his classes, and they had found themselves irresistibly attracted to each other from the first day. She'd been a top student: sharp, politically savvy, outspoken—and vulnerable to his virile masculinity. Her youth and enthusiasm had rekindled a flame which Ari had thought extinct. Her compassion and understanding, despite the 17-year age difference, had at last defined the word "home" once again for Ari—indeed, had given it new meaning. Now in residency as a neurosurgeon at a nearby hospital, she had shared his apartment from the moment they'd fallen in love. Six incredible years. Ari savored the thought for a brief moment, then put it out of his mind. He had to be mentally prepared for the serious—and dangerous—business ahead.

Turning right at the Seine, and checking the exact time on his watch again, Ari slowed his pace to stroll along the Left Bank past its tiny kiosks ingeniously attached to the wall bordering the river. Locked up at night, they were now unfolded, with lids propped up high and astonishing amounts of wares exposed within and displayed on the pavement outside under the watchful eyes of each proudly independent owner. This was capitalism in its simplest, purest form. The narrow sidewalk was jammed with tourists pausing here and there to finger an ancient volume or glance at a clever political cartoon or other bit of the flotsam and jetsam of printed matter that had somehow come to be the peculiar product offered here.

Timing himself carefully, Ari turned left to cross the Seine over Pont au Double to Ile de la Cité. He paused to curse the endless lines of tour buses converging there, belching dark clouds of foul-smelling, poisonous fumes as they stopped to disgorge or swallow up their cargo of tourists. And he took another moment, face uplifted, hand sheltering eyes from sun, to peer up at the massive Gothic facade of *Notre Dame* for at least the thousandth time. The repulsive, bird-beaked, evil-eyed, rodent-eared gargoyles with human torsos and arms, perched everywhere on the cathedral, were another contradiction that held a peculiar fascination for him. If such a place as hell existed, then these monsters surely represented its denizens.

Demons stationed on the parapets of a *church* to protect it from evil? Talk about the fox guarding the henhouse! Yet the same contradiction was repeated endlessly in governments around the world where the "welfare of the people" was in the hands of leaders who cared only for themselves. His life was devoted to eventually replacing what he called the "government gargoyles," beginning with Marxist regimes, and not sparing the West, from Paris to Washington.

Given over to momentary disgust, Ari moved on another hundred feet toward Pont D'Arcole. The perpetual hordes of visitors always milling about the cathedral made this a good meeting point. One could get lost in the crowds.

Of course *they* followed him everywhere he went and knew every move he made. It was for his own "protection," so he was told when he complained. Sometimes he caught a glimpse of his "guardians," as he had of those two today when he'd come out of the university, but usually he saw nothing. He just knew, even now as he stood on the curb across the street from the front entrance of the massive 13th-century cathedral, that somewhere in the crowd close by was the "security" he had not asked for, didn't want and certainly didn't trust. He was an expert at losing them when he wanted to, but that only made the committee angry and created more tensions.

Ari glanced at his watch again and waited. Out of the corner of his eye he saw a cab slowing. That was his signal. A quick wave of an arm, a dash between the parked cars into the street as it came to a stop, and he was inside.

The back seat was already occupied by a tall, lean, well-dressed man with sharp features and a self-possessed air. He could have been German, French, Dutch—a true international who could fit in anywhere and spoke eight languages fluently with flawless accent. No one would have suspected that he was from, of all places, *Texas*—until he spoke to them in English.

Except for a trace of gray in his crew-cut blond hair and a few new creases across his forehead, Roger Dunn's physical appearance had changed little since Ari had first met him in East Berlin 26 years before.

Without so much as a flicker of recognition, as though he were a total stranger, Ari greeted his fellow passenger in French with a hearty, "Thanks for sharing the cab." To the driver he added, "*Tour Eiffel.*"

"*Tour Eiffel*," returned the cabbie.

A Matter of Principal

For years, Ari had not heard from Roger since being taken from his apartment at gunpoint—nor had he attempted to contact him, suspecting that his mail and phone lines were under Stasi surveillance. Then one day, unannounced, the remarkable Texan had walked into Ari's office at the university. What a deliriously happy reunion that had been!

Roger told how he had diligently pursued every diplomatic channel in an attempt to learn what had happened to Ari after his arrest, but without any success. He had eventually assumed that Ari had been executed. It had been nearly 13 years later, while watching a French news program he sometimes picked up from a satellite dish, that he had recognized Ari in a feature story about the Sorbonne. Not long after that the American had come to Paris to present an irresistible offer to his old friend from East Germany.

Roger had revealed at their first meeting in Paris that for years he had represented a mysterious group of secretive and extremely wealthy and powerful men who controlled a multibillion dollar international banking conglomerate. This consortium was interested in financing viable efforts to bring down communist regimes around the world—which explained Roger's interest in Ari when they had originally met in East Berlin.

Though millions of dollars had been expended, none of the efforts of these financiers had brought any success. Something more than money was needed. Through their CIA connections, the syndicate had begun to suspect that a well-organized, clandestine student organization with the same goals as theirs was operating internationally. Yet even with their Interpol contacts, all attempts to infiltrate or even to contact the leadership of this impenetrable network had proved futile.

Then came Roger's chance discovery that Ari was alive and teaching at the Sorbonne. He immediately suspected that his old friend might be the one heading this intriguing student movement and came to Paris to find out whether that was the case. Ari was careful to reveal nothing, but he did admit to Roger at their first meeting that he was indeed the man who was running the operation that had so intrigued his colleagues and which the CIA had been unable to crack.

The conglomerate not only had CIA connections, but its influence reached into the highest levels of governments around the world, from the White House to the inner circle of the Kremlin itself. Roger explained to Ari that there were men rising to the top in Soviet leadership who were very much in sympathy with bringing down the Wall, liberating Eastern Europe and destroying Marxism. The question was how to do it—and Ari's group seemed to be the answer for which they had searched for so many years.

The international bankers wanted their organization and themselves individually to remain anonymous, even to Ari, because the men involved were household names worldwide. Ari suspected that Roger's father was among them, and perhaps the leader, but their identities were immaterial. What mattered was their wealth and their willingness to use it in the right way.

Through Roger, this unusual group had offered virtually unlimited funds to finance Ari's operation. While this was exactly what Ari needed, he had pretended reluctance to accept the offer. "I don't want to be indebted to anyone," he had told Roger. "Financial partners eventually make demands for information and participation that I can't—and will not—agree to."

"That's exactly the way we want it," Roger had assured him. "Take my word for it, these men have no intention of ever attempting to move in and take over. You'll have complete autonomy to run your program independently, no questions asked. Secrecy on both sides, and absolute trust—that's the only rule."

The arrangement had seemed to be ideal and had worked well for nearly ten years. The funds this group had provided had made it possible for Ari to greatly expand and accelerate his program. Unfortunately, the marriage of convenience had become increasingly strained in recent months. The partners no longer agreed on the principles Ari had once thought they held in common. The only bond that remained was *principal*—the huge sums of money which they controlled and were still willing to hand over to him, and which he desperately needed to hold his huge organization together. Ari had good reason to suspect, however, that even that bond was weakening—that the consortium was laying plans to eliminate him and take control.

To protect himself, Ari had, from the first day of their association, wisely begun a program of infiltration that had successfully penetrated the top levels of Roger's organization. One of the first findings his moles had passed on had confirmed his earliest suspicions—that Roger, unknown to the banking consortium and even to his own father, was actually working for the CIA. That startling discovery had raised serious questions concerning the very foundation of their friendship and had destroyed any hope that Ari could count on Roger's loyalty.

Ari had begun to sense a growing tension between Roger's professed friendship to him and his obligation to the consortium. While pretending to side with Ari at first—off the record, of course—Roger had stiffened his stance recently. New demands had been made by Roger on behalf of his superiors that were not in keeping with the original agreement. Today's meeting had been called to resolve some issues that threatened to destroy their relationship and its goals.

Ari settled back in the cab and stared out the window. Roger unobtrusively slid a thick envelope across the seat between them. Ari knew, without looking, what was in it: the usual 50 or so checks in odd amounts between $20,000 and $30,000 from a number of dummy corporations whose names kept changing and which, unlike automatic banking fund transfers, no one could trace. He had tried. He would deposit the funds over the next ten days in a dozen bank accounts he maintained around the city. Still observing the scenery out the window, Ari, with one swift motion, slipped the envelope into an inside pocket of his sports jacket.

"Good job!" murmured Roger softly in Russian. "It's going to break wide open in China—soon."

"And I'm *very* unhappy about it!" shot back Ari under his breath. Russian, forced on him in East German schools, was one of several languages in which he was fluent. It was the one he and Roger usually spoke whenever someone, even an apparently chance cabbie, might overhear them. "Your group is interfering... rushing it. It won't work. There's going to be a massacre!"

"Our intelligence—and we've got the best—says it's the right time and will succeed."

"It won't. You've got to call off your dogs... stop interfering!"

"What do you mean, *interfering*?"

"I'm talking about Chiang Lee and his cronies."

"Chiang Lee is a good man. Has the confidence of both the students and the workers. He's only trying to help you."

"I didn't ask for help."

"We thought you'd appreciate it."

"That's a violation of our deal. I'm supposed to run the operation—and Chiang Lee's involvement is a direct challenge to my leadership. It's going to bring disaster."

"Spell it out."

"You've got some greedy bankers who want to make money in China and can't wait. They're pushing it. This guy, Lee, is their man. Very charismatic. He's got the students excited. They're moving too soon. I'm telling you there's going to be a massacre!"

"You're convinced of that?" Roger seemed genuinely surprised and concerned.

"One-hundred percent," said Ari. "I was there last week."

"In Beijing? That's where you were when...?"

"When your goons couldn't find me for four days? That's right."

"You never cease to amaze me, Ari," said Roger grudgingly, but unable to hide the admiration in his voice. "Our best men... and you lose them... and they don't know how you do it."

Ari made no reply. There was an uncomfortable silence. At last Roger said, "You're not supposed to do that. Their job is to protect you...."

"So I've been told."

"It reflects on me!"

Ari frowned. "'Protection' was never part of the deal. I never agreed to it. So when I don't want them I lose them. You and I used to be close friends. I trusted you. Now I wonder: are you just naive... or are you feeding me a line?"

Roger hitched around in his seat to look Ari in the eye. "If you were in Beijing, how come none of our people there knew it?"

"Because I know who they are... and I wouldn't let them get within a Texas mile of me. Look, I know what I'm talking about... and I want Lee, that little *Caesar*, called off!"

Roger threw up his hands in helpless protest and fell back in the seat. "How did you get to Beijing and back without our knowing it?"

Ari laughed. "That's my secret. I met with my top leaders for two days... a dozen of them." His voice grew angry again. "They've lost control to this guy Lee, and they're worried about what's going to happen."

"Maybe Lee's gone beyond what we wanted him to do... even acting on his own. I'll look into it."

"Look, Roger, I know the situation! Your people put Lee in there, and they're backing him. That's a violation of our deal. No one's supposed to interfere! You put up the money—I run the revolution. Call him off *now*... before it's too late!"

"I'll check into it."

"Checking isn't enough! If he isn't taken out of Beijing within 48 hours at the most, we're finished. I'm going to lose my best people to slaughter or prison. They can't back away. They'd lose face... be dead for future leadership. Chiang is calling a strike they know will bring disaster... but they have to be in the front lines. Ten years of my careful work backed by *your money* is going to be wiped out!"

Roger looked worried. "I'll take care of it... if you're right. But my people have some complaints, too. They think you're dragging your feet—not just in Beijing but in Berlin and all over Eastern Europe. They want a schedule... and they want a list...."

"And I've told you they're not going to get either. If that breaks up our relationship...." Ari turned away to look out the window again.

"It's not unreasonable, Ari. We should be able to work this out. They're not asking for a complete list...."

"They were—and there's nothing to work out."

"That demand was a mistake. They've dropped it. They just want the name, address and phone number of your top man in each major center. In case of emergency. It takes too long to notify you and then have you contact your people. They want to be able to go directly. That's not unreasonable. It makes good sense."

"It makes no sense. I'm in charge, right?" snapped Ari. "I decide whether it's an emergency and I give *all* orders... *nobody* else! I've got to have complete autonomy and secrecy—and your people agreed. It took me 20 years to build this organization and I'm not betraying anyone...."

"*Betraying*? That's what you call giving us your key names? *Betraying*? You think we're the *enemy*?"

Ari turned and faced Roger. "You tell your bosses that they're not getting any names. Not one! That was our deal from day one and I've never agreed to a change—and I won't!"

Roger took a deep breath. "Circumstances have changed. It's been ten years, and we've invested hundreds of millions...."

"And we're just about there. Berlin has to come before Beijing...and if you interfere...."

"We've got the best intelligence in the world, and we think it has to be the other way around."

Ari pulled the bulging envelope from his pocket and put it on the seat next to Roger. "I got along very well without your money for the first ten years...."

Roger stared at the envelope in silence for a moment, then shoved it back toward Ari. "I thought you trusted me."

"I trust *you*, but I don't trust your bosses. They're the ones I worry about—the committee you report to...and the people at the top behind them. They know who I am; I don't know who they are...and they complain about not getting a list! They know where to find me at any hour of the day or night—their goons never leave me—and that worries me. I don't know where to find you until you tell me where we rendezvous next."

There was another long, uncomfortable silence. "Okay," conceded Roger at last. "I understand your perspective. I'll take your message, and do my best to persuade them...."

"*Persuade*?" interrupted Ari. "I'm not negotiating." He shoved the money back to Roger. "Take it!"

Roger quickly shoved the envelope back toward Ari. "Calm down. Your fuse is too short. I know my people. They're not trying to pressure you. They wanted to help—thought it would be an improvement. But they don't want to break the deal. They'll go along with it the way it was."

There was another long silence. At last Ari said, "I was reading a book the other day by an ex-CIA agent. It's banned in the United States, but available over here. It's called *Blowing the Whistle*...."

"I've read it," cut in Roger, "and it's baloney."

"Really? Are you an expert on the CIA?"

"You don't have to be. It's obviously sensationalism...yellow journalism. The guy's trying to make a buck."

Ari smiled and gave Roger a skeptical look. "Why are you so hot to defend the CIA?"

"I'm not defending the CIA. I'm simply telling you the guy's a screwball."

"I didn't read it that way," responded Ari, observing Roger closely. "I thought he sounded intelligent, knowledgeable. I must say I was surprised by his claim that the CIA has won the race with the KGB for psychic power, and that's why Gorbachev came up with *glasnost* and *perestroika*... but it does make sense."

"Make sense?" retorted Roger derisively. "Psychic powers? Sounds like science fiction. Like I said... the guy's a loony."

"Maybe. But what fascinated me the most was his claim that the CIA developed these psychic powers through contact with entities from another dimension...."

"Another dimension? What does that mean!" Roger was beginning to look uncomfortable. Was he really contemptuous of the book's theory, or was he trying to cover up?

"Something beyond the physical. After all, your top space scientist, Robert Jastrow—you know, he heads the Goddard Space Institute that sent out Pioneer and Voyager—claims there could be entities out there that have evolved beyond the need of bodies and are pure intelligence."

"Ghosts, right?" snorted Roger derisively. "You can't be serious!"

"Well, Jastrow is. Isn't there a worldwide program to contact extraterrestrial intelligences?"

"Yeah, Carl Sagan's pushing it—but I think it's a waste of money."

"That's your opinion... but some of the best scientific minds think it's worthwhile. So, getting back to the book, why couldn't the CIA be in touch with such entities telepathically... like the man said?"

"The guy's a kook!"

"Why are you so touchy on this subject?"

"I'm not!" snapped Roger, but there was no hiding the irritation in his voice. "We're wasting time. Get to the point... if you've got one."

"I'm just trying to explore a possibility. Those three Stasi agents who hauled me out of your apartment...."

"Rescued you," interjected Roger. "Remarkable."

Ari nodded. "And even more remarkable is the fact that one of them, the same character who haunts me in nightmares, showed up here in Paris. He was a German in Berlin, and here in Paris he's a Frenchman. Same guy... yet different."

"You've told me that. Why bring it up now?"

"Because this book gives a possible explanation. He said he was a 'mentor from another dimension.' I laughed that off at first, too, just like you're doing. But now this author claims that the CIA has made contact with something that sounds similar. It could be the explanation to something that's puzzled me for years."

"You're out of your mind!"

"And I think you're hiding something from me."

Roger looked pained but made no reply. He opened his mouth to say something, hesitated, then closed it again.

"I met them at your apartment."

"I was as surprised as you were."

"They appear when they want to and do what they please," complained Ari. "They invade my dreams... give me nightmares. I think they set me up at the Sorbonne. There's something weird going on."

"They looked ordinary to me... certainly not from another *dimension*," said Roger. "Rogue Stasi agents... working for the West. That's my guess. Maybe using mind control techniques...."

"Why rescue *me*? There's something I'm missing. They invade your apartment and haul me out, pretend to arrest me, then get me into the West. Then years later the head guy shows up here, gives me instructions... and then you come along to finance the operation. I think they've got some relationship with your group!"

Roger's discomfort was obvious. He shifted uneasily in his seat and retorted angrily, "Look, Ari, I'm not going to respond to your wild speculations, so let's drop it."

"Okay. But I still think you're hiding something."

Roger opened his mouth to speak, then clamped it shut and turned to look out the window. For some moments neither spoke a word

At last Ari broke the silence. "At least we got one thing settled. You'll make it very clear to the committee...."

"I will, and they'll go along," said Roger. "But they won't like it—not because they have any evil designs, as you seem to suspect. The only reason they wanted more information was in case something happened to you. What then? You know everything and nobody else knows anything. It's not good. That's what we worry about."

"So do I," retorted Ari quickly. "If your group knew what I know, they might get the dangerous idea that they didn't need me anymore. You need me more than you imagine—so tell them that."

Roger let out a long sigh. "You're a tough nut, Ari!"

"I'm a survivor. And I intend to stay alive long enough to see this thing through." Ari shoved the envelope back into his pocket.

The cab pulled over to the curb. "*Tour Eiffel*," called the driver. "*Vingt-six francs, si'l vous plait.*"

"You tell your bosses," said Ari quietly as he pulled a handful of change out of his pocket and handed the cabbie three ten-franc pieces, "it's got to be first Berlin, then Moscow... and only then Beijing! And I want Chiang Lee called off immediately!"

"Keep the change," he said to the driver, and climbed out of the cab without another word or a backward glance.

10

The Committee

Ari looked at his watch. In exactly seven minutes and 30 seconds he would make a call from a certain pay phone near the Eiffel Tower to another pay phone somewhere in Paris where Jean-André, one of his many couriers, would be at that precise time. Then he would go to another pay phone to make a similar call to a pay phone in his old town of Leipzig, where Heinz Buhne, his right-hand man in that area, would be waiting at that precise moment.

Coincidentally, Leipzig would be the center for the movement in East Germany when the time came—not because Ari wanted it that way for sentimental reasons, but because that was the way it was going to happen. There were 14 calls he had to make in the next three hours, each to a different country and from a different phone. That done, Ari would station himself at a precise time at yet another pay phone where his agents knew they could reach him if necessary. Tomorrow it would be a different phone and a different time for them to call, and so forth according to a schedule that was changed weekly.

In his briefcase, Ari carried the numbers and locations of about 300 pay phones in Paris, with an unpredictable calling schedule worked out for himself that he continually changed at random. Public phones were his communications hotline. Hundreds of *cartes telephoniques* that could be purchased in tobacco shops and had to be used in most public phones in Paris, along with coins or *jetons* for those instruments that still required them resided, with wrenching weight, in his briefcase as well.

Mail was a more difficult problem. Ari sent and received little, and never anything of great importance. Mail was far too slow and vulnerable. Fax machines were instantaneous, and it was impossible for the police or any other agency to monitor every fax machine. With an elaborate and changing schedule governing which machine to use, and messages to be picked up by couriers, Ari had kept such communications secure. Extraordinary precautions were absolutely essential in order to stay alive, and to protect his key people. Faxing was even a viable means of getting messages in and out of China, which had been a surprise to Ari when he had first discovered that welcome fact.

There was, of course, a pay phone where his directors of operations around the world could reach him at any hour of the day or night. It was monitored in shifts—8 hours on, 16 off—by three couriers who had a number where they could reach him at any time. They didn't know where Ari lived or who he was.

Any message they received at that phone would be in simple code either conveying urgent information or asking Ari to call immediately, and would be passed on to him verbatim.

How much easier it would have been to do all this from his own apartment. But Ari knew there was no such thing as a secure phone. What one genius could contrive another one could figure out—and the people he had to keep one step ahead of had unlimited resources and the world's most advanced technology at their disposal. What might be secure in the world of business would not make it in the world of international intrigue.

No, he could not afford to take a chance. *One* slip was all it would take. Roger was no real friend, but a triple agent, prepared to doublecross both him and the committee in order to fulfill CIA orders. Nor did that really matter. Roger could do nothing for him, even if he wanted to. The men over him, whether in Washington or Paris, were utterly ruthless. Of that Ari was certain.

— ✦ —

"Some publicity-hungry junior U.S. senator is pushing the investigation—and he's just ambitious enough to keep at it until he causes some real trouble." The speaker, a tall, intense man with chiseled features and aristocratic bearing, was sitting at the head of a long, ornately carved teak table in the opulent board room of the Paris office of one of the world's largest and most prestigious banks. The huge twentieth floor windows on two sides of the room looked out upon a panorama of the city from the Eiffel Tower to Sacre Coeur.

"Is that all you've got today, Jean—bad news?" complained a short, jowly man at the other end of the table. Nervously he shifted the dead cigar clamped between his teeth. "Are you saying that $100,000... or a high-class prostitute and a little blackmail won't take care of him?"

"Not a chance," returned Jean Bourbonnais gloomily. He was apparently in charge, though a formal meeting had not begun as yet. The five men seated around the table, all wearing conservative well-tailored suits, had been conversing casually, apparently waiting for someone to join them. "He's had a swarm of auditors from the world bank sifting through records at our Panama branch. They suspect our connections with Noriega. When Manuel worked for the CIA he was their fairhaired boy, but now that he's in jail they're scrambling to cover up and put the blame somewhere else."

"I thought our people in Washington had everything under control," objected a swarthy director from the bank's head office in Dacca, who was sitting just to Jean's right.

"In theory, Zaid... in theory," responded Bourbonnais. "But damage control never works as well in North America or Europe as in Pakistan. Don't worry," he added in a soothing tone, "nothing will come of it. And if it does... we have foolproof methods."

Jean Bourbonnais lifted a hand and waved a long, manicured finger in response to the worried expressions that followed his last remark. "Yes, I know... we've brought down enough passenger jets. That's still an option, but only in the rarest circumstances. There are ways that even an autopsy would never uncover. So relax. You look like a bunch of pallbearers."

"I may need some of that specialized help." The words came from the other end of the table. The cigar chewer was wiping beads of sweat from his forehead with a large initialed linen handkerchief. "They're sniffing around like bloodhounds on a hot trail... trying to trace drug money from New York back to Colombia through my branch."

"So, Barry, they've finally come to Miami? I'm sure they'll find your operation as clean as a hound's tooth!" quipped the short, stocky man to his left in a heavy German accent. "Just keep them away from Zurich as a personal favor to me."

"It's not a joke any more, Heinz!"

Bourbonnais glanced at his diamond-studded platinum Rolex. "We'll discuss these problems later. First of all, we want to get Dunn's report. He should be here any minute. We can't keep pouring millions in without some control."

"I've been saying that for years!" grumbled a short, portly man with a florid face and pompous expression across from Zaid. "It's a bottomless pit!"

"Agreed," conceded Heinz. "But nobody's come up with a solution. The guy always outmaneuvers us. How do we take control?"

"You've got to admit he's done an incredible job," suggested Barry.

"He *did*... for the first few years," complained Florid-face, "but I want to see some action! It's long overdue. *Patience*, he keeps saying, *patience*. I say we dump that arrogant Jew!"

Sounds of assent swept round the table.

"You're going to get some action in the next few days," put in Bourbonnais. "I just had a communique from Washington an hour ago. The CIA's in complete agreement with our appraisal. We're cleared to go ahead in China."

"It'll work!" exulted Zaid. "Any Asian could tell you that. Now's the time!"

"Chiang Lee has a huge student following," continued Jean. "They're going to take over Tiananmen Square. Mueller's top guys, whoever they are, have to go along with it. With Mao gone and a power struggle underway... and millions of workers ready to go on strike across China as soon as the students make their move... the regime will fall apart. They're already quarreling among themselves. There's new leadership in the wings ready to take over... not exactly what we'd want, but a big improvement."

"I know China," said Zaid. "I've lived there. And I know the way the Chinese think. Two steps forward, one step backward. Even if there is a crackdown ... with martyrs... if we can hold Tiananmen long enough for the people to get a strong taste of freedom... they won't forget. It will be the foundation for two more steps forward later."

"We'll do better than that," insisted Bourbonnais. "The old guard will be swept from power. This thing has incredible momentum. Chiang Lee has a genius for leadership. He may even end up somewhere in the top echelons of political power. So much the better for us!"

"So if we can pull this off without Mueller's people... why do we need him *anywhere*?" The question brought enthusiastic nods of approval and a fist slammed down here and there around the table.

"It's not that simple," Bourbonnais persisted. "This is the culmination of years of Mueller's work. He laid the foundation. Chiang would like us to believe that he's the whole show... but that isn't true."

"That's right," agreed Heinz. "The professor is still indispensable... for now."

"*For now*," repeated Zaid. "I can see the day coming—and it isn't far off—when we won't need that *yid* anymore...."

The door swung open and a secretary ushered in Roger. Glumly he settled into an empty seat across from Heinz.

"Well?" asked Jean Bourbonnais impatiently.

"He's not going to give us *any* information. *None*. Period."

"And you accepted that?" came the angry challenge from several voices at once, accompanied by expletives from around the table.

"You threatened to cut off his funds, of course!" Jean was clearly anxious.

"Sure I did. And he called my bluff. Handed back the money."

"He did? You didn't keep it!"

"I finally calmed him down and got him to take it. You can't pressure Ari. We've found that out before. He's like steel. The more heat you apply, the harder he gets."

"Oh, how I want to get rid of that snake!" growled Zaid through his teeth. "He's had us over a barrel for years...."

"Easy," cautioned Roger. "We can't get along without him... not yet... and he knows it. And he just might be able to get along without us. He threatened as much."

"He's made those threats before," grumbled Jean. "And I've never doubted that he meant it. We can't push him too far."

"But China... we're going to do it there," exclaimed Heinz with a note of triumph. "If there, why not elsewhere?"

"Not really," countered Roger. "Chiang is riding on Ari's coattails. Of course, if it works... then we'll have a pattern for elsewhere."

There was a long silence. At last Heinz spoke, "When the Wall comes down and Gorby's *perestroika* has come full circle, our arrangement with Ari *terminates*. He's finished—and good riddance!"

Zaid looked across the table into Roger's eyes. "You have any problem with that, Dunn?"

Roger shrugged his shoulders. "No, not at all. The guy's been a pain. He knows too much...and I suspect that he knows a lot more about our whole operation than we think he does."

"What makes you think that?" asked Florid-face, somewhat alarmed.

"Nothing in particular...just remarks he makes now and then."

"He's made his own funeral arrangements." Bourbonnais's words were cold, matter-of-fact. "I was at CIA headquarters in Langley last week. They're positive now that he's planning the same tactics in the West as soon as communism crumbles. He won't live to see it. We'll be finished with him by then."

"He's got his own agenda," added Heinz. "No loyalty to us. We've always known that. The sooner we get rid of him, the better!"

"Careful now," interjected Roger. "Don't rush it. We still need him. If someone takes him out too soon, everything could collapse."

"Langley knows exactly what to do, but they won't act until we tell them. When we all agree it's time...." Bourbonnais motioned with a closed fist and thumb pointed down.

He turned to Roger. "Something's bothering you?"

"Ari says Chiang's pushing it too fast and it isn't going to work."

Florid-face turned several shades redder. "Baloney! That's the same line we've heard from him for years. *Patience* and more *patience*! He's jealous of Chiang...afraid we can get along without him."

"The guy's an organizational genius," countered Roger. "He's incredible. Has his finger on the pulse...and he's always been right...."

"This time he's wrong!" cut in Jean sharply. "Has he brainwashed you, Dunn?"

"Look, I'm not siding with him." Roger shifted uncomfortably in his chair. "But I'd be remiss if I didn't pass on to you what he said. He warned me there'd be a massacre if we didn't pull Chiang off immediately. He said Berlin and Moscow have to come first...then Beijing."

"That's another nail in his coffin," snarled Bourbonnais, slamming his fist on the table. "He's always right. Nobody else knows anything. Well, this time he's wrong. When we prove it in Beijing...and the Wall comes down and communism collapses across Eastern Europe...it's 'goodbye, Professor Mueller'!"

Jean Bourbonnais put on his silver-rimmed glasses, opened a folder marked DAMAGE CONTROL that had been sitting on the table in front of him, and began to meticulously look through it while the others waited. "Now then," he announced at last, "we've got some serious problems to deal with...."

11

Nicole

"You're so quiet, Ari. Can't you tell me what's bothering you? Please, darling...."

Nicole tossed her long, blond hair back. It just touched the shoulders of the soft-pink silk suit that graced her slender, 5′8″ frame. With high heels, she was slightly taller than Ari. Meticulously groomed and a perfectionist with her makeup, she habitually wore the latest Parisian fashions, yet never seemed overdressed. She looked intently into Ari's dark and troubled eyes.

Ari avoided her gaze and turned to stare at the profusion of red and yellow tulips blooming next to the small sidewalk cafe where they were seated at Le Petit Pont. Just beyond the narrow strip of flowers and close-cropped lawn the heavy afternoon traffic crawled sluggishly along Quai Montebello bordering the river Seine. In the background rose the majestic spires of Notre Dame.

"It's nothing, Niki," said Ari unconvincingly, taking another sip from his glass and keeping his eyes glued on the traffic. "Nothing at all."

"Don't say it's nothing when I can see what it's doing to you!" Nicole's deep blue eyes searched his face in concern as he continued to stare past her in silence. "Please, love...."

A native of Paris, having graduated from the Sorbonne shortly after she and Ari had fallen in love and she'd moved into his apartment, Nicole was now doing her residency in neurosurgery. This evening was one of those special occasions when an opening in both of their busy schedules allowed them to relax over dinner together at one of their favorite sidewalk cafes. Ari had been careful not to embroil her in his revolutionary activities. She only knew, in the vaguest of terms, that he was passionately involved in some kind of international student movement that took far too much of his time. Exactly what that entailed and what his responsibilities were he had deliberately kept from her. It was best for her own safety if she knew nothing.

A barely audible sigh was her only answer. For a long time they sat in silence. "I'm sorry," Ari said at last. "It's no big deal. I'm just tired."

She reached over and straightened his open collar. "Darling, I don't believe you. It's got to be more than that. Something to do with that student movement you're so secretive about."

"You know why...I just don't want it to intrude into our private life."

"It does intrude—all the time. Like right now. Better that you should confide in me than this silence. And anyway, you know it's not healthy to keep everything to yourself."

"You don't tell me everything that goes on in the hospital."

"I would if it bothered me... like something's troubling you right now. You worry me."

"Look, there are things that I haven't been able to tell you. But I'm putting everything down in writing...."

"Why in writing?" interrupted Nicole. "Why not just say it... now?"

"You don't understand. It will all be in a sealed package... to be opened only in the event of my death... or disappearance. If certain people know that would happen... well, it could be a kind of, uh... life insurance."

Nicole leaned forward and looked intently into his eyes. "What are you saying? Someone might want to kill you?"

Ari shrugged. "Does that shock you?"

"It scares me! You can't just drop it there. I'm entitled to some explanation."

He reached for her hand. "Please, Niki, don't be afraid. Nobody's going to kill me, but there are some people I've worked with who would like to get rid of me, if they could. They need me desperately right now, so I'm in no danger... yet. But someday... fairly soon...."

"So that's why you're worried—and I was chiding you. I'm sorry."

"Actually, I wasn't worrying about myself. I was thinking of China. Something tragic is going to happen...."

"How do you know?"

"I go there once in a while. Two weeks ago, for example."

"You do? You told me you were going to Berlin... to lecture."

"Of course!" Ari forced a laugh. "The less you know, the better... for your own safety."

"Ari, this doesn't sound good. You've really got me scared."

"Now you know why I didn't tell you. I didn't want you worrying...."

"Well, I'm going to worry plenty if you don't come clean."

"Don't ask for that, Niki. Please! I'll tell you some things... but let's keep it the way it was and avoid this subject. You've got to trust me. Okay?"

"No girlfriends here and there?"

"Niki! You know me better than that. You've captured my heart so completely there isn't even the tiniest corner that anyone else could get hold of."

Nicole smiled. "I'm sorry, love. I was only teasing."

"I hope so!" Ari reached out to touch her cheek. She was not only beautiful and intelligent, but there was a priceless quality deep inside—loyalty, steadfastness, trustworthiness—that came through in their moments of intimacy. Their eyes met, comfortably, laughingly, and he knew again why this woman had his complete trust. Her keen mind, yet sensitive, gentle nature, had been both a challenge and a comfort to him.

"Ari," she persisted. "After what you've said, well...you have to tell me at least something, a little bit, now. Please, darling?"

He turned to focus on the rush-hour traffic again, hesitating. At last he said, "It's an unbelievable story." He paused for a moment, in an agony of indecision, then plunged on. "I shouldn't... but I will. It goes back 25 years. I was a kid of 20 then, idealistic, hating the lies and oppression in the so-called *people's democracies* behind the Iron Curtain. I can't go into the details, but there are some things you ought to know in case something... let's say... *unpleasant* happens to me."

"Ari, I love you with all my heart. I'll do anything, go anywhere... endure anything. You have to trust me. Please!"

He drained his glass. "First of all, Ari's my real name, not Hans Mueller."

"It's not a nickname just for me to call you?"

"No."

"If you're not really Hans Mueller...?"

"Look, that's a name I took as a cover. I didn't want you to call me *Hans*, but by my real name... so I had to tell you it was a nickname just between us. In fact, I don't even know my real last name."

"You don't? Go on... let's have it all." A different kind of fear was written on her face now.

Ari hung his head. "Niki... I'm sorry, but it was for your own good."

"So what's in your past that you had to cover up? You have to tell me."

"I escaped from East Germany in '64...."

"That's nothing to be ashamed of!" A great relief expressed itself in her relaxed features now.

"The *way* it happened, and *why*, is a mystery I've lived with all these years. To tell it might expose the three amazing characters who got me out to the West—which I mustn't do, in case they're still operating in East Berlin. That's where I first met *him*. He was the leader."

"*Him*? You mean the American you introduced me to as a 'business associate' that you used to know in East Berlin?"

"Roger? No. That's another part of the story."

"He's really a business associate?"

"Yeah, sort of. He represents an international banking conglomerate that's... well, frankly, involved in everything from laundering drug money to banking fraud and gun smuggling. So far they don't suspect that I know these things about them."

"And you're partners with them? Ari! So they're the ones who want to get rid of you?"

"They'd like to. But I'm not really a partner. There's money involved, but it's complicated and I can't talk about it now. Let's forget that for the moment, okay? I'm not talking about Roger and his group, but the three mysterious characters that got me out to the West. They seemed to be part of an anti-

Marxist faction inside the East German regime—at least that's what I was supposed to believe. I don't know what to think now, because four years later one of them showed up here at the Sorbonne... during the 1968 student riots. That was before your time...."

"I was seven years old," laughed Nicole. "An aunt sent me a Barbie doll from America for my birthday. How could I ever forget that? But go on."

"Well, briefly, I had organized student demonstrations around the world, from Berlin to Madrid to Berkeley—and then it got out of hand. Right here at the Sorbonne the students took over the university. Riot police came in with armored trucks, water cannons, tear gas. Ten thousand students fought back with Molotov cocktails. Eight million workers—half the French labor force at the time—went on strike. Took over factories. It was hell for a while. Students and workers marched through the streets of Paris smashing windows, burning cars, chanting, 'De Gaulle, *adieu*.'"

"I remember seeing that on TV!" exclaimed Nicole. "It was terrible!"

"Well, the students were given the most sweeping reforms since Napoleon. Workers got big raises, which, by the way, nearly bankrupted the country in those days. But it wasn't *adieu*. De Gaulle won the next election by a landslide. Politics is so corrupt... it has little relationship to things as they really are. But we students didn't understand that at the time. I learned a lot, I can tell you!"

"And *you* had organized this whole thing around the world?" asked Niki in admiration. "Already back then when you were still a student working on your doctorate?"

"Yes... to begin with. But I didn't have firm enough control, so it got out of hand. Lost its cohesiveness. Took on local issues, and in the end self-destructed. I learned plenty from that experience."

Ari stared off into the distance, reliving memories. "Well," he said at last, "as I started to say, that was when this same guy from Berlin suddenly showed up here in Paris. Came up to me one day on the street... said they were impressed with what I'd accomplished in just four years in the West... and that they had further plans for me. He even gave me some excellent suggestions that helped me found the organization I work with worldwide today."

"*They* had plans? Who're they?"

"I don't know. Sometimes I think I'm losing my mind. I'd seen him, *the very same man*, in nightmares that I'd had periodically for years... even before he arrested me—or pretended to—in East Berlin."

"In *nightmares*, Ari? The very same man? You're sure?"

"Absolutely! Be honest with me, Niki. Do you think I'm crazy?"

"Of course not! It's not unusual to dream of someone you may have seen somewhere... someone in a crowd, perhaps. You don't even remember, but the face made an impression. It's nothing to worry about."

"No, Niki, it's more than that."

"Why do you think so?"

"It's happened 20 ... 30 times. In dreams he stares at me. I'm totally helpless, sucked in, out of control. It feels like he's trying to take over ... think for me. I fight it ... try to break free."

He closed his eyes for a moment in pained memory. "It's even happened during the day lately. Suddenly I see his face and strange thoughts begin to race through my mind."

"Like what?"

"'Initiation' ... 'follow me' ... 'higher consciousness.' It feels like I'm being taken somewhere."

Nicole sat in quiet thought. At last she said tentatively, "It could be some kind of mind control. There's so much we don't know about the brain. Some of the operations I'm involved in.... Well, skip the technicalities—but we're considering the possibility that one mind can affect and even take over another ... from a distance. Is that what you're afraid of?"

Ari nodded. "It sounds bizarre, but I get the feeling that it's happening."

"And you think he's connected to Roger and his finance group?"

"I know he is—all three of the mysterious figures are. Roger won't admit it, but I'm sure he's lying. The CIA's involved with these ... whoever or whatever they are. And I've discovered that Roger is with the CIA, and the banking consortium doesn't know that's where his real allegiance lies. They arrested me—the three of them—at Roger's apartment in East Berlin. But Roger swears he was just as surprised as I was ... thought they were Stasi...."

"Is he telling the truth?"

"It's possible he didn't know anything at that time, but I'm sure he does now. One of these days I'll have all of the evidence ... not that it really matters."

Niki turned her empty glass round and round, staring at it thoughtfully. "I *think*," she suggested cautiously at last, "that they've been trying to take over your mind. Not entirely—that's not possible. I mean, it would be obvious to anyone who knew you if that happened. But to influence your thinking. To plant some thoughts, key ideas that would lead you in a certain direction. That would be much harder to detect."

"You really think that's possible?"

Niki nodded. "What I do in the hospital, of course, has nothing to do with what we're talking about, but I do a lot of reading just to keep up. It's hard to get data, because most of the experiments in this area are top secret ... involving the CIA or KGB."

Ari nodded solemnly. "That ties in with a book I read recently about CIA involvement in psychic experiments ... leading to contact with entities from another ... uh, dimension. What do you think of that?"

Niki sat up very straight, folded her hands on her lap, and spoke earnestly. "I'd take it quite seriously. We're spending millions trying to contact intelligent life somewhere in space...."

"Exactly what I told Roger the other day! He just ridiculed the idea, which makes me think he's hiding something."

"He must be," said Nicole thoughtfully. "Common sense would tell anybody that we're not the only *minds* in the universe. Suppose those three you met had been taken over by some *minds* from who knows where...out there somewhere...and the same entities...or whatever they are...are trying to take over your mind and body as well?"

"That's what it feels like. My God, I can't let it happen!"

Nicole's eyes expressed a concern beyond words. "Ari, I'm going to consult some of my colleagues—tomorrow."

"No! You can't do that, Niki."

"Relax. I won't say whom I'm talking about...just a patient. I want to get some opinions."

12

The East–West Connection

A discreet cough from the waiter caught Ari's attention. He approached their table, pencil and pad ready, and stood beside Ari in the distinctive dress of the *garçons* in this section of Paris: black bow tie and white shirt, black vest and crisply starched, spotlessly white apron reaching almost to the ground. "Are *monsieur* and *mademoiselle* ready to order dinner?"

"Someone else is joining us," replied Ari. He looked at his watch. "Any minute, now," he added with a smile.

"*Oui, monsieur.*" He leaned over to light the candle on their table and then withdrew.

They sat in silence for some time, both lost in thought. In the fading soft glow of rosy sunset reflected from the scattered clouds overhead, the candlelight seemed to accent the outline of Nicole's delicately prominent cheek bones. "Ari, how could you keep it a secret?" she asked him at last.

"What are you talking about?"

"Your escape from East Germany."

"Still thinking about that?"

"Of course I am! And it doesn't make sense. They wouldn't let you out of West Berlin without proper identification. You had to report to the authorities to get new papers. They must have known you'd escaped. And the Sorbonne... you'd need credit for your studies in East Germany."

Ari shrugged and rolled his eyes. "You're right—and I can't explain it. Somebody has incredible power... or influence... or something."

"What do you mean?"

"The three who 'arrested' me made me transfer my few belongings—some valuable papers and clothes—into a police briefcase. When I got to the West, besides the 50,000 West German marks they'd told me was in it, there were documents that I'd never seen before: a graduation certificate from Leipzig's Karl Marx University where I'd attended but hadn't quite finished, an official transcript of all my courses and grades, a West German passport in the name of Hans Mueller with *my picture*, and *a residence visa for France—also in the name of Hans Mueller*. So I didn't just make up that name—it was given to me."

"These were *official* documents?"

"Absolutely. They were the whole basis for my new identity in the West—and no one ever challenged them."

"You still have them?"

"Oh, yes. I have a French passport now, but I've kept everything I mentioned—just to make sure I hadn't gone completely crazy."

"Those documents were from *both sides* of the Iron Curtain? Incredible!"

"Both sides," repeated Ari softly with a half smile. "At the highest levels of government and banking there's been secret cooperation between East and West for years...in spite of the cold war, missile crises, threats of hot war, quarreling about the Middle East and Southeast Asia...." He shook his head in disbelief. "I still can't grasp it, but the pieces are beginning to fall into place."

Nicole was stunned. "What's their game...and who's playing it?"

Ari shrugged. "Obviously I don't have the whole picture. I do know that Roger's group is one important link between East and West in a behind-the-scenes battle for a New World Order and global control. With stakes that high, you can imagine the utter ruthlessness of the key players. Snuffing out innocent lives means nothing to them!"

Nicole sat quietly for a moment. At last she turned to search Ari's eyes pleadingly. "I have a horrible feeling. You've got to tell me the truth! Where does this 'student movement' you've organized fit into this whole picture?"

"There's a connection."

"Well, what is it?"

Ari took a deep breath. "My organization is being financed to bring down the Iron Curtain and destroy communism everywhere...even in China and Albania."

"That's impossible. You can't be serious."

Ari leaned forward, his eyes sparkling with a sudden surge of energy. "You wouldn't believe the structure I've built with the help of two dozen brilliant and dedicated men and women I'd trust with my life. They direct the day-to-day operations for me around the world. I've set the structure up in such a way that the CIA, the KGB...nobody can crack it. It took me 15 years to learn how and to build it cell by cell. I could make one phone call right now, and tomorrow a million students would take to the streets all over Eastern Europe. Three million in China."

"But to bring down the Wall!" Nicole protested. "In a hundred years, maybe...."

"One of the keys is Poland. After Solidarity was outlawed and the Soviets were threatening to invade Poland, Reagan and the Pope entered into a secret agreement in 1982 to support Solidarity and to make Poland the heart of a campaign to destroy communism...."

"I've never heard that," interrupted Nicole. "Where do you get this information?"

"You know I can't tell you that. We work with Solidarity in Poland...and with an incredible CIA-Vatican network involving hundreds of Catholic priests and churches that support Solidarity. You couldn't believe what's going on!"

"So what have they accomplished?"

"Plenty. Lech Walesa is out of prison. The Pope has visited Poland and was cheered by millions. The Vatican is now working with Bush. Strikes proved that Poland can't function without Solidarity—which Gorbachev admitted when he went there in '88. And now...just two months ago Solidarity was given full legal status. Open parliamentary elections are scheduled for next June. No doubt as to who'll be elected! The Polish communist regime and its sponsor, the Kremlin, caved in to the demands of the people—with massive secret aid from the U.S. and the active help of the Roman Catholic Church. It's the beginning of the end for communism in Eastern Europe." Ari leaned closer, his eyes narrowing. "The Pope's the most powerful man in the world. I really mean it—and I don't know where that fits in."

"You know history. Every emperor in Europe who amounted to anything had to work with the Church." Nicole looked at Ari closely. "And now you think history's taking a big leap...the Berlin Wall is really coming down?"

"It's just a matter of time—and it won't be long!"

Nicole shook her head, still unconvinced. "What's in it for these criminal bankers? Why would they finance the demise of communism?"

"Are you kidding? Free trade with Eastern Europe would mean billions in profits for them."

"And top Soviet leaders are involved?"

"Why not? Gorbachev and his inner circle have known for years that Marxism doesn't work. They just couldn't figure out how to dismantle it without creating chaos. I happen to know that Gorbachev and the Pope have made a deal. The Soviets and the Vatican...and the Americans...had plans for a New World Order long before Gorby wrote *Perestroika*. They've been working on it together for years."

Nicole looked at him skeptically. "Ari...you couldn't possibly have that kind of information!"

"Look," said Ari, leaning closer again and lowering his voice. "I *know* what I'm talking about...because the students I control are at the heart of the whole operation everywhere. Now just forget everything I said."

The sunset had faded and the street lights had turned on. Nicole sat watching the flickering candle, trying to take in what Ari had told her. "I'm not ready to forget it all just yet," she said abruptly. "Let's say the Wall comes down and communism collapses...then what?"

"I'm going to do the same thing in the West...overthrow corrupt governments."

Nicole reached out and put her hand on Ari's arm. "My God! They won't let you do that. They'll kill you!"

"Maybe," said Ari calmly, "but I have to try. I think of the suffering in the world, the poverty and malnutrition, children dying of starvation...doesn't that haunt you? Billions of dollars that could go for food and medicine and housing being spent to stockpile weapons so horrible....Niki, this planet is doomed—unless we stop this madness. The collapse of communism is just the beginning. I'm not going to stop until the job is done."

"But you said they're plotting to get rid of you—right now."

"Yeah, but they can't get along without me yet. And when the time comes... I'll survive."

"You're very brave, Ari... but the odds are impossible. That scares me."

"When I've put the whole picture together, I'm going to leave the evidence with you... and a few other trusted friends. That could save your life... and mine. If I turn up missing—or die, even though it seems perfectly normal—that's when you reveal the evidence to the world. It would send the leaders to prison for centuries. When they know that would happen... they're not going to kill me."

"They sure won't let you continue... not in the West."

"We'll cross that bridge when we get to it. By then this thing will have gathered such momentum that nobody can stop it!"

Nicole stared at Ari in speechless bewilderment. "This is such a shock," she finally stammered, struggling to find the words. "How you could keep this a secret from me all these years! And I thought you were off lecturing, debating... here and there."

"I do a lot of that," returned Ari quietly. "It's the perfect cover for most of my travels...."

"You lied to me... again and again!"

"Niki... *please.* I had to. It was for your own good... your safety."

She hesitated, looking into his eyes, then smiled and nodded. "Okay, I'll accept that... but to be in partnership with the monsters you describe... how could you, Ari?"

"Darling, I already said... it's not a partnership. They put up the money, but I use it as I please—no strings attached."

"It's filthy money, Ari! I wouldn't touch it."

He stared off into the distance for a few moments before attempting to respond. "I agree with you," he said at last, turning to look her in the eye. "It is filthy money—but not all of it. Maybe what I'm getting was earned legitimately."

She shook her head disapprovingly. "That's weak, Ari. It's all tainted...."

"Look at me, sweetheart," he said firmly. "I can't change how they get their money... but I can decide how some of it is spent. Why shouldn't I take evil money and use it for a good cause? I don't know where else I could have gotten the hundreds of millions they've given me. And without that... I wouldn't be on the verge of success today."

"Okay, so you're a modern Robin Hood. But on top of that, you've been spying on these drug-running, money-laundering murderers." Nicole was stupefied. "Ari, they'll find out!"

"They won't have to find out," he replied earnestly, "I'm going to tell them . . . at the right time. It's my only salvation. I have people in their organization feeding me information . . . people that I'm paying with *their* money . . . and they don't know it."

"When they find *that* out . . . they'll kill them and you!"

"Sweetheart, I just explained . . . I'm in no danger yet. They need me . . . desperately. Sure, they're trying to maneuver into the position where they know enough to get along without me. *That's* what I have to prevent."

"Can you?"

"I can, believe me. And, please, don't worry! I've survived this long. . . ."

They both fell silent and became absorbed in watching the ebb and flow of humanity along the crowded avenue.

Suddenly Ari smiled and waved to a rapidly approaching figure. "There's Abdul," he whispered. "I planned to recruit him after we all had dinner and you left for the hospital. But since I've told you this much . . . I'll just discuss it with him now. And, remember, not a word of what we've been talking about!"

13

Abdul

"Niki! Professor Mueller! Great to see you!" exclaimed Abdul after he had hurriedly squeezed between the patrons crowded around the closely placed tables, ducked under the rainbow-colored umbrellas above them and joined the waiting couple. "Sorry to be late. The traffic's horrible and parking's impossible. I should have taken the metro."

Abdul shook Ari's outstretched hand, then leaned over and kissed Nicole first on one cheek then the other.

"Wonderful you could join us, Abdy," said Niki with a happy smile. "It's been too long."

Ari motioned toward an extra chair he had pulled up to the small table. "Sit down and relax—we've got all evening. At least you and I have. Niki has to be at the hospital in an hour."

A 31-year-old, Jerusalem-born Palestinian Arab with irrepressible enthusiasm and outgoing personality, Abdul was passionately dedicated to the liberation of his homeland from the Jews. After his parents moved to Paris, he had attended the same high school as Nicole and they had been close friends for nearly 15 years. When he couldn't settle on a major in university, she had recommended that he try political science. "It fits your personality and special talents," she'd told him.

"Professor Mueller" had become Abdul's favorite teacher at the Sorbonne; so much so that he had urged Niki to take a class from "Mueller." Thus Abdul had played a key role in bringing those two together, another reason why Ari and Niki were so fond of him and had remained in close contact.

Since then Ari had become head of the Political Science department. Having worked closely with Abdul in his graduate work for the past five years, Ari had developed a great affection for this outstanding young man. Abdul's sharp mind, clear logic and near-photographic memory had made him one of Ari's prize students. He had just gotten his Ph.D. in political science, and Ari was trying to help him find a job worthy of his training and exceptional abilities.

"You've heard the news?" Abdul demanded breathlessly as he sat down and pulled his chair up to the table. In the soft glow of twilight, beads of sweat lent a sheen to his slightly pockmarked yet handsome features.

Ari had turned away to motion to the waiter but couldn't get his attention. Now that the sun had gone down and the light was fading, the overworked man was cranking in the large orange awning that extended from the front of the restaurant out over the sidewalk.

"About China, you mean?" asked Nicole.

"Right!" responded Abdul. "Isn't it incredible what's happening?"

"We picked it up on shortwave just before we came over here," commented Ari matter-of-factly.

"You're not excited?" demanded Abdul. "Fifty thousand students from Beijing University taking to the streets... ignoring threats of expulsion and cordons of police? The last I heard, 250,000 people had joined them. Numbers could soon reach a million... marching on Tiananmen Square... defying Deng's government!"

"For China," admitted Ari, "that's amazing... but it's premature—doomed to fail. Sorry to dampen your enthusiasm."

"I disagree!" exulted Abdul. "A French government Chinese expert—I forget his name—said Deng's government is caving in. They've agreed to talks with student leaders. The old guard will be swept out. There'll be fresh faces with democratic leanings. Thousands of workers are going out on strike to join the demonstrations. It's even spread to high schools, and into the country! There's a historic transformation going on."

"I'm with you, Abdy. It's almost unbelievable—but it's really happening!" Nicole turned to Ari with a frown. "How can you be so negative?"

"I'm just realistic," responded Ari quietly. "Give it two—maybe three weeks. Beijing's been caught by surprise and they're off balance for the moment, but when they recover... it'll be a bloody massacre."

"Deng wouldn't dare," protested Nicole. "The whole world would be outraged." Abdul nodded vigorously.

"This is China," Ari reminded them. "They're already isolated. World opinion means almost nothing."

"I'm optimistic," persisted Abdul. "So far it looks good. And if a billion Chinese could shake off communism... what an impact worldwide!"

Ari shook his head stubbornly. "The Soviets led the world into communism—and they'll have to bring it down. China can't be the one. Anyway, China's not ready yet. The protestors will pay a horrible price."

The expression in Abdul's dark eyes conveyed his keen disappointment. "How can you be so sure?" he asked Ari cautiously, hardly daring to contradict the professor who had taught him so much and whom he respected so highly. "You know something we don't?"

Ari shrugged. "Maybe. Remember the organization I've mentioned that needs your talents in the Middle East?"

"Yeah. I've thought about that. I'm interested."

"They've been involved in China for ten years. That's my information source." Ari caught the waiter's eye and motioned him over to their table.

"So, messieurs-mademoiselle. What will it be? The chef's special for tonight, perhaps... a very tasty *canard a l'orange?*"

"Just a cup of the soup *du jour* and a dinner salad with *vinaigrette* for me," said Nicole.

"And you, monsieur?"

"The duck sounds good," said Ari. "How about you, Abdy?"

"Why not! Make that two *canards a l'orange.*"

"Now I'm intrigued," said Abdul when the waiter had hurried off with the orders. "Tell me more about this organization."

Ari leaned back and smiled. "It's a worldwide student coalition headquartered in London. But don't think I'm of any great importance. I do some consulting... that's all."

Nicole gave Ari a what-a-liar-you-are look and turned away.

"What's their goal?" asked Abdul.

"The demise of communism... world transformation," said Ari confidently. "Is that big enough for you?"

"Too big. Sounds grandiose," returned Abdul, but there was definite interest in his voice. "How are they going about it?"

"Hundreds of underground newspapers—we have more than 100 in Poland alone—reaching millions all over Eastern Europe, in China and elsewhere, including the Soviet Union. Mimeographed bulletins and posters by the thousands... pasted everywhere. Producing videos and showing them to millions in secret gatherings of five, ten, a few dozen people at a time."

"Students doing all this?" asked Abdul, obviously impressed.

"Right. They're recruited through scholarships, fellowships, grants... special study programs in key universities. The ultimate weapon, of course, will be massive student demonstrations against oppressive governments worldwide. In the meantime, infiltrating and influencing the state media plays a big part—and takes a lot of money. Bribes... that's how communism works. Fortunately they're well financed."

"Sounds intriguing. Why haven't I heard of this group at the Sorbonne... if they're worldwide?"

"They keep a low profile. You wouldn't know they existed until they recruited you."

"Like you're doing now?"

"If you're interested."

"That depends. You say they need someone in the Middle East...?"

"Right. They've concentrated on communist regimes, so they've never been established in the Middle East. They need someone to get things started."

"I haven't lived there since I was a teenager."

"That's okay. A fresh look is what we want. You've got the languages."

"Arabic, of course. I'm rusty on Hebrew... but I'd pick it up again fast."

The arrival of their plates brought a momentary change in the conversation to topics of general interest. "I don't want Niki to feel left out," suggested Abdul between bites. "You and I can talk business after she leaves."

"You're always such a gentleman," said Nicole, leaning over to pat Abdul on the cheek. "Just like Ari. He won't let work interfere with our private lives. But I'm fascinated with the Middle East. So please carry on. I'll listen."

"Thanks, Niki," responded Ari and launched into his recruiting effort between bites. "To get started in that part of the world . . . the first thing we need is a thorough, on-the-spot survey of the major universities."

"What kind of survey?" asked Abdul.

"Student demographics. Live interviews. Student opinions on a variety of topics—from Arab/Israeli relationships to honest feelings about their own governments."

"Sounds intriguing. What's the purpose?

"Identify, recruit and train leaders. Then develop a strategy for recruiting Middle East students . . . organizing them into cells. . . ."

"This is the way it's been done elsewhere?"

Ari nodded. "All over Europe—East and West. Millions of students are involved in thousands of cells of about 25 each. No communication between the cells, no mass meetings. Orders come from the top. So if one cell is infiltrated it doesn't affect the rest of the organization."

"How is it all held together?"

"That's a secret they've never let me in on . . . but when the time comes for action, the sheer mass of numbers will be overwhelming . . . irresistible."

Obviously interested now, Abdul had momentarily abandoned his meal to listen. Nicole, too, was following intently. "You say, 'when the time comes for action,'" repeated Abdul. "What kind of action?"

Ari leaned forward and lowered his voice. "You know I wouldn't be associated with an organization involved in violent revolution. That only leads to more bloodshed and usually installs a regime more evil than the one being overthrown!"

"Of course," agreed Abdul. "So, like you said, the ultimate goal is transformation through peaceful demonstrations?"

Ari nodded. "On a scale so massive that they can't be stopped. That's the only way to achieve lasting change. And it *will* work!"

"That's what they're trying in China," interjected Nicole. "But you say it *won't* work."

"Darling, I thought I'd already explained. The timing is wrong. That's a key factor. And that's why this survey is so important in the Middle East."

The conversation died momentarily as they all concentrated again on their food. "How's the *canard*?" asked Nicole, soup spoon poised.

"Fantastic!" came the immediate response from both men.

As he ate, Abdul was deep in thought. "I'm a bit confused," he confessed at last. "I can see massive demonstrations in Israel. And it might work if not just Arabs, but Jews, too, were involved. But in the Arab countries...what's the aim there?"

"You should know that," chided Ari, "What's the trend in world governments today?"

"Democracy, obviously. The 70-year cycle favoring communism has ended. The pendulum is swinging back toward democracy."

"Exactly."

"But Marxism hasn't made much impact in the Middle East," protested Abdul. "There's been a lot of Soviet influence in some Arab countries... economic and military assistance...but nobody's buying their political system."

"No imperialism and totalitarianism?" demanded Ari.

"Yeah, Zionist imperialism. That's the problem. Israel has to give back the land she's taken!"

"Of course," agreed Ari. "But the Arab countries...can you think of one that has a democratic government...real freedom of the press and basic human rights?"

Abdul laughed uneasily. "I know what you're getting at. We've argued about this. You just don't understand the uniqueness of the Arab world. Islam rules. Whatever the secular form of government, the *mullahs* and *imams* and *ayatollahs* are the real authority. The Koran is the law."

"I've never denied that," countered Ari. "But whether the government is religious or secular—whether it claims to follow the Koran or the Bible or the Hindu Vedas or what—that's beside the point."

"It isn't beside the point," insisted Abdul. "In the Arab world the Koran is our lifeblood, our standard. It's God's word. There's no higher authority."

"Surely you don't defend the treatment of women in Arab countries!" cut in Nicole passionately.

"Husbands abuse their wives in Christian countries, too," responded Abdul with a confident smile. "It can happen anywhere."

"But the Koran condones polygamy and wife-beating," persisted Niki. "And the husband can divorce his wife by simply pronouncing it done. The woman has no rights. Isn't that true?"

Abdul cleared his throat. "It's not that black and white, Niki. There are cultural differences you don't understand. I don't think you or anyone else who is not a Muslim is qualified to pass judgment...."

"You're avoiding the issue, Abdy," scolded Nicole good-naturedly.

"We're not trying to jump on you," Ari assured him. "But the facts are pretty grim. Iraq and Iran have spent eight years torturing, gassing, bombing and slaughtering one another by the hundreds of thousands—all in the name of Allah! Saddam Hussein is a ruthless murderer...an Arab Hitler! Yet the majority of Arab leaders—who all claim to follow the Koran—hail him as a hero. And Kadafi and Arafat—are these human beings?"

"I'm not defending them," countered Abdul. "They're not good Muslims."

"They claim to be," retorted Ari. "I don't hear the mullahs and ayatollahs denouncing them as heretics. Facts, Abdy, facts. Arab countries, in general, have an abysmal human rights record. True?"

"There are problems... sure," agreed Abdul, "but they can only be solved within the context of Islamic law."

"Islamic law, it seems to me, *is* the problem!" cut in Ari. "The Iron Curtain is horrendous... but what about the Islamic Curtain? It has to come down, too! You can't even be a citizen of Saudi Arabia unless you're a Muslim. Talk about a denial of minority rights! It has to change."

"It's a religious matter for Muslims to work out," said Abdul, sounding offended.

"*Religious* matter? You can't cover up a denial of basic human rights with that excuse!"

"Saudi Arabia is an Islamic state," countered Abdul. "France isn't a Catholic state, and the United States isn't a Christian state. Don't you see the difference?"

"There's a world community of nations," Ari reminded him. "We need *world* peace... and we can't have it without full Muslim participation. Arab countries have to become democratic. It's that simple."

"I'm not arguing that," agreed Abdul. "But don't expect Muslims to abandon the Koran. Arab democracy has to take a different form than in the West. Don't try to impose a Western solution upon the Arabs. It won't work. There has to be an *Arab* solution for whatever may be wrong in the Arab world."

"Exactly," responded Ari. "There's no thought of bringing in outsiders to lead Arabs. A major purpose of this survey would be to find qualified Arab leadership among the students in Muslim lands."

"I'm glad to hear that."

"In fact," continued Ari, "we need Islam. That's why I'm concerned about its abuse of human rights."

"What do you mean, you need Islam?" demanded Abdul.

"I was telling Niki before you got here... how the Pope made a deal with Reagan back in '82 and how they've been working together to bring down communism in Eastern Europe. In fact, the Catholic Church is playing the key role. They kept Solidarity alive... and that's going to be the downfall of communism in Poland... and as a result, throughout Eastern Europe... and eventually the world."

"Interesting," mused Abdul. "I remember you talking about that in a seminar."

"And that's the kind of role that Islam and the local mosques have to play in the Middle East," continued Ari, "in bringing in democracy."

Abdul nodded, though not with great enthusiasm. "So long as Islam is effecting the change... I can't argue."

"Good." Ari paused and studied Abdul for a moment. "What I want to know is... could you spend the next six weeks in the Middle East heading up a survey team without letting any of your own opinions get in the way... and would you want to?"

Abdul was silent for a few moments. When at last he spoke it was with deep conviction and careful choice of words. "It would be a challenge I'd like to accept. I'm willing to take a fresh look at everything... and I think I could do a good job for... whoever these people are."

"Great!" exclaimed Ari, reaching out to shake Abdul's hand. "You're hired. Of course, you're on probation to begin with... and I don't know when you'll meet your real bosses. But if they're happy with this first job, then there'll be much more... probably involving moving back to Jerusalem."

"I'd love that! When do I start? And, well,... you never mentioned the pay."

"You start immediately. The pay is good... 30,000 francs for the six-week assignment plus travel expenses. Is that okay?"

"Yes, of course!"

Ari pulled a thick folder out of his briefcase and handed it to Abdul. "These people you'll be working for are well organized. Here's a complete schedule of where you're to be and when—hotel reservations with a payment method through a bank here in Paris—you just have to sign. There's a check for half of your salary plus another $10,000 for you to turn into travelers checks and use for hiring survey-takers in each location to assist you... for printing the extra forms you'll need, and for miscellaneous expenses. All of the instructions are in there, including several phone numbers to call in case of questions or any emergency."

"This is so sudden," stammered Abdul. "I'm overwhelmed...."

Ari paid the waiter and the three of them stood to leave. He put an arm around Abdul's shoulders and gave him a fatherly hug.

"You've got two days," Ari explained, "to study the material before your plane leaves Paris for your first stop in Damascus. Airline tickets will be delivered to you tomorrow morning."

"I'm excited for you, Abdy," said Nicole. "Send me some postcards."

"Remember, I'm out of the picture, now," Ari reminded him, "but when you get back to Paris, let me know how it went."

14

A Terrifying Possibility

"Ari! What are you doing?"

Nicole had awakened out of a sound sleep to find Ari sitting up in bed beside her in a yoga position, arms extended, palms up. From lips that only slightly moved came eerie, incomprehensible sounds.

She turned on the bed lamp and watched him in horror. Though his eyes were wide open, Ari seemed oblivious to his surroundings.

"Ari! Wake up!" Nicole grabbed his arm and began to shake him.

"No...no! I won't do it!" He flailed out wildly and almost knocked Nicole from the bed. The desperation in his voice impelled her to action. She grabbed him around the neck and hung on, yelling her loudest now.

"Stop it! Wake up! Ari! What's going on?"

He suddenly went limp and she loosened her grip. Ari turned and looked at her blankly. "Where did you come from?"

"Where did I come from! Don't you know where you are? Darling, you've been having a nightmare."

The man beside her seemed not to recognize her. He stared at her for another moment, then his eyes glazed over again and he began muttering in German. "Third level...chosen...special mission...no...no!" He shuddered violently as though some unseen hand had shaken him, then fell back on his pillow unconscious.

The clock on the bedstand stood at 3:21 A.M. Nicole turned off the lamp and pulled the covers up over her and Ari. What in the world was happening to him? Sleep was out of the question. She lay awake trying to understand what she had just witnessed. This was the third time she had awakened to such a scene. How many other occurrences like this had there been, unknown to her, while she had been sound asleep? What did it all mean?

She had only casually mentioned similar episodes in the past. Ari had denied remembering anything and had brushed the incidents off as meaningless. Was he covering something up...something else from his past, perhaps? She lay awake until dawn, determined that this time she would insist on getting to the bottom of it all.

—✦—

"You had another weird episode last night." Nicole faced Ari in the kitchen. He had just come in from his morning run.

"Got to get into the shower," he responded, wiping the sweat from his face with the front of his T-shirt and turning toward the bedroom.

"You didn't answer me," remonstrated Nicole, stepping quickly in front of him.

"I heard you—but I'm in a hurry. Got an early class today, you know...."

"Look, you're not putting me off this time," said Nicole firmly. "Six weeks ago I told you what some of the other doctors at the hospital said. There's something in your past that's trying to come out...."

"And I told you I'm not going to a psychiatrist for 'regression therapy'...."

"I didn't recommend that," she cut in quickly.

"Well, that's what one of the doctors said I needed. I tried it once, years ago, and as soon as the psychiatrist started to put me into this... this 'relaxed state' I could see *his* face. Look, don't trigger something, okay?"

"*His* face? The man from East Berlin that haunts your nightmares?" she persisted.

"Right. That did it for me. I'm not letting anybody hypnotize me—ever!"

"I think somebody *has* been hypnotizing you... for a long time," said Nicole solemnly, "and you just don't know it—or won't admit it to yourself."

With a resigned sigh, Ari relaxed and leaned against the door jamb. "Okay, what happened last night?"

"It was like every other time, when I've seen it. I don't know how often it's happened that I don't know about. You were sitting up in bed in a yoga position, hands extended, palms up, muttering in some strange language. Repeating the same words over and over... like a mantra, maybe."

Ari wiped his brow again and shook his head. "Honestly, Niki, I don't remember anything. I used to recall it all... clearly... remember seeing *him* ... but that hasn't been happening lately. It's different. I see him like a flash of insight when I'm awake... then it all goes away. Not often... once a month, maybe."

"I shook you half-awake this time—and you muttered some words in German."

"I did?"

"Yes. That figures. Anyone trying to take over your mind would communicate in your native tongue."

"What did I say?"

"I just heard a few words... but if you think about them, it may bring back a memory. Can we try?"

"I'm willing to try anything... except hypnosis. I know that opens me up to *him*."

"I wouldn't touch it either... totally dangerous. We'll talk about that some other time. Now, let's see if these words arouse a memory... if I can put it together in German. You said something like, 'third level... chosen... special mission... no... no!' Does that mean anything?"

Ari closed his eyes and tried to concentrate. "'Third level,' maybe. In the car in East Berlin... after they 'arrested' me... *he* said something about ten levels of consciousness. I thought it was a put-on."

"That was 25 years ago. What about since then?"

"It seems to ring a bell... but I don't know why."

"Concentrate. Think about it."

"I'm trying. I told you, when I see his face... just for a split second I get the feeling that I'm being pulled higher, almost like I'm going out of my body. That's when I fight it and the feeling goes away."

"You said something about 'initiation' before."

"Yeah, I get that feeling, too, sometimes."

"That ties in with 'chosen' and 'special mission.' Think about those words ... in German."

"It triggers something... but I can't get it," he said after a short silence. "It's like a name on the tip of your tongue. You know it, but can't say it. There's *something* there, but I can't quite reach it. It's maddening... so I just don't think about it."

"Try, Ari. Try. We've got to find out what's going on. Does it have anything to do with Roger's group... or your student movement... bringing down the Wall, the collapse of communism...?"

He stared at the floor in bewilderment. "It's odd. Sometimes I get the feeling—it surfaces from deep somewhere... then it's gone—that this whole thing that I've been pursuing with a passion for 25 years isn't as much my idea as somebody else's. There's something beyond it, some other purpose."

"That fits!" exclaimed Nicole. "You've been chosen for a special mission. But by whom... and what is it?"

Ari reached for her hand. His eyes were pleading with her. "You don't think I'm losing my mind? This sounds crazy. Maybe it's overwork... not enough sleep... an obsession that's driven me so long that I'm...."

"You're perfectly sane!" interrupted Nicole firmly. "Don't give that another thought. Brilliant people have weird experiences. Carl Jung had visitations from the 'spirit world.' Even had his own 'spirit guide.' Philemon, he called him. Said he was his guru, real as a person. Walked up and down in the garden with him, carried on conversations...."

"I'm not that bad off—yet!" laughed Ari. "That's a relief."

"In some ways your case is similar," said Nicole thoughtfully. "But what's happening to you is more subtle...."

"Maybe I've got some wires crossed. You admit there's a lot we don't know about the brain."

Nicole reached up and brushed the tousled, damp hair back from his forehead. "Love, nobody's messing with your *brain*—it's your *mind* they're after."

"Brain...mind...word games."

"Ari, I've tried to explain this to you before," persisted Nicole. "The *brain* is physical; the *mind* is not. It takes something physical—like drugs or electric shock—to affect your brain. Nobody's doing that to you."

"Oh, yeah? What about some kind of low frequency radio waves...or magnetic current beamed into this apartment...like the KGB aims at foreign embassies in Moscow?"

"Forget it. It would affect me, too—and I'm not having nightmares...or seeing *him*."

"Then what's happening? Somebody's doing something to me!"

"That's what we're trying to figure out. It's not your *brain* they're working on, but your *mind*. No one's slipping drugs into your food...or aiming microwaves at you. And even if they were, that wouldn't program you to do specific things."

"Specific things?"

"Right. The thoughts you get, the words you mumbled in German...*initiation, higher consciousness, chosen, special mission*...those all indicate some specific goal. It takes a *mind* to program that into you."

"So you think somebody's trying to do some kind of *mind control* thing on me...*telepathically*?"

"That's a possibility. We know that one mind can communicate with another—over any distance. That's been demonstrated halfway around the world. Some American astronauts sent telepathic messages back to earth while they were orbiting the moon...with pretty good success."

"But *mind control* from a distance—has that been done?"

"No question. Plenty of experimental data. The KGB's been involved in it for years—and the CIA. And right here in France...the same thing is going on. In hypnosis one person controls another by audible commands. That's why I'd stay away from hypnosis. But there's no reason that couldn't happen telepathically."

Ari gestured helplessly. "I think that's a little far out. Something is going on with my brain. It has to be...."

"Look, Ari." Nicole was exasperated. "Your *brain* is a *physical* conglomeration of *matter* inside your skull. It can be affected *physically*—by trauma, drugs, electromagnetic current. But that wouldn't make you think certain thoughts or do certain things. No *physical* influence—not even an electrode probing parts of your brain with your skull opened up on an operating table—conveys *specific ideas*. For that to happen, some *mind* would have to be involved." She waited for that to sink in.

"I'm not trying to be difficult," responded Ari defensively, "but you're the brain surgeon and you keep avoiding the obvious—that there's some malfunction in my brain. Electrical current, chemical reactions...isn't that how the brain thinks? Couldn't there be some imbalance...?"

"The brain doesn't think, Ari."

"Wait a minute...!"

"The brain is like a computer. It only does what it's told."

"Niki...this is really off the wall!"

"Then tell me...how does a brain cell decide what it's going to think about?"

"Some kind of stimulus, I guess. That starts the electric current going...."

"You can't believe that! A stimulus can trigger simple reactions...but not complex ideas. You think some 'stimulus' started electric current that told me to say this sentence? And if it did, where did the electric current in my brain get these ideas? Dreamed them up on its own? Come on, Ari!"

"But doesn't everybody believe that...that the brain thinks?"

"Just because everybody believes something doesn't make it true. I'm the neurosurgeon, and I'm telling you the brain doesn't think. The *mind* thinks and uses the brain, like a computer, to control the body."

Ari smiled in spite of himself. "My undergraduate degree is in physics, you know. I was taught that matter was all there was...that everything could be explained in physical terms—electric current, protein molecules, chemical reactions."

"Another common fallacy," interrupted Nicole. "You can't explain moral concepts, the idea of justice and truth as chemical reactions in the brain!"

Ari was shaking his head. "What you're telling me is intriguing—that *minds* aren't physical. So there must be a nonphysical dimension of the universe—whatever that means."

"There has to be. And you're right, we don't know what that means."

"That's exactly what *he* told me 25 years ago in East Berlin—and I thought he was crazy."

"*He* said that?"

"Exactly. Said I was a 'prisoner of the physical dimension' and that I didn't understand...but that I would some day."

"I don't know that we're exactly *prisoners*—but there's something beyond the physical, that's for sure."

"That's *revolutionary*!"

"To a physicist, maybe, but not to a neurosurgeon."

"That brings me back to that book by the CIA agent," mused Ari. "He says the CIA's in touch with nonhuman minds that don't even have bodies. Same thing Robert Jastrow and some other top astronomers suggest, but I never took them seriously. You've forced me to, now—and I don't like the idea."

"It makes me uncomfortable, too," confessed Nicole. "But I know that minds exist and that they're not physical. And I can prove it."

"Go ahead."

"Okay. You're dedicated to fighting for equality and justice. Those are abstract, ethical concepts without physical properties. So they couldn't arise from physical activity in the brain...could they?"

Ari thought for a moment, then shook his head. "A nonphysical concept like truth...I don't see how it could arise from physical stimulus of a brain cell. It just couldn't."

"Right. We can say that dogmatically."

"Keep talking."

"Surely you wouldn't accept that your determination to rid the world of Marxism and the horrible injustice and oppression it brings exists merely because some random electrical current in your brain makes you think like that."

"I'm not arguing that any more."

"So...like it or not, there's a *spiritual* dimension to human experience. You can't explain an appreciation of art, or philosophical concepts like truth, or good and evil in terms of electric current and chemical reactions in your brain."

"You already made that point. I'm convinced. But *telepathic mind control*," mused Ari skeptically, "how would that work?"

"*Influence*—not control. Total control would turn you into a zombie, and that would be obvious. Someone's trying to break your will...implant specific thoughts in order to get you to do certain things...use you for some 'mission.'"

"You really think so?"

Nicole nodded soberly. "I don't think there's any other explanation that fits the facts. I certainly wouldn't operate as a surgeon on your *brain* based on what I saw last night and what you've told me."

They stood there in silence, looking at each other sympathetically, holding hands. "There's something else bothering you," said Ari at last.

"We can't say that humans are the *only* intelligent beings in the universe," Nicole admitted somberly. "There must be *other minds* out there. And Jastrow could be right—some of them may not have bodies. Like what religious people call 'spirits.'"

Nicole paused for a moment, thinking it through, then went on. "And suppose one of *those minds...from a nonphysical dimension*—a dimension that could be right next door to this physical universe—suppose that entity, or whatever you call it, is trying to implant ideas in your mind...so it can use you for some purpose?"

"Exactly what that book said! And Roger pooh-poohed it. The CIA's got to be involved. Roger's lying to me. He knows what's going on."

"Never mind the CIA," said Nicole earnestly. "There's a much worse possibility than that...another dimension...and it's frightening."

Ari's eyes flashed with anger. "So, *they've* got a mission for me, have *they*? Well, I've got a mission of my own! Look, I'm drowning in sweat...and I've got a class." He gave Nicole's hand a quick squeeze and headed for the shower.

15

The Making of a Terrorist?

Ari gulped down the last of his orange juice and grabbed the kitchen phone at its first ring. It was just before 7:00 A.M. and Nicole mustn't be disturbed. An emergency operation had kept her at the hospital until after 2:00 A.M. She'd come home just before 3:00 looking completely exhausted.

"Hello," he said in a low voice.

"Professor Mueller, it's Abdy. Sorry to call so early...."

"That's okay. I was up."

"I just got back from Israel half an hour ago. I've got to see you right away."

"Is it that urgent?"

"It's *very* urgent!"

"Look... I was just going out for my run. I'll meet you at the Tuileries—the west fountain—in about half an hour. Okay?"

"I'll be there."

Ari's seven-mile running route took him straight down onto the narrow, cobblestoned Rue de L'Abbé, across the broad, tree-lined Boul'Mich and over the dew-dampened lawns of Jardin du Luxembourg. Exiting that huge park, he ran past the closed shops and small restaurants along Rue de Seine and crossed the river over Pont Royal, entering the nearly deserted Jardin des Tuileries at its southeast corner. When he came within sight of the western fountain in those spacious gardens, he could see Abdul already there, pacing back and forth in obvious agitation.

"You know about China!" Abdul called out as Ari came running up to join him.

Ari nodded as he took in deep gulps of air.

"They've massacred hundreds of students! The leaders are in hiding, and there's a big search on to find them."

"I won't say... I told you so," said Ari between gasps.

"It looked so good two days ago," lamented Abdul. "Three thousand students on a hunger strike... a million people joining them in Tiananmen Square. Thousands more surrounding tanks and troops miles away, so they couldn't get to the protesters. How could any peaceful demonstration be bigger or better? But it didn't work."

"Here's what I got straight out of China last night," explained Ari. "The army wouldn't fight the students. It was close to a military mutiny. So they brought in units from Mongolia. Didn't speak the language of Beijing. Knew nothing about thousands of workers supporting the students with strikes. Told these troops that the people in Tiananmen Square had some incurable, contagious disease."

"So that's why the carnage. Soldiers mowed those students down with machine guns...squashed them under their tanks like bugs!" Abdul choked on the words.

"It was horrible beyond description. But you didn't meet me here to tell me that."

"No. But it showed me that nonviolence isn't going to work...and that finalized my decision."

"I abhor the massacre as much as you do," replied Ari quietly, "but it doesn't prove that at all."

"I think it does...proves it to me!" Abdul spat out his disillusionment.

The rose-colored morning sun was just setting aflame the tops of the huge trees that lined the broad promenade through the heart of the Tuileries. Behind Abdul the towering obelisk of Place de la Concorde pierced the soft blue sky—and far beyond, the massive Arc de Triomphe loomed like some spectral shape in the early morning haze.

Numbed with the pain of the moment, Ari saw none of the beauty that lay before him. Instead, he saw hundreds of dead bodies and thousands of screaming young men and women fleeing the attacking Mongolian troops. Out of the horror stared faces of Chinese leaders who had been his students at the Sorbonne. These were young idealists he had recruited, trained and worked with for years...and dearly loved. Did they now blame him? Would he ever see any of them again?"

"I had to tell you my decision." Abdul's words brought Ari back to the present. "I'm done with it...finished. Nonviolence won't work."

"Wait a minute!" Ari put a hand on Abdul's shoulder. "Tiananmen Square doesn't prove that! I said there'd be a massacre. The timing was all wrong."

"There'll never be a time. Armed revolution is the only way."

"You can't be serious."

"Dead serious!" Abdul clenched a fist and raised it over his head. "If the students had been armed, they could have fought on their terms...and the fight would still be going on all over China."

"No, no! That would only have made the slaughter worse. Think, Abdy. Think! Where could civilians get the weapons to fight a modern army? How could you smuggle in the arms, train thousands of guerrillas? It would cost billions! It's impossible."

"It's not *impossible*."

"Of course it is. The day for armed revolution is over. There's a better way...and it *will* work. If I didn't believe that...I wouldn't have gotten you involved."

"I'm not blaming you. I just wanted you to know...."

"Tell me...how did the trip go?"

"I followed the schedule. Began in Damascus, then Beruit and other parts of Syria, Jordan and Egypt—mostly Cairo and Alexandria. Finally all over Israel, but most of my time was spent in occupied Palestine."

"Really? Why so much time there? That's a very small part of the Middle East."

Abdul looked away to avoid Ari's eyes. "It's such a hot spot...I thought it needed extra attention."

"You may be right," conceded Ari for the moment, but disappointed nevertheless. "Any major problems?"

"No. I think I did a good job—accomplished the major goals. I should finish writing up the report by tomorrow."

"Good. I look forward to reading it."

"Strange outfit you had me work for."

"Why is that?"

"Talk about secretive! I called some of the numbers you gave me, and nobody answers any questions. Wouldn't even trust me with an address where I should mail my report. Told me to turn everything over to you—that you'd mail it."

"I understand how you feel," said Ari sympathetically, "but they do have to keep their activities secret—and you were just new. That's reasonable, isn't it?"

Abdul nodded grudgingly. "Yeah, to some extent...but they went a little too far...like it was some international spy ring."

"Maybe some unnecessary paranoia." Ari shrugged. "You need a certain amount of it to be in that business—but I really don't know the operation. What did the survey uncover?"

Abdul took a deep breath. "The organization isn't needed in the Middle East—except in Israel. And it won't do any good there. You can't dislodge the Jews from occupied territory with words. It will take violence, outside help ...full-scale war."

"Was that the finding of the survey...or your personal feelings?"

"Well, the survey indicated just what you thought it would. Thousands of university students in every Arab country are discontented with their governments."

"They want democracy?"

Abdul avoided the question and Ari's eyes. "The common people want a return to Islamic fundamentalism."

"How'd you learn that? I thought you were only surveying students."

"The newspapers report it all the time...the shift back to fundamentalism."

"But your survey didn't support that idea," Ari reminded him.

"My survey was confined to university students."

"They're much better informed than other segments of society. Obviously the difference in mood depends on the level of education...and the propaganda people are fed. Uneducated Arabs don't know that Islamic law stands in the way of democracy and real freedom."

"I disagree." Abdul was growing increasingly uncomfortable.

"You're closing your eyes to the obvious."

"I'm not. We interviewed about 10,000 students at random in seven countries... and I'm giving you the facts. There was almost unanimous agreement that the real threat to peace in the Middle East is the existence of Israel."

"You can't be serious! Intelligent university students believe *that*?"

"Why not? It's true."

"Abdy! Arab nations fight among themselves... and do it in the name of Allah! You can't blame that on Israel."

"I believe in Allah, may his name be praised," returned Abdul. "Israel is *the* problem in the Middle East. She occupies territory that belongs to the Palestinians. Naturally, that creates tensions that even cause the Arabs to quarrel among themselves. Until that situation's made right nothing else is going to work out over there."

"I abhor Zionism," responded Ari. "And I'm sympathetic with the Palestinians. But Israel can't be that important. It's one of the tiniest countries in the world—hardly a speck on the map. And the Palestinians are just a small fraction of the Arab world. There are *global* issues to face. Israel and Palestine can wait...."

"With all respect to you—and I've admired you as my professor and mentor—you're wrong. That issue is central to everything else. Israel is a... a cancer in the Middle East. It has to be destroyed. Reject that idea and you can't do anything in the Islamic world. The survey proved there's only one cause that Arab students will rally around."

"The destruction of Israel?"

"Justice for the oppressed Palestinian peoples!"

"You're avoiding my question. By that phrase, don't the Arabs mean the destruction of Israel?"

"There's no other solution."

"And that's what Arab leaders mean by 'peace'?"

Abdul's face had darkened and his eyes flashed angrily. "Israel has committed atrocities against the Palestinians. You can't imagine how bad it is until you see it for yourself. I was almost out of my mind... especially when I talked with the Palestinians themselves in Israel. I promised them I'd fight for their cause. What else could I do?"

"What do you mean, 'fight for their cause'? With weapons? Attack civilian targets like they do? Become a terrorist?"

"You can call it terrorism... but it's war."

"I'm shocked, Abdy! Look, I'm not defending Israel. But we can't be partial in our justice. Worldwide terrorism... attacking or taking innocent civilians hostage who have no relationship to the Palestinian problem at all...you call that *war*?"

"Yes. It's war—and we're going to win!" Abdul was not backing down at all.

"Since when were innocent civilians the primary target in a war! Most of the terrorism in the world is orchestrated by Muslims... and in the name of Allah. Doesn't that bother you?"

"They've been driven to it," insisted Abdul, "by Israeli atrocities...bulldozing their houses if they sympathize with the Palestinian cause... expelling their leaders from the country...all in deliberate violation of their basic rights." Abdul threw up his hands. "You just don't understand."

"Well, I'm trying to," muttered Ari, "and you're not doing a very good job of explaining...."

"The key is Israel. Take care of that *cancer* and everything else will work out."

"That's too simplistic, Abdy. I'm disappointed in you. If this were your dissertation, I'd be embarrassed to be your sponsor."

"I didn't want to argue," said Abdul defensively. "I just wanted you to know my decision. When I finish the report, I'll give you a call and bring it by... with all the survey forms and a full accounting of all expenditures. There was about $3,000 left over."

—✦—

When Ari returned to the apartment and finished showering, Nicole was in the kitchen listening to the news while she sliced and buttered French bread and brewed the coffee for breakfast. The military crackdown, the massacre at Tiananmen Square, the return to a police state, the setback for human rights in China—the bleak recital of events blared from every station.

World reaction had been instant. And impotent. Shocked disbelief was followed by anger, then talk of retaliation and of sanctions to be taken against a despotic regime. Talk without action. Everyone knew that nothing would be done—not against China.

"Horrible," lamented Ari wearily as he slumped into a chair at the kitchen table.

Nicole turned off the radio and brought Ari a cup of coffee. Standing behind him, she put her arms around him, leaned down and kissed him on the cheek, her long hair falling down to caress his face and neck. He reached up and pulled her down again for another kiss, this one on the lips. How he loved this woman!

"But you predicted a massacre," she said sorrowfully, "so you're not surprised."

"Not surprised... but horrified. It was worse than anything I expected... and we haven't seen the end yet. They're still rounding up the leaders." Ari leaned on the table and put his head in his hands. "You can't know what this means to me, Niki." His voice was choked. "I knew so many of them—recruited them. Painted a picture of liberation. They believed me. And now....The timing was all wrong!"

"If this wasn't the time, why did they do it now? I thought you gave the orders."

Ari clenched his fists and slammed them onto the table in frustration and anger. "It was Roger's group...jumping the gun. Interfering...a flagrant breach of our agreement."

"You couldn't stop them?"

Ari shook his head slowly. "Not this time. I hope they've learned their lesson...but at what a cost!" They sat together in silence as Ari tried to confront a grief that was beyond words.

"The whole world's in mourning," sighed Nicole at last. "Nothing else on the news. Lots of noble 'condemnations' from political leaders, but no action. What can they do? It's maddening."

After another long silence, Nicole asked, "Have a good run?"

"I met Abdy in the *Tuilleries*. He called earlier."

"Thought I heard the phone. So he's back. How did it go on his first assignment?"

"First—and last. He doesn't want to work for the organization anymore."

"Why?"

"Says he's disillusioned with nonviolence. I get the feeling he's joined some terrorist group, but was embarrassed to tell me. He just hinted at it."

"I can't believe that! I know Abdy too well. He's sweet...and gentle."

"That's not the way he sounds now." Ari slid his chair next to Nicole's and stroked her hair thoughtfully. "I understand how he feels. I've felt the same way. Maybe you can talk to Abdy. He thinks so much of you."

"And of you, too, darling." She looked at him admiringly. Their eyes met and communicated without words the depth of love they had for each other. Ari leaned over and kissed her lightly on the lips again.

"I couldn't live without you!" he whispered.

"Oh, I think you could," she teased, "but I couldn't live without you!"

"I'm not the easiest person to get along with...I know that," confessed Ari. "But, you know, we've never had a fight in all these years. Some kind of record, huh?"

Nicole smiled. "What is there to fight about?" Her eyes communicated volumes—appreciation, admiration, commitment, love at its purest. "Back to Abdy," she persisted. "I'll give him a call my first free moment today and set up a time for both of us to sit down with him again. I know him too well to take this seriously. I think he's just discouraged...and so, my love, are you," she added tenderly. "What can I do to help?"

"Just...be here. Always." Ari groped for words. He took her in his arms and clung to her. "If you should ever leave me...."

Nicole held him tightly. "Never! You couldn't get rid of me if you tried."

16

Accusations and Denials

It was a blisteringly hot late afternoon in mid-July, but without the usual heat haze and smog. In spite of the lingering, oppressive humidity in the wake of a brief rain squall that had blown across Paris that morning, there was almost unlimited visibility under a pale blue sky. Across Pont Alexandre III hurried an endless throng of pedestrians, mostly eager tourists. They chattered noisily in a variety of languages, exclaimed over the magnificent, colonnaded design of this popular link between the two banks of the Seine, and paused now and then to aim their cameras in various directions from this strategic view point. The two figures standing off to one side near the center of the bridge and arguing guardedly didn't seem to belong in the same scene.

"This is insane, meeting out in the open!" Roger's voice crackled with suppressed anger.

Ari stared at him coldly. "I trusted you . . . all these years."

"And I've trusted you—so what's the sudden problem?"

Looking grim, Ari leaned against the low metal railing of the bridge and eyed his companion closely. Hiding behind dark glasses, Roger stood ill at ease and stared with unseeing eyes at the slowly flowing waters below. Beads of sweat glistened on his forehead and ran intermittently down his face and neck, soaking his collar.

"It took me a long time and a lot of effort to learn the truth," continued Ari evenly, watching Roger intently through half-closed eyes that squinted against the bright sun.

At the implication, a nervous tick tugged spasmodically at a corner of Roger's mouth. He dabbed at his face and brow with an already damp handkerchief. "We've met in cabs for years," he responded at last, deliberately ignoring the implied accusation. "Why the sudden aversion?"

"I've developed a terrible phobia about taxis. You never know who the driver might be—or where he might decide to go." Ari chose his words carefully. "A person could disappear . . . ."

"I resent the insinuation! After the years we've worked together? I can't believe it!"

"It's not that I don't trust *you*. It's who you work for . . . and I know you have to follow orders."

Roger's eyes blazed momentarily with anger, then he stifled a hot denial to say with forced calm, "Look, let's get off this bridge and into the shade. I'm dying out here. And the river's foul today—after that rain."

Ari made no move. "What's going to happen when the committee finds out who you *really* work for? Shall I tell them?"

"I don't know what you're talking about... and I don't like these persistent innuendos!"

"Then let me make it clear. Your real boss has his office at Langley...."

"Langley?" cut in Roger. "You're accusing me of working for the CIA?"

Ari nodded and stared at him coldly. "You've got it."

Roger's face reddened with anger. "You've been reading too many spy novels," he blustered. "You're paranoid!"

Ari's eyes narrowed again and a thin smile played across his lips. "Sure. And we're just a couple of tourists out here to take pictures. What would you like? The twin spires of Notre Dame behind you? Or how about over there, to your left, the dome of Hôtel des Invalides where Napoleon's body lies. *Paris le magnifique!*"

"Cut it!" snapped Roger. "I wouldn't think you'd be joking after what happened in China."

"Joking?" Ari's expression hardened. "You think I'm *joking*? I lost some of my best friends. Like Wang Weilin. Faced down a column of tanks and stopped them dead. Talk about raw courage from a 19-year-old! And those gangsters executed him." Ari thrust his face within an inch of Roger's. "I warned you...!"

Roger drew back. "And I told the committee exactly what you said."

"And those pigheaded idiots stuck to their own plans."

Roger shrugged. "It was a matter of opinion—and we were wrong."

"A massacre!" retorted Ari. "The whole program in China's been set back at least five years—maybe ten!"

"It could have gone the other way," argued Roger lamely, avoiding Ari's piercing eyes. "The students held Tiananmen peacefully for six weeks. No one could have known...."

"*I* knew—and I told you *exactly* what was going to happen! If the committee tries to run my end of the deal one more time...."

"They were trying to help," cut in Roger quickly. "They had a good man. The students followed him...."

"To their graves! Nearly all of the leaders I had trained!"

Ari turned away and stared in silence, following with his eyes a crowded tourist boat as it approached, then disappeared below the bridge, loudspeaker blaring descriptions and histories of everything in sight. "Eastern Europe's just about ripe," he said at last, and turned to face Roger again. "You tell Langley to keep its nose out!"

Roger shifted uneasily. "Langley has nothing to do with it, so drop it. Where d'ya get these crazy ideas?"

"You know that I know what I'm talking about. Now you go back and tell your bosses—in Paris and Washington—that at the first hint of interference, I'll shut the whole thing down. And I mean it!"

Roger made no response. He mopped his face and neck once more and stared down at the Seine flowing slowly below.

"Gorbachev and the Pope—they're the key," continued Ari after another long, uncomfortable silence. "Right?"

Roger's only response was to shrug his shoulders and to continue dabbing futilely at his neck and brow with the wet cloth.

"I'll spell it out," persisted Ari. "The Hungarians cut the barbed wire on the Austrian border back in May. East Germans are pouring into the West from Hungary—with Gorby's blessing. He's made a deal with Bush and the Pope. He had to. John Paul II has Poland in the palm of his hand. We both know Gorby's going to open the Berlin Wall... and then finish off Soviet communism. Right?"

"You're dreaming!" came the nervous reply. "Where do you get these fantasies?"

"Fantasies?" laughed Ari. "Stop bluffing."

"You're the one who's bluffing."

"Am I? I know *everything*—including what Bush doesn't know—the whole rotten corruption. The trail starts in Pakistan and leads through a network of banks—carefully avoiding implicating the Vatican bank—in more than 70 countries... and it's soon going to bubble up like a sewer overflowing the streets of Washington and pouring into the basements of Congress, the CIA, the White House...."

"What are you talking about?"

"You know very well what I'm talking about—multinational fraud on a scale never even dreamed of before. Bribery, corruption, gun running, drug smuggling, terrorism... financed by a string of money-laundering banks involving multiplied billions. I've got the details of drug deals, Noriega's part, the CIA's role... where you fit in...."

"You're mad!"

"You listen to me carefully," said Ari evenly, his finger on Roger's chest. "If some... let's say, uh... unfortunate accident should happen to me... or to any of my people... it would unleash a flood of embarrassing information with repercussions from Washington to Moscow...."

Roger was livid. "You've got spies inside...?" He clamped his mouth shut and fought to control his rage.

"Now that we understand each other," continued Ari, "let's move on. I was in that exclusive gathering of academics that met with Gorby at the Sorbonne last week. Liked what he said. He's obviously working with Washington and the Vatican. But don't let that deceive you. It isn't going to happen without millions taking to the streets... and that won't happen without my okay. Is that clear?"

"I don't have time," snapped Roger, "to listen to your wild speculations. Sure, Gorbachev and Bush and the Pope are friends. And that's good. Stopped the Cold War. But they're each doing what's best for the people they represent...."

"I thought the Pope represented God. How does that figure in?"

"What are you getting at?"

"The New World Order they talk about...who decides the details?"

"I thought we were all working for it."

"So did I. But lately I've started wondering whether we have different ideas about what that means."

"Don't give it a second thought," returned Roger soothingly.

"Oh, I'll keep giving it lots of thought—careful thought. You can count on that."

There was another long, strained silence. At last Ari added, "I'm ready to move on all fronts in Eastern Europe. The students are getting restless. Are your people going to back us at the highest levels—or leave us stranded?"

Roger glanced furtively around, pulled a fat envelope from an inside pocket and slipped it quickly to Ari. "There's double the usual in there. You'll get all the help you need. I'll be in touch." He turned abruptly and walked on across the bridge toward Grand Palais.

Ari stood some moments longer, watching Roger until he had disappeared from sight. Then he turned his eyes beyond the broad Esplanade to the expansive stone facade of Hôtel des Invalides. He recalled with a fleeting smile that in that vast military museum reposed the relics of Napoleon's disastrous retreat from Moscow in 1812. That historic debacle had led to the collapse of imperial France. Just the previous week, Gorbachev, when he'd met with President Mitterand, had enthusiastically hailed the partnership between the USSR and France. History was being turned on its head.

The smile broadened. Marxism had transformed Russia into the terror of the world. And now, at last, the tide had reversed itself. Solidarity, outlawed for seven years, but rescued and backed by the Pope, had just won nearly every seat in Poland's Senate and lower chamber. And what was Solidarity? An organization of *workers*—the very proletariat that Marx and Engels, in *The Communist Manifesto*, had exhorted to unite. Indeed, they had united...to overthrow Marxism itself! What irony.

We've come full circle! The communist oppressors will be swept from power all across Eastern Europe...and even in the Soviet Union itself, where the nightmare began. Eventually China will have to follow.

17

Opiate of the People

Taking advantage of the summer school holiday—and of his new understanding with Roger—Ari spent the next two months traveling. How he wanted to go back to China to seek out the few leaders whom he knew had escaped the purge! Yet to do so would only endanger them. He was getting money to them through established channels that were still functioning. Communications were coming out—but there was nothing else he could do to help at this time. The dark night of oppression had descended upon China once again. The entire country was in the grip of a terrible fear that was reminiscent of the worst periods during Mao's reign of terror. It was far too soon even to think of picking up the pieces of his shattered organization and starting over again. Though it had looked so promising a few months ago, taming the Dragon was now a lost cause.

Eastern Europe, on the other hand, was looking more exciting each day. Going through Check Point Charlie into East Berlin, Ari could sense the powerful currents of change just below the surface. East Germany was a dam about to burst. The same was true in Czechoslovakia, Poland, Hungary, and even the Soviet Union. The only exceptions, where the hardliners still held the people in their iron grip, were Albania, Bulgaria and Romania. Albania was too tiny, isolated and difficult to work in—it would follow when the other communist regimes fell. Bulgaria would come along, too.

Romania was Ari's big concern. There Ceausescu was taking an ever harder line against the tide of reform that was surging all around him and threatening to spill over from neighboring countries into his own. The handwriting was on the wall. Dictators who had been unchallenged for so many years suddenly knew their days were numbered and were beginning to soften in the hope of appeasing the rising tide of demands for more freedom from once-docile subjects. Ceausescu, however, was like a mad dog, determined that if he went down he would take the entire country with him.

"Play it cool," Ari warned his student leaders in Bucharest and Timisoara. "Don't push Ceausescu. His men will shoot you without any conscience. Let it happen in Germany, Poland, Hungary, all around you... then your chance will come."

Such wisdom was not easy to accept, now that the opportunity of a lifetime seemed within reach. Student leaders in Romania, like those with whom Ari clandestinely met throughout the communist world during those exciting two months in the summer of 1989, were euphoric. Freedom was in the very air they breathed, and Ari, in spite of his caution after so many disappointments down through the years, found himself caught up in the compelling sense of optimism. This time it would come to pass. The goal he had worked so hard to achieve was about to be realized, and nothing, absolutely nothing, could prevent it from happening. The time had come at last!

Returning to Paris in time to teach Fall classes, Ari found it almost impossible to suppress his excitement and keep his mind on his lectures. "I've never felt like this before!" he told Niki over breakfast the first morning he was back. "I was afraid the disaster in China would make it harder everywhere else and delay *everything*—but it's just the opposite. Eastern Europe's in the bag. All of it."

"Including the Soviet Union?" she asked skeptically. "The Red Army and the KGB... and those gangsters in the Kremlin... they're not going to roll over and play dead."

"That's what's so amazing." Ari shook his head in disbelief. He stood up and began to pace back and forth, gesturing fervently. "Gorbachev's been undermining the communist party, getting ready to dissolve the Warsaw Pact, making secret deals with the West—and the Kremlin leaders are following him like sheep! He's been talking about a 'united Europe from the Atlantic to the Urals' for two years. Nobody in the West—except Bush and the Pope—took him seriously. Now, suddenly, everybody's saying the same thing."

"*Especially* the Pope," added Nicole thoughtfully. "He used that same phrase just the other day in a big speech in Germany. Made the front page in *Le Monde*."

"I hope you saved the article."

"It's in there." She nodded toward a stack of papers on the other end of the table.

"The Pope! There's something I'm missing here," mused Ari. "My mother was a Catholic. I never took her religion seriously. A lot of superstitious hogwash. She was heavily into 'the Virgin'—'our Lady' of this and that, mostly Fatima...."

" 'Our Lady of Fatima' supposedly saved the Pope's life in that 1981 assassination attempt," mused Niki. "She appeared to him during his convalescence, gave him a mission and promised a miraculous sign that would cause the entire world to bow to his authority."

Ari leaned against the kitchen counter and laughed. "They print that stuff in newspapers and people believe it?"

"Somebody must believe it. I saved a stack of articles for you, all about Fatima—and I haven't seen any letters to the editor ridiculing it. The assassination attempt on the Pope occurred on the anniversary of the first apparition in Fatima, and John Paul's been back there several times to thank 'our Lady.' In fact, he dedicated the world to her 'Immaculate Heart.' She promised to convert Russia and bring peace to the world if the Popes would do that."

"This is the 20th century, not the Middle Ages!" retorted Ari.

Nicole nodded and smiled. "I agree. But read the articles. It's not just Fatima. The 'Virgin' has appeared all over the world and in some places appears daily. She's appeared right here in Paris; in Medjugorje, Yugoslavia; New York; the Philippines... you name it almost. And 900 million Catholics take it very seriously."

Ari resumed his agitated pacing back and forth. "It was Reagan and the Pope... and now Bush and Gorbachev and the Pope," he muttered, more to himself than to Nicole. "I always figured it was strictly a political arrangement... but obviously there's more to it than that. This superstition about the 'Virgin'... it fits in with the whole women's rights thing and goddess worship. It appeals even to people who aren't religious."

"Don't minimize the religious power," suggested Niki, probing her memory. "Take the 'Black Virgin' of Jasna Gora in Poland. I heard lots of talk about her when I was young. There's a huge shrine that's visited by millions of pilgrims. The Polish people have trusted her as their 'protector' for 600 years. The Pope is devoted to her."

Ari came back and sat at the table again across from Niki, a troubled expression on his face. "How do you fight superstition? Catholics are the major factor in Poland. All of my leaders there are Catholics, and I scarcely gave it a second thought. In fact, Solidarity's really a Catholic organization. I'm beginning to see things in a new light—and it's terribly disturbing!"

"The religious appeal is worldwide," added Nicole. "According to the newspaper articles I saved for you, hundreds of millions around the world are devoted to dozens of 'Virgins.' Fatima is the best known, but there's the 'Virgin of Lourdes,' of Guadalupe, Medjugorje... the list is endless. There's a 'Black Virgin' in Brazil that I had never heard of that's worshiped by millions."

"Niki, there's a powerful force here that I've overlooked!" Ari clenched his fists, and his eyes reflected a new and desperate understanding. "Communism was supposed to stamp out religion—but religion was too strong. That's power! Is that what's behind Gorbachev's strange moves? There are rumors that Gorbachev is going to visit the Pope... and Moscow is going to establish diplomatic relations again with Rome."

He stood up and began to pace the floor again. "I don't know what kind of a deal they've made... but something is going on between Bush, Gorbachev and the Pope. The Vatican is a key player in this thing—and I never saw it until recently! How could I have overlooked this for so long?"

"I was raised a Catholic." Nicole was staring out the kitchen window onto the tiny square below, seeing none of it, as long-forgotten memories surfaced. "I hated it. So did my father. My mother went along—fear, I guess. That's what my dad always said. But just before he died, he called for the priest. I'll never forget how he changed at the end. He wanted the whole religious trip—everything. And from the Church he'd despised!"

"I can't believe it!" exclaimed Ari. "All my life I've been trying to destroy communism—and all the time, right under my nose, was something even stronger and no less authoritarian! I never took religion seriously... a superstition for the gullible. But it's powerful! And I've just realized—probably too late—that it's going to cause serious problems down the line."

"Here's a thought for you," exclaimed Niki. "If you could get the local priests and bishops on your side—wow! There's a strategy."

Ari smiled with satisfaction. "We've already done that everywhere we could. The Catholic Church has been the major factor in Poland. Couldn't have gotten this far without it. But when communism falls, the Church will be stronger than ever." The worried expression had returned again. "Have I worked all these years just to get us back to the Middle Ages?"

"I think you're overreacting," countered Nicole. "The Church has always been there... and happy to work with whoever was in power."

"Cooperate? Only when necessary. The Roman Catholic Church *dominated* ... crowned and deposed emperors." Ari leaned against the kitchen counter and stared in silence at the ceiling with unseeing eyes for several moments, deep in thought. "Religion!" he mused half-aloud at last. "Who'd ever have thought that 'the opiate of the people' would come out on top against Marxism! Will it enslave the whole world in the end? What a scenario!"

"Ari, snap out of it," chided Nicole. "A little melodramatic, aren't you?"

"I wish you were right, but I don't think so. I've given my whole life to something that I suddenly realize could become a disaster. Are we going to destroy communism... only to see Catholicism fill the vacuum? Is that where we're heading? I've had a blind spot!"

"That reminds me—if you're worried about Catholicism... what about Islam? They've got 900 million, too. Abdy's become *extremely* religious while you've been gone. I tried to reason with him, but it's like talking to a programmed robot. I couldn't get anywhere."

"That worries me. He was always a Muslim... but not a serious one. I had hopes he'd moderate his position—but he seems to have picked up Islamic fundamentalism in his trip to the Middle East. I need him to open up that part of the world."

"You told me he refused."

"He was very emotional that morning. These feelings pass when reason finally takes over. Abdy's brilliant. Too smart to let his passions rule his head."

"If you thought he was emotional two months ago, you ought to see what's happened while you've been away. He's become a fanatic. 'Submission to Allah' is all he talks about. That's the New World Order he's dreaming about... a Muslim takeover of the planet."

—✦—

It took three days for Ari to get Abdul to return his call, and when he finally did the evasiveness couldn't be denied. Something was obviously wrong. The problem became clear when they got together at a small cafe a few days later. Abdul didn't want to join Ari even for a drink. Raw nerves were betrayed in every word and gesture.

"The faculty tell me they can't get in touch with you anymore," chided Ari. "I had to use a few connections to get your new *unlisted* number. And then you didn't want to see me. What's going on?"

Abdy leaned close and spoke in a half-whisper. "I think my new phone is bugged. Sometimes I'm followed."

"Who would do that?"

"The *Mossad*. The Israelis suspect me."

"Of what?"

"Forget it. I wouldn't have met with you for even a moment, but you've been my mentor. I respect... and *love* you... and especially Niki. But we can't have any more contact."

"You haven't joined the PLO!"

Abdul looked away and made no answer.

"Abdy! That's not the way to go!"

Abdul pushed his chair back and stood to his feet. His face was a mask of pain. "Don't try to contact me... *please*. It could be dangerous for you." He turned to leave.

Ari jumped up and stood beside him. "What about Niki? She's been like a sister. Will she ever see you again? You can't do that, Abdy! It kills me to see this happen."

"I... I'll try to get in touch with Niki." His voice was a hoarse whisper. There were tears in his eyes. "I want to see her, and explain... and say goodbye." Quickly he turned and threaded his way through the closely placed tables out onto the sidewalk and, without a backward glance, melted into the night.

18

Euphoria... and Despair

"That dinner was fantastic," exclaimed Ari, wiping his mouth with his napkin and pushing his chair back from the table. He stood up and reached for Nicole's plate. "Here, let me help you."

"Sit right back down," she ordered, then added with an impish look, "I've got a surprise for you."

"Shall I close my eyes?"

"If you like." She went to the refrigerator and brought out a Black Forest torte—his favorite. Cutting a huge piece, she placed it in front of Ari and sat down with a dazzling smile.

"You're not having any?"

"No. I'm watching my diet."

"Since when?"

"A few weeks ago. Just something I decided while you were away."

"You made this just for me? What's the special occasion?"

"Just a 'welcome home' to let you know how much I missed you. A week late, but I didn't have time to bake it until today."

"You shouldn't have!" exclaimed Ari.

"Well, then, don't eat it."

"Very funny." He was already digging in. "Mmm, wonderful!"

When the last crumb had been pursued and swallowed, Ari leaned back and sighed with satisfaction. "Niki, you're so thoughtful, always doing something special for me... in spite of your hectic life as a doctor. Where would I ever find another woman like you?"

"You'd better not be looking!"

Ari reached out and seized Nicole's hands. "How about a walk? I need it after that. Besides, it's a gorgeous evening."

"Great! I'll get my joggers on."

Once outside and away from the ever-present danger of bugging devices in walls and autos, Ari confided, "I've got a special assignment for you tomorrow afternoon. I hope you don't have something at the hospital."

"I'm off after three o'clock. What is it?"

"You bought a black handbag on sale at Galleries Lafayette yesterday."

"Yes?"

"If you have anything in it, empty it out tonight. Don't take it to work. When you come home put nothing in it. I'll have filled it with some very important papers. The same ones I put in that special place you know about...in case something happens to me."

"This sounds so mysterious. What's going on?"

"You're going to deliver the papers to an American. Used to be a student of mine years ago when her father was a pastor in Paris. Her name's Carla Bertelli.* She's a free-lance reporter now for *The Washington Post* and *The Wall Street Journal* with connections at *The New York Times*.

"Sounds impressive. Where do I find her?"

"Meet me at Cafe du Bois at seven o'clock. Bring the bag. My contact will come along about 7:30 and just 'happen' to recognize me. She'll come over and join us. You'll have put your bag down on the pavement beside you...on the right. I'll be on your left. Okay? She'll have a black one exactly like yours. She'll sit next to you and put her bag down beside yours. When she leaves she'll take yours with the papers in it...."

"How did you arrange this?"

"I just happened to see a write-up in *Le Monde* about a convention of free-lance writers, suspected she might be there...got in touch with her through a courier. Later we talked on the phone. It's all set."

They were walking past one of their favorite sidewalk cafes in the Latin Quarter. "Look," said Ari. "There's an empty table. Let's grab it."

"Two espressos," he called to the waiter.

They sat in silence, sipping their coffee and enjoying the endless parade of fascinating humanity hurrying past. "You've had something on your mind, Niki," said Ari at last. "I've noticed it—ever since I got back from Eastern Europe. What is it?"

Nicole hesitated. "I...oh, darling...." She reached out for Ari's hand as she struggled to keep her voice steady. "I've been waiting for the right time to tell you.... I...we're...well, I'm going to have a baby!"

She was too excited to notice the shocked look on his face. "I know we weren't planning anything like this...but since it happened, isn't it too wonderful? I found out just after you left!"

Ari put his hands over his eyes in an agony of disbelief. When finally he looked at her there was no mistaking his displeasure. But how could he communicate it tactfully to the deliriously happy girl beside him?

"But darling...," he began seriously.

Niki's smile faltered—and died.

"Look, we need to talk about this. It takes two...I mean, this just isn't the right time.... Maybe later." How could he get across to her that this must not be! "Darling, a little later it would be wonderful...but right now...it's impossible. Eastern Europe is about to break wide open!"

---

* Carla Bertelli is a major character in *The Archon Conspiracy* by Dave Hunt (Harvest House Publishers, 1989).

Somehow it hadn't come out the way he'd intended. The expression on Nicole's face told him he had bungled badly.

"Eastern Europe?" she managed. "I don't see the connection. That's reaching awfully far for an excuse...."

"It's the, uh...*timing*," he stammered. "So much is going to happen in the next few months...I'll need your support more than ever." There he went, putting his foot in his mouth again. How could he say it?

"But darling," responded Nicole softly, a tremor in her voice, "as for *timing*...it's almost too late for you already, you know. I wasn't going to say that...."

"Right now is just the *worst* time possible." He reached out for her, but she pulled her hands away. "I love you, darling...."

"So it just isn't *convenient* for you!"

"I didn't *exactly* mean that...."

"I have a career, too, you know...but I wouldn't let that stand in the way of something so important...something that ought to mean so much to both of us."

"It *would* mean a lot to me if we'd planned it...."

"Are you telling me to get an abortion? Is that what you want?" Nicole's eyes were accusing him.

Ari avoided looking at her as he carefully chose his words. "As a matter of fact—yes." He was trying to be calm, eminently rational. "Let's be reasonable about this, Niki, and not get swept away with emotion. Too much is at stake. The world is at a pivotal point...." Even as he said it, Ari sensed that Niki was on another track. He winced at what he knew would be her response.

"I don't believe what I'm hearing! Out to save the world, the environment, the plants, animals, and all of mankind—and you want to kill *our baby*!"

"Niki, listen to reason. We're not talking about a child...not at this stage, anyway."

Nicole stood to her feet uncertainly, her eyes blurred with tears. Desperately Ari jumped up and grabbed her arm. "Please, Niki! Let's talk it over," he pleaded.

"I think we've talked enough. I understand perfectly." She pulled herself free, ran across the street and disappeared among the crowd. Stunned and drained, Ari looked longingly and helplessly at the spot where he had last seen her.

Ari sank back at last into his chair. Looking around in embarrassment, he motioned for the waiter to bring the bill. Nicole would calm down. It would take time, but when she got back to the apartment they'd get it all sorted out.

She was a realist. It would be a hard decision, but she'd see that it *wasn't* convenient. Some other time, but not now.

—✦—

After her hurried departure, Nicole soon changed to a slower pace. They'd *never* had a fight. Nothing like this in all the years they'd lived together. How could he, the *father*, the man she loved so much, even think for one moment of an abortion! This was *their child!*

Of course she'd calm down, go back to him—but not yet. She needed space. Time to think. Aimlessly she wandered along the streets toward the Seine. From the sheltering maze of the Latin Quarter's narrow lanes she came out at last to traverse the left bank of the river and the ancient Ile de La Cité along Boulevard du Palais, then across the other arm of the Seine.

There were so many memories to sort through—the bitter and the sweet. Until tonight she'd found her only security, her only link to unconditional love and acceptance, in Ari. Now she must face a reality with no options. Did Ari's love have a price tag—one that she couldn't pay? That had never seemed possible. In despair, she sobbed aloud.

At that moment a voice intruded on her consciousness. "You can't explain the life that develops in the womb as a mere physical conjunction of sperm and ovum." Nicole's mind reeled under the impact of the words. "No, the incredible development of bones and nerves and brain and the trillions of cells in their intricate organization are all too marvelous to be explained by chance."

She had awakened as from a deadly sleep. Tearing her gaze from the sidewalk and daring to look up, she saw before her, at Tour St. Jacques, a small, attentive crowd gathered around someone whom she could hear but not see. Edging closer, wiping her eyes, she strained now to catch every word as the speaker continued.

"That fact alone should be enough to prove that we're not the product of random evolutionary forces, but of a blueprint so ingenious that only God Himself could be its designer. But there's much more involved than incomprehensible mechanical genius. Each of us is more than a highly organized conglomeration of cells. You can't account for the human personality, the qualities of love and hate, the esthetic appreciation of music and art, the recognition of truth and justice, of right and wrong, in terms of protein molecules and chemical reactions. These are *spiritual* qualities totally unexplainable in relation to the *material* composition of our bodies, which itself is marvelous beyond comprehension."

Nicole sensed the communication of an unusual calm and confidence as she listened. She was captivated by the logic and quiet power of the compassionate yet firm voice. At the same time, however, she felt herself repelled. Someone was trying to convince this crowd that God existed! How could he dare—in Paris, of all places. She knew that the overwhelming majority of Parisians, like herself, were too intellectually arrogant to believe in God. It was unthinkable to any educated person in the 20th century—intolerable—to be accountable to some "Creator."

Torn between the commonsense power of what was being said, and her reluctance to accept it, she began to move away. "You'll never know why you're here on this planet until you know your Creator. If you miss His purpose for your existence, you'll be forever frustrated and empty, no matter what you try in your search for fulfillment...." The words faded as she quickened her pace, strangely fearful of what more she might hear.

"Excuse me...."

Startled by the voice just behind her, Nicole turned to see a woman of about her own age hurrying to catch up with her.

"I couldn't help noticing...you've been crying. May I help?" There was a winsome tenderness about her that was immediately attractive.

"It's kind of you...." The empathetic eyes encouraged Nicole to continue. "I just had a quarrel with my fiancé."

"Is there anything I can do?"

Nicole shook her head, feeling foolish for having said anything. "No, thanks. I'll be okay."

"You're Dr. Lalonde, aren't you?"

"How did you know?" Nicole asked in surprise.

"I've seen you at the hospital."

Nicole looked at her more closely. "I've seen you there, too! You're a nurse...?"

She nodded. "Yes. I'm Francoise Duclos."

"Of course! Your husband is Dr. Pierre Duclos...chief of staff. Is he the one who's speaking back there?"

"Yes, we come down here quite often."

"I thought there was something familiar about that voice!"

"If Pierre and I can help in any way...," persisted Francoise.

"What your husband was saying...about, uh, life forming in the womb...." Nicole hesitated. "That caught my attention."

"You're pregnant?"

Nicole nodded. "Two-and-a-half months. I needed someone to talk to...." She started to break down and caught herself. "I've admired your husband...."

"Your fiancé isn't happy about the pregnancy?" asked Francoise gently. "Wants an abortion, perhaps?"

Nicole steeled herself. "I'd rather not talk about it." She took a halfhearted step to leave. "It was nice meeting you...."

"Can you believe it was only a coincidence that you came along just at the time when my husband was speaking about what concerns you so much at this very moment?" Francoise's voice was tender but compelling.

Nicole found herself suddenly overcome with emotion, unable to answer. *Coincidence? Maybe...maybe not.*

"Do you remember what he was saying?" continued Francoise gently.

"I shall never forget," confessed Nicole, barely managing to hold her voice steady. "No, I think it was not a coincidence. You're as persuasive as your husband." She held herself together with great effort. "I do need someone to talk to," she added, dabbing at her eyes.

Francoise put an arm compassionately around Nicole and guided her toward a nearby bench. "Then why don't we just sit down over here and you tell me what's on your heart. I'm a good listener."

19

To Be— Or Not To Be

For a long time Ari lay awake, starting at every real or imagined noise, and rehearsing with painful clarity the evening's debacle. So often during these past years he'd heard the reassuring sound of key grating against lock that had meant Nicole had returned safely from a late night at the hospital. Now he listened in vain. If only he'd been more sympathetic, more sensitive.

At last, sometime after midnight, he fell asleep. At 3 A.M. he awoke with a start. In a panic he realized that her side of the bed was still empty. She'd be sleeping on the couch, of course. But when he tiptoed quietly into the living room, it was empty.

Should he call the police? He picked up the phone, then put it down. No, she'd probably stayed at a friend's house. She'd lay a guilt trip on him... teach him a lesson. He should have remembered past discussions... that she had wanted to have a baby, and that he had always put her off. This pregnancy, even though unplanned, obviously meant a lot to her. He just wasn't the diplomatic type. Everything was so black and white to him, so obvious. That approach wouldn't work in this situation. He could see that. Still, she would eventually see the wisdom of getting an abortion. Having a child now was absolutely out of the question.

There was still no sign of Nicole when he awakened again around 7:30 A.M. and got up to shave and shower. He was gulping down black coffee and dry French bread and gloomily pondering whether he should notify the university that he was unable to teach his class that day when he heard a key turning in the front door. Nicole! Should he rush to greet her? No, this night's pain had been her responsibility. Now it was up to her to explain herself and make the first move toward reconciliation.

"Is that you, Nicole?" he called, unable to suppress his sudden relief.

"No, it's just one of the burglars who have a key to the apartment," came the quick response. That typical retort was a good sign. Footsteps approached, and there she was standing in the kitchen doorway. How very tired she looked. When their eyes met Ari knew that time had not healed the hurt.

"Where have you been?" Ari's voice shook. "I almost called the police...."

"I'm sorry. I should have phoned...."

"Well, I'm sorry, too. I was too abrupt. I should have given you time to think...." As soon as the words were out he knew he'd made things worse again, even before he saw her stiffen.

"There's really *nothing* to 'think' about," she responded quickly. "Abortion is totally *unthinkable*...." She sat down wearily at the table.

"Let's not start off arguing," pleaded Ari. "Can't we wait? I think you're still too upset to discuss this rationally."

"I'm not arguing," countered Nicole, controlling her voice with great effort. "And I'm quite rational. There's no *discussion*. Period. I'm just stating the simple facts. There's a child growing inside of me, Ari—*our* child with *our* genes. It will look like us... have our traits. I love that child... and I'm going to keep it!"

"So it has to be *your* way... without even hearing *my* side. No willingness to talk it over...."

Nicole stood to her feet. "You don't *reason* about something that's clearly wrong. You're talking about murder!"

"Terminating a pregnancy isn't *murder*!" he retorted defensively. "But let's drop it for now, okay? Later...."

"So that's how it becomes ethical! Even the Mafia avoids the word *murder*. They talk about *terminating* someone. So you just want to '*terminate* my pregnancy.' I have another name for it."

"You should have been a lawyer, Niki. But please, not now. You need to get some sleep."

"I had some sleep—enough, anyway. I have to be at the hospital in 40 minutes. Any calls?"

"No. Am I allowed to ask... where you spent the night?"

"After I left you I ran into a couple from the hospital. He's chief of staff and she's a nurse. I desperately needed someone to talk to... and after we talked for a while on the street I went home with them and we talked some more. It was too late to come back here. I think I settled a great deal last night."

"Settled a great deal?"

"A lot of things that I've wondered about for years fell into place. I do want to talk to you about all that... but I really must jump in the shower and get to the hospital."

"Well, I'm glad you want to talk things over," responded Ari, brightening a bit. "I was in agony last night... imagining the emptiness of life without you."

Nicole stood quietly in the doorway of the kitchen looking at Ari. He could see tears glistening in her eyes. "I felt the same pain," she said at last, "of being without someone I already love very much." Unconsciously, Niki's hands touched her belly.

"Niki, let's talk this out right now!" he pleaded, sensing a growing chasm between them and changing his mind.

"Later, Ari, like you said. Please. There isn't time right now. I'm scheduled for surgery." She hurried from the room.

— ✦ —

Ari spent the day in a tumult of conflicting emotions. Would Nicole leave him? If she did, it was totally unjustifiable under the circumstances. Had she hinted that she was *thinking* about it? He couldn't remember her exact words—but it seemed a separation was implied by her inflexibility. That fear haunted him.

In painful candor he scrutinized their relationship. Looking back he could see that he had too often taken her for granted. But, then, wasn't that a natural concomitant of the perfect love and trust they'd had for one another? He sensed, uncomfortably, that perhaps it wasn't quite that simple. Clearly, he hadn't given her as much of himself as she deserved. He'd been driven by a passion that left little time for the loving sharing of life together that she longed for and that he really wanted to give her.

She'd never complained. With a surge of emotion, Ari recalled the ever-ready sympathy she'd always been so quick to show, the encouragement when he was down. Was *she* ever down? It had never seemed so, but now he wondered. Were her unfailing good spirits more an act of love than a reflection of her true feelings? Could her pregnancy now have triggered resentments that had smoldered beneath the surface for months or even years? Guilt, self-justification, bittersweet memories chased each other in ever broadening circuits through Ari's mind.

What of those "friends" she'd "talked it over with"? How long had she known them? It seemed odd that she'd never mentioned them before. Obviously they were the ones responsible for the strange way she was now thinking and acting. Yes, in some subtle way that he couldn't articulate she seemed to be *different*. She'd been vulnerable, and they had taken advantage of her emotional state to brainwash her.

There was some small comfort in believing that the cause of Niki's stubborn narrowmindedness lay in something outside the bounds of their relationship with each other. That was an important point to bring up tonight. With trepidation Ari's thoughts turned to the evening's assignment. Would Nicole let him down? Surely not. She wouldn't let personal feelings stand in the way of something this important. She'd be at the cafe. If not, what would he do?

— ✦ —

When Ari arrived, he saw to his relief that Nicole was already seated at a choice outdoor table with a good view of the passing crowds. It was just the right spot for Carla, strolling by, to "happen" to notice him. Seeing the black handbag sitting on the pavement to her right, he took the chair to her left, giving her a light kiss on the cheek as he sat down. She endured it, but the warmth was missing. She was wearing his favorite perfume. Was that a good sign? For a brief moment he felt the old intoxication, the rush of nostalgic memories associated with that aroma, but her coolness quickly sobered him.

"Thanks for coming, Niki," he said as he settled himself beside her, trying to be low key.

"I wouldn't let you down, Ari. I know how important this is to you."

"It could save my life some day. . . ." He cut that little speech short and changed the subject. "You look terrific. . . as usual." If he could only forge a link with the past. It would be a mistake to launch right into a heavy discussion. He'd chased her away last night. He'd be careful not to make the same mistakes again.

Ari waited for Niki to say something in response, but she just sat quietly, seemingly absorbed in watching the passersby. He could tell that her eyes were seeing nothing. Finally he asked, "Did you get to the hospital on time?"

"Yes."

After another uncomfortable silence he tried again. "Everything okay over there?"

"Yes. . . everything's okay."

The arrival of the waiter relieved the embarrassment for a moment. Nicole ordered her usual soup and salad. "Maybe I'll just go with that, too," said Ari. Couldn't she see what she was doing to him?

There was another long silence. At last Ari said, "Look, Niki, it's only making matters worse for us just to sit here and say nothing. And small talk is dishonest. . . ."

"I'm willing to talk."

"Well, you said you'd come to some important decisions last night and that you wanted to discuss them. Can we start there?"

"Your friend will be here soon. Shouldn't we wait until after. . . ?"

"I can't wait. Please, what's going on in your head. . . and heart."

"I'm afraid you're not going to like it, Ari." She paused, searching for words.

"Is it that bad?"

"No, it's good, actually. The best for both of us, I think. . . in the long run, at least."

"In the long run? What about right now? What are you going to do?"

"Ari. . . I'm not the same person I was yesterday. It's difficult to explain. Things I used to believe no longer make sense. . . and other beliefs, solid ones, have taken their place. For one thing, I'm not an atheist anymore."

"Well, I *never* was," countered Ari, feeling relieved. At least she hadn't blurted out that she was going to leave him. "So that's no problem. But I don't see what it has to do with our situation."

"But it does. Whether God exists has everything to do with it."

"I'm willing to concede that there's some 'creative force' out there somewhere. So go on. . . ."

"You say you were never an atheist, Ari. But you weren't any more willing than I was to be morally accountable to God. 'Higher power,' yes. 'Creative force,' sure. But a personal Creator who made us for a purpose and who sets the standards of morals and ethics... did you ever believe in *that* God?"

"Really, Niki, I find this irrelevant...."

"No, it's very relevant. What we do is decided by what we think is right or wrong... but who decides that? Where do morals and ethics come from? That question always bothered me. Then I studied medicine and learned how intricately designed the human body is... even a single living cell is more complex than all of Paris. We can't possibly be the product of chance...."

"I don't have any problem with that," cut in Ari impatiently.

"Well, wouldn't right and wrong be equally a matter of God's design? Wouldn't He establish moral laws to govern human behavior just as physical laws govern the material universe?"

Ari sighed with resignation. "I don't see that this philosophical discussion is getting us anywhere."

"Ari, it's the crux of the problem! Right and wrong don't depend upon whether something's convenient or appealing to us...."

"So you're going to tell me that God says abortion is wrong. Is that it?"

Nicole nodded. "That's part of it."

"And now that you've got God on your side... I guess I'm outvoted two-to-one. That's pretty tough opposition."

"You don't have to fight God, Ari." Her eyes were imploring him. "Why not come over on His side?"

"What do you mean, *His* side? You weren't on his side yesterday morning! How can you change sides so fast?" Ari's bitter response was cut short by the waiter arriving with the soup.

An embarrassing and frustrating helplessness swept over Ari. To philosophize, theorize, discuss on an impersonal level man's godlike propensities and potentials was one thing. But to stand exposed and vulnerable to the personal probing of this woman, who had been his lover and was now a total stranger, was intolerable.

Nicole's eyes were pleading with Ari. "What happened last night was that I... well... came to the point where I was willing to swallow my pride and admit the truth... to myself first, and then to others."

Ari was losing patience. "We'd had a misunderstanding," he responded abruptly. "You were vulnerable—in an emotional state where you were looking for simplistic answers."

"I was in an emotional state," said Nicole softly. "That's true. But the rest of it isn't. I was seeking genuine answers, deeper and more honest than I'd ever been willing to face before in my entire life. And I thank God that my concern for the child inside of me brought me to that point."

"You've become a religious fanatic, Niki. In one night! I can't believe it. We've discussed the power of religious superstition... something that I forgot to factor into the equation... but I never thought *you'd* fall for it.

"It didn't all happen last night. I've wrestled with these questions for years. Last night was the culmination . . . the pieces finally all fell logically into place."

"I don't know of anybody of any intelligence who believes what you're trying to dump on me!"

"I don't think I'm ignorant and uneducated—or stupid."

"I'm not saying you are. It's because you aren't that I can't understand how you'd fall for this!"

"Well, Ari, the man who very kindly gave me all the time I needed last night and prayed with me and counseled me from the Bible happens to be one of the most brilliant surgeons in the world. Certainly the intellectual equal of anyone I know . . . you or anyone else."

Ari cut an expletive off in midair. "All right," he muttered, "put this on hold. Here she comes!"

20

"If I Die"

Ari had caught sight of Carla in the distance, her long, naturally wavy auburn hair bouncing with every step. *These tall Americans! They stand out in any crowd. And that self-confident stride, the look....* Ari pretended not to see her, and she made as though she were walking past. Casually she turned in his direction, stopped as though taken by surprise, and waved.

"Professor Mueller!" she called.

Ari looked up and saw her, as though for the first time. "Carla!" he cried as he jumped to his feet.

The tall American squeezed her way between the closely packed diners to his table, where Ari gave her a welcoming hug.

"I was going to call you, but I'd lost your phone number," she exclaimed. "What a lucky coincidence!"

"Nicole, this is Carla Bertelli. Nicole is my fiancée. I don't think you've ever met."

"You've mentioned her," said Carla, "and I've been looking forward to this."

Nicole smiled warmly and pointed to the chair beside her. "Please join us. Can you?"

Carla glanced at her wristwatch and hesitated, playing Ari's script to the hilt. "I'm on my way to a meeting, but this is too wonderful an opportunity to pass by. I can be a few minutes late." She sat down and placed her black handbag next to Nicole's.

"Something to drink?" asked Ari.

"Some iced tea would be nice."

Ari motioned to the waiter. "Some iced tea for the lady," he said. "With lemon."

"*Oui, monsieur.*"

Ari turned to Nicole. "Carla was a student of mine the year I started teaching at the Sorbonne. That was nearly 17 years ago. Her French was unbelievably good...and not a trace of that disagreeable American twang."

"I already noticed," said Nicole. "Flawless Parisian!"

"Well, I grew up here as a teenager," responded Carla modestly. "Professor Mueller was the best teacher I ever had...."

"Every student that's ever taken one of his classes says the same thing," added Nicole proudly. "That's how we met. I was also his student—in one class. After your time, I guess."

"About two years later," said Ari with an embarrassed laugh. "All this flattery is a little too much. I remember very well being *extremely* nervous that first year. It was such an honor to be on the faculty of France's most prestigious university!"

"You fooled me," laughed Carla. "I thought you'd been there forever."

"*Voilà, mademoiselle,*" said the waiter, placing the drink on the table.

"That was fast," said Carla with a smile. She took a sip. "And delicious, too."

"A combination that's not too easy to find here in Paris where dining is a time-consuming art," remarked Ari.

Nicole turned to Carla. "So what brings you back to Paris?"

"A convention of journalists. Tonight's the last meeting."

"I understand that you write for several newspapers. Any particular specialty?"

"Yes, parapsychology."

"*Really.*" Nicole's interest was now aroused. "I suppose Ari—Dr. Mueller—"

"*Hans* Mueller," interrupted Carla. "Where does the *Ari* come from? I never heard that before."

"It's a nickname I had in Germany as a boy," explained Ari. "Only Niki calls me that."

"Anyway," continued Nicole, "I suppose Ari hasn't mentioned that I'm doing my residency in brain surgery...with a growing interest in your subject."

"No, he didn't. Well, I'm fascinated with your specialty, too. If I can help you...send you some articles...."

"That would be wonderful."

"You know, there's a general consensus now that there's a significant relationship between our two fields."

"Yes, I'm aware of that. It's very kind of you to offer some help. Does Ari have your address?"

"I don't think so," responded Carla, reaching into the pocket of her jacket. "Here, let me give you my card. I'd love to keep in touch."

"You keep surprising me, Carla! When did you get into psychic phenomena?" Ari asked in surprise. "That wasn't your interest the last time I saw you."

"Quite recently, actually. I'm still feeling my way. My, uh...ex-boyfriend got me started. He's probably the top parapsychologist in the world. An incredible genius."

"You mean Ken ..., Ken...."

"Inman."

"Yes, Ken Inman. I remember meeting him at Stanford University...the one time I was out there. You broke up?"

"Well, not exactly. Nothing final. We just sort of drifted apart. He's got some top secret research that takes his attention 24 hours a day. I think we still love each other, but...well," she winked at Nicole, "a woman doesn't want to be taken for granted."

"A chronic complaint," agreed Nicole with an understanding smile.

"I wasn't going to sit around and wait," continued Carla, "while Ken pursued his work so passionately that he had no time for me. He just seemed to think I'd always be there whenever he wanted me. So I left him in California and moved to Washington, D.C."

"Did that bring him to his senses?" asked Nicole.

"It took two years. But he's flown out to see me twice in the last month. In fact, he's coming in again as soon as I get back from this trip."

Carla glanced at her watch again. "I'd really love to stay and talk, but I must get to that meeting."

"Remember," said Ari, leaning forward and lowering his voice. "Get that data as quickly as you can into the safest place possible. If I die . . . or disappear . . . no matter what the circumstances . . . you know what to do."

"You can count on me."

"What I'm giving you is hot . . . world-class stuff," confided Ari. "Believe me, it would shake a lot of governments, from Moscow to Washington."

"If it's that important," said Carla, "I can put it on the front page of every major newspaper in the world!"

"Hopefully, you'll never need to publish it—because that would mean *they've* done me in."

"Who are *they*?"

"You wouldn't believe it if I told you. But now you'll have all the proof. You'd be absolutely astonished to know the alliances that are working for a new world order . . . and what they're doing to accomplish it."

"So that's what the material is all about?"

"Partly. It's amazingly complex, but I've laid it all out with documented proof so you won't be afraid to publish it . . . if the time ever comes."

"Sounds fascinating! I'd love to see it published . . . but not over your dead body."

"If you published it now, I would be dead. But if you hold it, that could save my life."

"Well, this was a wonderful surprise, Professor!" exclaimed Carla, pushing her chair back. Reaching down, she smoothly took Nicole's bag, then stood to leave. "I really have to go. It was nice to meet you, Nicole, and to see you again, Dr. Mueller. If you ever get over to Washington . . . or when I'm next in Paris . . . we must spend some time together."

"We'll do it," promised Ari.

"Yes," added Nicole, "we must keep in touch. And please send those articles."

Ari watched Carla until she'd been swallowed up in the mass of humanity crowding the streets. Then he turned to Nicole. "Thanks, Niki. I really appreciate your doing this. It went off perfectly. Carla's a smooth operator."

"I'm glad I could help. She is a charming woman . . . and I hope we can keep in touch."

There was a long embarrassing silence. At last Ari volunteered, "Well, back to square one. So you believe in God, Niki. As I said, I don't have any problem with that."

"Let's be honest, Ari. You do have a problem with a God who sets the standards of human behavior... you're just not admitting it."

"We've been over that before—and it leads nowhere. What other crucial decisions did you come to last night under the influence of those... uh, those...."

"Friends. Please, you don't know anything about them, so it's not fair to make insinuations."

"Well, they obviously took advantage of your emotional state."

Nicole stood to leave. "You wanted me to explain some things, but I really don't think you're in any mood to take me seriously." Before he could reply she was walking away.

Ari waved a 100-franc note frantically at the waiter, then dropped it on the table and ran off in hot pursuit.

"Where are you going?" he asked apprehensively when he'd caught up with her, then added, "*again*" with some irony. She was leaving their apartment farther behind with every stride.

Nicole stopped and turned to face him. "I... I'm not sleeping with you anymore. I can't... not until we're married... if we ever are. And that's in God's hands now."

"So that's it! Come on, Niki! Where did you get these prudish ideas? Those *friends* have sure done a number on you."

She put a hand on his arm. "I love you, Ari. Very much. I don't want to hurt you... but I just can't violate my conscience. It always bothered me...."

"Sleeping with me?" he interrupted in astonishment. "It did? Why didn't you ever say so?"

"I was confused... didn't want to hurt you... rationalized that my feelings of guilt were brought on by old-fashioned ideas. You know, stuff I'd learned in childhood. The usual rationalization."

"You never told me anything about feeling that way! Why now?"

"I wanted to get married right from the beginning. Remember? You talked me into living with you for 'just a short while'... to see whether we were compatible. Then you decided that a marriage certificate was 'just a meaningless piece of paper'...."

"So, what's the big deal... whether we're married or not? Would that change anything?"

"Yes, it would."

"What—and how?"

"Ari, it shows a commitment for life."

"I love you, Niki! I'd never leave you! You know that. I've told you so... *many* times!"

"But you wouldn't stand in front of witnesses and say it and make it official."

Nicole's lips were trembling, and in the fading light Ari could see tears welling up in her eyes. How he longed to hold her in his arms. "I would be willing," he stammered, "but it never seemed that important."

"Every society has marriage... for its own stability... laws that forbid the arrangement we've had. It isn't good for lots of reasons... and it's especially bad for any children that come along. Look at us right now."

"So you're afraid we're going to get arrested? Come on!"

"There's something worse than breaking man's laws, and that's breaking the laws of God. That's why I have to leave, Ari. God knows I love you as much as ever and I hope we can get married... but I can't push that on you."

"Well, I'd be willing to get married... if we could agree on something else...."

Nicole's eyes lit up with anger. "This is *our* child that I'm carrying, Ari. But if you don't want to be bothered with it, then I'll take care of it alone. I'm certainly not going to allow you to talk me into *terminating* it!"

"You have a way with words," muttered Ari. "It's so incredible that this ...*accident*...could shatter the perfect relationship we've had for six years!" Unbearable agony was etched on his face. "Where are you staying tonight?" he stammered, searching for words.

"With the same friends."

"I'd like to tell them what I think of them!" Agony had turned to fury. "They've warped your mind!"

"I'm sorry you feel that way. I'll be coming by tomorrow to get my things. I'm not sure when...." She turned and walked away.

21

Sweet, Sweet Success

The next few weeks were bitterly lonely ones for Ari. He hadn't been there when Nicole had come to the apartment to pick up her things. Perhaps that had been best. But how he missed her! The last six years—his happiest—couldn't be so easily negated. The vivid memory of her face and enchanting voice, of her lilting, contagious laugh and graceful feminine movements, of the very fragrance she exuded, of the comfort of her presence and the love they had shared, made the present emptiness maddening. But even as the pain eroded all sense of peace, his resolve remained firm.

He could not, must not, give in on the abortion issue. It was a pregnancy they had not planned, and as such it should be immediately terminated. Nothing could be more logical. Much as he longed for a reconciliation, Ari was determined, as a matter of principle, that the only way it could happen would be for Nicole to yield to reason—which she showed no sign, at least on his terms, of doing.

They still kept in touch periodically by phone. She had called him for the first time at the apartment one evening a few days after she'd moved out. "Just wanted to be sure you found the keys I left on the sink," she'd said.

"Yeah, thanks," Ari had responded glumly.

"Any time I can help in any way, Ari, just let me know. I want to keep in touch. My phone number is 28-52-59."

"Where are you living?" he'd asked.

"I've got a small apartment near the hospital—it's adequate, and close enough to walk."

"Any address?"

"I hope everything's going okay. I guess you're happy about developments in Eastern Europe."

"Yeah, it's going great. Thanks for calling." Ari slammed the phone down angrily. She had ignored his question, and that hurt.

He stared out the window at the small square two floors below. It was like a stage on which one could watch a microcosm of Parisian life portrayed. He had often thought that each face was like a mask hiding the real person. Now he was one of them. Who could suspect his real thoughts? Outwardly he projected success and fulfillment. The campaign he had waged for so many years was at last producing tangible results. But inside he felt a painful emptiness—like he'd been severed from part of himself. *She's not coming back. God, I can't bear it!*

— ✦ —

In October 1989, the time seemed ripe to turn up the heat throughout Eastern Europe, with special pressure on East Germany. Ari began to make regular weekend trips behind the Iron Curtain, leaving at noon on Fridays right after his last class, and returning early on Mondays in time for his first class of the week. It was as much a matter of personal revenge as strategy that caused Ari to base the final phase of the long-planned student revolution at his old university in Leipzig.

Student "freedom marches" were inaugurated to take place each Monday. Starting out inauspiciously, they proved to be the spark that would ignite East Germany. In harsh response, the Communist Party's aging 77-year-old boss, Erich Honecker, ordered the police to use all necessary force to clear the streets. For awhile it looked as though Leipzig would become a bloody replay of the massacre at Tiananmen Square.

Ari, however, now in constant touch with Roger, and having received his repeated assurances of what was happening behind the scenes at the highest levels, urged the students forward, confident of the outcome. In a surprise move, pressured by Gorbachev and with promises of his own elevation to the Party's top post, Egon Krenz, head of the dread State Security forces, persuaded Honecker to discontinue the use of violence and brutality against the student demonstrators. The Soviet leader's secret plan was now in full swing with the special help of the Vatican.

Riding the swelling crest of his personal popularity, Gorbachev's *glasnost* and *perestroika* had, by this time, gathered such irresistible momentum that nothing could stand in the way. It was no coincidence that the Soviet president made a well-timed visit to East Germany on October 7, ostensibly to celebrate the fortieth anniversary of the communist state. Nor was it mere serendipity that a few days later Honecker was forced out and replaced by Krenz. On the surface that move seemed to be a setback. However, based on inside information from Roger, Ari pressed ahead boldly, knowing that, contrary to widespread fears, Krenz would be the unlikely man, in cooperation with Gorbachev, to bring down the Berlin Wall.

The Monday demonstrations in Leipzig, always taking place a few hours after Ari had departed for Paris, grew in size and boldness, from 200,000 on October 23 to nearly a half million on November 6. On November 8, 1989, Ari suddenly announced the cancellation of his classes for the rest of the week because of urgent business in Berlin. He knew that the despicable Berlin Wall was coming down the next day, and it was only fitting that he should be there when it happened. The following week the students in his classes would ask in astonishment how he happened to be on the scene at that historic moment. A "lucky coincidence," of course, would be his explanation. His irrepressible elation, however, continuing unabated for days, caused more than one student and faculty member to wonder what personal stake he could have had in the collapse of communism to cause such extraordinary jubilation.

All animosity and distrust between them seemingly forgotten, at least for that glorious moment, Ari and Roger played the part of comrades in arms, as together they watched the Wall come down. While euphoric Berliners on each side chipped away at the hateful barrier that had so long separated families and friends, the two conspirators from the West congratulated and slapped each other enthusiastically on the back as though they had played a major role in this historic event, as indeed, though unknown to those around them, they had. Ari was bursting with a sense of triumph that words were inadequate to express. *At last!* No one could possibly have understood how he felt to be a part of that exhilarating scene.

"It's coming down...coming down...bring it down...," Ari kept telling Roger, as if he couldn't see for himself. Gesturing with clenched fist over his head, he danced with any one of the hundreds of wild celebrants, men or women, who came within arms' reach.

"You bet it is, you all!" Roger yelled in his broadest Texas drawl. "It's happening! We did it! Hooray!"

Intoxicated with joy, Ari and Roger mingled with the frenzied crowd to greet the surging masses of humanity pouring through the breeched Wall in both directions. Pandemonium reigned as these two nonresidents of Berlin, to a background of rockets, flares and firecrackers, were swept up in a rampage of sweat-drenched and screaming humanity suddenly gone mad with ecstasy.

The hated Wall was no more! And it was indeed Krenz, the head of the equally hated secret police, who had given the command to remove that infamous barrier. By that grand concession he hoped to appease the marching masses. Instead, he, too, was forced from office three weeks later.

Communist regimes were now falling like dominoes across Eastern Europe. And everywhere it was Ari's students who led the way, followed by the workers and masses. Even Bulgaria's evil regime, considered one of the toughest, collapsed the day after the Wall became a relic of the past at the mercy of the hammers and chisels of souvenir collectors. In short order, Bulgaria's entire Stalinist leadership was purged. Early in November 1989, participants in the first student demonstrations in Czechoslovakia were attacked, beaten and arrested by riot police. There, too, Ari urged the students on, confident of the outcome. Within ten days it was history.

The climax came on November 24 with the triumphant appearance of Alexander Dubcek on a balcony above the thousands of wildly celebrating demonstrators below. The hero of Prague's Spring of 1968 had been vindicated at last. Twenty-one years earlier, as the newly elected head of the Czechoslovakian Communist Party, Dubcek had attempted to give communism a human face. That courageous but foolish and premature move toward freedom and reform had been crushed by Soviet tanks and 500,000 Warsaw Pact troops moving in "to prevent an invasion by NATO forces." Now the Warsaw Pact was in disarray, about to be dissolved under Gorbachev's amazing orders. The new freedom had the Soviet leader's full blessing—but that astonishing fact seemed to have lost its significance. It was the common *people* who had triumphed and were now exerting their will at last. Gorbachev was about to work himself out of a job.

Developments previously unthinkable followed swiftly in dizzying procession. There was no stopping the revolution now—and in every country Ari's students had played a leading role in unleashing it! On December 3, the entire East German Communist Party leadership resigned under public pressure. Within a few more weeks more than half of its 2.3 million members had turned in their party cards. Unification of Germany, so long thought impossible, was suddenly and obviously inevitable.

Ironically, it was the masses of common people, the proletariat on whose behalf the communist revolution had allegedly been waged, who, in the end, rose up and rejected it. The fact that the "worker's paradise" which had been 70 years in building was a shameful fraud could no longer be denied. All that had seemingly been set in concrete was changing. Even the once fearsome Warsaw Pact, which had joined together the armies of the Soviets and their puppets to oppose NATO, was finally dissolved by that amazing man from the Kremlin, now known affectionately worldwide as "Gorby."

To the astonishment of a watching world, East and West, the twain that were never supposed to meet, began to form a new partnership. The European Economic Community would no longer be confined to the West. It would encompass a hitherto unimaginable Europe—a Europe that would be united, as Mikhail Gorbachev, George Bush and Pope John Paul II had already agreed, "from the Atlantic to the Urals."

Though unknown at the time, it would later come out that the Vatican had been a major player behind the scenes, working closely with the CIA. The role of Roger's group and Ari's secret and far-flung student organization, however, would remain an unknown element of history, hidden from even the most diligent scrutiny.

22

Farewell to Love And Friendship

Because of his intensive travel schedule into Eastern Europe during those busy months, Ari had lost touch with Nicole. Then one evening in mid-December she called and asked to meet him the next day at their favorite restaurant on Boulevard du Port-Royal. Of course he had agreed, trying not to sound too eager. At least she had initiated the get-together. Was this a good omen?

Ari arrived first and took an inside table beyond the bar in a secluded corner. He had been waiting only a few minutes, when Nicole came up quietly behind him and kissed him lightly on the cheek. Her long silken blond hair caressed his neck and the fresh-scrubbed scent of her presence overwhelmed him with tender memories. With a swish of her full silk skirt, she sat down beside him, more radiantly beautiful than ever.

She was seven months pregnant and looked it. Obviously he had lost the abortion battle and resented that. Just seeing her again, however, brought back the old magic feeling—the same giddy attraction he'd felt the first time he'd laid eyes on her that unforgettable day nearly seven years ago.

Ari felt his heart suddenly racing as old passions were inflamed again. "I miss you!" he blurted out. It wasn't at all the opening he had so carefully rehearsed. He felt flustered just being with her—like he'd felt on their first date. It was almost as though their relationship were starting all over again. How he wished it could.

"I miss you, too, Ari," she responded quickly. "Very much."

"Then what are we doing apart, eating our hearts out?"

"I feel the same way," she said earnestly, "and that's why I wanted us to get together... to talk."

"Well, you've had your way," began Ari, "so I guess it's too late to talk about that." Not knowing where to go from there, he paused and waited.

"I worry about you, Ari."

That remark surprised him and put him on guard. "*Worry* about me?"

"You work so hard, day and night... and I don't think you take very good care of yourself without me."

"I eat... I sleep. That can't be what you're concerned about."

"Of course, I am. But there's more. I'm concerned that you're putting your energy into something that won't work."

"Won't work? I guess you haven't heard the news lately. You're kidding, of course."

She tossed her hair back and leaned forward, elbows on the table, chin resting on clasped hands, and looked at him intently. "I know the Wall came down and communism's collapsing—at least in Eastern Europe—but those are superficial symptoms. The disease rages on untouched."

"You surprise me, Niki. You've never expressed these sentiments before," replied Ari warily, beginning to have a bad feeling about their getting together. "Is this another result of your new way of thinking?"

She nodded almost imperceptibly and pressed on. "You mean well, Ari. You've devoted your entire life to creating a new world order of peace and plenty for everyone. I admire you for that passion. But it's doomed to fail—in spite of what seems like such astonishing success at this moment."

"Isn't that rather dogmatic... and sweeping?" asked Ari, puzzled. "We've talked very little about this in the past. Of course I didn't want my work to intrude into our private lives."

"Oh, I'm not concerned with the details of how you're going about it—especially now. I just know that you can't possibly achieve your heart's desire. That's what troubles me, and that's why I wanted to talk about it. You're going to be disillusioned one of these days."

"And you asked me to meet you so you could tell me *that*?"

"Just listen to me, Ari—please! It's not easy for me to articulate... I'm so new at this. But... well... you're not going to solve the world's problems by cleaning up the environment or changing the social and political systems. The root of the problem lies much deeper than that. We're all sinners. People have to be changed on the inside... and only God can do that."

The waiter had been hovering nearby ready to take their orders, but Ari waved him away. "So you're saying that the problem is not with society and political systems but with people? I think it's both. And, please, if you want to call yourself a *sinner*, go ahead... but don't include me in that clan of evil. Okay? I don't have anything to be ashamed of in my life... I can hold my head high. God knows I've expended myself for what I thought was right!"

"Ari, I'm not taking anything away from your sincere efforts. They're admirable, as I already said. But, to put it in medical terms, your *diagnosis* has been wrong. You haven't recognized the real malady that plagues this planet. *All* of us... you and me, and everybody else... are rebels trying to play God... in different ways. Until we let the one and only true God direct our lives... there'll never be real peace on this earth."

"Look, darl-... Nicole," interrupted Ari in an agitated tone, "if you want to believe those childish tales, go ahead, but I've already told you I won't communicate on that level!"

"I know—and that only proves what I'm saying. I felt just like you do until five months ago. The last thing I wanted was for God to run His world—or my life. Our efforts at creating a peaceful world are attempts to prove that we don't need Him."

"Precisely! I don't need an imaginary deity telling me what to do. I've gotten along okay without that crutch." Ari's voice was getting louder and other patrons were stealing curious glances at this pair that was apparently having a lovers' quarrel. "And I resent being brought here to have your religion forced on me!"

"Calm down, Ari," said Nicole softly. "We're attracting attention. I'm sorry if I come across like I'm preaching at you. It's just that I want so much for you to have the same peace I've found... a peace and joy inside like I never thought was possible."

"You've achieved your peace by destroying mine," he flung back bitterly, then hurried on. "That proves nothing. Any placebo would have the same effect if you really believed in it."

"No, Ari, I'm relying upon irrefutable facts and impeccable logic. And it rings true to my conscience, as well... to what I know inside of me is truly right."

"Niki, you're wasting your time. We could be talking about something really significant, something we can find common ground on...."

"Oh, Ari!" she exclaimed passionately, "face the facts! Here you are expending yourself to convince students that something's *wrong* with the world and enlisting them to make it *right*. Yet at the same time you deny an infallible standard of right and wrong! So why should anyone go with *your* definition of what's wrong in society and how to make it right?"

"It's common sense. Everybody recognizes tyranny and injustice and...."

"True," cut in Nicole. "And where did this universal standard of right and wrong come from? Not from the configurations of atoms in the brain! You just admitted what the Bible says—that God has written His moral laws in every person's conscience...."

"The *Bible*? Come on—you don't believe those fables!"

"You've never read the Bible, much less studied it. Now what would you think of someone who condemned a book without ever reading a word of it or knowing anything about it except by hearsay?"

"I know enough about it!"

"Ari... have you ever read *any* of it?"

There was a long silence. "As a matter of fact, no," he conceded at last.

"Your conscience would have bothered you if you'd lied to me. Right? And your conscience also tells you that you haven't lived a perfect life any more than I have. We've broken God's moral laws."

"Like living together without being married?" he retorted contemptuously. "Is that what you're trying to convince me of? Well, I won't buy it. I'm not going to let you lay a guilt trip on me just because it makes you feel good to call yourself a 'sinner'!"

"I wasn't even thinking of that, Ari, honestly. We're sinners in lots of ways. And you can't pay for breaking God's laws in the past by keeping them perfectly in the future. That's why God became a man through the virgin birth... why Jesus Christ died for our sins... so we could be forgiven.... Ari... what's the matter?"

"*Jesus Christ!*" With barely controlled anger Ari spat out the words "You're going too far. Do me a favor... don't mention that name again!"

Nicole opened her mouth to reply, then thought better of it. She regarded Ari for a few moments in silent anguish, then stood to her feet and walked slowly out of the restaurant. He made no attempt to follow her.

— ◆ —

Ari had hoped that the remarkable progression of events in Eastern Europe would have convinced Abdul that nonviolence had now proved to be eminently effective, yet so far it seemed not to have swayed him at all. Something had to be done to persuade him. The Middle East was one place where Ari still had the green light from Roger's group, and he remained convinced that Abdul was the ideal man to head up the work there—if only he could be returned to reason.

Several weeks after their last futile meeting in the restaurant, Ari swallowed his pride and called Nicole to enlist her help in one final attempt to bring Abdul to his senses. Because of Abdul's long friendship with her, Ari was hopeful that Nicole could get him to at least listen to reason. Perhaps together they could rescue him from the whirlpool of hatred and violence that they both suspected had caught him in its vortex and was sucking him down to destruction.

Nicole was able to persuade Abdy to meet them both a few days before Christmas, 1989, at his choice of location. The arrangement was made on the condition that each of them would take a separate circuitous route to get there and make certain that no one was following. The demand sounded like paranoia, but they were willing to meet his terms in order to see Abdul face-to-face once again.

So it was that the three formerly close friends, now seemingly worlds apart, met one last time on a busy platform of the Paris Metro. Niki was due to give birth in a few weeks. She looked extremely tired, and Ari's heart went out to her. He felt overwhelmed by the impulse to hold her in his arms and speak some comforting words, but their alienation was now so complete that no hope of reconciliation remained. The three of them found an empty bench at the end of the platform and sat down together.

"Fantastic what's been happening in Eastern Europe!" was Ari's opening comment, after they had engaged in small talk for a few minutes. "Communism is being overturned, dictatorships thrown out in exchange for democracy ...and all by nonviolent means!"

"I'm happy for you, Ari," responded Nicole. "This should be very gratifying after all those years of hard work."

"There are 60 million Muslims in the Soviet Union still being treated like second-class citizens," was Abdul's disheartening response.

"That's going to change," Ari assured him. "Everything can't happen overnight. But what about the suppression of basic civil rights in Muslim countries? That's where I'd hoped you'd be involved. You could play such a key role in a historic transformation. . . ." He didn't want to be drawn into an argument, but Abdy's challenge couldn't go unanswered. And how else could he be persuaded?

"That's Western propaganda!" Abdul's retort was by now predictable—almost programmed. "There is no suppression of human rights in Arab lands."

"Just answer me honestly, Abdy," insisted Ari. "Has the situation improved or worsened in Lebanon since the Muslims gained control?"

Abdul's face darkened. "You keep forgetting that the whole cause of the problems there is Israel!"

"Suppression of human rights *inside Arab countries* is the fault of Israel?" asked Nicole incredulously.

Abdy stared away in silence. "I should not be talking with you," he said at last. "It's only because we've been friends for so long. But we can't meet again."

"You can't be serious, Abdy!" pleaded Nicole. "After all the years we've been like brother and sister to each other? I can't believe it!"

"I love you, Niki, but I'm a Palestinian . . . and I have to do my part to liberate my people."

"And so you've joined the PLO. Is that true?" demanded Ari.

Abdul made no reply.

"The PLO charter calls for the total destruction of Israel," said Ari evenly, trying unsuccessfully to make eye contact with Abdul. "How can you now contemplate the extermination of Israelis? That's not the solution!"

For one uneasy moment Nicole's thoughts went back to a more personal problem. *Extermination, darling . . . ? Wasn't extermination your 'solution', too?* She bit her lip to keep from saying it.

"We don't advocate killing *all* Jews," insisted Abdy. "Yasser Arafat is not a Hitler. . . ."

"I just reminded you," interrupted Ari pointedly, "the PLO charter calls for the destruction of Israel."

"That's right. The problem is the *state* of Israel. It's illegally occupying Arab land and has no right to exist. All we want is our land back . . . and a Palestinian state with its capital in Jerusalem. Some Jews can continue to live there after all Arab lands have been restored. . . ."

"And you're committed to accomplish this by terrorism against innocent civilians?" demanded Ari.

"Civilian casualties are inevitable in any war."

"Abdy, I've never been a supporter of Israel—but the more you justify this fanatical position, the more my sympathies begin to shift in that direction."

"They *stole* that land!"

"I beg your pardon. Palestine was partitioned by the United Nations. But I'm not even talking about that. Let me ask you a more basic question: Would you rather be an Arab living in Israel, or a Jew living in Lebanon, Syria, Iraq, Iran or even Jordan or Saudi Arabia?"

Abdul stood angrily to his feet. "It isn't so . . . so simple," he protested. "There are complex issues rooted in the past. The way you phrase your question betrays your prejudice and ignorance of history and your tolerance of injustice."

Ari stood also and put an affectionate hand momentarily on Abdul's shoulder. "I thought I knew you," he said sadly. "I thought we had the same ideals . . . and I know we did, until you came under the influence of Arafat and his gang of thugs."

Lightly but affectionately Abdul kissed Nicole on both cheeks. "I will miss you—very much. And I will pray that Allah will bless you both with a good child."

He took Ari's outstretched hand. "I don't want to part as your enemy. We have been like brothers for too long. Someday you'll understand. . . ." Spontaneously they fell into one another's arms. Then Abdul tore himself free, turned and walked resolutely toward the platform exit.

A Question of Survival

On February 20, Nicole gave birth to a healthy baby boy weighing just under eight pounds. Ari learned of the event a week later when he received in the mail an announcement of the birth of Ari Paul de Benoits. Enclosed was a picture of mother and child taken in the hospital. Nicole was looking proudly and protectively down at the small bundle in her arms.

Along with the vital statistics was this note in a familiar hand: "He looks so much like you, Ari! And he's such a good baby. You'd be proud of him. Would you like me to bring him over sometime? Lots of love, Niki."

Eyes blurring with tears, Ari read and reread the note, coming back again and again to those words, "He looks so much like you, Ari!" The woman he had passionately loved had given birth to *his* child—the baby he had wanted her to abort. Perhaps he had been wrong to insist upon that invasion. Yes, he'd made a tactical blunder. It had been a monumental folly that he'd come to profoundly regret.

How he missed her! Yet he had never admitted his remorse to Nicole. He'd been prevented from doing so by circumstances beyond his control—and entirely her fault. Nicole's newfound religious zeal had grown into an irrational fanaticism that made reconciliation impossible. Even in this, however, he had to shoulder much of the blame. There was no escaping the fact that he had driven her away—and into the arms of these religious fanatics.

His all-consuming passion to bring down the Wall had numbed his own natural feelings and left him sadly out of touch with Nicole's feminine emotions. Looking back, as he so often had during these lonely months, Ari could see with crystal clarity that he had driven her into this religious obsession. But after that it had no longer been his doing. An alien force with which he was incapable of coping had taken over.

Nicole was in the grip of a powerful superstition that was driven by primal instincts deep in the collective unconscious of the human race. Such was the only plausible explanation for the otherwise inexplicable madness that drove the zealots of all religions—whether Catholics and Protestants in Ireland, the Shi'ites of Iran or the Muslims and Hindus in India—with a blind passion that no other power on earth could command.

Nicole's totally irrational and unjustifiable commitment to Jesus Christ made it impossible for Ari to live with her in any kind of harmony. Religion had erected an insurmountable barrier between them. On that issue she was now more stubborn than he had ever been. That unyielding stance made his pain the more unbearable.

That this worse-than-imposter "Christ" figure—a fabrication of the warped minds of power-hungry religious leaders—stood as an alien between them was maddening. Ari found it unbearable that another man had stolen Nicole's affection—a man who had possibly never lived, whom she had certainly never met, but about whom such fantastic tales had been told that he was now a cult figure with hundreds of millions of followers. It was insane.

Ari had never denied the hypothetical existence of some "higher power" behind the universe. But if this "God" of Nicole's was indeed in charge of human affairs, as she insisted, then it was *he* who had ordained the birth of this unwelcome child. If Nicole could prove beyond reasonable doubt the existence of this "God," whom she seemed to equate with Jesus Christ ("O, yes," she'd told him with childish confidence, "God became a man to show us His love.") it would only have justified Ari's hatred of him.

In spite of the excruciating pain the decision brought to him, Ari had concluded that it was clearly best—yes, even for the child's own good—for him never to see this little son who bore his name. As for Nicole, it was also better never to see her again. The only hope for full healing of that emptiness inside would be to put her completely out of his mind. That was also the only way of preventing her from pressing her religious ideas on him, which she seemed unable to refrain from doing whenever they met, in spite of his strongly worded objections.

That Nicole had become a Christian gave Ari more sorrow than if she had died. He couldn't bear to think of her the way she was now. What a contrast the past years of happiness were. Yes, it was as though she had died already. And instead of mourning, he would let the past be as though it had never been.

That settled, Ari slipped the birth announcement and picture between two volumes on the top row of the book shelves over his desk, determined to put the past behind him and never to look back. Not an easy thing to do, but by sheer willpower he would accomplish what logic dictated as the only course to take for his own emotional survival. It would be best for Nicole as well.

— ✦ —

The bleak days of winter merged and passed in gray and dreary progression as Ari mechanically went about the management of his ever-shrinking sphere of influence. It was a labor now devoid of joy, though not of passion. He found himself engaged in consolidating his power in Eastern Europe and laying plans for extending the mushrooming reforms into the Soviet Union. When that task was accomplished, he would take his revolution to the West. There were, however, troubling signs that his days of usefulness were numbered. Subtle at first, the indications grew clearer that his position was weakening. The harbingers of serious trouble became increasingly ominous.

The student demonstrations that had at last proved so effective and had vindicated his vision of more than 25 years desperately needed to be taken into the Soviet Union. That vast conglomerate of republics was clearly heading for economic and political disaster. The only way to avoid chaos would be to pressure the Kremlin into taking the right course—but his hands were tied.

Roger's group had from the very beginning steadfastly refused to allow Ari to extend his efforts into the USSR. Obviously, they were protecting their partner, Gorbachev, just as they were protecting the United States and Western Europe from the same disruptions. Elsewhere, in the former Soviet satellite countries, the student protests had done their work and were obsolete. The unsung genius who had engineered so much of the success was beginning to feel like a man out of a job.

There was only one thing to do. He had to make his break with the Committee that had financed him—and he must do it without further delay. Knowing full well the extreme danger and the impossible odds, Ari began to lay his plans.

On a blustery afternoon in early March, Ari, with the tickets in his pocket for a flight to Moscow the following morning, sat hunched against the cold near a phone booth close to the Château de Vincennes Metro station. He had been waiting for more than 30 minutes without receiving a single call. This was one of more than two dozen such locations he had frequented for years on his changing coded schedule—public phones that were seldom used by the general populace and which, in the past, had kept him busy answering incoming calls at predesignated times. Now, however, it was rare for him to receive any communication at all.

Inconspicuously sitting on a bench within earshot of the phone booth, Ari was absorbed in studying a book documenting Vatican-controlled secret societies. It contained some fascinating insights that seemed to fill in gaps in the information he had been gathering through his spies inside Roger's group. There was no doubt that the Vatican-Washington alliance had only grown stronger following the key role Rome had played in saving Solidarity from extinction and in establishing Poland as a central base of resistance within communist Eastern Europe. The Vatican's almost incalculable wealth and influence—and its deliberate actions, both openly and in secret—made it a major player in the international network that was setting the stage for a new world order.

Ari was now convinced that Christianity and Islam, in a modern version of the Crusades, would fight it out once again, this time for world dominion. And Christianity of all stripes and denominations, so his research had indicated, was heading for a worldwide alliance under Rome that would include all religions except Islam—and, of course, Judaism. Israel would be a thorn in both sides and increasingly isolated.

Perhaps the Israelis would be cured of their stubborn Zionism, which he had never been able to stomach—the preposterous pretension that they were a special "chosen people" with preemptive rights to Arab land! And now, months after Abdul's defection, he was still looking unsuccessfully for someone to head up the strategic work that was so badly needed in the Middle East.

Putting the book back into his briefcase, Ari stood up and stretched wearily. It was time to leave—and not even one call had come through. Pulling his full-length leather coat close about him, he turned to lean into the stiff wind that had been howling down the broad avenues and lanes of Paris for the past three days. He was just starting to walk away when the phone rang. It was a minute past the scheduled time slot for calls at this phone booth. Probably it wasn't for him. On the unlikely chance that it might be a late call, Ari turned casually back and picked up the receiver.

"Hello?"

"This is Paxson," announced a voice vibrant with suppressed alarm. "It's late here."

"Later than you think," said Ari quickly, giving the emergency identifying response and feeling his heart start to beat faster.

"They're going to terminate you! I said, *Terminate*! I think they're on to me, too. I've got to go underground. I need 300,000 francs in cash... at the drop ... tonight."

"I'll take care of it. Listen! Everyone pull out! Pass the word!"

Instead of shock, Ari felt almost relieved. Of course, he'd known this was coming. They couldn't let him proceed with his plans. Moscow—and everything that trip would have led to—was suddenly, and with shattering finality, a lost dream. Someday... maybe. But now there was only one goal—survival. It would be the focus of all of his attention, energy and skill. And to pull it off—if it could be done at all—would involve a dangerous gamble.

First of all he had to shake the shadowy "protection" that dogged his every step. He had not bothered to lose them for at least six months, so they wouldn't be likely to expect him to do so now. Surprise was worth two or three minutes, and that could be crucial. He knew exactly what he would do, having planned the necessary steps for every location that he frequented.

There was a public toilet that backed up to an alley not far away, and Ari headed for it at a brisk pace, though not so fast as to arouse suspicion. If those two behind him knew of the order to terminate him, at least they weren't the ones assigned to do the job or he wouldn't still be alive. That meant he had some time, but at best very little.

Entering the W.C., Ari noted with relief that it was empty. There was a small window in the rear over one of the toilets, through which he quickly crawled, dropped down into the alley and ran to a main street 50 yards away. Exiting the alley, he hurried toward a large intersection. Before reaching it he had flagged down a passing cab. Once inside, he slumped down low in his seat and carefully peered out the windows. There was no sign of his "protectors," who must have been, by then, in a panic.

"Banque Francaise Internationale," said Ari, giving the cab driver the name of the closest bank where he had a large account.

When they had reached that destination he handed the cabbie a 500-franc note. "I've got several more stops to make," Ari announced in a trusting tone. "I'll only be a few minutes. Wait for me, okay? I'll make it worth your while."

"*Bien sûr, monsieur,*" responded the driver eagerly.

It was midafternoon and the lines at the tellers' cages were frustratingly long. Rather than choosing the shortest one, Ari stood in the queue leading to the teller he knew best, a pleasant young woman who was familiar with his account and would recognize him. Not only did Paxon need cash, but so did he. This would be the last chance. There was a balance of about 1.5 million francs. He'd leave enough not to attract undue attention.

While standing in line Ari took from his briefcase the checkbook for this particular bank. Here he was known as Jean-Claude Hébert and, of course, had all of the necessary identification to prove it. He wrote a check to himself for 1.2 million francs and presented it to the teller when he finally reached her.

"*Bonjour, Monsieur Hébert!*" she greeted him warmly. "Haven't seen you in several months. Been traveling again, I suppose."

"Yeah, too much," responded Ari dryly, "but you have to make a living. *C'est la vie.*"

"Do you want a cashier's check?"

"No, I'd like it in cash."

"I'll have to go to the vault. Can I give it to you in 10,000-franc notes?"

"Okay... but give me 200,000 in 5,000-francs."

The teller punched his account number into her computer. "Let me just make sure you have enough to cover this...." Her eyebrows rose in surprise. "I'm showing that your account has been closed."

"Impossible! That account should have about 1.5 million francs in it right now."

"Oh, I see. There's a note in the computer to have you speak with the manager."

Ari was thinking rapidly. *It couldn't possibly be a mistake. They've wiped out all of my accounts! Having me speak with the manager is just a ploy to hold me here until the police... or the assassins arrive....* "You bet I want to speak with the manager—immediately!" replied "Jean-Claude" indignantly. "But I've got a taxi waiting for me outside. Let me tell him to go on. I'll be right back."

Hurrying out of the bank, Ari jumped into the cab. "Place Denfert-Rochereau," he said, pulling a distant location out of the air. Getting there would give him time to think. He had put 5 million francs away in a safe-deposit box at another bank, but it was too risky to go there under these conditions. He cursed himself for being lax. He should have been carrying his emergency fund with him.

Ari's mind was now a turmoil of both anxiety and anger. The irony was maddening. *Success put me out of business! I've lost the students I controlled. Most of the leaders I trained and worked with are running for political office in Eastern Europe's new wave of democracy. I failed to crack the Arab world and my organization was smashed in China. They're desperately afraid of what I might do in the Soviet Union—and in the West. They don't want me operating any more. I'm a threat. They've got to kill me.*

24

Man Without a Country

"Pull over at the next phone booth," Ari told the driver. "I just remembered an important call I have to make. See, that one up ahead... on the right. I'll just be a minute."

Inside the booth Ari dialed Roger's office at the consortium's headquarters—a number that Roger had never given him and would be surprised to discover that he knew. The receptionist gave him to Roger's secretary.

"I'm sorry, but Mr. Dunn is in a meeting right now. May I take a message and have him call you?"

"You tell Mr. Dunn that the man he's looking for is calling," said Ari evenly, "and if he's not on the line in 30 seconds, I'm hanging up!"

Roger was on the phone almost immediately. "Hello?"

"Good afternoon."

"How did you get *this* number? Where are you?"

"Why did you close my accounts?"

"I was going to explain that, Ari." The answer came too quickly, too smoothly. "I've been trying to get in touch with you all day. We need to get together to talk. There are some procedures we have to work out...."

"That's the last lie I want to hear! Now listen to me. I'm going to walk up to the front door of Banque du Monde Internationale in ten minutes. I want you to come from your office down to the street and meet me out in front with Jean Bourbonnais beside you."

"Bourbonnais?"

"Yes, Bourbonnais!"

"Why, he's... he's the chairman of the bank. I couldn't get someone like him to meet you... certainly not on such short notice... and in the street? Come on! He's got *nothing* to do with your accounts, anyway."

"I said *no more lies*! He's the chairman of the European branch of your group. I've had moles inside your organization for 15 years. I know *everything*. The order's been given to terminate me—right?"

There was a long silence. "Okay, Ari. You can't get away, so I'll admit it. I'm sorry it's come to this—but there's nothing I can do about it. You know too much."

"Wrong, Roger. You desperately need me... *alive*. Now you listen carefully. I know *everything*. If I'm killed... or if you harm anyone that you suspect of working for me...it will be the worst mistake you ever made. If I should die...*or disappear*...under any circumstances...there are half a dozen people in key places around the world who will immediately have access to data exposing your entire international network—and they'll publicize it in every major newspaper. I'm talking about everything from drug money laundering, to arms smuggling...selling poison gas technology to Iraq, helping Pakistan's nuclear arms program....I could go on and on."

There was a long silence on Roger's end.

"Am I getting through to you?" demanded Ari.

"I get the picture," came the glum response at last.

"Now, is there any reason why Bourbonnais can't meet with me in ten minutes?"

"He'll be there."

Ari jumped back into the cab. "Forget Place Denfert. Take me to the headquarters of Banque du Monde Internationale."

As the cab pulled up in front of the bank Ari surveyed the scene. Bourbonnais, a tall, thin man in his early sixties, with neatly groomed gray hair and mustache and aristocratic bearing, was standing out in front waiting for him. Roger was at his side scanning the traffic anxiously. The pedestrian flow seemed normal. Of course there would be security people scattered everywhere, but there was nothing he could do about that. They weren't going to shoot him in front of all those witnesses.

"This is it," said Ari. "I won't need you anymore." He handed the cabbie a 200-franc note and stepped out onto the sidewalk.

Bourbonnais was as suave and obsequious as a politician stumping for votes. He extended his hand cordially when Ari walked up to him and suggested in a cultured voice, "Professor Mueller! It's such a pleasure to meet you at last. Let's go into my office where we can talk things over in private."

Ignoring the proffered hand, Ari shot back tersely, "After we have an understanding." From an inside coat pocket he pulled out a dozen sheets of paper and unfolded them. "That's so you'll know I'm not bluffing," he said as he handed them to Bourbonnais. "The documents I've given to several people for safekeeping run to more than 250 pages, all of it packed with information and confirmation sources similar to what you're looking at now."

Bourbonnais skimmed the contents rapidly, with Roger looking apprehensively over his shoulder. "Where did you get this propaganda?" demanded the banker, his face red with anger, after he'd scanned the first three or four pages. "You can't prove any of this!"

"Keep reading," suggested Ari calmly, including Roger in his cold stare. "Gentlemen, you know and I know that you're sitting on the biggest banking and criminal scandal in history...and I've got it all laid out in spades. Those pages are just samples."

The two men went back to their reading, this time more carefully. Soon Bourbonnais's fingers were trembling as he turned the pages. At last he folded the sheets of paper and stuffed them into his pocket. The color had gone out of his face, and when he looked at Ari his eyes betrayed the fact that he was convinced and ready to negotiate.

"Okay," said Bourbonnais reluctantly. "You've got your life insurance. But we've got some serious problems to work out. Let's go to my office."

"You understand what happens if I don't come out of there alive?" emphasized Ari.

"I do—and we don't want that any more than you do." Bourbonnais looked at Roger for confirmation. He nodded grimly.

Once inside his spacious suite on the 20th floor, Jean Bourbonnais pointed Ari and Roger to a sofa and sat down to face them in an overstuffed executive chair behind his huge desk.

"Now, you say there's 250 pages. How do I know?" the old fox demanded, sounding shrewdly confident now that he was safely inside his lair.

"You're going to have to take my word for that," said Ari firmly.

"That's not good enough. I want to see them. I want proof."

Ari opened his briefcase, pulled out another 30 or 40 pages and threw them onto the banker's well-ordered desk. "That's all you get. I'm not telling you everything I know—but if you're looking for your name, you'll find it in there prominently."

Roger jumped up to look over his shoulder as Bourbonnais shuffled quickly through the papers, pausing now and then to read a paragraph more carefully, and cursing under his breath. Again his face turned varying shades from pink to crimson and, finally, ashen white. He let the papers fall from his hands onto the desk, leaned back in his chair and fixed Ari with a desperate stare. Roger gave Ari a look that was part loathing, part admiration, and returned to the sofa where he slumped down and looked expectantly to the man in charge.

"You've put your cards on the table," said Bourbonnais grudgingly. "It looks like a winning hand. You're a very clever man, Dr. Mueller—which is why we stuck with you all these years. But there are several concerns. Let's take them one at a time."

"Let's do that," responded Ari coldly.

"First of all, I give you my word that from this moment on we have no lethal designs against you. In fact, we'll assign some of our best men to stay with you day and night to make certain you're fully protected!"

"I wouldn't give you two *centimes* for your word," said Ari matter-of-factly. "We're talking this over because neither of us has any choice. Right?"

Bourbonnais nodded somberly.

"As for your 'protection'," added Ari testily, drawing his thumb quickly across his neck, "I've had it up to here—and I don't want one more minute of it!"

"Suppose someone else terminates you. . . ."

"I can take care of myself!" cut in Ari.

"Suppose you die from natural causes," argued Bourbonnais. "No fault of ours... but your friends, under the orders you've given them, so Roger tells me, will publicize this information. That's not your intent, is it?"

"If I'm dead, I couldn't care less. Just hope it doesn't happen."

"Wait a minute!" interjected Roger.

"Look... I'm still relatively young, in excellent health. And I intend to stay that way. But if it happens—you'd better be quick to prove it's natural."

Bourbonnais turned to Roger, whose only response was a resigned shrug.

"I don't like it," complained Bourbonnais, "but that's down the line. Our immediate problem is the matter of asylum."

"What do you mean, *asylum*?" demanded Ari quickly.

"Just that. We have to find a country that will take you."

"A country that will *take* me? What's wrong with France? I'm staying right here!"

"That's out of the question."

"What are you trying to pull?"

"Let me explain," said Bourbonnais in a patient voice, as though he were talking with an important client. "You've been at the top of the Interpol wanted list for the last ten years. That was part of the reason for the 'protection' you didn't like. We've held them off until Eastern Europe was behind us. There's no way you could stay in France... or any other country connected with the Interpol network."

"You're lying. I've committed no crimes!"

"You owe *millions* in back taxes and penalties to the French government for funds deposited in a number of accounts which you never reported as income. You've been living under false I.D. for the past 25 years, crossing borders with fraudulent documents, passing money internationally through illegitimate channels.... Do you need to hear more?"

"The money came from your companies... which incriminates you."

"Wrong. You're very clever... but we outsmarted you on this one. Those companies that gave you the money were all involved in illegal activities... but no one's been able to trace the people behind them. The canceled checks were recovered by the police in a shoot-out with a drug kingpin. He was killed and the checks were found in his briefcase. The bank accounts where they were deposited belonged to you... under fictitious names."

"And if I'm arrested, I'll tell them where it came from...."

"And we'll sue you for libel! You can't show any connection to us. We know you tried to trace those companies, and couldn't."

Ari stared out the window at the skyline of Paris stretching to the horizon. "Sounds like I'm a man without a country," he conceded at last.

"Believe me, we'd prefer to have you here," said Bourbonnais. "But it wouldn't look good, would it, if we tried to pull strings for such a criminal."

"Of course not!" responded Ari sarcastically. "I certainly wouldn't want that crime to taint your immaculate conscience."

"I'm glad you understand that everything has to be according to the law. That's the way we operate."

"Of course it is," returned Ari bitterly, "when you want to make sure I don't get back in business!"

"That's part of the deal—and we want that promise in writing...."

"Forget it!" snapped Ari. "I'm making no promises—and you couldn't enforce a deal, anyway. You going to threaten to kill me? If I die...or disappear...."

"We don't have to enforce anything." The confidence had returned to Bourbonnais's voice. "You're *persona non grata* all over Europe—East and West—the United States, South America. The Soviets won't let you enter their country. The visa you've got for your flight to Moscow tomorrow has been revoked. You couldn't have boarded the plane. And the Chinese know you were the foreign agent behind Tiananmen...we've seen to that."

"Thanks," said Ari, controlling himself with great effort. "Go on. I'm listening."

"Switzerland might take you," suggested Bourbonnais. "Or some island in the Pacific. Fiji, maybe, or New Caledonia—or even New Zealand. Some place far away, where you won't get yourself into any more trouble...."

Ari shrugged. "Okay, I guess I stay right here in this office under your 'protection' until we find a country that will take me. And if we don't?"

"We will." Bourbonnais picked up the phone and buzzed his secretary. "Get me the Prime Minister of Fiji...or the official in charge of New Caledonia. And if neither is available at the moment, then try the Prime Minister of New Zealand. Get them at home...or on a golf course, or yacht...anywhere you can reach them. It's an emergency."

He put the phone down and leaned back in his chair. "Let's hope this doesn't take too long," said Bourbonnais with a veiled smile. "What would you gentlemen like to drink?"

25

An Unhappy Compromise

Ironically, after more than six hours of sweating out negotiations conducted with numerous governments through Bourbonnais's top political contacts, tiny Israel was the only nation that was willing to admit Ari for immigration. And that breakthrough came only at the last minute when Ari brought up the possibility—and was finally willing to admit what he had spent a lifetime trying to deny and forget—that he was probably a Jewish survivor of the Nazi holocaust. Actually it had been Abdul's repulsive anti-Israel rhetoric, so reminiscent of the Nazi slogan, *Deutschland Erwache! Judah verrecke!* ("Germany Awake! Death to the Jews!) that had so recently stirred long-suppressed memories.

Israeli computers were able to verify enough of the story Ari told Bourbonnais to convince them of its authenticity. Yes, there had been one young Jewish couple of record—a Jacob and Elizabeth Thalberg, beloved schoolteachers—living in the small village in East Germany where Ari had been born and raised by his foster parents. And, yes, it was known that the Thalbergs had been taken from the village sometime early in 1944 and had perished at Auschwitz just before its liberation by the Russians in January, 1945. There was no record of any children born to the young couple, but there now seemed little doubt that Ari had been their only child.

And so the good news came at last when Bourbonnais finally hung up the phone and announced, "Papers are being drawn up in the name of Ari Thalberg to allow you to immigrate to Israel. As a holocaust survivor, they could not turn you down. Until then, you'll be kept in protective custody...." Bourbonnais pushed a button on his desk.

The door swung open and four plainclothes officers entered. Pulling snub-nosed revolvers from shoulder holsters, they advanced warily toward Ari.

"Put those guns away!" snapped Bourbonnais nervously. "He'll go with you. Anybody who lays a finger on him is finished!"

"What is this!" protested Ari.

"You'll be treated like a king," came the smooth answer. "A 'guest of the French government' until you're safely aboard El Al and on your way to Israel. You know we can't have you floating around out there."

"When do I get my personal belongings...from my office at the university, and from my apartment?"

"Everything will be packed and shipped to Israel—at our expense. You don't have to lift a finger."

"You'd better let me make some phone calls—right now," demanded Ari.

"That won't be necessary."

"My students... my contract... the university. I can't just vanish. Somebody's going to have to make an explanation."

"Roger has that all under control," countered Bourbonnais. "Right?"

Roger nodded. "I've already scheduled a press conference. Everyone will be notified."

— ✦ —

Nicole was nursing her two-week-old baby and watching the late evening news, when to her surprise she saw Ari being interviewed by the Israeli Consul General. The brief discussion revealed the recent discovery that Dr. Hans Mueller, a popular professor of Political Science at the Sorbonne and head of that department for the past five years, was in fact Dr. Ari Thalberg, a Jewish survivor of the Nazi Holocaust. The discovery had been made quite by accident only that afternoon. As a result, Dr. Thalberg had been invited by the Israeli government to immigrate to that country, was leaving his post at the university and would be flying to Israel within a few days.

The news that Ari was Jewish detonated in Nicole's consciousness like a bomb blast. Was that why he had such an aversion to Jesus Christ? How little she really knew about this enigmatic man! She called later that evening to wish him well in his new identity and country, only to discover that the phone in his apartment had been disconnected. The next day she called his secretary at the Sorbonne.

"Michelle, this is Nicole. I'm trying to get in touch with Dr. Mueller. I called his apartment last night, but the phone was disconnected...."

"We've been trying to reach him, too. He hasn't been in touch with us at all. The only thing we've heard was the announcement on the news last night. If you find out anything, let us know!"

Worried now, Nicole phoned the Israeli embassy. It was another stonewall job. Not one of the various persons to whom she was referred would admit to the slightest knowledge of either a Hans Mueller or an Ari Thalberg. At last she reached someone who admitted to knowing something, but was not giving out any information.

"I'm sorry, but Dr. Thalberg is in seclusion. It was a shock to discover his Jewish roots and the name and fate of his parents... and he has requested not to be disturbed."

"But I was his closest friend," protested Nicole.

"If that is the case, I'm sure he'll be in touch with you when he's ready."

"Well, when is he leaving? I could at least see him off at the airport."

"We don't have that information—and if we did, we couldn't give it out. Good day, *mademoiselle.*"

Nicole was now convinced that something had gone horribly wrong. She sat by the phone, pondering what to do. Then she remembered the emergency number Ari had given her months ago, found it in her purse, and dialed.

"Mr. Dunn is in conference with clients all day," his secretary announced. "Could someone else help you?"

"Tell Mr. Dunn," said Nicole in a conspiratorial voice, "that I have some information about Ari Thalberg that would be of great interest to him... and I must talk to him immediately."

Roger came on the phone almost immediately. "You have some information? To whom am I speaking... and how did you get my name and number?"

"Mr. Dunn," began Nicole in a cheerful Pollyanna voice, "we've met only once that I recall, but Ari has told me a great deal about you."

"Ari gave you this number? And who are you?"

"I'm Nicole. I lived with Ari for six years."

"Oh, yes, I remember." Roger's tone became guarded. "You had some information about him that you wanted to give me?"

"Before I get to that... Ari has disappeared, and I think you know where he is."

"I saw him on television just last night."

"And so did I. But he's not at his apartment, his phone has been disconnected... the university doesn't know where to find him...."

"You know more than I do."

"Let's not play games, Roger. I wasn't born yesterday. I happen to be one of those persons—and I know there are several others—to whom Ari gave a packet of documents that I know you don't want to be made public. And of course I won't do so except in the event of Ari's death—or *disappearance.*"

There was a prolonged silence. "You know what I'm talking about?" persisted Nicole.

"Yes. Go ahead."

"I wouldn't be so stupid as to tell you this without having made careful provision for those papers to be kept in a safe place and to be published—in spite of my death or disappearance—if and when the conditions Ari set forth are met."

"What do you want from me?"

"I want to see Ari."

"That's impossible."

"Then I have no choice except to follow Ari's instructions and to release the material."

"He's not dead!" declared Roger with finality.

"Why should I take your word for that? Dead or alive, he has *disappeared.* His instructions state explicitly that if he should *disappear....*"

"He hasn't disappeared. There's no reason...."

"Unless I have some proof," said Nicole icily, "I have no option except to follow Ari's instructions and release...."

"He's leaving tomorrow morning," interrupted Roger. There was a long pause. At last he conceded, "Okay, here's what we'll do. You be at *Orly Sud* at eight o'clock tomorrow morning and you can see Ari."

"Where? At the El Al gate?"

"El Al is not marked—for security reasons. Just wait outside the main entrance. I'll find you."

"I'll be there!"

26

"I'll Be in Jerusalem Before You"

When Nicole phoned Dr. Duclos and his wife to tell them the good news of the next day's meeting, they insisted upon taking her to the airport. "It's too much for you... to drive out there alone with the baby." Her objections were brushed aside. "It's all settled. We'll pick you up at 6:30 tomorrow morning."

It was just before 8:00 A.M. when they pulled up in front of Orly International Airport's south terminal. Nicole got out of the car, holding little Ari, and looked around. "We'll stay right here as long as we have to," Dr. Duclos called after her.

Nicole had only a vague recollection of Roger as a very tall Texan, but she was certain that he would know her. Nervously she walking back and forth near the car. Ten minutes passed. Could she have been deceived? Suddenly a tall man of about 50 burst out of a doorway and came directly toward her.

"Nicole?" he asked in an agitated voice, and when she nodded, he immediately shot at her, "Where've you been?"

"You said 8 o'clock—and I got here just before."

"They couldn't wait. They've already taken him through security." He seemed to notice for the first time the bundle she was carrying. "You can't take the baby!"

"Why not? This is *Ari's* son! He's never seen him."

"Impossible! Is someone with you?"

"In the car over there," said Nicole. "Please! Are you a human being?"

Roger had already grabbed her arm and was steering her toward the parked vehicle. A policeman was waving at the driver to move on. "Let them stay!" yelled Roger. He pulled something the size of a passport out of his pocket, opened it up and waved it at the officer.

"*Oui, monsieur*," said the policeman and motioned to Dr. Duclos to remain where he was.

Nicole opened the front door of the car and handed little Ari Paul to Francoise. "Here. Ari's already gone through security and they won't let me take the baby. If something should happen to me... remember, you're taking care of him..."

"Don't worry. We'll be right here... and we'll keep praying."

"Hurry!" demanded Roger. "His plane is about to board."

Nicole followed him inside, half running to keep up with his long stride. There was a lengthy line of passengers at *Passeport Controle*. Roger led her up to a dark-haired man in casual clothes who was standing to one side searching the faces of each person while seemingly not looking at anyone.

"Here she is," said Roger breathlessly, motioning toward Nicole. Then he turned and disappeared.

The blank expression on the man's face didn't change as he instantly looked her up and down, then asked for her purse. That expert search quickly completed, he said in a thick Israeli accent, "We'll give you five minutes with him. Follow me."

The Israeli agent led Nicole quickly back down the escalator then hurriedly through the crowd on the ground floor. They came to a lone policeman and another Israeli plainclothesman guarding a short passageway that contained an escalator that was off-limits to passengers. Without showing any identification and with a scarcely perceptible nod her guide was waved through.

"This bypasses the normal security and passport checks," he explained in a rare attempt at pleasantry.

The top of the escalator was guarded by another policeman. Nicole could see that she was now in a holding area filled with passengers who had cleared security, passport and personal baggage checks and were waiting for their planes to be announced.

"Over there," said her guide tersely and motioned across the room. Then she saw him. Ari was looking out a window, his back to her. Dejection and a great weariness were reflected in his sagging frame. For the first time she perceived him as a man in his forty-seventh year. He had always acted and looked so much younger than that—but at last his age seemed to have caught up with him.

Nicole turned with a questioning look to the man who had brought her. He nodded again in Ari's direction, then lit up a cigarette and leaned against a wall in watchful attention.

Nicole walked up behind Ari and laid a hand gently on his shoulder. He turned around slowly.

"Niki! How did you get in here?" Instead of reaching out to touch her, he seemed to recoil.

"I just had to say goodbye. I brought your son... but they wouldn't let me bring him in here."

For a moment Ari looked genuinely disappointed. Then he steeled himself again.

Something wasn't right. His cheeks were flushed but his eyes were devoid of life, his expression wooden. "Are they treating you well?" she asked anxiously.

"Oh, sure, I'm fine. But they wouldn't let me stay in France."

"You didn't expect they would, did you?"

A dejected look and a shrug were his only answer.

Nicole opened her purse, pulled out a folded piece of paper and handed it to him. "Here's my address. Will you write to me?"

There was a long pause before Ari replied. "I hadn't planned to. It's best for us to forget each other."

"And your son... will he never know his father?" She saw tears well up in his eyes as he reached out and took the piece of paper, then quickly looked away.

"There's something I *have* to tell you, Ari," she continued, looking at her watch and hurrying on. "I had a dream last night—and I wouldn't mention it... but it was so vivid, so real!"

He still seemed remote, preoccupied. "Are you listening," she asked. He nodded.

"You were on the other side of a deep gorge, calling to me. I was in a beautiful place—peaceful... protected. Somehow I thought it was Jerusalem and I'd gotten there ahead of you. It's crazy, but when I woke up I heard myself saying, 'I'll be in Jerusalem before you.' I kept repeating it—and then fell asleep again feeling so... so secure."

Ari turned and looked at her intently. The listlessness was gone and he was now listening with deep interest.

"That's not all. I dreamed the same thing again—but this time I saw flames and smoke behind you and heard loud explosions like bombs or shooting. It was getting closer. I knew you were in terrible danger. You were crying out for someone to help you. Then the strangest thing happened. Out of nowhere appeared a man standing on the edge of the cliff in front of me. He bent over, leaned far out to bridge the gorge, and you ran quickly across his back and into my arms...."

"Niki... Niki. Not more messiah madness... not in these few moments...."

"It was so real," she persisted breathlessly, "like it was actually happening. He put his arms around both of us... and I noticed the wounds.... Oh, Ari," Nicole finished helplessly.

Ari's face flushed. "Please, darling. Not *now*. Our last... maybe our last meeting—and this is all you have to say? Just leave it, Niki."

"Ari... I *had* to tell you." The words came in a sob. "I just know it means something important... for both of us!"

The tension between them was broken by the firm voice of the Israeli security agent addressing Nicole. "You'll have to come with me now."

Ari's expression softened. He reached out to touch Nicole's arm. "I'm sorry," he said. "I will write... and maybe you and our... our... son... can come to Israel some day...?"

At that moment the sharp staccato of automatic gunfire erupted from the floor below, bringing the buzz of conversation in the large room to a deathly silence. Out of the corner of her eye Nicole saw the policeman at the top of the side escalator she and the security man had used whirl around and aim his gun downward. In the same instant he was lifted off his feet and hurled backward by the force of heavy slugs slamming into his body. The scene before them metamorphosed into the agonizing slow motion of a nightmare. The *Gendarme* seemed to hang suspended in air, a red stain spreading over his uniform, before he came crashing to the floor.

"Down!" yelled the Israeli security man, motioning toward the floor. Like a coiled spring suddenly released, he leaped over a row of chairs and sprinted to one side of the escalator, pulling a revolver from a holster concealed under his loose jacket as he ran.

"My baby!" screamed Nicole.

Ari grabbed Nicole to pull her down to safety as four masked men exploded from the top of the escalator into the waiting room, spraying death from their submachine guns. Nicole was hit twice in the back, one bullet severing her spine and the other lodging in her heart, killing her instantly. Her body, which had shielded Ari, was thrown against him by the impact of the bullets, knocking him to the floor.

Pandemonium reigned. The screams seemed almost to drown out the gunfire. Ari saw five civilians standing nearby go down in rapid succession before he hit the floor. There he lay, Nicole on top of him, his arms around her. "Niki, I'm sorry . . . Niki . . . ," he heard himself say.

The shooting stopped as abruptly as it had begun. Ari rolled Nicole's lifeless form gently over onto the floor, raised his head cautiously and peered around. It took him a few moments to believe the unbelievable—that the attackers had been dealt such a swift defeat. With incredibly fine-honed precision, the three Israeli security guards who had been present had shot and killed three of the masked men and had taken the other badly wounded attacker captive. Within a matter of seconds it was all over.

His shirt and pants stained with Nicole's blood, Ari stood uncertainly to his feet and stared in shock at her dead body and the chaos around him. *My God, Niki's dead!* He seemed to consciously realize it for the first time. The stunning impact of death's finality and hopelessness staggered him. She was gone, and he couldn't bring her back. Along with the futile grief that constricted his chest and throat, a surging fury rose within him. What vile creatures would make such an attack upon innocent and helpless civilians?

Feeling strangely detached from the scene around him, only with difficulty did Ari become aware that the lone surviving terrorist was being led past him, black ski mask still hiding all but his defiant eyes. There had been no need to handcuff this despicable creature. Blood oozed through his shirt and sweater from a badly wounded right shoulder. His shattered left arm hung limply at his side.

As the wounded attacker was being dragged past Ari, an Israeli security man contemptuously ripped off his mask.

"Abdy!" The name came involuntarily in a hoarse whisper from Ari's lips. There was no mistaking the identity of the pain-racked but defiant face. For one moment of unspeakable despair that seemed an eternity, Abdul's and Ari's eyes met. In the same instant Abdul caught sight of Nicole's body lying face up in a pool of blood at Ari's feet.

"Niki!" It was a shriek from the depths of hell. "Niki!" He tried to pull free from his captors to fall beside her, but they jerked him violently away. As Ari watched in stunned horror, Abdul was dragged from the room, still fighting, still screaming, "Niki! Niki!"

"All El Al passengers proceed immediately through your gate!" The words were being repeated over and over on the loudspeaker, but Ari didn't hear. He had fallen to his knees beside Nicole's crumpled body and was sobbing uncontrollably. "Niki," he pleaded, "Niki, I'm sorry, I'm sorry... Niki...."

Ari became aware of a hand on his shoulder and looked up to see the Israeli guard who had accompanied Nicole to this last farewell. He was still holding a smoking .38 revolver. "They're boarding." His voice was gentle but firm. "You've got to get on board quickly for your own safety."

Desperately Ari pulled away from him. "She was my fiancée! And the baby... my son... where is he?"

Another security guard stepped up quickly, and the two Israelis yanked Ari to his feet and shoved him toward the gate. "I'm sorry," the first one muttered, "but the plane must leave with all able-bodied passengers. There could be another attack."

"My God, man! I can't leave!" argued Ari, digging in his heels. "I've got to find my son! He's got no one now! I've got to find him... I can't leave!"

Just then Roger came running up, relieved to see that Ari was unharmed. "Get him aboard!" he ordered.

"You scum!" Ari turned on Roger, waving an accusing finger. "You ordered this attack!"

"You're crazy!" shot back Roger. "Of course we didn't!"

"Just a coincidence that they happened to attack *my flight*?" Ari's eyes were blazing and his mouth was trembling. "They killed Niki!"

Roger glanced down at the lifeless form, then quickly back to Ari. His face registered genuine sympathy. "I'm sorry—but we're not behind this. You know we've got selfish reasons for wanting you to stay alive."

"He's asking about a baby," interrupted the Israeli security guard hurriedly.

"She left it with friends outside." Roger turned to Ari. "The baby's safe. That wasn't part of our deal. Now get aboard... we think there's going to be another attack."

"We've got to get this plane out of here fast!" The two Israelis grabbed Ari again and pulled him toward the gate. "Here's your bag. Get moving!"

"Niki... I'm sorry. Niki. Nikeeee!" The soundless cry deep inside screamed a last agonized farewell.

27

"Welcome to Israel"

ISRAEL—1990

A hysterical passenger in his early seventies, his expensive tailored suit spattered with blood, was being taken off when Ari boarded. He had finally convinced a flight attendant that his wife had been killed in the attack. Though overcome with shock and his own grief, Ari, after long years of training and practice, instinctively absorbed and evaluated every part of his surroundings and the swiftly moving events. He marveled at the speed and skill with which the superbly trained and prepared El Al crew controlled what would otherwise have been utter chaos on the plane. Speaking with absolute authority and assurance as they went up and down the aisle seeing to special needs, the flight attendants brought a sense of calm and safety to the passengers, many of whom were in a state of near-collapse when they came aboard.

The Orly control tower gave the ill-fated flight priority, clearing all other planes, both arriving and departing, out of its path. Ari had hardly settled in his assigned window seat when the plane rumbled down the runway, climbed aloft and headed for Israel. Four dead and seven severely wounded passengers had been left behind. As soon as the plane was safely in the air, the captain came on the intercom to share some confidential information in explanation of the quick departure in the wake of such unspeakable tragedy.

"Just before the attack, the French police received an anonymous tip that it would happen," declared the Captain in a firm but sympathetic voice. "The informant said there would be two groups of terrorists... four each. We could take no chances... had to get the plane aloft. We're now safely en route to Israel. Although Israel is constantly targeted by terrorists, you'll be safer there than almost anywhere else in the world. An attack like this could not happen at Tel Aviv's Lod Airport, where you'll be landing. We'll keep you advised of our progress...."

Sunk deep in his seat, Ari tried to distract himself by idly watching the changing panorama of fading French countryside playing out far below. He was in an agony of despair. Into the dark pit of his soul were compacted, in sledgehammer blows of memory, every endearing moment of the brief but sweet life he and Niki had shared as lovers. As the joyous and beautiful facets of their six years together passed in pain-ridden review, he gave in to a consuming guilt. The tragic ending was all his fault. He'd been proud and stubborn. She had been so loyal, so true, so ready to be everything he needed.

Of course, he had planned to marry her when the time was right—but that time just hadn't come. Why? *Why?* If only he had made the commitment years ago that she had so ardently desired! That would have been more honorable and might have changed everything. Maybe they would have let him stay, since Niki was a native of France—or at least that might have changed the time factor. He probably wouldn't have been scheduled for this ill-fated flight and Nicole would still be alive.

It was impossible to believe that Niki was gone—and that the passionate purpose to which his life had been devoted for the past 25 years had died as well and he was now going into exile. If only *this* or *that* had or had not happened or he'd had a different attitude or made a wiser choice here or there. The turmoil of regret and self-accusation was endless. *And Abdul! Could his gun have killed her? How could he have ended like this!*

Scenes from the past followed quickly on the heels of one another in anguished procession. And always that indelible vision of Niki's lifeless form in a pool of blood returned with searing clarity. And her last words—there was something arresting and haunting about them.

I'll be in Jerusalem before you! His initial revulsion at the spiritual implications was now replaced by a burning need to know what that dream had meant. Her messiah madness had been a central part of the story . . . so there was an underlying *religious* meaning. That would have been more than enough cause for him to dismiss the whole thing—but her vivid dream had been so unusual, so gripping. He wrestled with the strangely compelling words—*I'll be in Jerusalem before you.* He tried to tell himself that it meant nothing, yet at the same time he felt irresistibly drawn by the thought that there was some mysterious meaning behind it all.

Nicole had become a fanatical Christian, which made everything she said suspect. Yet the conviction in her voice had not been fanaticism, but something very different—something that had captivated him in spite of his skepticism. He owed it to himself—but especially to her memory, now—to fathom that mystery.

To Ari, the cult of the crucified Jew was a demeaning religion. What little he knew repelled and offended him. Yet those words—*I'll be in Jerusalem*—had a strange power that he couldn't explain. Somewhere he'd heard that Christians associated Jerusalem with "heaven." Had Niki had a premonition of her death? Was that possible? Could *all* such connections between intuition and subsequent events in the exterior world be explained as mere coincidence? Could something more be involved? Carl Jung, among many others, had seen a relationship. The idea was becoming more acceptable even among physicists. But what could be the connection between the material universe and that nonphysical dimension that Nicole had believed in as a medical scientist even before she had become a Christian? He had to know.

Once the plane had reached its cruising altitude, Ari jumped out of his seat and hurried to a restroom. There he washed Niki's blood from his hands and face and out of his hair, and tried to get the worst of it off of his shirt and pants. As he scrubbed and dabbed and wiped himself dry—and watched Niki's blood go down the drain—Ari was reminded that the red stain which had covered him had saved his life. Had Niki not been in the path of the bullets that killed her, he would have died. He wished it could have been the other way. She had abundant reason to live—he no longer had any. Tiny Israel would be his prison. And little Ari Paul—what would become of him?

Returning to his seat, Ari had to slip past a doctor and two nurses who were moving down the aisle, taking blood pressure, calming fears, giving tranquilizers, finding only a few superficial cuts and bruises to deal with but much lingering hysteria. An identical team was working its way down the opposite aisle, ministering to the needs of the passengers in the same way. The most popular remedy, however, was the wine and hard liquor that was being passed out liberally and without charge as token compensation from El Al for the trauma everyone had suffered.

Midway in the flight, overwhelmed by the enormity of his tragedy and his inability to cope with the complexities involved, Ari drifted into a troubled slumber. Completely exhausted by the events and stress of the previous 48 hours, it was only when the intercom crackled loudly over his head and the pilot announced their final approach into Tel Aviv that he at last came out of a profound sleep. When the plane penetrated beneath the low cloud cover, just before it touched down, Ari caught his first glimpse of his new homeland. So this was Israel. A feeling of revulsion was his only reaction as he took in Tel Aviv's drab Lod Airport and the desert-like landscape surrounding it.

The plane had no sooner rolled to a stop near the terminal than it was boarded by a dozen or more men and women, none of them uniformed, who said little but watched every move the passengers made. One of their number, apparently in charge, spoke over the intercom briefly: "Welcome to Israel, ladies and gentlemen. We profoundly regret what happened in Paris, but since it did occur we must deal with that fact. You will all be taken to a debriefing room. That phase shouldn't take long. Your baggage will be held for you. Now please follow me."

Coming off the plane, Ari fell in line with the other passengers making their way as directed toward the terminal under the watchful eyes of young soldiers armed with Uzis. Ari immediately noticed and tabbed as a Mossad agent a muscular man in jeans and flowered shirt open at the neck who was standing to one side and scrutinizing each passenger. His eye caught Ari's.

"You! Thalberg!" he yelled and motioned for Ari to fall out of line and follow him. "Welcome to *Eretz* Israel," he said tersely when Ari had joined him. "My name's Ariel," he added, reaching out to give Ari a warm handshake. "Sorry about Orly. Now you know just a little bit what it's like to be a Jew." He set off at a fast pace and motioned for Ari to follow. "You get to have your own private debriefing," he explained.

Inside, the terminal was awash with immigrants, principally from the Soviet Union. Bewilderment, ecstatic joy, stoicism and a dozen other emotions were written on the faces of these homecomers to the "promised land" of their forefathers. Here was the sanctuary of the chosen—at least that was the hope in their hearts, the faith that they would find a place of refuge at last.

As his escort pushed his way through the churning mass of humanity pressed into the small terminal, the alien sounds of Hebrew and the electric excitement of the new arrivals left Ari feeling all alone in spite of the jostling crowds that surrounded him. There was no way that his deportation to this uninviting and isolated land could bring him any joy. He would never have chosen to come here. For him, this was a place not of promise but of exile. How long would it be his prison? Would he ever be able to leave? To gain entrance he had been forced to admit his Jewishness to the world—a heritage that was still a source of shame to him.

What irony that he, who had hated Jews and especially Zionists, should have been forced to throw in his lot with these despised people. Ari was well aware that anti-Semitism was on the rise everywhere. At the same time that the Berlin Wall was coming down, bringing new freedom and democracy to millions, neo-Nazism had been on the rise and Jewish cemeteries throughout Europe were being defaced with swastikas. He had seen some of them. On his last trip to Warsaw he'd also seen the venomous epithet resurrected from the past—"Jews to the ovens!"—newly spray-painted on the Jewish State Theater. How could he take his place as one of these persecuted people! Better that he had died at Orly and Nicole had lived.

To make matters worse, he was now consigned to live among them in Zion. The very claim that this minuscule land was some foreordained "sanctuary of the chosen" was repugnant to him. Chosen people indeed! By whom and for what? In actuality they were an abominated race surrounded by 200 million Arabs who were sworn to their (and now his) extermination.

Ari absorbed every detail of the people and events around him even as he was hustled through the airport. He noted and marveled at the rapidity with which the continual influx of Jewish immigrants arriving from the Soviet Union and elsewhere was organized into small groups and funneled outside to several desks, where they were processed and taken off to temporary accommodations. At Orly Airport, on the plane, and now here he had already seen enough to admit begrudgingly that Israeli efficiency was worthy of his admiration.

After they had passed through the terminal, Ari's guide led him down a short, narrow hallway, where he stopped at the open door of a small, sparsely furnished office. A depressing greenish-yellow hue reflected from the dingy walls and ceiling. The lone occupant was a bright-looking young man of about 30 years of age. He looked up from the papers he was working on and stared at Ari coldly, his face an expressionless mask.

"Here's your man," said Ariel. With a perfunctory "good luck" to Ari he disappeared back down the hallway.

"Come in and sit down," said the young man, motioning the new immigrant toward a shoddy straight-backed chair, one of three lined up just in front of his desk. He scrutinized Ari closely as he seated himself, then continued to look him over in silence as though he were some specimen in a jar. Was it a test of wills? *If he thinks I'm going to say the first word, he'll wait a long time!* thought Ari, deciding that he was going to dislike Israel even more than he'd imagined.

"Well, you got quite a send-off at Orly," the young man said at last matter-of-factly, without the slightest tinge of sympathy in his voice.

"Are you suggesting it was aimed at me?" Ari was determined to match his inquisitor's aloofness.

"No. A random strike as far as we know. PLO. You were aware of that?"

"I presumed so. Then the pilot confirmed it about an hour out of Paris."

"And you knew the one who survived? Abdullah Mustaf?"

Ari raised his eyebrows in surprise. "How did you know that?"

"That was obvious from both your reactions."

"I suppose that astute observation is already in my file," commented Ari dryly. "Yes, I did know Abdul. I have nothing to hide. I sponsored him for his Ph.D. He was a good person...until he got mixed up with some Islamic radicals."

With a slight nod the young man continued. "He certainly knew Nicole—the girl you lived with for six years."

"Are you trying to impress me? I hope you haven't believed everything Interpol has to say about me. I was set up."

"We do our own work—and verify everything passed on from outside sources. We've kept a growing dossier on you for the last 20 years. It takes up an entire file cabinet."

"Then I guess you don't need to ask me any questions," declared Ari sarcastically. "You must already know everything that's worth knowing. Maybe more than I know."

A thin smile momentarily unfroze the young man's mouth, then gave up the effort. "Perhaps. By the way, you can call me Uzi."

Woodenly Ari took the outstretched hand, which gripped his firmly. Uzi? The name of their famous submachine gun? Was that his real name, or was he being funny?

Uzi reached out and turned on a small tape recorder that was sitting on top of a stack of papers on his desk. "When was your last contact with Abdul?"

"About six weeks ago."

"Where?"

"On a platform in the Paris Metro."

"Which one?"

"L'Etoile."

"That's an unusual place to meet."

"It was Abdul's choice. We were lucky to get him to meet at all—but we failed in our mission."

"And what was that?"

"Nicole . . . well, she and Abdy had been like brother and sister. I had Abdy as a student before I met Niki. In fact, he introduced us." Ari turned away momentarily to get control of his voice, then continued. "We met with Abdy to try to talk him out of what we suspected was a growing involvement—though we didn't know for certain that it was—with the PLO."

"And he wouldn't be persuaded."

"Obviously not."

Uzi turned off the recorder and made a few notes on a piece of paper. That finished, he looked up and smiled at Ari, this time with obvious warmth. "Okay. Let's talk about your situation here. You're a holocaust survivor. That makes you someone special in Israel. You're the youngest I've met. They're dying off, you know."

"I'm sure they must be. Even if my parents had survived Hitler they'd probably be dead by now. If not, they'd be in their late seventies. . . ."

"Your Israeli citizenship and passport are being held up on a . . . technicality. Obviously you can't leave the country. That's not our doing, you understand." He shrugged sympathetically.

"I understand," said Ari. "What about jobs? They must be scarce here . . . with so many immigrants."

"It depends. In your case, there just happens to be an opening in the Political Science Department at the Hebrew University in Jerusalem. They'd like you to come for an interview."

Ari sat in thoughtful silence for a moment. "No," he said at last, "I'd rather not."

"It's a very prestigious position," pressed Uzi enthusiastically. "Of course, if you'd rather live somewhere else. . . ."

"No, I'd like to live in Jerusalem. But I've had my fill of the academic world . . . and teaching politics."

"So? What do you have in mind?"

There was a long pause. "I'd like to write," said Ari tentatively, " . . . political trends . . . analysis . . . commentary—that sort of thing."

"Books?"

"No. Articles. Magazine . . . newspaper. . . ."

"And you want to live in Jerusalem?"

"I think so. What about the *Jerusalem Post*?"

"You've never written for a paper. . . ." Uzi's voice had lost its enthusiasm.

"That's true . . . but I've been analyzing the world political scene for years for the courses I've taught . . . and the work I *used* to be involved in." Ari thought it best to add that last phrase, just to remove any questions.

Uzi furrowed his brow and stroked his chin thoughtfully. At last he shrugged expressively and said, "Well, why not apply?"

"I just go there?"

"I'll give them a call . . . put in a word for you . . . and let them know you'll call them tomorrow." He flipped through a card file on his desk, wrote something on a slip of paper and handed it to Ari. "Here's the number . . . and the personnel director's name. You'll be living in Jerusalem. Call him first thing in the morning."

"Thanks," said Ari. Uzi was a human being after all.

"Now about housing," added Uzi. "We've already assigned you to an apartment in Jerusalem. You'll have to share it with. . . ."

"Share it? With whom?" cut in Ari sharply.

The young official leaned back and laughed. "Hey, we're talking Jerusalem, not Paris. Immigrants are pouring in faster than we can build apartments. . . ."

"I had hoped to have my own place," said Ari with great disappointment.

"Impossible! But don't worry," Uzi assured him with another warm smile, "you'll like this guy. He's easygoing—and quite a character. His name is Yakov Kimchy. He's 83, one of the last surviving Haganah fighters from the 1948 War of Independence. A national hero. Fascinating. Was a close friend of David Ben Gurion and Golda Meier. And you'll be inside the old city, which is a fantastic place to live."

28

The Old Warrior

Nothing Uzi might have said could possibly have prepared Ari for the little gnome of a man who answered to his knock a few hours later. A very round, wrinkled face topped by unruly white hair and punctuated by the brightest of blue eyes peered out through the doorway and sized up Ari in one glance.

"Come in, come in," came the hearty greeting in barely understandable English and in the thickest of accents. "You must be Ari Thalberg. I've been expecting you. I'm Yakov Kimchy. Welcome to Israel!"

Ari felt his hand gripped in a bone-tingling handshake. The man was a bundle of energy with the enthusiasm and strength of someone 30 years younger—and his smile was contagious. For the first time since boarding the plane, Ari felt his pain-ridden defenses relax in a very slight yet discernible way. This infectiously happy man was a new breed in Ari's life, a man he liked and trusted instinctively from his first greeting.

Sensitive and responsive to Ari's somber mood, Yakov put a hand gently on Ari's shoulder as he entered the apartment. "You've been through a horrible ordeal. It's been on the news. PLO attack at Orly. Disgusting! I understand that was your flight."

Ari nodded. "Yeah. My . . . uh, girlfriend—we just had a son that I've never seen—was there to see me off. She was killed."

"I'm so sorry." The deep sympathy in the old man's voice and eyes was obviously genuine.

"I'd rather not talk about it," added Ari. "You probably know more about it than I do, anyway, from watching the news."

"I've killed a few terrorists in my day . . . quite a few. It's a terrible thing to have to kill someone . . . ," mused Yakov, then seemed to shove the past back into its niche in his memory and abruptly returned to the present with that bright smile. "You'll like it here in this rebuilt section of Old Jerusalem. No happier place to live in the whole world!"

"I could think of a few," responded Ari glumly. "But here I am . . . and very grateful to you for taking me in."

"Well, let me show you the place, such as it is," chirped Yakov cheerily. He led Ari down a short hallway. It took off from the tiny entry that opened onto the living room in the other direction. "It's not a large apartment," went on Yakov, "but it's comfortable . . . and you can't beat the location."

There were two bedrooms off the narrow hall. Yakov pushed the first door open. "Here's your room. It's about the same as mine... a place to sleep and think. Drop your bag in there and we'll go on."

Not expecting much, Ari peered inside. Opposite the single bed stood a small desk and chair under a long, narrow window. One needed to stand on tiptoe in order to see out of it, which was just as well since it looked straight at the cracking, bare stone wall of an adjoining house about two feet away. At the foot of the bed was an ancient wooden clothes cabinet and beside it a small four-drawer chest topped by a mirror. It would do.

"Home, sweet home," said Ari graciously, dropping his bag onto the floor. "Thanks again for taking me in. You're very kind."

"Not much closet space," admitted Yakov apologetically, "but you're welcome to half of the coat closet in the entry."

"This is more than I need right now. Everything I have is in this small bag. They're supposedly shipping my other things... but I won't hold my breath."

The tiny kitchen boasted an adjoining eating area and next to the table a small window that looked down on a narrow cobblestone street below. "It's all yours just as much as mine," said Yakov generously. "We'll split the expenses."

"Sounds good to me. I just hope I can find a job."

"You'll find one. There's always room for a good man who isn't afraid to work. Now, how about a drink? I just made some lemonade... my granddaughter brings the lemons up fresh from the kibbutz near the Sea of Galilee...."

"Sounds great."

Drink in hand, Ari followed Yakov back through the tiny entry hall and into the living room. "Sit down and relax for a moment," said Yakov, motioning toward a sofa that faced a large picture window. He seated himself in an ancient wooden rocker nearby, which also faced the window. "This is my favorite spot," he added with evident satisfaction. "How's that for a view!"

There, spread before his eyes Ari had his first glimpse of the Temple Mount, but from a different angle than he'd ever seen it in pictures. Down below, at the Western Wall, the faithful were in clear view bobbing up and down in the fervor of earnest prayer. Just beyond and above them towered the soaring Dome of the Rock, its golden cupola dominating the skyline. The last rays of the setting sun gave it a soft, ethereal sheen. Jerusalem the Golden. He'd heard the phrase somewhere.

Ari felt compelled to get up from the sofa, where he had just seated himself. Lemonade in hand, he walked over to stare out the window in speechless awe, overwhelmed by his first sight of the temple mount topped by that golden dome. "I'll be in Jerusalem before you," he murmured under his breath. What could it possibly mean? Ari sighed and turned back toward Yakov. Listlessly he listened.

"What makes Jerusalem so impressive is the history behind everything here." With that brief introduction, Yakov launched into Ari's education in things Jewish in general and Israeli in particular. It was a process that the old Zionist would pursue with an almost fanatical fervor in the ensuing months.

"There's a big rock inside, directly under the dome," explained Yakov. "That's where the Arabs say Abraham offered Ishmael. They claim this land was promised to him and to them as his children. In fact, it was Isaac who was offered by Abraham on that mount—Moriah it's called—which is why Solomon built the original temple there. And it was to us, the Jews, Isaac's descendants, not the Arabs, that this land was promised by God."

Ari's attention focused briefly. "You really believe that 'chosen people' stuff?"

Yakov smiled. He had met Ari's kind before—lots of them in Israel. "Of course. History proves it. Our people lived here for centuries before they were carried away to Babylon... for their sin against God—exactly what the prophets warned would happen. The prophets also said that one day God would bring his people back to their land—and here we are!"

"Religion's off limits to me," said Ari half apologetically, hoping not to offend Yakov, but wanting him to know.

"Impossible!" responded the old man with a twinkle in his eye. "Religion is what the conflict in the Middle East is all about."

"Really?" Ari's question was halfhearted. How could this tiresome old man carry on so incessantly? "Sure," he added, trying to show some interest, "there's the Islamic fundamentalists and the Orthodox in Israel... but they're fringe elements. How could the Middle East conflict be *all* about religion?"

"Bothers you for religion to be that important?" asked the old man perceptively. He leaned back in his rocker and laughed. "Let me prove it to you. Although the Koran—in Sura 5:21—admits that this land belongs to Israel, Islam teaches that Allah gave it to the Arabs. So the very existence of Israel makes Allah a phony god and Islam untrue. Unless the Arabs can put an end to the state of Israel, Muhammad was a false prophet. That's how high the stakes are! And any talk about 'peace' that ignores the challenge Israel's very existence poses to Islam is dishonest."

"Maybe," conceded Ari reluctantly. "I don't deny that religion has a role... at times perhaps even a major one, but I still think you're making it much larger than it really is."

"You'll understand better after you've lived here awhile."

Ari returned to his seat on the sofa. They sat in silence for a few moments, sipping the ice-cold lemonade. Again Ari's gaze was drawn to the magnificent and intriguing panorama.

"Refresh my memory. What else makes the Dome of the Rock so important?" asked Ari at last.

"From that rock under the dome, Arabs say Muhammad ascended to the 'seventh heaven' on a winged horse with the face of a woman."

"I remember now. But isn't his body buried in Mecca?"

"No. In Medina, in Saudi Arabia. So... if he went to heaven he left his body behind."

"I don't think that matters to a Muslim, does it? There's no logic—which is why I avoid religious quibbling."

"You're right. If it were a matter of logic, Muslims would abandon Muhammad for Christ. He resurrected and went to heaven bodily... leaving behind an empty grave."

The old man seemed to be watching Ari closely through half-closed eyes. Surely an Israeli war hero couldn't possibly be a follower of that despised *Christ.* Was Yakov testing his reaction? It was too soon after Nicole's death to endure this conversation. Ari felt like telling Yakov to shut up. Then again, maybe a good discussion was just what he needed to get his mind off the immediate past. He decided to opt for the latter—but to avoid any reference to Jesus. Niki's death and her belief were still too raw.

"I guess that site right in front of us is central to your religious conflict thesis," suggested Ari. "It's sacred to the Israelis because that's where their temple was—but now the Muslims claim it's sacred to them because of the Dome of the Rock. Is it built right where the temple used to be?"

"That's a matter of controversy. As you look at it right now, I think the temple was to the left." Yakov stood up to point. "Three temples, actually—Solomon's original, then the one that was rebuilt by Ezra after the return from Babylon, and finally Herod's temple. That's the one we know most about." The old man was gesturing enthusiastically now. Obviously this was a subject that he enjoyed immensely.

"Down there where you see the people praying," continued Yakov, "men on the left, women on the right—that's the wall that Herod built to support the landfill when he expanded the mount to make room for his enlargement of the temple and its grounds. That temple was destroyed in 70 A.D. by the Romans—and the Arabs built the Dome of the Rock in the seventh century to prevent the Jews from ever rebuilding their temple again."

"I thought they built it because Muhammad, like you just said, had been there... something about Al-Aqsa...."

Yakov shook his head vigorously. "Al-Aqsa is mentioned in only one verse in the Koran—Sura 17:1. It's the place Muhammad supposedly journeyed to from Mecca on his magical horse. But Al-Aqsa was never connected with Jerusalem—certainly not when that was built. Sura 17:1 is missing among the many verses from the Koran inscribed inside the Dome. Get an Arab guide and go in there and ask him to find Sura 17:1—and he'll tell you it isn't there."

"That's odd." Ari got up from the sofa again and joined Yakov at the window to better see the view.

"Actually, it isn't odd at all. Jerusalem was never considered sacred by Muhammad—nor by any Muslims for 13 centuries after his death. No Muslim ruler ever used Jerusalem as his political capital or even as a religious or cultural center—even after Islam had conquered this entire region. You know, not too long ago Jordan controlled Jerusalem for 19 years...and the Saudi monarch never visited even once!"

"Then why do Muslims consider it so sacred today?"

"Because of a very clever lie." Yakov's eyes gleamed with just a trace of anger. "In the 1920s Yasser Arafat's uncle, Haj Amin Al-Husseini, spread the myth that the Dome of the Rock had been built over the fabled Al-Aqsa. He popularized this lie in order to increase his own importance as the Grand Mufti of Jerusalem—and especially as a means of recruiting Arab support for the removal of any Jewish presence in the Holy City."

"I remember vaguely. He fled to Germany, didn't he?"

Yakov nodded. "He was pro-Hitler and told the Arabs, 'Kill the Jews wherever you find them. This pleases God and religion and saves your honor.'"

"Incredible. Sounds like Hitler."

"Exactly. And don't forget, Arafat—and most Arab leaders—still subscribe to the same creed."

"That baffles me," remarked Ari gloomily, reminded of his own identity with them now, "why the Jews have been so hated throughout history. It's incomprehensible."

"I've lived through a lot of that hatred," said Yakov quietly, "and there's only one explanation."

Ari's attention was riveted at last on the old man's wrinkled but bright face. It was marked by a passion and a conviction that promised the answer that Ari desperately needed.

Slowly Yakov enunciated the words: "Like I already said, the Bible calls the Jews God's 'chosen people.' That's why they're hated."

"As simple as that?" smiled Ari indulgently. "You really believe that, don't you."

"I didn't use to—because I didn't believe in God. But I've lived through four wars right here in Israel, and I've seen events that you'd have to call 'miraculous.'"

"Such as?" queried Ari pointedly.

Yakov looked at him with compassion and understanding. "I know what you're thinking. I was a skeptic, too. I'll just tell you the first 'miracle'—the one that got my attention. A company of Haganah that I was commanding was about to storm an Arab position. Suddenly a wind blew across the no-man's land right in front of us. It was so strong and stirred up such a sandstorm that we couldn't move. It only lasted a minute, then stopped as suddenly as it had begun. And there in front of us we saw dozens of mines exposed, the sand that had covered them completely blown away. If it hadn't been for that wind, the mines would have wiped us out."

"A lucky coincidence," suggested Ari with a cynical smile.

Yakov burst into a quick, good-natured laugh. "I know dozens of similar stories... incredible events that defy normal explanation and that saved Jewish lives. These incidents are talked about with awe in the Israeli military, but not publicized. They convinced a lot of us who fought in the wars that the God of Abraham, Isaac and Jacob was fulfilling His promises to His ancient people in a peculiar way at this time in history."

Ari made no response. He continued to stare out the picture window at the Dome of the Rock, now fading in the gathering dusk. There was intriguing mystery here that he'd enjoy investigating some day—but it was too much to be confronted with all at once. It was difficult enough to face his Jewishness without this fervent Zionist so persistently hammering away at the religious implications.

Finally Yakov broke the silence. "I saw the world look the other way during Hitler's attempt to exterminate the Jews. And now I see the same attitude. It isn't just the PLO charter that demands the destruction of Israel—in the name of 'peace.' The spirit of Hitler lives on in the cries of Arab leaders for a holy war to exterminate Jews. That call to arms screams daily from mosques and from political forums throughout the Arab world. Yet pressure grows for Israel to give back land it took in self-defense... in order to create a Palestinian state that the Arabs have sworn to use as a launching pad for the destruction of Israel."

"Watch what you're saying," protested Ari. "You're getting into politics ... and that's my field." The discussion had taken a more comfortable turn, and he decided to jump back into it. "The Jews forced the Arabs to leave and then took over their land and houses. That property has to be given back!"

"Where did you hear that?"

"It's common knowledge." The patronizing tone was obvious.

"I was there," said Yakov, his face suddenly flushed with anger. "There may have been a few incidents like that. But I can tell you as an eyewitness that we pleaded with our Arab neighbors to stay."

Ari could scarcely contain a skeptical smile.

Yakov faced him now, eyes blazing. "I'm giving you the facts. You read about it... but I lived through it. The truth gets suppressed... and the world seems unwilling to hear it. I remember seeing notices placed on doors of businesses, homes, mosques, saying something like: 'We begged our Arab neighbors to stay. This is not our property, but theirs. Keep it safe for them until they return.'"

Discomfort was plainly written on Ari's face. How could he respond to this man who had *lived* the history that he had only read about. There was no doubt that he had taught secondhand versions, and apparently—unless Yakov was lying, which seemed unlikely—some perversions with rather glaring deficiencies.

"There's a lot of prejudice out there," Yakov continued heatedly, "and it's not easy to correct lies once they've been widely published and accepted. We didn't want the Arabs to leave...but they did...about 800,000 of them."

"I'm not arguing with you," countered Ari cautiously, "but what you're telling me doesn't make sense. Why would they leave?"

"Arab High Command radio announcements...day and night...warned them to get out *temporarily* for their safety. Seven Arab nations were going to attack. The Jews would be driven into the Mediterranean. And the Palestinian Arabs were promised that in a few days they could all return to their homes and farms...after the new state of Israel had been eliminated!"

"That makes sense," admitted Ari. "And instead, tiny Israel won a stunning victory against impossible odds."

"Impossible is an understatement." Yakov was grinning again. "I was there—and I can tell you it only happened because of a lot of miracles!"

"What about the hard work, bravery and Jewish ingenuity?" demanded Ari. "Isn't the saying, 'God helps them who help themselves'?"

"I'm not taking anything away from the bravery of the men and women I fought with." Yakov was silent for some moments, seemingly lost in his memories. Ari waited. He was so talkative—but one had to respect this old warrior. One of Israel's most famous heroes—wasn't that how Uzi had put it? He certainly avoided taking any credit himself.

"Back to what we were talking about...this whole Palestinian problem," said Yakov at last. "You can imagine the disillusionment and anger among the displaced Palestinians when the promises of the Arab High Command turned out to be so much hot air. At first, they were angry with their own leaders. But the lies that were told eventually turned that anger—and the anger of the whole world—against Israel, as though it were our fault that the Arabs attacked us and we had to defend ourselves."

"What about those notices not to take over Arab property?" demanded Ari, turning from the faded view in the now darkened window to face Yakov. "Instead, you kept it after all! And you took a lot of land that was never part of what Israel was given by the UN partition. Why didn't you give that back?"

"Arabs were welcome to return to their homes, but few did. And as for the territory we'd taken in self-defense, it would have been suicide to give it back. We couldn't return to the original borders the UN had given us—they were indefensible. We were forced to hold a limited portion of additional land for strategic purposes...self-preservation. We knew—and the Arabs kept threatening it—that they'd attack again and never quit until we'd been annihilated."

"And you fought in that first war in '48?" asked Ari.

Yakov nodded. "And in '56, and '67 and '73. We *had* to win each time," he said matter-of-factly. "The Arabs can lose and come back to fight again. Israel can't. One loss would finish us forever."

"You've given me a lot to think about," confessed Ari somberly. "I was head of the political science department at the Sorbonne, but I've never heard this side of the story... at least not as well put as you've just presented it."

"With each new war, the very survival of Jews everywhere is at stake." There was a powerful conviction in Yakov's voice that gave his statements the ring of authenticity, as though he were speaking for the entire Jewish race, past, present and future. "We've sworn there will never be another Holocaust! But I can tell you that without God's intervention we could not survive."

"Was 'God' on our side when Hitler slaughtered us?" retorted Ari. "That's how I lost my parents... and I suppose a host of relatives—aunts and uncles and grandparents and cousins—that I'll never know even existed."

A sad and gentle compassion now replaced the anger in Yakov's voice. "That's a difficult question. I lost many relatives, too. The Torah warned our people that we'd be scattered around the world and that God's judgment would fall if we disobeyed Him. Our ancestors disobeyed... and exactly what God warned about did happen. You can't get away from that."

"But the Holocaust... !" protested Ari.

"It was too horrible! I don't understand. But I know there probably wouldn't be an Israel today, a sanctuary for the Chosen People to take refuge in, if it hadn't been for the extermination camps. So that horror may turn out in the long run to have saved more Jewish lives than it cost."

Again Ari smiled. *"Chosen people, indeed!"* he muttered under his breath. "Well," he said aloud to Yakov, eager to escape from the recurring and annoying religious theme, "we've gotten into a pretty heavy discussion before we're really even acquainted. Now how about agreeing that we disagree on religious issues—and then let's forget that subject. I'm just not interested."

Yakov shrugged good-naturedly. "If that's the way you want it. But that won't change the fact that the persistent hatred of our people would have wiped us out long ago if God hadn't protected us. You'll understand that better after you've lived here awhile and know what it feels like to be threatened with annihilation from every side. If the God of Abraham, Isaac and Israel doesn't exist and doesn't help us, then we'll be exterminated. There's a growing international anti-Semitism that reminds me of the Germany of the '30s. World sentiment is again turning against Israel. You'll begin to feel it, too. You'll see."

For another moment Yakov stared at Ari as though he were looking into his very soul. Then he switched on a light and headed for the kitchen. "Sorry that I talk so much. You must be hungry... and tired. Let me fix something to eat, then you can catch up on some sleep."

"Maybe I'll just lie down for a minute. You can call me when it's ready." Ari started across the living room toward the hallway. At that moment there was a knock.

"Wait a minute," Yakov called after him, hurrying to the door. "I know that knock. I want you to meet someone."

29

A Metamorphosis

"David!" exclaimed Yakov as he pulled the door open. "Great to see you! I've got a roommate—all the way from Paris. This is Ari Thalberg. Ari, meet David Kauly."

Ari felt himself instantly and comprehensively scrutinized, analyzed and memorized by the slightly balding, stocky man of medium height in his mid-forties who catapulted himself through the doorway and grasped his hand.

"So you've moved to Israel." It was more a statement than a question. Ari was immediately alert. Who was this man with the quick eyes and noncommittal expression, and what did he know? He decided to keep that question alive for future consideration.

"Yes. Just arrived a few hours ago. Yakov's good enough to share his flat with me."

"This is the place to be... in the Old City. Keep your eye on the old man, though," added David, tilting his head in Yakov's direction and winking at Ari. "He may need some help getting up and down the stairs."

Yakov snorted. "David was one of my lieutenants in the '67 war. Couldn't keep up with me then, and he's still jealous. Works for the Defense Department. One of these days I'm going to march in there and clean out some of the dead wood. It's not like it used to be in the good old days."

David grinned. "That's why I drop in once in a while—to be reminded about how superior the 'good old days' were and to pick up some of Yakov's nuggets of wisdom. He has plenty to spare. We have some great discussions. You're welcome to sit in any time—right now, if you wish."

"Thanks. I'm still trying to digest all the erudition he's been pouring into me since the minute I arrived. Good to meet you. I'll look forward to seeing you some other time." Ari turned and headed down the hallway to his room.

Closing the door behind him, Ari stretched out on the bed, feeling totally exhausted. Could it be that his age was catching up with him? Age? Forty-six wasn't so old. He'd get back to running, find a good gym and get back in top shape. There might even be a karate studio where he could earn some extra money as a part-time instructor. He needed to enter some tournaments and beat some of the local competition, make a name for himself... then the students would come flocking.

It was hard to believe he was actually here, in Jerusalem, the very place he least wanted to be. At the moment he was a ward of the Israeli government, with no job and a decent, but apparently religious, old bore for a roommate. He was a stranger in a strange land, with nothing to look forward to or to live for. Committed to revolution all of his life, he was now an old war horse put out to pasture. Could life ever have any purpose again?

Still, the sharpness of despair had lessened to a small degree. Should it, he wondered? Was he being untrue to Nicole in this first slight healing? Yet one could not go on living in the past. To continue to blame himself for her death could not help Nicole. She was gone, and it would only make his new start in Israel more difficult to bear if he kept looking back.

But what about little Ari Paul? How he wished he had the picture Niki had sent. Would Bourbonnais be true to his word? Would they really pack up his things and send them here? That picture, casually thrust between two volumes—would it be lost, or packed up with the books and arrive safely? It was all he had. Of course, little Ari wouldn't look like that any more. He'd been so tiny then. He'd be several weeks old now and growing each day. Soon he would be learning to walk and talk and respond... all without his father there to share those moments. Who was raising him? Would he ever know who his father was? Would father and son ever meet? He owed it to Nicole to find Ari Paul and raise him in her memory.

Ari fell asleep wondering when and how he would be able to bring his son to Israel. As the child's father, he must have some rights. Surely he could take custody of his own offspring. He'd have to get a job first and establish himself here in his own apartment... or perhaps even a home out in the country where the child could grow up in the fresh air, learn to ride horses.... It was a dream worth dreaming, something he could do for Nicole.

— ✦ —

When Ari called *The Jerusalem Post* the following morning he discovered that Uzi had already arranged an appointment for that afternoon with the editor-in-chief himself. The reception given him was beyond his expectations as a complete newcomer to the field of journalism.

"Uzi told me you were the head of the Political Science Department at the Sorbonne. Is that right?" The chief seemed greatly impressed.

Ari nodded modestly. "Yes, for the past five years. I taught there for almost seventeen. Published lots of articles..."

"You're really way overqualified for anything I can offer you. But we'd like to have you join the staff. I've been thinking for weeks about a new feature—a twice-weekly news analysis column—and wondering who I could get to write it. How would you like to take that on?"

"It would be an honor... and a challenge," responded Ari enthusiastically. Maybe there was something to live for after all.

"That should still leave you time to teach a class or two at the Hebrew University, if you're interested," the chief added.

"That's a possibility." Ari didn't want to dampen the chief's enthusiasm. But in his heart he knew he was finished with the world of academia. He couldn't bear to be around students and not involve them in that cause to which his entire life had been devoted. And that, of course, was out of the question. He had a whole new life to begin.

Ari was hired on the spot. As he signed his contract he could imagine Yakov's triumphant and predictable pronouncement—"It's a miracle!" So be it. He had a job.

True, the starting salary wasn't anything to brag about, but it would pay his half of the rent and utilities, with a little left over for some minimal personal spending and even a small savings. A man starting life all over again at his age couldn't expect much more. At least it was a first step in the right direction that he hoped would eventually see his son in his care. Perhaps fate would begin to smile after all.

In the days that followed, the job grew on Ari. He was on his own with no one looking over his shoulder, able to express his personal opinions with only minimal suggestions from the top. After all, it was a new experience for him, and he was thankful for constructive criticism and advice. The other staff were generally congenial and some of them, especially an attractive young reporter who reminded him somewhat of Nicole, made decidedly friendly overtures. As for Ari, office camaraderie was okay, but nothing more—not yet.

Perhaps the void left in his life by Nicole's death could be filled after all... but it couldn't be rushed. He'd be cautious, slow to establish close friendships, knowing that they could become a minefield of danger. That restrained attitude was a carryover from his years of secret work. It was difficult to shake habits that had been so deeply ingrained.

Ari wasn't at all happy with the way events were proceeding in Europe. Let Bush and Gorbachev—and the Pope—take the credit. It was their New World Order, not at all what he'd had in mind. He was washing his hands of it all, determined to clean every vestige of the past out of his briefcase—and mind. Carefully he burned page after page of names, addresses and phone numbers. His lieutenants throughout Eastern Europe and Asia must be wondering what had happened. He hadn't even been able to get a message out to them. They were on their own now.

One of the blessings of the new job was that Ari could deal with current issues in his column. His third feature was a three-part in-depth analysis of the Stasi, its destructive effect upon East German society, not only in its heyday, but the traumatic continuing repercussions since the Wall had come down. Paid informers had been everywhere. No place had been safe, from the schoolroom to the pulpit. Even the Roman Catholic confessional, through hidden microphones and corrupt priests, had been used by the Stasi for its evil work. And now that the truth was coming out at last, friends and families were being torn asunder as they learned that some of their closest and most trusted companions had for years been well paid by the Stasi to inform upon and betray them. Divorce, suicide and even murder of betrayers in outraged revenge for years spent in prison were the continuing fruit of past decades of treachery.

There was another side of the story, too, that Ari also laid out as one of the results of German unification. In the new Germany, ex-Stasi agents who had escaped the accusations of victims were becoming private detectives, a profession unheard of under Marxism, but suddenly in great demand under capitalism. Some of the work involved getting the goods on their old comrades. Freedom came with a heavy price tag.

There was a great deal of popular demand among readers for commentary on new trends in Europe—with special interest, of course, upon anything related to Israel and worldwide Jewry. With unification, the former East Germany was becoming a breeding ground for hate groups that were growing increasingly powerful and violent. Ari did a two-part series analyzing the rise of Neo-Nazism, with special emphasis upon anti-Semitism. The chief was more than pleased with his new recruit and so were his readers.

"I like what you're writing better now than I did a month ago," Yakov told Ari one evening as they were eating supper together at the small table next to the kitchen. "I can see a slow but steady metamorphosis in your thinking."

"I must admit," confessed Ari, "that living in Israel has given me an entirely different perspective than I had before. I'm beginning to see things in a new light, though I still have problems with Zionism—and the 'chosen people' thing."

Yakov's round face lit up with a brighter-than-usual smile. "You're a fair man, Ari. You respect facts. I like that. You'll come around."

"I see the news coming in on the wires and satellite daily. Not just from news bureaus... but we pick up raw stuff through our own people out there. It's been an education. Incredible... the outpouring of hatred and threats of extermination against Israel from the surrounding Arab states!"

"Yet the world ignores it. We're the bad guys for wanting to defend ourselves...."

"I don't think most of the world knows the truth... or maybe even wants to. Most of this stuff never gets off the wires into a form that reaches the average person. They're kept in ignorance."

"Those are not idle threats," Yakov reminded him. "They seem to be when nothing comes of them... but that's only because the Arabs have been defeated in each war and the Soviets are reluctant to back them in another. They're hoping to win a propaganda war to establish an independent Palestinian state as a base inside Israel. In the meantime, even while crying 'peace,' they try every possible means of terrorism against us from outside."

Ari nodded his agreement. "At first I was critical of the military presence. It's everywhere. Planes overhead, sonic booms, helicopters always on some mission, soldiers in the streets. You really have to *be* here awhile to understand it."

"You'll be a real Israeli soon!" exulted Yakov with approval.

"Not so fast, you old war horse," laughed Ari. "I'm still concerned about the siege mentality among you Israelis. It could breed a destructive paranoia... an extremism. I see some signs of it in the Knesset from time to time... and in some of the political parties that are jockeying for power. That worries me."

"And me as well," agreed Yakov.

"Really!" Impulsively, Ari reached across the table and shook the old warrior's hand vigorously.

— ✦ —

David dropped in at the apartment about once a week. He and Yakov seemed to have a genuine friendship that indeed went back for decades. Yet there was something odd about the visits that puzzled Ari. The man was intelligent and knowledgeable, a good talker on almost any subject, but very vague on personal matters. Ari had given him several opportunities to elaborate even slightly on what he did at the Defense Department, but David adroitly sidestepped each one.

Ari suspected that David had something to do with Israeli Intelligence and that Yakov's sharing of his apartment was part of a plan to keep their eyes on him. He could understand why the Israelis might want to do that, considering his past, the circumstances under which he'd been sent to them and the fact that he'd been on the top of the Interpol wanted list for years. So what did it matter? Let them watch him—if that's indeed what they were doing—until they tired of it. They'd soon be convinced that he had nothing to hide. Not any more.

— ✦ —

"Ari, my son! My son!" Ari heard himself muttering the words in agony as he struggled into wakefulness early one morning after he'd been in Israel about six weeks. Little Ari Paul was on his heart and conscience day and night. How desperately he wanted to bring him to Israel! Yet there were so many practical problems standing in the way. He had no money for what would undoubtedly prove a costly custody battle in the French courts. Couldn't even hire a lawyer to look into it as yet. Moreover, given his present living arrangements and minimal salary, and his past 'criminal' record, he wouldn't seem very well qualified in the eyes of the court.

Common sense, however, was overridden by passion. How he longed to see his son, to hold him in his arms, to protect him and care for him. This natural desire was intensified by an overwhelming sense of guilt that continued to torment him. The fact that he had insisted upon an abortion and had refused to take any responsibility for Niki's pregnancy continued to haunt him. The child was *his*—and his alone now that *she* was gone. He owed it to *her*, to Niki, to find *their* baby and raise him in her memory.

There was another consideration that troubled him. An increasing risk was involved the longer his child remained separated from him. What if Roger's group should try to use the baby boy as leverage? They might threaten to kill the child if any information was leaked about them. Certainly it would be insane to contact these old associates, and now antagonists, in attempting to locate his son.

Ari remembered that Niki had come under the influence of a doctor and his wife, a nurse, whom she had known at the Paris hospital where she had been doing her residency. She had stayed with them in the process of leaving him and finding an apartment of her own. It would seem likely, then, that they were the ones who had driven her to Orly to see him off. If so, she had left the baby with them when she'd come inside the airport to bid him farewell. At least it was a starting point. They would know something—if they'd tell him.

"Of course you're welcome to call Paris or anywhere else," Yakov readily told Ari when he asked about using the phone. "We'll look at the bills when they come in and settle up."

It was no problem getting the number from the international operator. Ari quickly dialed the hospital and made his inquiry. There were several married couples who both worked there, but only one doctor-nurse team. Their name was Duclos. It rang a bell immediately.

"Dr. Duclos," Ari said when he'd gotten him at last. "My name is Ari Thalberg, formerly known as Professor Hans Mueller at the Sorbonne. I was engaged to Nicole. She probably mentioned me. You know of her tragic death...."

"Yes, I do. We were with her at the time. We brought her to say goodbye to you at Orly."

"I thought so!" continued Ari hopefully. "Then she must have left our child with you. How is he?"

There was a moment's hesitation. "Yes, she did," said Duclos guardedly. "He's a beautiful, happy baby. He's doing very well with us."

"He's *my* son!" Ari blurted out, unable to restrain himself. "Could you send me a picture?"

"Certainly. What's your address?"

Ari gave him the number and spelled out the street name. "One day, when it's possible, I'd like to have him here with me."

This time there was a longer silence on the other end before the doctor replied. "I don't want to deceive you by holding out any hope on that score," he said at last. "You wanted her to abort the baby, I believe."

"What we may have discussed when she first realized she was pregnant is irrelevant now. Niki had the baby. I'm the father, and I have a parental interest in my son."

"Yes, I'm sure you do," came the placating response, "but there are legal avenues. You weren't married. . . ."

"We're not discussing moral issues," cut in Ari.

"No, of course not. I'm simply telling you the facts. Since you weren't married to Nicole, you'll need to provide some proof."

"You know I'm the father. Niki must have told you."

"I'm not the judge. It's a matter for the courts to decide. To be very frank, the mother's wishes will have prior claim. She made arrangements for us to keep the baby and raise him."

"Can you prove that in court?"

"We already have. Nicole must have had a premonition of her death. She said something about a dream. It was so real to her that . . . well, she wouldn't leave for the airport until she'd written and signed a simple statement asking us to raise the child . . . in the Christian faith. . . ."

"That's a violation of his ethnic origin!" spluttered Ari, then fell silent in frustration. So it *had* been a premonition of death. "Jerusalem" . . . the name turned to bitter gall. Yakov would call it another "miracle," a "sign" that God was at work. But what kind of a "God" would rob him of his dearest love and was now keeping him from his son?

Almost unheard was the doctor's calm and inexorable logic: "The courts will decide any future guardianship changes. In the meantime, we've been awarded legal custody. As for the child's faith, he'll decide himself, when he's old enough. Better just leave it at that, Professor Thalberg. Oh yes, I'll send those pictures right away."

For some time Ari sat staring at the silent phone. No, he wouldn't fight the Duclos. Not yet. At least he knew who had his son. Let them keep him for now. Eventually he would gain custody. And if they did raise him as a Christian during his impressionable years, it would be simple enough to teach him otherwise when he was older and could think for himself.

Elor of the Nine

Life in Israel was settling into a routine of near-boredom. So Israel was surrounded by enemies who might attack at any moment. So what else was new? Terrorism, yes, but a major attack, no. Not without the Soviet Union to back the invaders, and that was no longer feasible. Gorbachev's *glasnost* and *perestroika*, just as Ari knew had been the plan all along, had given the Soviet leadership so many internal problems that helping the Arabs in a war against Israel was out of the question—at least for the foreseeable future.

Ari was running out of hot issues to write about. Then along came Saddam Hussein's brutal takeover of Kuwait in August, 1990, and Ari's job as a political columnist became exciting for him once again. *The Post* had connections high up in the Mossad, which gave Ari access to certain intelligence data that would not expose agent sources and was periodically earmarked for publication in his columns.

It was common knowledge that Kuwait had been a haven for terrorists of every stripe as well as the chief paymaster to the PLO. It was Mossad data, however, that Ari used (without revealing the source) to tell how the PLO had repaid the Emir's longtime favors by giving Saddam the detailed intelligence for his invasion of Kuwait. There was no honor among murderers and thieves, and this latest duplicity was going to have lasting repercussions.

In his column, Ari predicted that Arafat had cut his own throat by siding with Saddam, an inhuman monster whose crimes not only against his own people and Kuwait but against all of humanity were so great that when the truth was known the entire civilized world would abhor him. Neither Kuwait nor Saudi Arabia would any longer support the PLO when the coalition forces chased Saddam's vaunted army back to Iraq, as they surely would. Democracy would have to come—slowly, but inevitably—to both of those Islamic dictatorships. When that happened it would send shock waves throughout the entire Arab world that would lead to greater freedom and eventually bring down the Islamic Curtain as had already happened to the Iron Curtain.

—◆—

Early one evening, Ari set off on one of his aimless, leisurely strolls through some of the narrow back streets of the Old City's Arab quarter, savoring the exotic sights and sounds and stopping in a shop now and then to browse among its intriguing wares. He had just downed a cup of fresh-squeezed orange juice purchased from a street vendor and was walking away when he realized that someone had come up beside him and was matching his steps.

Ari turned to give the man a questioning look. He appeared to be Jewish, in his early thirties, of medium height and build, with a neatly trimmed dark beard and wearing a well-tailored beige linen suit.

"I hope I'm not intruding...," the stranger began apologetically. "I'm one of your admirers... read your column religiously. Your thinking is very stimulating."

"That's kind of you to say." Ari stopped and reached out to shake the man's hand. "And your name?"

"Elor. It's such a pleasure to meet you. I had a question, if you don't mind."

"No. Go ahead."

"Your articles about the Stasi were excellent. I wondered, however, why you didn't bring in something personal. Would have made it even more interesting... and authentic."

"Personal? What do you mean?"

"Oh, perhaps how you escaped when the Stasi came to your apartment that night in Leipzig, or maybe how you threw those two off the train...."

"Who are you!" demanded Ari. "How do you know that?"

"Just a friend... and admirer."

"Look, if you're with the CIA... or the banking Consortium... this was not part of the deal. The past is behind me. I'm not getting involved anymore...." Ari stopped in mid-sentence. The eyes. There was something about them. Where had he seen this man before?

"You were in the backseat of that car when I was 'arrested,'" began Ari uncertainly. Could this be the same man? It couldn't be—but it was. "Then later in Paris... and you've haunted my dreams!"

The man made no reply. He just stared at Ari. The look on his face was pleasant enough, friendly... but there was no mistaking those hypnotic eyes. With great effort Ari broke away from the stare that had caught him unawares and had locked their eyes together.

"What are you doing here in Israel!" hissed Ari. "Who are you!"

"A mentor... from a higher level," came the enigmatic reply. "As I told you in Berlin."

"What do you want? Why don't you leave me alone?"

"Have you not seen a pattern? That at times of crisis or significant change in your life I have appeared to give you help and guidance?"

"Help, yes... once. But *guidance*? No."

"Never?" The man's eyebrows rose ever so slightly in mild reproof.

"Yes," admitted Ari grudgingly, "you did give directions for getting out of East Berlin... and you made some astute comments in Paris... but beyond that no 'guidance' that I recall."

"There have been other times of which you were not aware...."

"You've been playing with my mind!" cut in Ari angrily. "Is that what you mean? I haven't appreciated that!"

"We've been preparing you."

"*Preparing* me? For what?"

"That you are a Jew—and a very special one—is most important. Intuitively you know that, though you have resisted admitting it to yourself. What you do not know is that you were chosen at birth for a mission involving Israel."

"Sure. And the moon's made out of green cheese. What's your game?"

"If you weren't skeptical, but fell for flattery, we wouldn't be interested in you. I have come not to flatter but to explain your mission. The appointed time for its fulfillment is fast approaching. That's why we brought you here."

"Ridiculous! It's a fluke that I'm here."

The man caught Ari's evasive eyes. His smile was unlike any human expression Ari had ever seen. It communicated a peace and power and confidence that seemed to be superhuman. "We've guided your entire life step by step. It was always the plan that you come to Israel. That was necessary for your mission. Next you go to the United States to meet a man whose destiny is interlocked with yours."

"That's impossible. I can't leave Israel. My days of jetting around to accomplish grandiose missions are past. My entire life's work has fallen into the hands of others who are abusing the powers I labored to give them."

"You're discouraged—and you're wrong. You've done well. Don't grieve for Nicole. It was her karma. You will meet her again in another and better life. Your personal mission for this life, however, has gone according to plan to this very day...and it will shortly proceed to its successful conclusion."

"Either I'm crazy, or you are," muttered Ari. "And, frankly, I don't know which is the truth. Maybe we're both crazy."

Again that peaceful smile of total confidence. "You will understand when you go to America...to California. Then you will trust us. For your further progress total trust is absolutely essential. We have reached the limit of what we can do through telepathy and dreams. For your mission to be fulfilled you must believe what we say and willingly follow directions."

You are crazy! thought Ari, staring at him in silence, avoiding his eyes. The situation was bizarre beyond belief, but this...whoever or whatever he was... couldn't just be dismissed. There was a question that had come up at that deportation meeting in Paris in Bourbonnais' office, which they had sidestepped, and it had bothered him ever since.

"What's been your connection to Roger's group?" demanded Ari. The response was a surprise. It revealed secret knowledge and insight that gave a further sense of legitimacy to this mysterious figure.

"As you yourself discovered, Roger works for the CIA, with whom we maintain contact on another level. You'll be initiated into it soon. You were wrong in not trusting him, but you had no other choice. The Paris group are pompous fools. Roger is simply using them for Langley's purposes. You passed a major test by handling that ambitious cartel well. They have delusions of taking over the world, which would be a disaster. They would fight among themselves. We're tolerating them only as long as they're useful—which will not be much longer."

"Your analysis of the Paris group is accurate," admitted Ari guardedly, stunned by the matter-of-fact authority with which he spoke. "And you obviously know Roger's true mission and loyalties." The man was earning his respect, but he remained an impenetrable mystery. "Don't you think it's time to tell me who you really are?"

"I have told you. My name is Elor. I'm one of the Nine—the Archons. We put mankind on this planet 20,000 years ago. The experiment will end in disaster unless your race takes a new direction." Again that smile of utter confidence and power.

"You're 20,000 years old? Sure, and I'm Napolean! You make sense for awhile... and then you sound crazy again."

"How old did you think I was when we had our first face-to-face encounter in East Berlin?"

"About 40, maybe 45."

"That was nearly 30 years ago. How old do I look now?"

"Early thirties," admitted Ari, bewildered.

"Am I the same person?"

"Your features change... but your eyes are the same. I'd know them anywhere."

"Why do you think it so fantastic when I say we put mankind on this planet 20,000 years ago? Did you not admit in a discussion with Nicole that humans are not the only intelligences in the universe? And did you not quote Robert Jastrow in his belief that more highly evolved beings must exist... perhaps as far beyond man on the evolutionary scale as man is beyond worms? And did not Nicole admit this possibility as well?"

Ari nodded slowly. "The *possibility* exists... but to run into someone on the street who makes this claim—that's too fantastic to be true! It's like running into someone who claims to be God."

"There is no 'God,'" came the quick, almost derisive response. "We are all gods. Look up quickly!"

Ari looked up to see a beautiful white dove fluttering down. It landed upon Elor's head, remained for a moment, then vanished.

"Now look at the wall above and behind me!" Elor commanded.

To his utter astonishment, Ari saw one of the masonry stones in the side of the building behind Elor come out of its place, hover in the air, then return, restoring the wall as it had been. The mortar that had held the stone was seemingly undisturbed and as sound as before.

Elor held out his right hand and a flame about six inches high began to burn in his palm. Immediately Ari could feel the heat. Elor grabbed Ari's hand and held it in the flame. Now his sensation was one of pleasant and soothing coolness. The flame vanished and Ari looked at his hand. It had not been burned.

"Be not deceived," counseled Elor, seeing Ari's dismayed expression. "These are not miracles, as some misguided souls imagine. There are no miracles—only natural phenomena produced by universal laws of which the inhabitants of this planet remain almost totally ignorant. Your science is still very primitive because it has concentrated entirely upon the physical universe. You, too, can do what I have just done—and more—once you have been initiated into the secrets we hold. But the time for that is not yet."

Ari was standing open mouthed, unable to comprehend what he'd seen with his own eyes. Was he having a nightmare, from which he'd soon awaken? Had he been hypnotized? Was Elor exercising some kind of mind control in order to deceive him? He stepped forward and examined the wall carefully, then turned to orient himself with his surroundings. He was standing at a familiar corner. The streets in all directions looked the same as he remembered them. People were coming and going, paying little attention to him and Elor. Ten yards away an elderly Arab squatted in front of a shop and puffed on a cigarette. In the other direction he could see several children playing and could hear their shrill voices. Everything seemed normal.

"We've met before—in my dreams. I was terrified then," confessed Ari, turning to Elor. "Why not now?"

"That is why I have not visited you in your dreams for many months. You were projecting your own immaturity and fears upon me. I have not changed, but you have. Soon you will be ready."

Elor put his hand on Ari's shoulder and held him with his eyes. "You will be the leader of a New Israel that will be purged of its Zionist ambitions and delusions of being 'God's chosen people.' Only then will Israel take its place in the New World Order of nations and live in peace... a peace such as the world has never known."

Ari stood stunned... speechless. Once again the man sounded insane. He wanted to tell Elor that he was repelled by such unbelievable flattery. Instead, he heard himself stammer, "Why me?"

Elor patted Ari affectionately on the arm. "Your heart is right. You've proved your willingness to expend yourself for the good of mankind, asking nothing for yourself. It was part of our plan to allow you to do that, though we knew it would only fail."

"What do you mean by that?"

"Changing the government, even bringing freedom... as you can now see in Eastern Europe... is not the answer. There must be a change in spirit. We've come to instill genuine love in mankind. Only then can we trust your race with the power it needs to rescue this planet from ecological collapse... and a total psychotic breakdown of society."

"I can see the truth in what you say," conceded Ari, "but how it can be done... that seems impossible."

"We have a plan, and you are essential to its success."

"I can't believe that."

"You must. Earth's computers and knowledge of the cosmos are not sophisticated enough to verify the fact that there is a cycle in this galaxy of 1,997 earth years. I cannot explain it further, but we can only act during a narrow window of time at the peak of the cycle. The plan will work at no other time. If we fail this time... your world will not last another 2,000 years, of that we are certain."

"You put an awful responsibility on my shoulders. What do you expect me to do?"

"Nothing at the moment. You will learn more in California when you meet the other man who, along with you, holds the key. But we must have your willingness."

"How can I give it to you if I don't know what I must do?"

"Are you willing to save your race?"

Ari looked at Elor closely. "You're serious, aren't you."

"We are. Forgetting the details for the moment... if you could be the one to save mankind, would you be willing?"

"Of course, I couldn't say no to that... but I still think it's too fantastic to believe."

"You do not realize the importance of your Jewish birth... nor of your being here in Jerusalem. This city is the key. At the moment it is the source of controversy between hateful religions. That is all the result of our failure last time."

"Last time?"

"Yes. As the cycle approached its peak nearly 2,000 years ago... right here in Jerusalem I made the same offer to a young carpenter. He chose, instead, to become the founder of a new religion that only made matters worse—the world already had too many religions. Your aversion to religion is one of your strong points."

Elor paused for a moment to give Ari a chance to absorb what he had said. Then he added, "Are you willing?"

Ari did not hesitate. "You may be crazy, and probably are. We both may have lost touch with reality. I don't know. But if I can do anything to rescue this planet from destruction... then, of course, I'm willing. How could I say no?"

Elor looked pleased. "I must warn you," he added in a soothing voice, "do not mention this to anyone, especially to the old man you are living with—the foolish one who talks of God and miracles. It was not our doing to have you meet him."

Not their doing? Then whose could it be, if they control the universe? Ari was trying desperately to think clearly, to evaluate what was being said. With great effort he turned away from Elor's piercing stare. Immediately he became dizzy and had to reach out to support himself on the building beside him to keep his balance.

"Be patient." Elor's voice was persuasively hypnotic. "You will know the truth after you have met the One who is the reincarnation of the Christ Spirit for this Aquarian Age—the one who will rule the New World Order. He is our main contact with the CIA. You will go to his facility near Stanford University soon, to become his right-hand man. Afterward you will introduce him to Israel. But before that can be done, a great sign will occur that will cause Israel to embrace you as its new leader. You will be mourned as dead—but on the third day you will be resurrected."

Ari stared at Elor in bewilderment. The whole thing was preposterous. Yet there was such power in this man. No, he was much more than a man!

"I'm willing to do what's right," declared Ari. "But supposing, when I learn more, I don't like your plan? What if at that point I don't go along with it?"

"Moses said the same, did he not?" Elor's smile was confident and captivating. "Yet Yaweh—He is one of us—compelled him. The Bible has been perverted, so it no longer tells the true story. Like Moses, you have no choice in this matter. We have decided that you are the one—and you will soon desire to fulfill our will."

"So your New World Order is to be built upon coercion . . . ?" began Ari in protest, only to realize that Elor had vanished. He was standing in the middle of the narrow street talking to himself and drawing curious glances from passersby.

31

Miriam

As the weeks turned to months, Ari's strange street encounter, instead of fading into the past, seemed all the more vivid and troublesome. There was no way he could deny its reality, though he wasn't sure what that meant in relation to an "intelligence" that could take on different forms, do the impossible, and appear and disappear apparently at will. His undergraduate work in physics had, in a sense, prepared him for something so bizarre. In the world of subatomic particles the impossible happened all the time. But to see it in the mundane world of everyday experience was boggling.

It was also very disturbing. So much that Elor had said made good sense. There was no doubt that the new freedom in Eastern Europe wasn't the cure-all. Though bastions of freedom, Western democracies were seething cauldrons of racism and bigotry with increasing crime and mushrooming debt and monumental selfishness that left little hope of ever seeing the kind of compassionate caring for others that was so obviously needed. The transformation of the heart that Elor spoke of with such conviction was definitely needed, but he had declined to explain how that would come about.

Ari was most uncomfortable regarding the role that had supposedly been assigned to him. Yes, it did fit ideas which he had already formulated—that Israel had to give up its "chosen people" delusion and Zionist madness. That confirmation gave him a good feeling about Elor, but it hardly made up for the nagging apprehension. This business of "higher" consciousness, traveling to California to meet the man who would oversee this new world of love and brotherhood, and himself becoming some kind of "messiah" . . . all of that made him feel uneasy. In the meantime, life went on and he continued to enjoy his work and build a loyal following of admiring readers.

The enigmatic David Kauly dropped by frequently in the evening for the discussions with Yakov that both seemed so much to relish and into which Ari had increasingly been drawn despite his initial reluctance. No matter where their conversations started these days, they always came around to the same argument: whether Israel should ignore the wishes and assurances of the United States and make a preemptive strike on Iraq's scud missiles before Saddam used them against Jerusalem and Tel Aviv, which would certainly be his primary targets. David and Yakov were in full agreement that Israel would eventually have to act, but could not decide upon the timing.

"A preemptive strike would be a disaster for Israel's public image," argued Ari one evening. The three friends were seated comfortably in front of the picture window watching the lights go on one by one across the city as the dusk deepened. Ari had become increasingly dogmatic in arguing against a preemptive strike. He had just written a persuasive article presenting that viewpoint. It had brought more critical letters than the *Post* had received in years. "There is just no doubt," continued Ari, "that such unilateral action would split the allied coalition confronting Iraq, putting that effort in jeopardy. And for sure it would seem to justify the animosity of the Arab coalition partners against Israel. Saddam would become a hero again. You'd have rabid crowds demonstrating in every Arab city of any size!"

"You may be right about that," conceded David. "But the safety of our civilian population is the number one priority."

The three of them sat in thoughtful silence for a few moments. At last Ari asked, "How is it possible to live in Israel without becoming paranoid? That question has been bothering me lately."

"What do you mean?" demanded Yakov a bit testily. "Are you suggesting that it's paranoia to take steps to prevent Saddam from using his missiles in a chemical attack against Israel? He's repeatedly threatened to do exactly that!"

"In the Defense Department," cut in David, "we take the threat very seriously."

"I didn't mean that specifically," said Ari. "I'm talking in general terms. I've been here nearly eight months now, and I find myself developing more of a siege mentality every day. I sense the same attitude among people in the streets... like the whole world is against us."

"Maybe they are," responded Yakov solemnly.

"See, that's what I mean!" retorted Ari quickly. "It's a paranoia that goes with being here—and I don't want to be caught up in it."

"And you don't think there's sufficient justification to have a siege mentality when you're surrounded by enemies who are just waiting for the chance to destroy you? I thought you'd begun to see that months ago." There was disappointment in Yakov's voice.

"I'm not denying that there's *some* justification," conceded Ari, "but you can live with a chip on your shoulder and blame everyone else for the inevitable feeling of hostility. It's in the air here in Israel. Just let anyone dare to knock it off!"

"There's some truth in what he's saying," admitted David. "We've talked about that for years. We probably made some mistakes in what we did in Lebanon. Hair-trigger reactions are dangerous."

As time had passed, Ari had come to the conclusion that David wasn't a Mossad agent after all. He was convivial, urbane, well-informed and widely traveled, and just plain "normal" in an engaging way. He was also a fountainhead of extremely interesting information both about Israeli and Arab politics. That know-how had been a great help to Ari in understanding the Middle East better. Ari had even used some of David's ideas in his newspaper columns. David had, in fact, become a good friend.

Yakov ignored David's attempt to be agreeable. One had to beware of being too soft on new immigrants. "Have you ever been to Yad Vashem?" he asked Ari.

"Yad Vashem?"

"The Holocaust Museum."

"I've been avoiding it," confessed Ari.

"How can you write for *The Post* if you don't thoroughly understand the Holocaust? In fact, you can't!" Yakov sounded irate.

"You've commended me," responded Ari defensively. "I've gotten lots of letters from readers who like what I'm writing."

"Yes," said Yakov in a more conciliatory tone, "you've done a good job . . . up to a point. And I know you're gaining a following—but there's a missing dimension of deep conviction in some of what you write. You need to go to Yad Vashem!"

"I know, I know. I should . . . and I will," conceded Ari ungraciously. "But the Holocaust's been dealt with . . . again . . . and again. It's not healthy to be forever dredging up the past. Adds to the paranoia. I'm writing about current events."

"The world must *never* forget!" countered Yakov heatedly. "The victims died for nothing unless their memory can be kept alive. It's the only way to prevent another horror of the same dimensions. *Never again!* is our motto and determination. That's the message of Yad Vashem. You *must* see it—soon!"

A knock on the door punctuated the urgency in Yakov's voice. The old man jumped up with a cry of joy and hurried into the small entry hall. He seemed to recognize every visitor's individual knock. He opened the door to a smartly dressed woman in her late thirties with long, curly, jet-black hair and dark, twinkling eyes amazingly like Yakov's. Her face seemed to light up when she smiled. "Surprise!" she exclaimed.

"Miriam!" bellowed Yakov, as though he were announcing her arrival to all of Jerusalem. They fell into one another's arms, embracing with great fervor. Although she was several inches taller than he, Yakov's ardent hug lifted her off her feet.

"Come in, come in!" he cried, taking her by the arm and leading her into the living room. "This is my granddaughter, Miriam Zeira, from Tiberias," he announced proudly. "You know David, of course . . . and this is Ari Thalberg from Paris, a Holocaust survivor and my new housemate. Remember? I told you about him."

Miriam smiled and nodded a greeting, then reached out and shook hands with David and Ari.

"Am I interrupting some important meeting?" she asked apologetically, stepping back as though to leave. "I can come back later. . . ."

Yakov took her by the arm again and propelled her into an empty overstuffed chair next to his ancient rocker. "Don't you dare try to escape! When do I ever see you any more? You'd think Tiberias was on the other side of the world!"

"Now, Grandpa," she protested. "I get up here quite often."

"You do? Well, Ari's never met you, and he's been here eight months."

"I just spent six months in Europe on my sabbatical, remember?"

"Yes, and you've been back more than a month, and this is the first time you've gotten up here. Are you staying at Deborah's?"

Miriam nodded. "Yes. This is a long weekend for the school system." She turned to David and Ari, who were still standing and looking a bit awkward. "I must have interrupted an important discussion, if I know Grandpa...."

"Yes, we were having a go at it," said Yakov quickly, "and we're going to carry on. Sit down, you two." He turned to Ari. "Miriam teaches in a high school. She could give you some lessons about Israel's history that would be very helpful...."

"Now Grandpa, don't start bragging about me. I'm sure he knows a lot more about history than I do. I read his columns in *The Post* and he seems very knowledgeable...."

"Knowledgeable?" cut in Yakov. "He's abysmally ignorant about almost everything that's important in relation to Israel!"

Miriam turned to Ari with an apologetic smile. "By now you must be used to the dear man's scoldings. He does that with everyone. I feel sorry for you." The look of affection that passed between Miriam and Yakov belied her words.

"Let me bring you up to date, Miriam," continued Yakov. "We were discussing whether Israel ought to make a preemptive strike against Saddam's scuds. Ari thought we were paranoid even to suggest it... and when you knocked, he was just telling us that the Holocaust is ancient history that would be better forgotten."

Miriam was too well-bred to looked startled. That observation embarrassed Ari momentarily.

"I didn't exactly say *that*," protested Ari, feeling compelled to explain. "Your grandfather is twisting my words... which he does frequently. You probably know he's a master at that." To his surprise, he was suddenly concerned that this personable woman whom he had just met should not have a bad impression of him.

"I'm shocked that you'd make such an accusation!" interjected Yakov, pretending to be highly offended.

"I was just commenting," continued Ari, defending himself to all three, "that... well, I wouldn't dare express it journalistically, of course, but it seems to me that the Jews—at least a great many of them—have a persecution complex. I've developed one myself since moving here. I know there's a fresh wave of anti-Semitism sweeping the world. But I keep coming back to the question: Why should *Jews*, any more than any other minority group, feel so threatened? Does our paranoia help to bring at least some of our problems upon us?"

"Yes, why *Jews*?" returned Yakov bitterly. "We have to face that question. Are we so loathsome? Is that why we've been hated and hounded to the death down through history? That was the first thing we talked about, Ari. Remember?"

Ari nodded, regretting that he had raised the issue, sensing that he was going to get another religious lecture.

"You can't deny the universal animosity toward us," continued Yakov earnestly. "And I defy anyone to come up with any explanation for such hatred except the one presented in both the Torah and many other parts of the Bible, including the New Testament. We're hated because we're God's chosen people ...and we disobeyed Him, and this is His judgment upon us."

"Pretty harsh judgment!" muttered Ari. "Is that the only benefit of being 'chosen'...to be punished?"

"'To whom much is given, of him shall much be required,'" said Miriam softly. "That's what Jesus of Nazareth, the greatest of the rabbis, said."

Jesus of Nazareth? Ari immediately recoiled at the name. He glanced over at David and with satisfaction noted that he looked uncomfortable as well.

Yakov continued as though he and Miriam had rehearsed it all ahead of time. "Moses said that through Israel the Messiah would come and all the nations of the earth would be blessed. That's a heavy responsibility. And to fail to live up to it—and Israel has failed—must carry severe consequences."

"And I'm no more ready to accept that myth now than I was when we first met," countered Ari irritably. He looked over to David for support, but he just threw up his hands and shrugged.

"A journalist should respect the *truth*," replied Yakov quietly.

"You call it a *myth* that God chose Abraham, Isaac and Jacob and gave their descendants this land?" asked Miriam in genuine surprise. "We study Jewish history right out of the Scriptures. It's accepted in Israel's school system as accurate, or we wouldn't use it. In fact, it's the most accurate record we have."

"I'm not a total atheist," muttered Ari lamely.

"But he's close," countered Yakov quickly. "He's very touchy about the idea that a personal God might have some definite plans for mankind...and especially that we Jews could have a special role to play in that plan."

"Maybe I'm overly sensitive," admitted Ari, "but it upsets me to see anyone taken up with superstition in a scientific world."

"I'll drop the subject," promised Yakov, "because I know it makes you uncomfortable. But it's unfair to call what I believe superstition without proving that it is, which you can't. And I can prove it's not superstition, if you're inclined to listen some day. I'm simply stating the undeniable fact that the descendants of Abraham, Isaac and Jacob have always been persecuted and hounded to the death like no other people. That's history—and the present reality." Here Yakov turned to David. "You'd agree with that, wouldn't you?"

David nodded. "I'm with you that far. No ethnic group in the history of the world has been persecuted so consistently over as long a period of time as the Jewish people."

"Okay," said Yakov with an air of triumph. "In that respect, at least, we all agree. The evidence is irrefutable that the Jews are absolutely unique in the persecution they've received down through the centuries. The phenomenon is too consistent to be explained by chance, so there has to be a reason. And until you have a better explanation, I'll stick with mine."

"But the world has come a long way since Hitler. There couldn't be another Holocaust today!" insisted Ari.

"There *won't* be," cut in David, "but only because we won't allow it. *Never again!* We're now capable of defending ourselves. We couldn't in the '30s and early '40s. And we're not going to let the world forget the unthinkable evil that happened then. That's why Yad Vashem was created. Yakov's right—you need to see it."

"Okay, okay," responded Ari defensively. "I'll go—and report back on my impressions. How's that?"

"Just don't put it off," chimed in Yakov. "Get to it!"

Ari looked at Miriam in mock pain. "You can see how they batter me around. Who knows what consequences I'll suffer at their hands if I don't get to the Holocaust Museum immediately."

"Let me rescue you, then," offered Miriam. "Why don't I take you? Can you go tomorrow morning?"

"I don't want to put you to that trouble," demurred Ari, feeling embarrassed as their eyes met.

"No trouble at all," insisted Miriam. "It would be my pleasure. It's a huge place . . . more than just the main building. Most of the exhibits only have a title to identify them, with little or no explanation. You really need a guide . . . unless you'd rather be alone."

"No, I'd rather be with you than be alone . . . I mean, it's nice to have someone explain things. It would be very kind of you."

"Done," Miriam said with a gracious smile. "I'd consider it a privilege to take a Holocaust survivor through Yad Vashem. It will be a wonderful experience—for both of us. How about ten o'clock tomorrow morning?"

"I'll be ready," agreed Ari gratefully. It would be the first time he'd been alone with a woman since Nicole had walked out on him.

With a quick hug for Yakov and a promise to see him again before she returned to Tiberias, Miriam was gone.

Bar Mitzvah—At Last

The next morning found Miriam, with Ari beside her, expertly threading her small Fiat through the maze of streets in the Old City and out to the hilltop Holocaust Museum not far from the Knesset. As they drove, he learned that she was a widow, having lost her husband of six weeks in the 1973 Yom Kippur War. They'd had no children, and she had never remarried. Sitting next to her he felt a sense of easy and pleasant camaraderie between them, as though he'd known and respected this admirable woman all his life. And he sensed that she felt the same way about him.

"It's going to be horrifying," Miriam warned Ari as they left the car in the parking lot and walked toward the sprawling complex, "so just be prepared. It's beyond anything you could imagine. I never cried so much... I mean, really wept... as the first time I went through."

"Really?" he asked, not knowing how else to respond.

"Of course, I lost a lot of relatives, some of whom I had known... and then, well, you're a man... and that makes a difference."

"It's not sensationalized, I hope."

"Not at all. I think you'll agree, when you see it, that the terror and repugnance of the Nazi Holocaust are presented solemnly, and without vengeful rhetoric or the least bit of sensationalism."

Ari was skeptical. Of course Miriam couldn't be objective. She was born and raised here in Israel. Entering the grounds, he could see in the faces of many who were already leaving the museum that they had been traumatized by the enormity of the evil documented within those halls. It had to be sensationalized. He would tell her gently... point it out as they went along.

"We'll go to the Children's Monument first," said Miriam, taking Ari by the hand and leading him in that direction. It seemed such a natural thing to share in this way, as only a son and daughter of Judah could, the horror they were about to witness.

"It was erected in memory of the 1.5 million children who died in the Holocaust," said Miriam in a voice tender with emotion as they approached the entrance.

Ari's attention was first arrested by some photos and names of only a very few of the young victims. Then, in bold print, were emblazoned the words from the Proverbs of Israel's King Solomon: "God's candle is the spirit of man searching the inward parts of the belly."

"What does *that* mean?" Ari asked Miriam as they paused before entering.

"I can't explain it. You'll see," was all she would say.

"And *God*—why mention *him* here?" persisted Ari. "If he exists and these were his 'chosen people,' how could this have happened to them? Surely the Holocaust ought to be all the proof anyone needs that no god who cares about mankind exists—and Yad Vashem should be considered a memorial to that fact!"

"There is much I don't understand, but I know that God loves me," came the quiet response. "And He loves you, too." She gave his hand a squeeze and pulled him gently forward.

Stepping inside the darkened building, Ari was glad to have a hand holding his. He stayed close beside Miriam as she led the way through a labyrinth of pitch blackness that was illuminated only by the flame of a single candle. That tiny pinpoint of light, reflected in unseen mirrors, seemed to occupy a thousand places at once, floating eerily close at hand and fading off into the unmeasurable distance. Ari became aware of a voice echoing softly around him, moaning out in measured cadence the names and ages of the young Holocaust victims. Each had been someone's beloved child whose once happy young life, filled with hope and promise, had been stamped into oblivion by heartless monsters—monsters who represented the most scientifically advanced and cultured nation on earth at that time.

As the voice moaned relentlessly on, Ari felt the impact of each name like a sledgehammer blow to his soul. Innocent, tender, trusting... betrayed, each had been a unique child. One-and-a-half million of them! What terror those young minds had endured, what torment and agony. What joys they had missed. And what inventions, and cures for disease, what art, and unimaginable potential of every kind the world itself had lost in the snuffing out of those young lives!

Staggering out into the blazing sunlight again, Ari's voice broke. "I could have been a name spoken here," he whispered.

Miriam put an arm around him. "By God's grace you were spared." The words came softly, confidently, matter-of-factly.

Why wasn't he angry? He should be. Was it, after all, God's grace that let millions of others be tortured and die?

Miriam's words anticipated his unspoken complaint. "None of us deserves to live. God must have had something special for you to do."

Elor claims that the Nine rescued me—that they have something special planned for me. How do I know what's true? Is life itself a dream... a nightmare? Do we ever awaken?

Taking Ari's hand, Miriam pulled him along again. "This grove of trees that you see winding its way through the entire grounds," she said, waving her free arm, "is of special importance. Each one was planted in memory of one of 'The Righteous,' someone who saved Jewish lives. Some of the stories are beyond belief—yet they are true. They would make you weep!" She stopped next to one of the trees. "We can't look at them all, but this one is very special."

Ari looked down at a name identifying the one in whose memory the tree had been planted. It was Raoul Wallenberg.

"I'm sure you know the story better than I. Refresh my memory," he asked reverently.

"I teach the amazing story in school," replied Miriam. "All Israeli children know Wallenberg! He was a young man from a prominent Swedish family—brilliant, talented, handsome, with a full life ahead of him. He used his position as a diplomat in Budapest to issue false documents and rescue nearly 50,000 Jews from the extermination camps. When the Russians 'liberated' Hungary in January, 1945, Wallenberg was arrested and two days later he was reported dead. In fact he had been taken to a Soviet labor camp where he spent some 20 years. Two months after his death the Soviets admitted that they had held him all that time. It's so tragic...."

"His crime?" asked Ari rhetorically, knowing the answer.

"You can imagine," replied Miriam. "The communists couldn't afford any heroes on the wrong side."

"It's ironic...Stalin's labor camps killed far more than Hitler's ovens," declared Ari numbly. "In both cases the world stood by and did nothing. Communism grew, became the darling of Western liberals, was praised by university professors and students around the world even though it went on to slaughter at least another 50 million after taking over China and Southeast Asia. It's repugnant—beyond belief!"

Ari turned to Miriam with an inner rage that could not be suppressed. Rage against the perpetrators of such unmitigated infamy and against those who never raised a voice or a hand to stop it. "Really, where is justice in the world? Is there any hope?" It was a question he had asked himself repeatedly—and in vain.

"Not in this world," Miriam replied simply. He knew what she meant without further explanation. Was she a believer not only in God but in Jesus, too, like Nicole? She reminded him of Nicole. She exuded that same peaceful assurance that he had sensed in Niki after her conversion.

The two paused next in front of a weathered bronze monument alive with small faces that reflected pathos, terror, anguish. "It's dedicated to the memory of Janusz Korszak, the principal of a Jewish orphanage in Poland," explained Miriam. "He was given the chance to save his own life, but he chose to stay with his children. For that he was sent to Auschwitz, where he died. Here he is, immortalized in bronze, embracing his beloved orphans."

Together they wandered on to pause transfixed before the "Silent Cry," the blackened bronze figure of a man weeping for a grief so great that it could not be voiced. Startled, Ari felt a warm trickle spill over and course down his cheeks.

Miriam was weeping softly as well. Tenderly Ari put an arm around her. How long they stood there in shared grief he did not know.

The immensity of evil this place represented was far more than the mind and emotions could endure. Most repugnant was the fact that the Holocaust had been carried out methodically as official government policy and with the full power of state bureaucracy, ideology and technology. Ari felt overwhelmed by despair for the future of mankind. The perfectibility of man was a sham, a mockery. If there was any hope, he found it in the fact that for every Nazi murderer there was someone who had risked his or her life to rescue the innocent victims of the most heinous crime in history.

Inside the huge memorial housing the eternal flame Ari stood with head bowed, reading on the floor in front of him in large letters the names of the infamous Nazi extermination camps and killing fields: Belzce, Lwow, Janowska, Drancy, Bergen-Belsen, Treblinka, Buchenwald, Babi-yar.... At the latter place, in one huge ditch, 150,000 Kiev Jews had been shot and buried where they fell.

In the main museum, which Miriam had visited many times, she waited patiently at his side while Ari carefully read every document and description. He found the sights and sounds and the painstakingly detailed horror almost beyond belief. The exhibits documented the progressive steps the Nazis had taken in their attempt to effect a "final solution to the Jewish problem."

First came the economic boycotts against the Jewish populace. Then followed the "Aryanization" of Germany, which stripped Jews of property, jobs and social status. How efficiently and meticulously the Germans had dehumanized the hated race. Technology, psychology, brilliantly and diabolically conceived pogroms had all combined to perfect the holocaust juggernaut.

Ari had encountered people in Europe who insisted that the Holocaust had never occurred—and there had been the time when he had half believed that evil theory because he had wanted to believe it. Here in Jerusalem, however, there was no denying the truth. One of the most stirring exhibits contained 129 pictures taken by one Heinz Jost, a German soldier, on September 19, 1941. In stark black and white detail the photos documented the horrible reality of starvation and death in a Jewish ghetto. Corpses were lying in the streets where they had dropped and would remain until they were piled on carts and hauled away for mass burials. The helpless, hopeless expressions on the children's faces told the story more poignantly than words.

The pathos of that silently endured terror and death, when the world closed its eyes, seemed to wring from Ari the last remaining emotion of which he was capable. These were Jews, *his* people. To his surprise he had found himself making that identification at last.

A fierce pride stirred within as Ari read the description of the terrible slaughter of Jewish men, women and children at Dubno in October, 1942. The account was written by Hermann Freidrich Graebe, who had witnessed the occurrence from beginning to end. Graebe reported that as they were faced with death not one cried out in fear, not one pleaded for mercy. Silently they embraced and kissed each other, said goodbye, then stood mutely awaiting their fate. Reading Graebe's account made Ari proud to be Jewish. Surely his parents had endured their fate with the same unbending spirit. These were *his* people! The same blood flowed in his veins!

And with that long overdue admission of his true racial identity came a renewed indignation that the world had not only stood by and done nothing, but that Britain, theUnited States, even neutral Switzerland refused to give refuge to many Jews who had escaped, and turned them back to Nazi ovens! Help for the Jews came only as a by-product of the Allies' protection of their own interests and in retaliation against Hitler for his aggression. Nazi doctors performed inhuman experiments of which the West was well aware. The unashamedly obscene speeches of Nazi leaders telling what they were doing were no secret. He stood transfixed as he read the blatant, murderous intent expressed by Heinrich Himmler in a Party speech at Posen, October 4, 1943:

> The Jewish race is in the process of being exterminated. Well, that's all right, that is our programme—extermination of the Jews—and we are doing it, we are exterminating them.... this thing is a splendid page in our history which we will never write and which shall never be written.

Yad Vashem had written that terrifying history large for the world to see at last. Would the message be heeded? Having labored for years to effect an idealistic renewal of civilization, Ari now felt a helpless pessimism for its future.

Near the end of the exhibits, Miriam pointed out an account of the dark role of Haj Amin el-Husseini, Grand Mufti of Jerusalem. "I especially wanted you to see this," she whispered. "He was Yasser Arafat's uncle—and the PLO still embodies his destructive passion."

"Your grandfather mentioned him," Ari responded quietly and turned his attention to the exhibit under the glass. There he read Haj Amin's May 15, 1943 letter to German Foreign Minister von Ribbentrop, requesting German intervention in the Balkans (especially in Bulgaria) in order to prevent the Jews from leaving for Eretz-Israel. The mufti assured Ribbentrop that the Arabs supported the Axis Powers in their "final solution" to the problem of the Jews, the common enemy of the peoples of Europe and the Arab nations.

In the same display was a copy of a cable from Himmler to the Grand Mufti on the anniversary of the Balfour Declaration, November 2, 1943: "The National Socialist Party has inscribed on its flag 'the extermination of world Jewry.' Our party sympathizes with the fight of the Arabs, especially the Arabs of Palestine, against the foreign Jew. Today, on this memorial day of the Balfour

Declaration, I send my greetings and wishes for success in your fight." (signed) "Leader of the S.S."

Haj Amin, an admirer of Hitler, especially for his Jewish policy, had managed to flee to Germany. On March 1, 1944, over Radio Berlin, the mufti issued his inflammatory call: "Arabs, rise as one man and fight for your sacred rights. Kill the Jews wherever you find them. This pleases God and religion. This saves your honour. God is with you." There it was, the horrifying reality, all documented under glass.

After reading those appalling words, Ari pulled Miriam close to him and whispered, "I'm almost persuaded that your grandfather's right. Such unbelievable hatred has no ordinary explanation."

Miriam nodded. "We're God's chosen people... and we rebelled against Him... and He isn't going to let us go!"

"All I know," replied Ari, "is that nothing has changed. The same murderous obscenities calling for the destruction of Israel still blast forth from loudspeakers in mosques and radios in the streets and Arab houses—and the world is just as deaf and blind to those threats as it was to Hitler's."

Silently Miriam clung to Ari. Barely audibly she heard the words, "*Never again! Never again!*" Softly she repeated the same heartbreaking refrain.

As the two stood transfixed by what they had just read, an elderly orthodox Jew with long beard and flowing black coat came up and stood beside them. He began quietly reading aloud in a solemn voice Haj Amin's radio message. Then Ari noticed that a young boy and girl of about 10 and 12, apparently his grandchildren, were standing just behind him and listening in wide-eyed horror.

When the old gentleman had finished reading, he half-turned to Ari and Miriam as though to include them as he told the children: "That man's nephew, Yasser Arafat, heads the PLO. Its charter today still calls for the destruction of Israel. Nothing has changed since Hitler announced his intentions to the world—and no one pays any more attention now than they did then. One day Israel will have to fight the whole world!"

Is that paranoia or realism? Ari pondered the question as he and Miriam stood silently watching the old gentleman and his two grandchildren move slowly on.

"I don't know whether he came to that conclusion from his own convictions, or from the Bible," whispered Miriam. "But he's right. Hebrew prophets in the Old Testament warn that in 'the last days' all the nations of the world will attack Israel hoping to destroy her... and the Messiah will intervene and save His people."

"And you believe this?"

She nodded. "Of course. It's true, Ari. It's true."

On any other occasion Ari would have made a derisive comment. But not here at Yad Vashem. The horror was so overwhelming and the forces still arrayed against the Jewish people so powerful and their relationship to what happened under Hitler so undeniable... that only a Messiah could save them from total annihilation.

And I thought it was paranoia! mused Ari as they left the museum and walked silently and slowly, hand-in-hand, back to Miriam's car. *If it's paranoia, then I'm becoming crazy, too. Never again!*

Words seemed almost sacrilegious on the short drive back to the old city. What could one say after such an experience?

"Sensationalism?" Miriam asked at last.

"Please forgive me," was the quiet response.

Vehicular traffic could only come within two blocks of Yakov's apartment, and there was no place to park in the busy, narrow street. Miriam stopped to let Ari out. "Why not park somewhere so you can come in for a few moments?" he suggested hopefully.

She shook her head. "I've hardly been with my cousin. I must spend some time with her." She was avoiding his eyes now.

Reluctantly Ari climbed out and closed the door. Leaning in through the window he asked anxiously, "When will I see you again?"

She turned toward him and smiled. "When would you like to?"

Their eyes met. "As soon as possible," he said as he returned her smile.

"Well, Grandpa has my address...."

"I've never been to Tiberias," he stammered, "and I have no car."

She laughed. "There's a bus. Something you really want is worth the effort, isn't it?"

A chorus of horns was sounding. Miriam reached out and touched Ari's arm. "I've got a car. How about next weekend?"

"Friday night?"

"Friday night. It'll be eight before I can get here. I'll come to Grandpa's apartment and we'll go out for dinner. Okay?"

"You shouldn't have to drive all the way up here...." A taxi driver had jumped out and was running toward them, cursing loudly and flailing his arms as he ran.

"I've got relatives in Jerusalem that I ought to visit," replied Miriam, raising her voice above the bedlam. "And you heard my grandfather scold me for not coming often enough."

"I'm with him on that!" yelled Ari as she drove away. He stood there looking longingly after her car until it disappeared, aware that her departure had left an aching emptiness in his soul.

— ✦ —

Yakov took one look at Ari when he arrived at the apartment a few minutes later and knew that a profound change had come over him. "Now you know," he said simply, "like the rest of us."

"Yes... yes, now I know," responded Ari somberly. "It's maddening. That the world could let this happen! Doesn't speak too well of evolving man," he added with a bitter irony.

"And the world has not gotten better," remarked Yakov sadly. "Israel can't count on any friends to rescue her—not even the United States. She has to be strong, ready to defend herself."

"I think I'm paranoid, too," added Ari. "*Never again!*"

"Spoken like a true Israeli!" exclaimed Yakov, lighting up with that contagious smile and patting Ari affectionately on the shoulder.

Today I feel like I've had my Bar Mitzvah at last!" declared Ari enthusiastically. "I'm proud to be a Jew," he added almost fiercely.

Yakov reached out to shake Ari's hand, but felt himself enclosed in a bear hug instead.

33

Abducted!

The aerial bombardment of Iraq began on January 15, 1991. Ari wasn't surprised at the uncompromising stand taken by the U.S. President and his coalition partners in their pursuit of Kuwait's liberation. He was surprised, however, at the overwhelming superiority of American technology, resulting in such astonishingly few allied losses. The allegedly invincible Republican Guard was pinned down and pulvarized. Allied air power was making certain that the ground war, once it began, would produce a swift and stunning victory.

Based upon inside information from *The Post's* Mossad connection, Ari had predicted in his column that Israel would not retaliate after Iraq's primitive scud missiles began dropping hit-or-miss on Israeli civilians. The Butcher of Bagdad had invited Israel to dance, but she didn't like the tune. Her leaders were too clever to play into Saddam's hands. This was exactly the position Ari had taken months before, and for which he had been soundly taken to task by a number of readers, including members of the Knesset. Now he had been vindicated.

Iraq's cold-blooded leader had threatened to "burn Israel with chemicals." Thus, every scud attack carried the potential of unleashing poison gas or biological warfare against defenseless civilians. It was a time of great trial for that beleaguered nation, especially since its vaunted military, which had always been swift to take revenge in the past, was not allowed to retaliate. Such inaction created a national sense of helplessness. Ari learned firsthand a further lesson in what it meant to live under the constant threat of a war of extermination against the tiny nation that had finally become his own.

Miriam was now coming up from Tiberias each weekend. She and Ari spent every possible moment together. It seemed rather obvious to Yakov and other relatives in Jerusalem, who saw little of Miriam on these regular visits, that something serious was brewing between those two. As for Ari and Miriam, neither of them was willing to think of their relationship as a "romance." Not yet.

"We happen to have lots of common interests," Ari told Yakov, "and we find each other intellectually stimulating."

"No more than that," nodded the old man vigorously, pretending to be convinced.

"Right. We just enjoy one another's company."

Yakov smiled. "So much that you can't get enough of it in a weekend? What's going to happen when school lets out for vacation!"

On weekdays, Ari began to walk each evening through that part of the Arab quarter where he had encountered Elor a few weeks previously. He would even buy a cup of orange juice from the same street vendor and stand nearby, drinking it slowly, warily, in the hope that this amazing person or entity or whatever he was might make another appearance. It would be most interesting to get Elor's views on the Gulf crisis—perhaps a fresh insight that he could even put in his column without, of course, divulging the source.

Then one evening, about three weeks into the air war, it happened—but not in the way Ari had anticipated. He had just enjoyed the fresh-squeezed orange juice to the last drop, thrown the empty cup into a trash barrel and resumed his stroll along the narrow street when a man in a business suit came up and began walking alongside him. Turning in excitement, fully expecting to see Elor, Ari noted to his dismay that the man matching his stride was an Arab and wearing a *kafiyeh* and an obviously unfriendly expression. In that instant, he became aware that a second Arab had simultaneously come up close behind him.

"Keep walking straight ahead," said the man beside him in a low, menacing voice. "My friend has a gun pointed at your heart."

Ari obeyed, but slowed his pace to kill time, hoping for an Israeli patrol to appear. He had gone only a few paces, however, when the man behind him hissed, "To your left, quickly, into this shop."

The door to the small souvenir shop, which had been closed, swung open at that moment. *Better to resist out here in the street than inside.* Ari turned his head slightly to see where to send his lethal feet, but the man with the gun behind him had cleverly pulled back out of kicking range. *They're pros... know exactly what they're doing!*

Reluctantly Ari obeyed and entered. No sooner had he stepped inside and his two abductors behind him, than the door was shut instantly and locked.

"Keep going. Straight ahead." It was the first man who was giving the orders.

In the semidarkness of the dimly lit interior, Ari became aware that several other Arabs had been waiting inside. They fell in with Ari and his captors as they moved between two rows of merchandise toward the back of the long, narrow store. Through another door they entered a low-ceilinged room where Ari was ordered to sit on a lone wooden stool in the center of the room, while his captors gathered around him. He was blindfolded and, with a jerk, his hands were secured tightly behind his back with some kind of hard plastic that cut painfully into his wrists.

I lost my only chance... no way now. Who are these guys? What do they want?

"We read your newspaper column." The words were spoken with evident sarcasm by someone standing directly in front of him. Again it was the voice of the Arab who had first accosted him in the street and who seemed to be in charge.

"I'm glad you do," said Ari. "I work hard writing it, so it's nice to know that I have some readers."

A smashing blow to the head from behind rendered Ari senseless for a moment. He would have fallen from the stool had not strong hands supported him. "We do the talking here," growled the voice in front of him. "You answer only when you're told to, understand?"

There was an ominous silence. Then the same voice continued. "We don't like what you write. It's Israeli propaganda. Prejudiced. No sympathy for Arabs... especially Palestinians."

"I try to be objective," insisted Ari.

Another blow, this time from the front, left his head spinning and his ears ringing and the taste of warm blood in his mouth.

"Let's finish him right now and be done with it," said someone to his right. "Why waste time with this scum?"

A low murmur of heated conversation ensued. Even with his limited knowledge of Arabic, it became apparent to Ari that more than one of his captors were urging his immediate execution.

"Calm down, brothers," ordered the man in front, switching back to Hebrew. "When we get through with him, he's going to be a big help. He's going to write for us—give his readers a new perspective on the Palestinian problem."

"You think the paper will print my column if it becomes a mouthpiece for the PLO?" demanded Ari.

"You're intelligent... educated... clever," came the quick response. "You can make it subtle at first, okay? A little here... a little there... nothing too obvious."

"As a journalist, I write what I think is true," interrupted Ari defiantly.

"Shut up! You'll write what we tell you to. You've got no choice. You're on the PLO's death list—and there's only one way to get out of here alive. We have guaranteed ways to persuade you. Better do it the easy way. It's not so messy. Agreed?"

"Suppose I say 'okay.' You let me go—but I don't write what you want. What then?"

"The whole Israeli army can't protect you. We'll get you, and when we do you'll wish you'd never been born!"

So this was what it was like to face death. Niki... and now it was his turn. At least hers had been instant. These monsters knew how to extract the last agony from their victims. And Miriam... just when they.... Never mind. He'd go standing for his principles. He wished he'd done a better job of that in the past. But now... at least now....

With great effort Ari pulled himself upright on the stool. "Go ahead," he said. "Kill me. I won't be your mouthpiece!"

"Oh, we wouldn't kill you." The voice was a smooth as oil. "That would be too easy. We have other methods."

Ari clamped his mouth shut. He would not say another word. There was no point in it. That was part of their game, to get him into some bargaining discussion and bit by bit bend his will. Never!

"You have a son in Paris. Ari Paul. He'll soon be a year old...."

Ari sank down in despair. *My God, they mean it! If I had my hands free for one minute, I'd take some of them with me!*

"We could have him here tomorrow. We have a little game we play. You watch and we torture. We have a soundproof room—babies scream a lot. What do you say?"

A long, terrifying silence followed. Ari thought carefully. There was only one way to save his son. He would get these men so enraged that they would kill him right now...then his son would no longer fulfill any purpose for them.

"I'll tell you what I say." Ari steeled himself. His hands were tied, but he had two free feet. "You know what I think of monsters who would torture a baby?" He jumped up from the stool and his knee went instantly into the groin of the man in front of him. Swiftly he lashed out with his other foot where he thought someone had been standing just behind him, but found only empty air. A blow from the side knocked him to the floor.

A tremendous crash and a chorus of shouts seemed for the briefest of seconds to be ushering Ari into some otherworldly hall of fame. It wasn't his own heroics, however, as he immediately realized, that were precipitating this commotion. Stampeding boots, yelled commands, oaths, a brief scuffle and it was all over. Four strong hands lifted him to his feet and pulled the blindfold from his eyes.

Ari looked around in astonishment. To his great relief, he saw a dozen Israelis in plain clothes with Uzis and now clearly in charge. The Arabs were on the floor with guns at their heads being handcuffed, a look of stunned disbelief frozen on their faces.

"You're a lucky man, Thalberg." The speaker was tucking a .22 caliber Beretta, the preferred weapon of Israel's Mossad, as Ari mentally noted, into his belt under his jacket.

"How...how did you find me?" gasped Ari. His head was aching and he felt on the verge of losing consciousness.

"We've been watching this place for weeks. It's a PLO safe house. Had it bugged. Just happened to be listening when they brought you in—or you would have been a dead man. You couldn't take them all on blindfolded and hands tied."

"I'd rather die than make a deal like that."

"They would have tortured you first. You're a tough customer...but they would have had you screaming."

"I wanted them to kill me—then my son wouldn't have been of any use to them."

Already the commander was on his hand-held radio. "We've got six of them. Thalberg's okay, but he's hurt. I want an ambulance outside the Damascus Gate immediately. Out."

The commander was clearly in a great hurry. "Okay, let's get these guys out of here—the back way. Schwartz and Lemke . . . pick two other men and stay behind. The next shift will come in the back door at 4:00 A.M. They'll open the shop in the morning. I want everybody arrested who comes into this place—customers, anybody—no exceptions for any reason."

A man on each side supported Ari as they hurried to follow the commander of the unit out the back way. Following a narrow passageway between buildings, they arrived at the next street. Six unmarked cars were waiting.

"Not a word about this to anyone," cautioned the commander as he helped Ari into the back seat of one of the cars and climbed in beside him. "It never happened. Okay? We're still working on the case. This isn't everybody, and we don't want any leaks."

"Okay," said Ari. "But I'd sure like to thank you publicly. You guys deserve it. I owe you my life."

"We're not in this for thanks, just survival."

The Mossad

So it was possible to be abducted by PLO terrorists right in the heart of Jerusalem! That alarming experience served as a solemn warning to Ari. Indeed, he had been *very* lucky. So—he was on the PLO hit list because of what he wrote in his column in *The Post*! No doubt he'd now been moved up a little higher in targeting priority. That was not a comforting thought. How he wished for his old faithful Luger, left behind in France. Any pistol would do, but there was no way the Israeli government would license him to carry a concealed weapon.

What he really needed was a bodyguard. Certainly the Mossad agents who rescued him must know that. However, the Mossad hadn't offered him any protection. He could hardly ask for it, because the surveillance of the PLO group that had abducted him was a top secret operation, under total wraps. So it couldn't be mentioned to the police or even to other Mossad units. He wanted to discuss the need for protection with Yakov and David, but without knowing about his abduction, they'd think he was paranoid for sure, an accusation he had so recently made against others.

Ari decided to avoid the Arab quarter, at least when he was alone. And he determined to put into practice certain defensive strategies for his own personal safety. During the years he'd headed the underground student movement Ari had read everything in print on the CIA, KGB, Mossad and other intelligence agencies. He had memorized their tactics, knew all of the most effective surveillance techniques—and know how to keep from being followed. As often as it had suited his purpose, he'd given Roger's group fits by dodging the tails they put on him. That experience would now prove invaluable.

The first day he began his new *modus operandi*, he discovered that he was being followed! Moreover, whoever was on his trail was using highly sophisticated methods. It had taken every tactic he knew and even then he had almost failed to detect them. He ruled out the PLO. Intuitively he felt it just wasn't their style. Nor was it the Mossad, because they had learned of his abduction only through a bug they had planted in the souvenir shop. Had they been the ones tailing him, he would have been rescued even sooner. It had to be Roger's group. Who else could it be? And why would they have him under surveillance? It didn't bode well, no matter who was doing it.

During the next week Ari carefully learned all he could about his shadows in an attempt to identify the organization that was following him. They picked him up first thing each morning, and were there every afternoon when he left his office to catch the bus home, watched him get off the bus and made certain that he went to the apartment. Only someone who was a top expert—and Ari considered himself to be that—could have detected the operation.

When he went out for his evening stroll they picked him up again. He was under 24-hour surveillance! Obviously the house and phones must be bugged as well. So what? He had nothing to hide. But he was determined to find out who was doing all this, and why.

It took him nearly two weeks to learn the details of the operation. Annoying—and potentially dangerous—as it all was, he couldn't help admiring the teamwork involved. These guys were the best. It was all directed from a vehicle whose make and color were changed every day. When it was a van, Ari was especially wary. Vans were the vehicle of choice for abductions. There were three men on foot. In that way they didn't have to follow so closely, but could anticipate his route and pick him up at strategic points. All those involved seemed to be Israelis, which puzzled him, since he had eliminated the Mossad as a possibility.

Why was such a sizeable and expensive operation devoted to him? Ari pondered that question for days without finding an answer. Surely they weren't after information about him. There was nothing to learn. He did the same thing every day, week after week. It had to be Roger's group. They were probably "protecting" him to make certain that he stayed alive... unless they had some more sinister motive.

After learning the surveillance procedures and making certain that he did so without being detected, Ari decided one evening to turn the tables on his shadows. He suddenly veered from his usual route and headed up a very narrow, steep street that was impassible for vehicular traffic. The command car would have to drive several blocks out of the way and hope to pick him up where the small lane bisected a larger avenue.

As soon as he entered the narrow street, Ari turned casually into a variety shop, taking considerable time to browse. Other shops followed at the same leisurely pace. Having set that pattern, he went into a shop on his left near the end of the street. He'd first met the owner a few months ago and they had become friends. The man had once lived briefly in the south of France and Ari had offered to coach him in French, dropping in now and then to do so.

The shop was long and narrow and full of nooks and crannies that could not be seen from outside. Ari knew that his tails were keeping a safe distance and wouldn't enter the shop unless they became concerned at the length of time he was taking. By then it would be too late.

"I need to ask a favor... trying to avoid this woman," Ari said apologetically to the owner in French. "Give me a sales pitch on something out near the front of the store. I'll pretend to be interested, but it won't be exactly what I want. You'll lead me to the back of the store to show me something else. Don't ask me the details right now—I'll explain later—but I must get out your back door and over to the next street."

"D'accord," said the proprietor with a wink. Then he began talking in a loud voice, motioning to Ari to follow him toward the front of the store. There he went through the requested routine. Ari haggled, and finally the owner loudly declared that he had some other selections of the same item in the rear of the store. Once in the back and out of sight from the street, Ari slipped out the door while the proprietor kept up a running and enthusiastic dialogue with his now vanished customer.

Once outside, Ari went through a gate in the rear courtyard, then ran along the top of a stone wall until he could squeeze down between two buildings and out onto the next street. Hurrying to his right, he reached the next corner quickly and peered around it cautiously. Just as he had thought, there was the command car pointed away from him and in the direction of his presumed route, where they expected him to emerge from the street he'd been on. Sprinting up behind the car on the blind right side that had no mirror, Ari quickly opened the rear door and looked in. His jaw dropped. Totally speechless, Ari stared at the two men sitting in the back seat.

"You're a clever devil!" exclaimed David in embarrassment. "How did you manage this?"

"I don't owe you any explanations," replied Ari angrily. "You owe me some. Why am I being followed?"

"Get in," said David, motioning to Ari and sliding over into the middle of the seat. "We'll go somewhere to talk."

"Why not your office in the Mossad building?" asked Ari, climbing in beside him.

"When did you figure that out?" asked David with genuine admiration in his voice.

Ari ignored his question and addressed the man sitting next to David. He had been the commander of his "Arab abductors" and the one who had so viciously interrogated Ari in the back room of that souvenir shop.

"You son of a . . . !" Ari had leaned over to look the man in the eye. "What did you think you were doing? I had a headache for a week!"

The man nodded toward David. "It was his operation," he said quietly, looking guilty and repentant.

Ari fixed David with a cold stare. "I don't enjoy having guns jammed in my back, being tied up and knocked around just for fun. What was that—a training exercise for Mossad recruits?"

"We've lost him!" crackled the radio. It was a transmission from the team that had been following Ari. "He went in this shop and must have gone out the back door. . . ."

The driver picked up the mike to reply. "Let me have it!" said David quickly, taking it from him. "You say you lost him?" he shouted in agitation. "Then *find* him! Move!" He winked at Ari, but the angry expression on Ari's face didn't soften in the slightest.

"Well?" said Ari, looking right through David, "let's hear it. And you'd better make it good. Your friend can tell you that the pen is mightier than the sword. He reads my column."

David laughed. "You've sure got more than your share of *chutzpah*. Look, Ari, I apologize, but there wasn't any other way. We needed to recruit you—so obviously we had to be sure you were clean. We also had to make certain that you had the wits and the guts to carry out the assignment . . . even though our files said you did."

"I hope you're convinced. How'd you like to have me put you through that torment!"

"Look, Ari, we need you . . . and we didn't have any choice. We had to be sure."

"You must have come to your conclusions long ago. Why am I still being followed?"

"Actually, we were going to discontinue the surveillance—but we realized you knew all the tricks . . . so we've used you to train some of our newer men and to improve our techniques."

"Thanks a lot. You guys put me through hell . . . wondering who was after me and why. I should have been on salary for the Mossad! I can tell you every car and van you used, describe every man. Did you know I was watching your team?"

"We suspected you were, but we only caught you at it two or three times. That's why it was such an invaluable training exercise. By the way, I'm not usually with the team, so you just happened to catch me today."

"So what's this about recruiting me?"

"You've got some information we need."

"What are you talking about?"

"We need data on the group that financed your student movement."

"I thought you were part of that East–West Consortium."

"Why would you think that?"

"Everybody else is. You know it's a joint U.S.–Soviet operation. The U.S. supports Israel. Even the Soviets now have diplomatic ties with Israel . . . no more Cold War."

"That's what everyone's supposed to think. But who's really going to risk relations with 200 million Arabs . . . with their oil . . . and a billion Muslims . . . . for 5 million Israelis?"

"Pretty heavy odds," conceded Ari.

"So that's why we need your information."

"Surely the Mossad has done a better job of penetrating their organization than I did. You must have plenty. . . ."

"If you don't know anything that we haven't already discovered, then we don't need it . . . but there's only one way to find that out."

Ari shook his head. "Sorry. No deal."

"You're turning us down?"

"Not for lack of loyalty to Israel. I think you know that by now."

"Then what's the problem?"

"I've placed the full exposé with several trustworthy people... for release if somebody does me in. That's my life insurance. If I give it to you... then those gangsters wouldn't have any reason for keeping me alive, would they."

"They wouldn't know that we know."

Ari thought about that for a moment, then shook his head again. "I know how the Western intelligence community operates. Information is continually exchanged... or leaked. I can't take that chance."

"Okay," said David. "I understand. We won't press you."

"It wouldn't do any good," responded Ari firmly. "But you still didn't answer my question. You said something about *recruiting*—that involves more than just giving you old information."

"We've got a job for you. It's dangerous—but you're the ideal person to do it."

"So?"

"Look, I'm stuck with this team. I'm going to really chew them out for losing you. I'll come by the apartment tomorrow evening about eight o'clock and we'll go into it in detail."

"Okay. What about Yakov?"

"No problem. He's worked with us for years."

"I suspected that." Ari shook David's hand, then leaned over and shook the hand of his companion. "No hard feelings," Ari assured him. "I just wish your men hadn't been quite so conscientious."

"Sorry... we had to make it realistic."

Ari reached over to open the door to get out. David grabbed him. "Get back in here! One of my men might see you."

To the driver he said, "Heim, take us to Ari's apartment—fast. We'll let him out over there and then come right back."

35

Recruited

David showed up promptly at eight o'clock and joined Ari in the living room, sitting next to him in front of the picture window. He wasted no time getting down to business. "There are some bizarre aspects to what I'm going to tell you," he began, leaning forward and punctuating the tension in his voice by stroking the knuckles of his strong, restless fingers. The lights had just gone on, illuminating the Dome of the Rock and the Western Wall, but the magnificent view was lost on these two.

Yakov could be heard rinsing dishes at the sink in the kitchen. "Come on in here!" yelled David, a slight edge of irritation in his voice. "Stop pretending you're so busy. You'll be giving advice soon enough—so you might as well get in on the beginning."

"I'm not *pretending*. I *am* busy. But I'll join you since you insist." Grinning widely, Yakov came into the living room, wiping his hands on the apron he was wearing, and sat down in his favorite spot in the rocker. It was an unwritten law that no one else used that special chair.

"First, some background," began David. "You know, of course... at the highest levels there's a secret partnership between East and West... to form a New World Order. And it goes beyond anything Bush or Gorbachev or the Pope imply in their public statements."

"I'm aware of that. All they've said so far," agreed Ari, "is that Saddam Hussein's fate will be shared by any other aggressor. We've entered a new era of peace. No tolerance of aggression. And a new era, too, of international banking and trade cooperation and shared wealth with developing nations. That's basically the New World Order as it's been publicly presented."

"But, in fact," continued David, "what they have in mind is a world government with its own military and police force."

"Exactly. That's what the consortium that financed me is all about. But I never got that impression from them. I had to find it out for myself."

"Okay, we all know that." David leaned back in his chair and spoke slowly. "What if I told you that extraterrestrial intelligences are involved in this whole picture?" His eyes, under the half-closed lids, were watching Ari's reaction closely.

"Sure—little green men," said Ari with a quick laugh. *He can't be referring to the Nine or is he? How could he know about them? I can't ask him—I've been sworn to secrecy!*

"No, I'm serious," said David without changing his position or relaxing his veiled gaze. "Do you have a problem with that?"

"Well, I thoroughly infiltrated the group that financed me and nothing like this ever came to my attention."

"It's not known at that level. This is the CIA's most closely guarded secret. We think it's being kept from President Bush—at least he doesn't know the full extent of ETI involvement."

"I suppose it's theoretically *possible*," admitted Ari, "but it still sounds like science fiction...or the stories cooked up by lunatics...you know...beamed aboard flying saucers and all that garbage."

"They're not *all* crazies. We happen to know that the United States is in touch with ETIs at a top-secret psychic research center south of San Francisco near Stanford University. That contact put the Americans far ahead of the Soviets in the race for psychic power. In fact, it's no contest any more."

"You've got solid evidence?" countered Ari cautiously.

"I can't even hint at what it is—it could jeopardize our agents. But to answer your question, yes, we have."

"If this is really true," exclaimed Ari, "it's the most important development in the history of the planet. It would change everything."

"It already has. Why do you think the Soviets had to abandon their plans for world conquest and enter into a partnership with the West? Sure, most of the old-line Party members and military men don't know the truth...and the KGB is mostly in the dark. That makes it tough for Gorbachev. He learned about the ETI involvement with the CIA several years ago. How he learned it, we don't know, though we suspect he's had direct contact himself...."

"You really think so?" interrupted Ari, fascinated by what David, a high-level Mossad agent, was telling him.

"There's no other explanation why he wrote *Perestroika* in '87, brought the Berlin Wall down and dissolved the Warsaw Pact. His fear of these entities—who have chosen to work only with the United States so far—has colored every move he's made since then. They're literally forcing earthlings to get together."

"If that's true," mused Ari, "it would answer some questions. I never could understand what motivated Gorby...why he'd tear down everything 70 years of communism had built. Of course Marxism didn't work—but I thought he'd keep the Kremlin old guard in power and move into a modified socialism. And I couldn't buy the Golitsyn scenario, that it was all a KGB plot...to get the West to finance their troubles, then nuke us. Anyway, it's gone too far now. They'll never put Humpty Dumpty back together again."

"Yes, and no," countered David. "As far as we're concerned, Anatoly Golitsyn is legit. There's no doubt he was near the top of the KGB when he defected. We've got confirmation of his story...that the KGB planned to dupe the West into financing bankrupt Eastern bloc satellites by giving them freedom, uniting East and West Germany, bringing down the Wall...."

"Solid confirmation?" interrupted Ari.

"Yep. But we think Gorbachev used that KGB plot as a cover for his own plan. How long he'll retain power as the USSR unravels is anybody's guess... and it isn't all that important. If he's ousted by some internal power play, that might even increase his popularity worldwide... which is where his real interests lie."

"ETIs sharing their power with the CIA," mused Ari thoughtfully. "Sounds like a sci-fi thriller—but it does put some of the pieces of the puzzle together."

Ari and David sat in thoughtful silence. Yakov had reached out to take a large volume from the coffee table and was leafing through it noisily.

"So—you think ETIs are actually directing international politics through the U.S., from behind the scenes... and Gorbachev has had to go along with it," summarized Ari slowly. "Awesome, unbelievable...!"

"It is awesome," agreed David. "Terrifying. In fact, that's the major problem the U.S. faces—how to reveal this contact without causing worldwide panic. Solving that problem is a primary goal of the CIA installation near Stanford."

"So what's Israel's special concern?"

"The ETIs are very much anti-Israel."

"You're kidding!"

"No, it's a fact. And recently Hafez Assad has been stating publicly that he believes in UFOs and that ETIs are the only ones with the capability of achieving a peaceful settlement in the Middle East."

"I remember reading the interview where he first said that and wondering whether he'd gone out of his mind. Is it possible that the same ETIs that the CIA is in touch with have made contact with Syria—and perhaps other Muslim countries?"

"We don't know. But these statements that Assad's been making in interviews with the international media are giving us fits."

"Maybe it's just a personal opinion, another one of the kooky ideas that grow out of being President of Syria. I don't see why ETIs—if they ever got to earth—would be on Syria's side against Israel. Why would they be anti-Israel?"

David gestured toward Yakov. "He could explain that better than I could, because he reads the Bible all the time. He even believes it—from cover to cover, as he hastens to tell everyone. Amazingly, these entities see the Bible as a great threat to the New World Order...."

"The Bible says," broke in Yakov, "'the demons believe, and tremble.' They've got enough sense to take the Bible seriously... which is more than can be said for either of you!"

"Are you saying the ETIs are *demons*... and that's why they take the Bible seriously?" demanded David.

"I am."

"Even if that's so, which I think is nonsense," countered David quickly, "that doesn't mean the ETIs think it's true. I'd agree that the ETIs take the Bible seriously—but *only* because nearly 2 billion people believe it. Millions of people accept the fable that the Jews are God's chosen people and that their Messiah is going to rule the world from Jerusalem. I think that's what concerns the ETIs... or Gorbachev or the Pope or anyone else interested in forming a New World Order."

"And with good reason," added Ari. "Obviously, anybody who's expecting some resurrected 'messiah' to rule the world from Jerusalem is at odds with the Bush-Gorbachev-John Paul II New World Order that you think the ETIs support."

"You know what I think of this," cut in Yakov, taking advantage of the opening David had given him. "There are no created beings outside this planet except angels or demons. Angels don't pose as ETIs... but it would be an ideal cover for demons. That's who the U.S. is dealing with... and the whole world is going to fall into the trap!"

David winked at Ari. "We humor him when he talks nonsense, because in the next breath he'll come up with something brilliant."

Ari gave Yakov an incredulous stare. "You're saying there couldn't be highly evolved humanoid creatures on even *one* of the millions of planets in the universe that must be orbiting around suns similar to our own? Come on, old man!"

"It's the only reasonable conclusion based on the facts," replied Yakov unhesitatingly. "The same Torah that gives us the only sensible explanation for Jewish uniqueness and persecution throughout history says that God created man. I can believe that. But I can't believe that life and intelligence evolved from a 'Big Bang' of energy. Pure chance could *never*—not in trillions of years—produce even one living cell much less the human body and brain... much less individual personalities and abstract concepts such as beauty, truth and justice. You don't get an encyclopedia from an explosion in a print shop! Evolution is a myth. Only an Infinite Designer could produce the intricately designed organisms living on this earth." There was passion in his voice.

"Okay," countered Ari. "Suppose your 'god' created life on this planet. Why couldn't he have done it on some other planets—and why couldn't such creatures have developed a technology for visiting earth just as we've been able to visit the moon?"

David rose abruptly from his chair, went over to stand in front of the window and stared sullenly into the night. Obviously he hadn't suspected Yakov would take this tack, and didn't want any part of such a discussion.

Motioning to Ari to ignore David, Yakov continued. "Creatures anywhere in the universe with the power of choice would rebel against their Creator, just as we've done. God doesn't have to 'experiment' by creating humanlike beings on other planets to see what would happen. He already knows. According to the Bible, this planet is unique... the focus of God's battle with Satan for control of the universe. There's no hint that similar creatures live on other planets."

"You can convert him when I'm not here," grumbled David impatiently, turning around to face Ari and Yakov. "My time's limited and I stopped by tonight with a specific purpose in mind. Can we get on with it?"

"Go ahead," said Yakov in a voice edged with misgiving. "Recruit Ari. I'm not stopping you. But I just want him—and you, too—to know what you're going to be up against on this particular project."

"Let's forget the ETIs for a minute," continued David. "We'll come back to that later. Would you be uncomfortable working for Israeli Intelligence?"

"The Mossad?" asked Ari, wanting to be precise.

"That's a word we don't speak here in Israel because it doesn't exist," countered David quickly. "Let's call it 'the office.'"

Ari thought about it for a minute. "I don't mind working for 'the office,'" he said at last, "but it depends upon what you have in mind."

"We need information—the kind that doesn't come over the wires at the *Post*."

"I hope you don't mean the data I gathered on the consortium," said Ari warily. "We settled that."

"Of course not. Something else, and perhaps even more important in the long run."

"I don't see that I'm in a position to gather any information. I thought that was a speciality of that unmentionable organization."

David laughed. "How do you think we get our intelligence? We have very few highly trained officers. We call them *katsas*. But we have thousands of unpaid volunteers—*sayanim*—around the world. They're our lifeblood. You can see why. I doubt that we've got 1,500 employees on the payroll in the entire world, including secretaries and janitors. Compare that with 25,000 just at the CIA's Langley headquarters, and 250,000 KGB employees worldwide. So we have to rely heavily on volunteers. You'd simply pass along certain information. We'll teach you how to gather and transmit it."

"I can't travel abroad," responded Ari pessimistically. "What information could I pick up for you here in Israel?"

"You'll be traveling," said David matter-of-factly. "I've already cleared that. Just before coming to Israel you had contact in Paris with a former student... Carla Bertelli. Is that right?"

"What about her?" Ari asked uneasily. *Could they possibly know about the exchange of purses... the data I gave her?*

"We want you to write to her. Phoning would be too pushy. Let her know where you are, that you're writing for *The Post*. That should interest her—and cultivate her friendship."

"Why get in touch with *her*?" Ari's suspicions were aroused once again. This didn't look good.

"She's involved in that CIA psychic research lab near Stanford where they're in touch with ETIs."

"*Carla* is? She told me she was reporting on psychic research . . . but I had no idea she'd hit the jackpot!"

"Of course she wouldn't tell you . . . but she's in this up to her eyeballs. If you play the game right, she'll pass on the information we need. We'll give you plenty of help."

Ari was breathing a bit easier now. "So that's where I come in . . . my connection to Carla. Okay, I'll do my best. What are my orders?"

David turned back to the window and stared into the distance in silence. "There's more to it than that," he said at last without turning around, "but I can't explain that right now. Your immediate goal is to get an invitation to visit her."

"In the States?"

"In California . . . at the psychic research center. The first step, of course, is to get back in touch and renew your friendship. Write to her today. Let me know how it goes."

36

Déjà Vu

The ground war in the Gulf was over almost before it had begun—in 100 hours. Was this just a good round figure that appealed to President Bush when he gave the cease-fire order—or was something more involved? His generals in the field had been unhappy at calling off their forces prematurely and thus leaving Saddam, an Arab Hitler, still in power. Why had the decision been made at that exact point?

After raising that question, in one of his columns Ari had pointed out another side to the story. Bush's order, ending Operation Desert Storm at midnight February 27, had made a prophet out of the Lubavitchers' Rabbi Menachem Schneerson, who had predicted an end to the conflict by Purim, which began on February 28. Was that merely conincidence?

There was more. For some strange reason, a joint resolution of the U.S. House and Senate had declared the Rabbi's eighty-ninth birthday to be "Education Day-U.S.A." The Lubavitchers had suddenly become influential. Why? Ari offered no answers, only raised the questions—and suggested that the Lubavitchers were worth watching.

Iraq's vaunted war machine, including its tanks and artillery and supposedly invincible Republican Guard, was totally devastated, while coalition losses were unbelievably low. The small number of Patriot antimissile batteries moved in from the United States—too few to cover all of Israel—had intercepted many but not all of Iraq's scud missiles. A few had gotten through, with horrible enough results, though again the casualties were relatively low. However, with Saddam humiliated and forced to accept a harsh surrender, the scuds were finished as well. Israeli news coverage for February 24, 1991, had begun its evening broadcast with these words: "God bless America!" That had expressed very well the sentiment all over Israel.

Kuwait had been liberated after seven months under an Iraqi regime that proved to be even more brutal than that of the Nazis. Before they fled, Saddam's defeated forces, upon his personal orders, had wantonly destroyed as much of that country as they could. Even historic objects of Arab and Islamic art and culture were looted or smashed and the museums wrecked in a final act of barbarism. Not even the zoo was immune. And by setting Kuwait's oil wells on fire, Saddam Hussein had the distinction of creating the worst environmental disaster in human history. It was a heinous crime against all mankind, including generations to come.

The fact that such wanton, unmitigated evil had been perpetrated by one Muslim nation upon another in the name of *jihad* or Holy War shook the faith of many thinking Arabs and brought deep division in their ranks. It did not, however, decrease the Arabs' united hatred of Israel nor their determination to see her destroyed. If Saddam had done to Israel what he'd done to Kuwait, the Muslims would have praised his action as fully justified. And, unfortunately, so would a growing number of non-Muslims in the rest of the world.

Shortly after the war had ended, rather unsatisfactorily as time would prove, U.S. Secretary of State James Baker toured the Middle East, meeting with coalition partners to discuss establishing a permanent peace for the entire region. He came to Israel as well. Pressure was building for Israel to make a deal with the Palestinians, giving them back the West Bank and the Gaza Strip in exchange for "peace." Few Israelis had any illusions that the PLO would remove from its charter the provision calling for Israel's destruction—or that any promises it might make about "peaceful intentions" could be trusted.

The determination of the United States and her coalition partners to bring peace to the Middle East was, oddly enough, the beginning of one of the most perilous times in Israel's history. Ari could feel the tension build. And, of course, he was analyzing the dangers in his twice weekly column in *The Jerusalem Post.*

— ✦ —

"You've disrupted my whole life—suddenly and completely!" Ari declared in mock reproof as he put his coffee cup down and looked across the elegantly laid table at Miriam. It was a Saturday afternoon, about the twentieth consecutive weekend they'd been together since they'd first met. The soaring splendor of the King David Hotel's tea salon seemed the perfect backdrop to Miriam's dark and animated beauty. Adding dramatically to the romantic atmosphere was the expansive view of the Old City beyond the windows of the venerable hotel.

"Look what you've done to *me*!" she responded with a laugh in the same feigned tone. "I'm driving up here every weekend—hardly the role of the woman! When are you going to get a car so you can come down to see *me*?"

"Yeah, *when*! On my pitiful salary...and with the impossible price of cars. ...Look, darling, can't you transfer to a school here in Jerusalem?"

Miriam looked down at the table in front of her. Picking up a spoon, she began stirring her coffee slowly, giving it all her attention. At last she looked up at Ari. "I...I love you," she said with a slight tremor in her voice. "I've never been smitten like this. You're a wonderful person underneath that agnostic bluster...and I've enjoyed being with you so much! But...I...well, I should have made it clear sooner that...."

There was a long silence. "That *what*?" The anxious question hung in the air as Ari waited for an answer.

"Like my grandfather, Yakov, I'm a follower of Messiah Jesus...."

"Well, I knew that," responded Ari with obvious relief. "You made no secret of it. A few months ago I wouldn't have taken it so calmly. I've come a long way. Don't you think so?" he added wistfully. "A lot more broadminded, thanks to you." He smiled tenderly. Certainly she couldn't view her religion as a serious concern if he didn't. Had he taken that attitude with Nicole, everything would have been different. Wouldn't it?

Miriam reached out and took his hand. "That's the problem, Ari. You don't understand. It *does* matter—and I should have explained how important it was from the very beginning. But I told myself I was just going out of my way to be nice to a new immigrant...a Holocaust survivor...." Her voice wobbled.

Ari gave her hand a squeeze and laughed. "Are you kidding? Something happened between us the first time our eyes met...that day when Yakov introduced us. You remember...you know what I mean."

Miriam nodded. "I know—but that's the way it happens in fairy tales, or the soaps. I tried to tell myself that it wasn't real."

"Wasn't *real*! You're in my thoughts day and night! So what's the problem?"

"Jesus is my Savior, my Lord," Miriam blurted out, "my whole life. If you don't have that same relationship, that same love for Him...it just wouldn't work, and I couldn't...."

"Couldn't *what*?"

"Couldn't marry you...."

"You would if I had the same religion?"

"It's not *religion*, Ari. It's a very personal *relationship* I have with God through the Messiah. I don't like to keep saying it, but you really don't understand. And it isn't fair to you. I should never have let it go this far. I don't want you to be pressured to make some kind of commitment to Jesus just for my sake. That wouldn't be genuine."

Ari's eyes reflected his confusion and disappointment—but at the same time his stubborn determination. "I'll never believe in your Jesus...and I wouldn't pretend that I did. But I don't hold your beliefs against you, so why should you cut me off if I don't become a believer like you?"

Anxiety was plainly written on Miriam's face. "It's my fault. I'm sorry. There's just no way you can understand this...unless...."

"Unless what? We love each other so much...I don't see why...."

The first tear spilled over and traced a path down Miriam's cheek.

Gently Ari dabbed at her cheek with his napkin. "Let's get out of here." Quickly he called the waiter over and paid the bill, and in silence they walked out into the deepening twilight.

Once in the street and heading toward the Old City and Yakov's apartment, Ari gave vent to his confusion, "Look, Miriam, we love each other. I couldn't live without you...and I know you feel the same way about me. Then why, just because I can't think in the same groove on one isolated issue...?"

Miriam stopped abruptly, pulled her arm loose from Ari's, and turned to face him. "We're not talking myths or alternate belief systems, Ari. Jesus is alive! I know Him personally. He means so much to me that I couldn't possibly share my life with someone who didn't have that same relationship!"

"*Déjà vu,*" muttered Ari, more to himself than to Miriam. "I don't believe it."

"What do you mean, *déjà vu*?" asked Miriam. "Has this happened before?"

"Come on, let's keep walking and I'll tell you about it."

Miriam slipped her arm through his once again and they continued slowly down the hill toward the Hinnom Valley. "I was engaged... well, we lived together for six years... and, uh... I know that's offensive to you..."

"She was a follower of Messiah Jesus?" asked Miriam in surprise.

"Not at first. But she became one—and wouldn't live with me any more.... By that time she was pregnant. I wanted her to get an abortion. It was the only sensible thing to do. Having a baby would have disrupted her career –she was doing her residency as a neurosurgeon at a top hospital—and I needed her just to be there to help me. It was a time of crisis in my own work."

"The baby... did she have it?"

"Yes, a boy. She named him Ari Paul. I've never seen him. We were estranged at that point. She had become a Christian—and I was outraged. Like you, she said she couldn't marry me if I didn't share her faith."

"Good for her! And she's raising the baby alone in Paris?"

"She's dead."

"Oh... I'm sorry."

They walked for some time in silence. Finally Miriam asked softly, "How did it... happen?"

"She was killed by Arab terrorists. PLO. The ones who attacked the El Al flight I was boarding. You saw it on the news... and you remember I told you something about it... but not this part." He choked on the words. It was some moments before he recovered enough to continue. "She had come to say goodbye to me. I wish they hadn't let her... but who could have dreamed what would happen! One of the killers had been her closest friend. I'm sure he didn't know that I was catching that flight. He went berserk when he saw Niki lying there...."

Again silence enveloped them as they walked on together. Not knowing how better to share his grief and to express her sympathy, Miriam clutched his arm more tightly.

"And the baby?" she asked at last.

"A Christian doctor and his wife are raising him."

"Thank God for that!"

"I don't. Why should I? They'll indoctrinate him... and that makes me angry."

"You're the most stubborn person I've ever met!" exclaimed Miriam. "Do you think my grandfather and I have less intelligence because we believe in Jesus?"

"No, but you've somehow been persuaded, for some strange reason, to believe in something totally contrary to your cultural integrity. I suppose it must be appealing to trust in some 'higher power'... for protection... answers to ultimate questions...."

"Do you know what it costs an Israeli to believe that Jesus is the Messiah?"

"I know it isn't popular...."

"That's a cosmic understatement! Our little group of believers in Tiberias has been stoned, spit at, bricks through the windows... they even burned down the place where we met for worship, just like they did to the Baptist Church here in Jerusalem. Holocaust survivors said it reminded them of *Kristallnacht*."

"I thought Menachem Begin apologized for that..."

"He did... officially. But it didn't change anything. We now meet in secret in the forest overlooking the Sea of Galilee. We of all people shouldn't persecute one another! The treatment of believers in Jesus here in Israel awakens memories of the rising anti-Semitism in Germany during the 1930's. Our phones are tapped, mail opened, letters and checks removed... we get empty envelopes. I only say this so you'll know that Grandpa and I... and a lot of others here in Israel... wouldn't enter lightly into this relationship with Jesus, who is so despised not just by Jews but by most of the world."

Ari didn't know what to say. All he could think of was that he was about to lose the woman he loved, just as he had lost Nicole... and he couldn't understand why or what to do about it.

At last, Miriam broke the silence. "I'm not complaining. Jesus said it would be this way for His followers. I just wanted you to know that it costs plenty for an Israeli—I'm a Sabra, a native-born Israeli, you know—to believe in Jesus Christ. So you know that Grandpa and I, and any other Jewish believers, would have to be fully convinced that Jesus was Israel's Messiah, that He died for our sins on a cross just outside the wall of the Old City, and that He rose from the dead and is alive today."

"But Miriam, love, of course you *believe* it—but that doesn't make it so. Think about it."

"How about you? Are you willing to *think* about it... to examine the evidence?"

Again Ari made no response. How could he possibly deal with such single-minded devotion to an outmoded fable? It was the one flaw in this otherwise lovely and lovable creature.

"I'd like to take you to the Garden Tomb—the grave where Jesus was buried. Of course, it's empty. Will you come with me tomorrow?" Miriam was looking at him beseechingly.

"Maybe... reluctantly."

"Let me ask you something, Ari. Have you ever read the Bible?"

"No... but there are lots of books I haven't read."

"The Bible isn't just another book. It claims to be God's Word—which is reason enough to at least check it out. And if you would read it you'd know that every word is true. It lays out the history, the evidence, the facts—even foretells the future without ever making a mistake. Don't you think it's rather stupid to come to a conclusion before you've even examined the evidence!"

"*Déjà vu* again. Niki told me the same thing."

"Too bad you didn't take her advice. You've read far more books than most people—why not the Bible?"

"I don't have time."

"I think you're running from God... like Jacob and Moses and Jonah did...."

"Jacob, Moses, Jonah... how do you know they ever lived?"

"There isn't any doubt. The school children here study the history of Israel from the Scriptures. You need to do the same! You don't even know the history of your own people. You're an Israeli now. You've come to Israel... yet you don't have a clue why this is our land or what amazing things God did in the past to bring our people here."

"Middle East history wasn't my field," he responded lamely.

"Well, now it should be... since you're living here."

"That wasn't my choice, but I'm glad I am... for several reasons. You're the most important one."

"You've always been vague about what brought you here," said Miriam, "and I didn't want to press you... but I've wondered."

"I was deported... and Israel was the only country that would take me... but I can't tell you any more than that."

"You—a criminal? I don't believe it. Were you framed...?"

"I was... but it's more complicated than that. Someday maybe I'll be able to explain... but I can't now. Your grandfather might be able to tell you. I'm sure David knows. He said the Mossad has a file on me that takes up an entire cabinet... and they let me in... so that must say something."

Lost in their own thoughts, they walked in silence the last few minutes to Yakov's apartment. When they arrived he was sitting in his favorite rocking chair in the living room reading his Bible. Ari found the peaceful sight particularly annoying this night.

With a winsome smile, Miriam appealed to Ari. "See, Grandpa's reading his Bible... and he's got plenty of them around here, so you don't have any excuse...."

"Some day, maybe," replied Ari.

"Stubborn, isn't he?" complained Miriam to Yakov.

"A real Jew!" exclaimed Yakov, with an unperturbed smile. "Like Rabbi Saul of Tarsus... it'll take a Damascus Road experience to convince him—and he's going to have it one of these days. Let's not give up on him."

37

Progress and Peril

The following Monday Ari received a response to the letter he had written to Carla. It was enthusiastic and gave promise of further contact.

"How good it was to hear from you," her letter began. "And how sad I was to have confirmation of Nicole's death. I saw her name on the list of victims in the news, but wasn't sure whether that was the same person to whom you had introduced me. I tried to phone you at the Sorbonne, and that's how I learned you'd gone to Israel. They could give me no forwarding address or phone number. So that's why your letter was such a welcome surprise.

"And how excited I was to learn that you have a newspaper column of your own—and in such a prestigious paper as *The Jerusalem Post*! Yes, it was a surprise to learn that you were really Jewish, a Holocaust survivor. I guess that makes you very special in Israel. I can understand why, when you discovered your roots, you wanted to live there. It seems strange to call you Professor Ari Thalberg now after knowing you as Professor Hans Mueller all these years, but I'll get used to it."

Carla went on to tell how she had broken up with her fiancé, Ken Inman, but that it was for the best. He was the one who had gotten her into the field of parapsychology,but he had recently abandoned it. By contrast, she was getting more heavily involved. In fact, there were some spectacular developments that she would soon be revealing to the world. Since breaking up with Ken, she felt a new freedom in her work. She gave no details about that work, but did hint again that she would be doing a special report—something momentous—soon, and that she might even give Ari a scoop for his paper.

Ari brought Carla's letter to David at his office the same day it arrived. Her references to parapsychology, to her work, to the new developments and the possibility of giving Ari a scoop were, of course, of special interest to the office. Only after its experts had meticulously analyzed the contents was Ari given the okay to respond—and of course they told him exactly what to say.

"This is a great start," exulted David, when he returned the letter a few days later to Ari at Yakov's apartment, along with the detailed instructions for replying to it. "We're very pleased. She's given you this opening to ask what the nature of this big news might be, and whether it involves some American breakthrough in psychic research, since she told you that was her new field."

"No problem. She was quite open and enthusiastic about her interest in parapsychology when we met last in Paris," recalled Ari.

"Then you have every reason to mention that subject specifically without appearing to be prying."

"No question about it."

"Now here's what we're going to do. One of our writers will do an article about the possible involvement of ETIs in the area of psychic power. It will be published in *The Post* next week. Include a copy of that with your letter, and ask her whether she thinks there's any truth in it. But play it cool. Don't sound too eager. When you have the rough draft of the letter ready, give it to me and I'll have our people fix it up."

"I just wonder whether we're kidding ourselves," said Ari thoughtfully. "If these ETIs are really so far advanced psychically, wouldn't they be able to read our minds and know what we're planning and doing?"

"I'm not sure whether they can," replied David somberly. "Anyway, that's a chance we have to take. We can't just sit back and do nothing."

"I guess you're right... but it's frightening."

"Now here," said David, handing Ari a piece of paper with a map and directions, "is where and when you report. Memorize everything before you go to bed, then tear it up and flush it down the toilet."

— ✦ —

A few days later, an excited and eager recruit reported to Mossad headquarters on Tel Aviv's King Saul Boulevard. Ari was to live with other recruits in a nearby apartment while he underwent intensive Mossad training that would completely cut him off from contact with the outside world for three weeks. He was assigned to receive special instruction in *Mishlasim*—gathering and communicating information—at the large, two-storied *Midrasha*, the Mossad training academy. It sat on a hill just outside Tel Aviv, overlooking the road to Haifa.

The training was thorough and concentrated. When finished, Ari would be able to pass along, secretly and in the various prescribed manners, to the appropriate people in the organization whatever information he gathered. Though David had said no more about it, Ari was now confident that he was definitely going on that special assignment to the United States. Otherwise the Mossad would hardly have invested this time and effort in his training.

Ideological discussions formed the framework for the day's practical instructions and took up most of each evening. Ari learned that Israel, while grateful for the help it had received from the United States in the past, was fearful that it was being gradually abandoned by its old ally. The recruits were told that there were elements within the United States who considered Israel's very existence to be a threat to Middle East peace and the promised New World Order. Such parties, the Mossad was thoroughly convinced, were, together with the Arabs, plotting Israel's destruction behind the scenes.

No mention was made of the influence of ETIs. Apparently that topic, which had concerned Ari ever since David had raised it, was still too clandestine even to be voiced outside of the Mossad's innermost circle. He had been told of it only because of his relationship to Carla and the Mossad's hope to use him in getting information out of her. David claimed she was directly and personally involved in developments at the CIA lab. Ari, however, found it hard to believe that Carla could be involved in any other capacity than as a journalist. Was it possible that she was working with the Nine—the same ETIs that Elor claimed to represent? If so, what about the "life insurance" papers Ari had given her? It seemed impossible to unravel the web of intrigue that was being woven about him.

According to his Mossad political instructor, there was growing sentiment in the U.S. that Israel's military had become so strong that it posed a real threat to world peace. Her nuclear capabilities caused the gravest concern. No one believed that Israel would surrender her nuclear arsenal even if the Arabs promised to recognize her right to exist. Nor did anyone in the U.S. or anywhere else imagine that the Arabs would really stand behind such a pledge of recognition and peaceful coexistence if they made it. Yet Israel was criticized for not being willing to make such a suicidal deal. Small wonder, then, that his Mossad instructors projected a desperate sense of "us-against-the-world" and expected fanatical dedication to Israel's security in those they carefully tutored.

— ✦ —

When Ari returned to Jerusalem, David carried on his highly specialized and enlightening political education once a week. It wasn't that so much of what David revealed was new, but that his insights were unique. He analyzed and explained the importance of events with which Ari, as a professor of political science, had been in varying degrees familiar, but whose hidden significance, even as a news analyst, he had failed to comprehend. Certainly he had not put the information together in the insightful and intriguing way that David now presented it.

"The Cold War's out, cooperation's in," David began one evening when he came over for a visit about a week after Ari's return. "The question is why. The players in the game have their own reasons. The Soviets are working with the West for the formation of a New World Order—or so it seems. Both are courting the Muslims, who have their own plans to take over the world. To abandon that goal they'd have to renounce Islam and Muhammad—not likely."

Ari was nodding, listening carefully, completely absorbed in the rapid-fire analysis. "There's a fourth group, however," continued David with an air of mystery, "perhaps even more powerful and potentially dangerous than Islam. It wields a pervasive, behind-the-scenes influence in both East and West, and it also has its own agenda for world domination." He paused for a moment to let Ari ponder his words. "Any idea what it is?"

"Another world player...perhaps more powerful than Islam?" Ari mulled that over for a few moments then shrugged his shoulders. "I've got my own ideas... but you probably wouldn't agree. You tell me what you have in mind."

"I'll give you a hint. It's about the same size as Islam—nearly a billion. The two of them fought for centuries, but they're now 'dialoguing' about what they have in common."

"So we do think alike!" responded Ari. "You must mean the Catholic Church. Right?"

"You got it. The largest and most powerful Christian church in the world—and it has never recognized Israel as a nation, and like Islam, rejects Israel's right to exist."

"Odd, isn't it," reflected Ari. "Christians use the same Hebrew Scriptures, and traditionally have been the strongest supporters of Israel."

"That used to be the way, but it's changing now. Even hard-core Christian fundamentalists have been turning against Israel lately. But it was always that way with the Catholic Church...."

"Now you're talking about something that I spent a lot of time investigating when I was in France," enthused Ari. "I have no doubt that the Pope is the most powerful leader on earth today. Bush and Gorbachev consult him weekly... they work closely together for their New World Order, just as they did to rescue Solidarity and bring down communism in Eastern Europe."

"But they each have their own agenda, in spite of the apparent cooperation at this stage," cut in David.

"Exactly. And I think, when it comes to power, the Pope definitely has the edge!"

"Well, we agree on that. Rome intends to establish its own world government—the 'kingdom of God' under the Pope."

"An idea from the Middle Ages," mused Ari, "coming back to haunt us today. Incredible! And this worries Israel, I'm sure."

"Big worries. The Catholic Church has a long history of anti-Semitism. It claims to be the true Israel with a divine mandate to rule the world. That's why it has never recognized Israel."

"I don't think the average Catholic knows this," suggested Ari.

"You're probably right... which is why the Pope has to work through secret Catholic organizations. Their tentacles reach into the highest circles of power worldwide. Even here in Israel their wealth and influence is at work—openly and undercover."

Ari nodded. "I researched some of those organizations. There are dozens."

"It's the major ones that worry us." David's mood and expression had turned solemn. "The big three concern us the most: the Jesuits, Opus Dei, and the Knights of Malta. The Knights, for example, are like another CIA or KGB."

"I was just beginning to really get into the Knights," said Ari. "Studied their history and what they're doing now. I know they're a big factor not only in

Europe, but in America—North and South—especially in the United States. But I hadn't looked at them in relation to Israel. Are they anti...."

"Is the Pope Catholic?"

"It's that definite?"

David nodded emphatically. "From their history you'll recall some particularly intriguing incidents...."

"Go ahead and refresh my memory. I don't know exactly what you have in mind."

"Let's take a couple of examples right out of office files. Toward the end of World War II, the Office of Strategic Services—forerunner to the CIA—made contact with Reinhard Gehlen, then Hitler's chief of intelligence (the Schutzstaffel or SS) on the Eastern Front. Out of that meeting came a secret agreement transferring control of Gehlen's organization into the hands of the OSS. After the war it then became the postwar intelligence agency of West Germany, the BND."

"I remember," said Ari. "Incredible! But go on."

"The OSS and the BND," continued David, "worked together to pull off a brazen scam code-named 'Project Paperclip.' A wealthy industrialist in America—a Knight—was also involved. Remember, this was a just-defeated Nazi Germany full of war criminals with varying degrees of complicity in the murder of 6 million Jews, and millions of non-Jews. Project Paperclip involved the smuggling of some 900 German scientists into the United States."

Ari was nodding solemnly, his anger growing. "Yeah. Snatched many of them right out from under the noses of the Russians before they could take them off to the Soviet Union. Never mind the murdered Jews at this point. Something else was more important, specifically the U.S. rocket program... which meant there were more than a few missing defendants and witnesses at the Nuremberg Trials."

"Right. But the most intriguing part is the involvement of the Catholic Church in this rotten mess," continued David. "Gehlen's brother—remember, Gehlen was SS head on the Eastern Front, who worked a deal with the American OSS, now the CIA—was secretary to a top official at the Knights of Malta headquarters in Rome. Another deal was struck—to use the Knights to help thousands of Nazis, many of them war criminals such as the infamous Klaus Barbie, escape to South America. A number of Roman Catholic monasteries and convents acted as safe houses in the underground railway known as the 'Rat Line' that passed these Nazis along to safety."

"My blood pressure's going up," muttered Ari angrily. "The Holocaust... and now this! I'm vaguely aware of what you're saying, but never saw much about it in print. Wasn't interested..."

David looked grim. "What I'm telling you is all fully documented. I could give you lots of details from office files, including hundreds of names. Baron Luigi Parrilli, a Knight, who took part in the negotiations that set up the deal,

Prince Valerio Borghese . . . and others. But the names mean little now. By the way, Borghese was saved by the OSS from being arrested for war crimes by the Italian resistance. It's no coincidence that he was high up in the Knights. His exact title was Bailiff Grand Cross of Honor and Devotion."

David stood up and began to pace the floor as he continued. "Now listen to this. Borghese gave Nazi SS leader Gehlen and certain American leaders the Knights of Malta Grand Cross award. Among the American recipients was President Harry Truman's envoy to the Vatican, Myron C. Taylor." He turned to face Ari, anger written all over his face. "Enough of such details. They're not important. I just wanted you to get a picture of the power, the sickening duplicity, Nazi cooperation and anti-Jewish bias of the Catholic Church—and especially of the Knights of Malta."

"No wonder Israel thinks the whole world is against it," muttered Ari furiously, more to himself than to David.

"You see now why we trust no one? If we're to survive, we have to be able to defend ourselves against the whole world."

Ari nodded. "But now you say that ETIs are mixed into this soup . . . working with the Americans. What defenses do we have against *them*? And whose side are they on?"

"I don't know. It's a puzzle, and we haven't been able to fit the pieces together. The Americans and Soviets are now working together as never before in history, but they also double-cross each other. In spite of Gorbachev, the Soviet military and KGB have their own agenda. So does the Pope. Each rival is maneuvering behind the scenes to come out on top. The ETIs are working through the CIA at the moment, but they obviously have their own agenda, too. And though we don't know exactly what their plan is, you can be sure it isn't favorable to Israel . . . for the reasons I've already given."

David sat down again, looking like a man unburdened, drained. There was a long, thoughtful silence. At last Ari raised the question he had been afraid to voice but couldn't hold back any longer.

"The ETIs," said Ari, trying to sound casual, "is there some name they go by?"

"Yeah, 'the Nine' . . . or 'Archons'," came David's immediate response. "That's fairly fresh information, and it has some mysterious significance that we're not sure of yet."

The Nine . . . ! Oh, my God! Ari's worst fears had come true. He turned quickly away to hide his consternation. Hopefully, David hadn't noticed his reaction.

"Look, don't mention this to anyone," added David, "not even someone inside the office. We have a mole at the secret CIA lab. You have to know that because you'll need to make contact when you get out there."

A Dangerous Assignment

Yakov had been idly rocking back and forth in his favorite chair, eyes closed, listening carefully to all that David had been telling Ari. Now he came back to life, sat up straight and turned abruptly to Ari. "Stay out of it! The CIA's being set up. 'The Nine' aren't ETIs."

"Come on, Yakov," returned David uneasily, "let's not get sidetracked onto that demon thing again... okay?"

"You just listen to what I have to say," returned Yakov impatiently, "and you'll learn something. I used to practice cabala... heavy occultism... and I'm telling you that 'the Nine' are well-known in occult circles. They've been making contact with spirit mediums in seances for centuries."

"So?"

"They never posed as ETIs until recently. Used to pretend to be 'ascended masters' who lived thousands of years ago. Only lately have they claimed to be highly evolved extraterrestrials... but they're still 'channeled' the same way, through spirit mediums."

"Give us an example," demanded David.

"It was the Nine who put Andrija Puharich, an American medical scientist, onto psychic research and Israeli psychic Uri Geller. The Nine were even listed in an Esalen catalog as teaching a course in Gestalt therapy through a resident medium...."

"Esalen?" asked David.

"Yeah, I've heard of it," volunteered Ari. "Almost visited it the one time I was in California, but I was too busy at Stanford. It's kind of a New Age think tank south of San Francisco where the Human Potential movement got its start."

"Right," continued Yakov. "Anyone knowledgeable in the occult would tell you that the Nine have been known for centuries as spirit entities, not as ETIs."

"It doesn't necessarily mean they're the same entities just because they have the same name," objected Ari.

Yakov shook his head. "If these 'ETIs' are so all-powerful, do you think they'd let some other entities use their name and cause that kind of confusion?"

"I thought seances were a hoax," put in David, but his voice lacked conviction.

"Most of them are," agreed Yakov, "but not all of them. Any grade school child in Israel can tell you that the Torah forbids seances and all attempts to contact 'spirits.' You remember King Saul went to the witch of Endor, and his dabbling in the occult brought destruction to him and his army. The CIA's fate will be the same if they keep this up!"

"So why does the Torah forbid seances?" asked Ari, becoming interested in spite of his rejection of the Bible.

"Because, as I tried to tell both of you the other day, the 'spirits' contacted in seances—and the supposed ETIs that science believes in—are actually *demons* bent upon deception and destruction!"

There was a long silence. David and Ari exchanged uncomfortable glances, but said nothing. They seemed to be taking Yakov's pronouncements about demons at least somewhat seriously for the first time.

"By the way, the New Testament mentions the Nine... even calls them 'the Archons' in the Greek."

"You're putting us on," laughed Ari. "Chapter and verse... okay?"

"Laugh if you want, but I'm warning you...." Yakov looked over his glasses like a schoolteacher scolding his pupils. "'The Archons' is an expression in the Greek used by one of Israel's greatest rabbis, Saul of Tarsus. He lived in the first century and hated Christians with a passion. Had them imprisoned and killed. Then he suddenly turned 180 degrees... became the world's leading Christian of all time... the Apostle Paul."

"Why this sudden change?" asked Ari. David was looking increasingly uncomfortable, obviously displeased with Yakov for persistently bringing in religion.

"He claimed that Jesus had proved His resurrection by personally appearing to him," said Yakov, "and he began to preach that Jesus was Israel's Messiah."

"You take his word for it?" demanded Ari.

"Testimony like that would stand up in any court! You've got to be blind or perverse to deny it. Jewish history admits that Saul, a leading rabbi who hated and persecuted Christians, suddenly became one of them, exposing himself to imprisonment and eventually his own martyrdom. Why? It doesn't make sense, unless his story is true."

"It could have been a fantasy... a hallucination."

Yakov smiled patiently. "Saul of Tarsus was not given to fantasy. He was a brilliant man, a hard-headed rabbi and utterly opposed to Christianity. It took something supernatural to change him so suddenly and completely. His life and teachings have impacted mankind more than anyone else's except Jesus Himself. To say it was all based upon a fantasy isn't rational. He had to be convinced beyond a shadow of a doubt that Jesus had been raised from the dead and was Israel's Messiah... or he certainly wouldn't have become one of the believers he hated."

David had been listening to Yakov with growing exasperation. "Is this your way of announcing that you, like Saul, believe Jesus was Israel's Messiah?" he demanded.

"I've told you that before," said Yakov calmly.

"Hinted at it."

"No, told you—but you didn't want to hear it."

"If this gets out," countered David in dismay, "it will be a terrible blow to the military. One of Israel's last living heroes of all five wars betrays her...."

"It's not a betrayal!" shot back Yakov quickly. "You keep forgetting... Jesus was Jewish!"

"Look," interrupted Ari, "we were talking about ETIs. You brought up this Saul of Tarsus because he'd said something about the Nine."

"That's what I was getting to," said Yakov, settling back in his rocking chair. "The Apostle Paul mentions these entities in one of his letters to the early Christians."

"Tell us about it."

Yakov began to read from the open Bible he was holding. "'We wrestle not against flesh and blood, but against principalities, against powers, against the rulers of the darkness of this world, against spiritual wickedness in high places.' The Greek word Paul used for 'rulers' was *kosmokrators*, an epithet for Satan. And the word for 'principalities' was Arche— or Archons."

"He wrote about *Archons* 1900 years ago?" Ari was astonished.

"Exactly. And what he said explains something about them. In Paul's day the nine magistrates who ruled Athens were called Archons, which is why these entities call themselves 'the Nine'...."

"So the Nine were people, not ETIs," interrupted David. "I don't see the connection."

"Let me finish. Paul was talking about Satan and his demons... and he said that just as there was a hierarchy of nine men who ruled Athens, so a hierarchy of demons were in control of the evil that rules this world. And he argued that these evil beings, not other humans, were the real enemies of mankind."

"How do we verify that?" demanded Ari, intrigued now.

"Look the word up in any dictionary," countered Yakov with a confident smile.

"I'll do that!"

There was a long silence. Ari became aware that David had been watching him intently.

"Tell me," said David at last, "why the name 'Archon' means so much to you."

"I find it intriguing," responded Ari quickly, playing it cool. Should he tell them the truth? He had been sworn to secrecy. But what was his obligation to Elor? He glanced over at Yakov. "You must see some significance, or you wouldn't have gone into this long explanation. Right?"

Yakov made no reply. He, too, seemed to be regarding Ari with unusual interest.

"There's more to it than that," insisted David. "What is it?"

"I've debated whether to tell you. One of the Nine... I guess... at least that's what he claimed to be... has already contacted me."

"When was that?" demanded David sharply. "You should have reported it immediately!"

"I was sworn to secrecy."

"You don't have any secrets from the office!"

"That was long before you recruited me... before I even knew you worked for the office."

"Well, you're with us now. Let's hear about it."

"They've haunted my dreams most of my life, tried to control my thoughts... and I've fought it. Nearly drove me crazy at times. The first waking contact came almost 30 years ago in East Berlin. The next one was a few years later in Paris. The third time was here is Jerusalem about four months ago. This well-dressed Israeli businessman came up to me in the street...."

"Medium height, about 40, in a beige linen suit?" asked David incredulously. "And he suddenly disappeared?"

"Yeah," replied Ari in surprise. "How did you know?"

"Some of my men were following you. That was before you got onto us. They didn't know where this guy came from—said he just suddenly appeared—or where he went. They claimed he just vanished. I didn't believe the report. Chewed them out... almost sacked one of them. They said a huge white dove settled on his head while he was talking to you, then it was gone."

"So your men saw it too!" exclaimed Ari. "Then I'm not losing my mind. That's not all the guy did. He pulled a large stone out of a building without touching it, then put it right back into place. A flame suddenly ignited in the palm of his hand. It wasn't phony, I could feel the heat. Unbelievable—but I *saw* it!"

"And he said he was an Archon?"

"Yeah. Called himself 'Elor, one of the Nine.' Could read my mind. I'm dead if I double-cross him. How can I get Carla to give me information about the Nine without them knowing what I'm doing? They probably already know what we're planning. There's no way you can fight them!"

"Did he say he was going to contact you again?" asked David.

Ari nodded. "Soon. But I don't know where or when."

"Okay, when he does," said David cautiously, "take a direct approach. Ask him what they're up to with the CIA. He might tell you. In the meantime, keep working on Carla. You're making good progress, judging from the letters she writes, but there isn't much time. We think something big is about to break."

Ari made no response. How had he gotten himself into this? He was working for the Mossad... and at the same time the Nine. According to David they were against Israel... yet they planned to use him to rescue Israel from its "chosen people" delusion and from Zionism. That sounded legitimate and beneficial. It was the only way to bring peace in the Middle East. The Mossad must be misinformed.

David's concerned voice brought him back to the present. "I know what you're thinking. It's an unusually dangerous assignment, but we'll give you the training...and the backing...to carry it out successfully."

Yakov snorted in disapproval. "You're sending him up against demons! He needs God's protection, not some irrelevant spy training!"

"I appreciate your concern, Yakov," said David evenly, "but not your interference in office business."

Yakov was not backing down. "I'm warning you both, you're up against demons! Satan's preparing the world for the Antichrist—and Israel is a special target for his seduction. She'll be cleverly deceived into embracing her enemy as her Messiah...just because he'll guarantee her safety and bring peace!" Here he looked squarely at Ari with anguish. "And you could well play a part in her destruction."

"Enough of this religious paranoia, Yakov!" David sprang to his feet and stormed out of the room. Pausing for a moment in the small entry hall, he called back to Ari, "Don't forget your assignment. I'll check with you later." He slammed the front door behind him and was gone.

"I'm going out for a walk," said Ari, rising to his feet. "I know you mean well, but I get tired of always having your religion pushed on me. I thought you would have given up by now."

Yakov regarded Ari with compassion. "I'm sorry you feel that way. I wouldn't want to push anything on you. It's your choice. But I'm warning you—don't get involved in this without God's protection. If you do...you're finished. Count on it!"

Back in the Saddle

By the time Ari returned, Yakov, who usually retired early, was already in bed and sound asleep. His peculiar whistling snore could be heard as Ari tiptoed down the hall and into his own room. Whatever his eccentricities, the old man's religion had definitely cleansed his conscience and given him peace of mind. He seemed to drop off quickly and sleep soundly all night—and scarcely expressed a worry since Ari had known him. "The Lord's will is always best," was a standard response when any difficulty did arise.

In contrast, Ari lay awake for a long time that night trying to fit the pieces of the puzzle together. He found himself in the uncomfortable but exhilarating position of being a double agent. Life had purpose once again... and excitement. That was what he loved. Danger was nothing to fear; it was a challenge to face and conquer. How to handle what lay before him was the question that troubled him now, and he lay awake turning the convoluted scenario over and over in his mind.

Out of loyalty to his adopted country, as well as the desire to do something worthwhile, he had accepted an assignment with the Mossad that had turned out to be far more dangerous and significant than he had imagined. Too late he had learned that it would involve spying not only on the CIA but on their mentors, the Nine, who had been watching over him as well since earliest childhood. These mysterious entities, who claimed to control the universe, had chosen him as Israel's "Messiah"—to lead her into her proper position in the New World Order. They even claimed to have brought him to Israel for that purpose.

The idea of a savior—Messiah madness, he had called Nicole's belief in Jesus—had been repugnant at first. With the passage of time, however, and a greater insight into the Arab-Israeli conflict of interests, it had begun to make sense. And after Elor had demonstrated his incredible powers, there seemed little doubt that if the Nine so desired they could make it all happen, including the "resurrection" Elor had mentioned. Of course, that idea wasn't to be taken literally, but it would be "as though" he had come back from the dead. Certainly whatever they did would be impressive.

The Mossad, however, was convinced that the Nine were anti-Israel—that they were planning to destroy her. Did that mean that the Nine were deceiving him? Did they, perhaps, intend to use him in some ploy that would actually annihilate Israel? Where was the truth? Did he dare confront Elor with this question the next time they met? But didn't Elor already know his thoughts—and thus that he had agreed to work for the Mossad against the Nine? Ari went over his options carefully.

To make matters more confusing, Yakov swore that the Archons were demons and that without God's protection, Ari would be "finished" if he got mixed up with them at all. David had promised the Mossad's protection in his assignment. But from what Ari had already seen, there seemed to be no way humanly possible to defy the Nine. The Mossad would be finished, too. Yet a maxim he had adopted as a teenager, which had helped him confront an abusive foster father then and had guided his life since, was this:"Never accept defeat: with enough guts and brains, anything is possible!" It was still true.

Now he was facing the most difficult challenge of his life. That made it worth accepting! After being exiled to Israel and seeing his life seemingly brought to a dead end, the future had suddenly brightened. Perhaps he could have a powerful impact upon this planet's destiny after all. Opportunity had knocked, and now it was up to him. His loyalties were with neither the Mossad nor the Nine, but with mankind. He was working for the good of all humanity. And to do that he would play both sides, while remaining his own man, true to his own ideals. It was a great sensation to be back in the saddle again!

Assured that life had a purpose once more, Ari lingered for some moments in that nether land of half-consciousness, his eyelids heavy at last. He was drifting off to sleep when the sudden appearance of a brilliant light beside his bed startled him. He sat straight up, instantly fully awake. It was more than a light—an overpowering *Presence* filled the room!

"You wanted to ask me something." More like a command than a simple statement of fact, the words came in a vibrant, full-throated, almost musical voice out of the shimmering radiance. The interior of the light began to take on shape. Elor! Although he did not appear as a human now, but in a translucent, transcendent form, there was no mistaking who it was. "*Now, my son*, don't be afraid. Ask me whatever you will!"

In spite of his brave thoughts of facing and conquering any challenge, Ari found himself confronting something not of this earth that was terrifying in a way he had never imagined. Elor's "don't be afraid" had only increased his fear. Heart pounding and breath coming in short, convulsive gasps, Ari struggled to slow his breathing and get control of his thoughts. David had suggested the direct approach. Why not?

At last he managed to get the words out, "The Nine are working with the CIA... is that true?"

"The preservation and good of all creatures on this planet is our goal," came the oblique response. "We have no favorites. Yes, we work through America's Central Intelligence Agency right now, but eventually we'll be in constant touch with every individual on this planet. The Mossad has nothing to fear from us."

"They think you're anti-Israel." There it was. He had blurted it out and now must take the consequences.

"It was good for you to say that. The Mossad seeks to defend the twin myths of 'chosen people' and Zionism. You yourself know that these delusions stand in the way of peace. We are Israel's true friends, as we are of all mankind. Would we have chosen you, a man who now loves Israel, to be her leader in the New World Order, if we did not have Israel's best interests in mind?"

"No, surely not." Ari felt somewhat relieved. "The world is bigger than Israel. She must take her place in the family of nations without expecting special preference. But she shouldn't be the object of special hatred and attack, either."

"Well spoken. When Israel drops her claim to favoritism, then anti-Semitism will cease. There is no 'god' in the heavens. But if there were, why should he have favorites? Why should there be any 'chosen people'? This desire to be preferred above others is the root of all problems on earth. Do you understand?"

"I do. I can see that you're right."

"It is also the jealousy that comes from fear that others may be preferred by Allah or Yaweh or some other fabled 'god' that causes strife. We favor neither the Jews nor the Arabs—nor the Americans. Why should we? We are so highly evolved that we have all power and all possessions and need nothing. Earthlings have no treasure to offer us to buy our favor. One of the delusions of religion is that the 'gods' want to be worshiped and give help in exchange for gifts given to them. How foolish! We are gods . . . and so are you, but you, like the rest of mankind, have not yet awakened to your own potential. We need nothing and want nothing from mankind—only to prevent a disaster here that could set back the karma of the entire galaxy. That is our only concern."

It was a long speech, but the tone of voice had been sympathetic and sincere. It made sense and put Ari's mind somewhat at rest. "Could I bring that message to the Mossad?" he asked Elor. "It might calm some of their fears."

"No. Don't reveal this contact to anyone. The next contact will take place soon, and you may report it—but not this one."

"Can you tell me any specifics concerning your work with the CIA and how it will benefit . . . ?"

"Not yet," cut in Elor impatiently. "You will go to the United States soon to see for yourself. Informing you about that development is not my mission now. I have come to warn you."

"Warn me?" asked Ari apprehensively.

"Yes—that the woman you have fallen in love with is deceiving you. You must not become further involved." He paused for a moment, then added bitterly, "It was not our doing to have you meet her—or her grandfather!"

"Not your doing?" asked Ari cautiously. "But I thought you were in control...."

"There is One who is our Enemy... and he is yours as well."

"Who do you mean?"

"They call him the Christ... but he's a usurper. One day we will destroy him. But until then he has much power. She and her grandfather are on his side, working against us. Do not believe their clever lies."

"Are you saying that this one they call 'the Christ' actually lived here in Israel... that he was a historic person?"

"We gave him the same mission then for which we have now chosen you. He was to teach love for all creatures, the brotherhood of all mankind and the infinite potential within all. We initiated him to the tenth level—as our representative in California will initiate you. But he took that power and used it to start the most narrow-minded, bigoted religion in the history of the universe. He claimed to be the only way to God—even that he was God. And instead of teaching acceptance of all, he condemned those who did not live by his narrow-minded code... and even claimed that he would die for 'sinners.'"

"And it was here at Jerusalem that he was crucified... and resurrected? Is that what happened?" asked Ari.

"That is a myth created by priests to keep the common people in bondage. Jesus did not die on the cross. The Muslims have that one right. There is no death. It seems to be real only to those who accept it in their minds. Evil, like beauty, is 'in the eye of the beholder.'"

"Then what about the empty Garden Tomb that Christians say proves his resurrection?"

"Another invention of the clerics!" Elor's voice was heavy with contempt. "Jesus of Nazareth simply used the mind-power of the tenth dimension to demonstrate the potential that resides in every person. He discarded the body he had temporarily taken and ascended to the astral plane. In doing so he demonstrated the Christ-potential that resides in everyone and showed the way for all mankind to escape the wheel of reincarnation. Unfortunately, he now opposes us... but he is doomed to fail."

At that moment Ari heard his bedroom door swing open and he turned to see Yakov standing just inside the room, taking in the scene. Anger suffused the old man's face. With an unwavering finger, he pointed at Elor.

"In the Name of the Lord Jesus Christ," declared Yakov with an authority that unnerved Ari, "get out!"

To Ari's astonishment, Elor and the light that surrounded him vanished instantly.

"Demons have no place in this apartment," declared Yakov simply. With that he turned abruptly and left the room, shutting the door quietly behind him.

—✦—

That night Ari's sleep was disturbed by terrifying dreams. Always Elor was the central figure, commanding, pursuing, relentlessly hounding him in a phantasmagoria of surrealistic visions. By the time Ari encountered Yakov in the kitchen the next morning, the visit of Elor and Yakov's dispatching of him had all but merged into the nether world of nightmares. Ari was too embarrassed to mention the episode and hoped that Yakov would ignore it, too.

"Had a rough night?" asked Yakov pointedly, when Ari finally put in his appearance.

"Nightmares... visions... weird stuff. I can't tell what was real and what wasn't. It was horrible."

"Have you had these visitations often?"

"Visitations? You mean like what you saw in my room? No, it never happened to me before."

"That was Elor... right?"

"I... I think so."

"I thought you said he'd appeared to you several times."

"Only in the form of a man... and in broad daylight," replied Ari reluctantly. "Never like this...."

"Now do you believe what I said... that these creatures are demons?"

Ari thought about that for a few moments. At last he replied, "I don't think last night proved it. He claims to be so highly evolved that he no longer has a body... and that he can take on any form. That's a scientifically acceptable explanation."

"Ari, you amaze me. You're so skeptical of what the Bible says, yet you accept the theory of a few scientists without any evidence. Theories are just that until proved... and for this one there is no proof."

"A friend of mine in Paris, a professor of astrophysics at the Polytechnic Institute next to the Sorbonne, hypothesized the existence of beings that he said were probably as far beyond man on the evolutionary scale as we are beyond worms. He thought they'd seem like 'gods' to us if we ever encountered them."

"Hypothesized. No proof. Not even a shred of likely evidence pointing in that direction." Yakov was trying to speak patiently and finding it difficult.

"Elor has certainly demonstrated to me that he has godlike powers.," returned Ari quickly. "I can't explain that away. He says there is no God, that we're all gods, and that he's just higher on the evolutionary scale than the inhabitants of this planet... and that explains his powers. It seems to me to be consistent with what a number of astrophysicists have hypothesized."

"Evolution is a myth—with a diabolically clever purpose. The perfect setup for demons. One day the scientific community is going to make contact with demons masquerading as ETIs—and the whole world will be deceived."

"Even if you were right, you couldn't prove it."

"I proved it last night."

"How?"

"I commanded your diabolical Elor, in the Name of the Lord Jesus Christ, to leave—and he did. That ought to tell you something about his identity!"

"I admire your courage," conceded Ari. "I'm terrified of Elor. I wish I had your influence over him."

"It takes no courage to stand up to demons when the God who created the universe is protecting me. You need His protection, too."

Ari made no reply. How could he argue with this old man who was so sure he had 'God' on his side—and whose life seemed to prove it? He busied himself beating an egg, dipping bread in it, and frying himself some French toast, while Yakov cooked his usual oatmeal with dates and raisins.

After a long silence Yakov volunteered, "I was reading the other day that anti-Semitism is even sweeping Japan now, in spite of the fact that there aren't any Jews over there."

"I think I saw the same article," responded Ari, happy that Yakov was not lecturing him further about demons, and eager to move the conversation in another direction. "It mentioned a recent best-selling Japanese book claiming that Japan was the victim of an international Jewish conspiracy?"

"Right. In fact that book together with another by a former Diet member, titled *The Secret of Jewish Power to Control the World*, sold almost 2 million copies. It sounded a lot like Hitler's propaganda. In the last five years there've been more than 200 books about Jews flooding Japan, many of them openly anti-Semitic. Don't you think that's rather amazing?"

"I still can't fathom this persistent, worldwide anti-Semitism!" exclaimed Ari in frustration.

"I know you don't want me to keep harping on this," said Yakov half-apologetically, "but there's only one explanation that makes sense. The Jews are God's chosen people. If Satan—he's the leader of the Nine—could destroy Israel, then God could not fulfill the promises He made through the Hebrew prophets that the Messiah would one day rule over Israel from David's throne."

"There's actually a prophecy about the Messiah ruling on David's throne?"

"*A* prophecy? Lots of them."

"Someday, maybe, you could... uh, mark them all in a Bible so I could look them over?"

"Sure. I'll do it right away. You'll have it when you come home from work this evening."

"I still think there's got to be another explanation for this universal anti-Semitism," insisted Ari.

"I'm waiting for you to tell me what it is."

Ari remained silent. Just when he'd thought life was at last coming together for him, his props were being swept away by an invasive *Presence* against which he had no defenses.

The Israeli Connection

On May 13, 1991, an unusual news item came across the wires at the *Jerusalem Post.* Ari's first reaction was to dismiss it as simply bizarre. The more he thought about it, however, the more intrigued he became. Late that afternoon, after some intensive research, Ari walked into the office of his editor, Ruta Cohen, and sat down to discuss his findings with her.

"What's on your mind, Ari? Onto a scoop? I know that look," said Ruta, when Ari had settled himself in a chair in front of her desk. Adjusting the oversize silver-rimmed glasses that lent her rather tall and very lean frame a scholarly look, the editor fixed Ari with the direct and piercing gaze that intimidated most of those under her.

"Don't laugh," said Ari tentatively, knowing Ruta well enough to suspect she might reject his proposal immediately. "I'm intrigued by that item on the wire today about the Pope."

"Refresh my memory. I've been busy...."

"Well today, in Fatima, Portugal, the Pope put a diamond necklace on a small statue of 'Our Lady of Fatima.' And in the necklace was one of the bullets that Mehmet Ali Agca, the Turkish gunman, pumped into the Pope's body exactly ten years ago. You know... the assassination attempt."

"Why the necklace? And why the bullet in it? By the way, would you like some coffee... or something else to drink?"

Ari shook his head. "No, I'm fine. It was because the Pope is convinced that 'Our Lady of Fatima' saved his life... and this was one way of thanking her."

Ruta waved her secretary away. "He's serious?" she asked.

"Very definitely."

"And you were thinking...?"

"Of doing a feature on it."

"Do it! No mercy... do it." Ruta was a colonel in the reserves and ran her department as though it were part of the Israeli Army and the country was at war. Ari, however, felt perfectly at ease with this imposing woman—one of the few staff members who did. She, in turn, respected him for his ability to stand up to her.

"Actually, I think there's something to the story," Ari countered.

"You do?" That seemed to be a thought entirely outside the bounds Ruta had set on the possible, but now that Ari had stated it without backing down she was willing to reconsider. He knew her as a very reasonable person if one had convictions and the courage and ability to substantiate them. Otherwise she was like a tank rolling over the opposition.

"If you remember the background, it's rather intriguing."

"I vaguely recall," responded Ruta thoughtfully, "that the assassination attempt occurred on the anniversary of the first appearance of 'Our Lady of Fatima.'"

"Yes, she first appeared on the same date, May 13, in 1917," interjected Ari.

"Right. Probably a coincidence. No one could prove it wasn't—and so what?"

"If that were the whole story, I'd agree with you and make a good satire out of it, which my readers expect from me now and then," returned Ari respectfully. "But there's a lot more to it. I've been researching it all day—and the more I've dug out the more intriguing it's become."

"Go on."

"The fact that there are so many alleged appearances of 'the Virgin Mary' all over the world. Even if most of these apparitions are written off as hallucinations, there's still a core that can't be explained away."

"Sounds like what the kooks say about UFOs."

"Not just the kooks—that's too simplistic. Some of the most credible researchers have pointed out similarities between UFO appearances and the apparitions of Mary."

"That doesn't impress me. Next you'll be saying she rides in UFOs."

"That's not the point. Let me remind you that in this woman the Roman Catholic Church has a secret weapon with a powerful worldwide appeal even to non-Catholics—something that fits the mood of the times. You know, feminism, women's lib, goddess worship...."

"I wouldn't call virginity very popular," came the quick response. Knowing Ruta, Ari took that sarcastic remark as a warning sign and hurried on.

"Let me finish. There's much more. The Pope believes in many of these apparitions of Mary and is devoted to her in their various forms—like the Black Virgin of Jasna Gora...that sort of thing. She's been the patron saint and protectress of Poland for 600 years. The Poles really believe that. The Pope's going to lead a huge pilgrimage to Jasna Gora in August. They expect more than a million...mostly young people, from around the world. Pretty impressive, right? Millions have visited Medjugorje, Yugoslavia, where the 'Virgin' supposedly appears every day. These apparitions have a huge following!"

Ruta started to drum impatiently on the desk with her fingers. It was her way of saying that the subject matter hadn't caught her interest and the interview was about to end.

"Look, you can't just brush this off," insisted Ari. "The Pope is today's most highly respected world leader. He's consulted by Bush, Gorbachev and a host of others, such as Arafat. You've got to take this man seriously. You can't just dismiss his beliefs as ludicrous."

Ruta gave Ari a you-can't-be-serious look. "You mean you have to accept all that the Pope believes and become a Catholic just because he's a highly respected world leader?"

Ari leaned back in his chair and laughed. "Very funny. Of course not. These appearances are something specific, unique. They're not dogmas pronounced by the church. They're *events* that either happened or didn't. *Something* caused millions of people to think they happened. And if they did, then it seems to me we've got something here worth investigating."

Ruta stopped drumming and placed her hands in her lap. "Okay, convince me."

"On that day ten years ago, as the Pope was moving along through the crowd, he noticed a young girl with a pendant around her neck. It held a small picture of 'Our Lady of Fatima.' He leaned over to bless her. Wham! Two bullets that would have killed him tore through empty space where his head had just been."

"A *lucky* coincidence."

"That's what I would have said—but there's more," persisted Ari. "While he was convalescing from the assassination attempt, the Pope had a personal visitation from 'Our Lady of Fatima.' She gave him a 'sign' and promised that one day in the not-too-distant future she'd give a spectacular sign to the entire world that would cause all of mankind to recognize and submit to the Pope's supreme spiritual authority."

"Too incredible for belief," said Ruta brusquely.

"Agreed. And that's why it's so intriguing—because the Pope obviously believes it totally, and I still say he's too credible a world leader to dismiss this as nonsense. I don't think he's hallucinating. As for the world recognizing his spiritual authority, Gorbachev—he's an avowed atheist—already has. He introduced the Pope to his wife, Raisa, as 'the highest spiritual authority on earth.'"

Ruta turned her swivel chair to one side and stared out the window in silence. That was a good sign. It indicated that she was thinking seriously about the proposition.

"And remember," Ari hurried on, "whether something is true or reasonable doesn't matter as long as millions think they have some basis, no matter how bizarre, for believing it. Listen to this. 'Our Lady of Fatima' said that if the Popes would dedicate Russia to her 'Immaculate Heart,' she'd convert Russia and turn back the tide of communism from taking over the world. Now who do you think is getting the credit for bringing down the Berlin Wall, delivering Eastern Europe from communism and breaking up the Soviet Union?"

"That's ludicrous."

"You think so, and so do I—but if millions of people believe it, that gives it tremendous power to mold opinion."

Ruta was still looking out the window, apparently lost in thought. At last she asked the inevitable question, "Where's the relevance to Israel?"

"The Israeli connection is rather ominous. As you know, the Catholic Church has never recognized the right of Israel to exist. In fact, it's been our secret—and extremely powerful—enemy. I don't have to persuade you of *that*."

Ruta swung around in her chair to fix Ari with a skeptical look. "And you think these apparitions of Mary have something to do with that? Come on!"

"Let me finish. Syria's Hafez Assad insists that ETIs in UFOs are going to establish peace in the Middle East. And according to the experts, as I've already said, there's a relationship between UFOs and apparitions of Mary. The Vatican, which promotes Mary, takes the side of the Arab nations against Israel...."

"Too tenuous!" interrupted Ruta forcefully. "We couldn't print something like that!"

"You still haven't let me finish. Millions of people are convinced that they've seen UFOs and apparitions of 'Our Lady' of this or that. Do you admit that?"

Ruta nodded. "They *think* they have."

"That's all that's necessary," argued Ari. "They only have to *believe* they've seen something inexplicable or 'supernatural.' It's not inconceivable that whatever is the source of these 'signs,' which have convinced millions that UFOs exist and that Mary is appearing, might also produce a far greater sign that would convince hundreds of millions... perhaps even billions of people around the world."

Ruta again gazed out the window. Ari continued.

"And if it happens, it could be very bad if the sign the world receives seems to favor the Arab and the Catholic opposition to Israel...."

"Who says there'll be a sign? Suppose there isn't—and I don't think there will be."

"This is where the plot thickens," said Ari, rushing on before he lost her. "Fatima was the name of Muhammad's favorite daughter. He said before his death that she would be the highest lady in heaven... *except for the Virgin Mary....*"

Ruta turned to face Ari. "I wasn't aware of that," she said. "So 'Our Lady of Fatima' has a special appeal for Muslims...." For the first time since he'd begun sharing his idea, Ruta's eyes had that bloodhound look. She was at last on the scent of something worthwhile.

"You've got it! Listen to this," continued Ari. "I've been watching reports coming across the wire about the reception the statue of 'Our Lady of Fatima' gets among Muslims in Africa and India. They come out by the hundreds of thousands... and bow down and worship her! And in a popular book way back in 1952, a highly-regarded Catholic bishop—Fulton J. Sheen, I think it was—predicted that it would be 'Our Lady of Fatima' who would unite the Muslims with the Catholics worldwide!"

Ruta stood to her feet abruptly. Ari did the same. "I'm still not convinced," she said, then added grudgingly, "but I think you may be onto something worth exploring. Go ahead and do some more research, and let me know what you come up with."

— ✦ —

That night, intrigued by his new project, Ari worked later than usual. It was such a beautiful evening that he decided to walk all the way to Yakov's apartment instead of riding the bus. It would take him less than an hour, and he needed the exercise. The weather had turned hot recently, but with darkness settling and a moderate breeze blowing up from the Mediterranean, the temperature was dropping and the evening was now very pleasant. It was more than a year since Ari had arrived in Jerusalem. He had to confess that the city had grown on him. It had a vitality, a sense of expectancy, of being on the verge of something exciting that he had never experienced anywhere else in his years of traveling the world.

Darkness had descended and the street lights had come on by the time Ari, coming down Shlomzion ha Malacha Street, reached the junction and turned onto Mamilla. Crossing the Hinnom Valley, he thrilled to the sight of the Jaffa Gate straight ahead. David's Tower rose on the right and the parapeted city wall dating back to Crusader times stretched out on either side. With the floodlights illuminating it, the ancient wall looked unreal, like a giant movie set. As he approached, it loomed above him in timeless beauty.

Choosing not to use the Jaffa Gate—he wanted to avoid the Arab quarter—Ari proceeded to his right along a narrow path that zig-zagged its way up Mount Zion. Reaching the base of the ancient wall he joined a broad walkway that would take him into the Old City through the Zion Gate, still pockmarked with bullet holes from the Six Day War of 1967.

Ari had not gone far along the deserted promenade when he noticed the familiar figure standing in the shadow of an Armenian monastery about 50 feet ahead, obviously waiting for him. As he drew closer Ari felt the hair rise on the back of his neck. There was no doubt that it was Elor, but this time appearing as an Arab in flowing white robe and Bedouin *kafiyeh* such as he might encounter at the Sheep Gate of the Old City.

"So, my friend," the mysterious entity began, when Ari had reached him, "you're going to devote one of your columns to apparitions of Mary. Does it disturb you that I know everything... even your most secret thoughts?"

"Easy," said Elor quietly in response to Ari's speechless anger. "You forget that we're billions of years ahead of you on the evolutionary scale, so your private thoughts are of no interest to us. Unless, of course, they oppose our plans for the good of this planet...."

"And do your plans involve 'Our Lady of Fatima'?" asked Ari, getting control of his outraged feelings. It was frustrating to be at such a disadvantage in a contest of wits. In fact, it was no contest.

"It was I who appeared at Fatima as 'Mary,'" responded Elor matter-of-factly. "Yes, 'Our Lady of Fatima' will play an important role in the transformation of consciousness that mankind must experience for peace to reign. But all of this will become clear to you in exactly two years and one month. That is when you will arrive at a secret location near Palo Alto, California for a historic event—and you will not see me again until after that trip has been successfully completed."

"California?" asked Ari cautiously. Then Elor knew everything! "Are you referring to the mission the Mossad's sending me on?"

Elor's laugh sent the hair rising on the back of Ari's neck again. "Let them think they are sending you. It is to the same place and at the same time that we have planned. You will do *our* bidding... and you will find that it will coincide with their objective. You will be able, *as an eyewitness*, to tell the Mossad all that they want to know."

Ari was speechless. Could the Nine really predict the future... perhaps even make it happen? Elor had hinted at that in the past, but never had he been so specific as now.

Elor put his hand on Ari's shoulder. "You wonder whether I really know the future. I'll give you a sign. The Israelis and Arabs will come to the peace table for face-to-face talks before the end of this coming October... and they will do so in Madrid. In December the talks will move to Washington, D.C."

Ari could only stare at Elor in wide-eyed bewilderment.

"You may confidently make that prediction in your column in the *Post*, if you wish," continued Elor. "However, I would not advise it."

"So, you're not certain...?"

"On the contrary... but how would you explain yourself?"

"Why should I?"

"You would be asked. And if you have no reason, then even when it happened it would be nothing more than a lucky guess."

"Of course," responded Ari after a moment's hesitation.

"The sign I have given shows our deep interest in Israel reaching a peaceful settlement with its neighbors. In fact, we are the ones who will bring it to pass."

"So there will be a peace agreement between Israel and the Arabs?"

"Eventually. But no more about that now."

Ari struggled to make sense of what Elor seemed to be saying. "Are you telling me that you somehow guide human history?"

"Not entirely. That was our plan—but like yourself, most human beings are stubborn and don't accept guidance readily. They can only learn the hard way... and some never learn."

"Give me an example of your influence," Ari challenged him.

Elor smiled and released his grip on Ari's shoulder. "There are so many lies. Religion is such a fraud. Our plans to transform this earth have been frustrated by selfish religious leaders who keep their followers in bondage by promising them a mythical 'heaven.'"

Ari nodded. "I agree!"

"Buddhists are the closest to the truth. The Muslims are somewhat further from it. The worst delusions came through those who call themselves Christians. Christianity quickly became a complete perversion of the original teachings of the Christ before he rebelled. The primordial pagan religions had been far closer. This ancient wisdom would have been lost with the coming of the science that accompanies your so-called advancements of civilization. So we inspired the formation of many secret societies, such as the Freemasons and Rosicrucians, to preserve the ancient mysteries until the day when the power of the gods would pass to men and a New Age would dawn."

Elor took Ari by the arm and gently propelled him forward. "Come, my friend, let us walk together."

Ari obeyed as in a dream, perplexed beyond words. There was silence for a few paces. Then Elor continued. "The Emperor Constantine followed much of our guidance... blending Christianity, which had wandered so far astray, back into the mainstream of paganism. It became known as Roman Catholicism. For peace to prevail on earth, all religions must yet be united under one head, and we have chosen the Vatican to be the headquarters. The present Pope is on the right path. Mary is the key. The genuine apparitions are appearances of one of the Nine, and will yet play a major role in effecting religious unity. Your interest in this subject indicates that you, too, are on the right path."

Ari shook his head in bewilderment. "You speak in riddles."

Again that confident, all-knowing smile from Elor. "It only seems so at this time. When you are in California and meet the One we have chosen to rule the New World Order, you will begin to understand. He is a Jesuit. He will use the Roman Catholic Church and its Pope to effect worldwide unity of religion. And then, my friend... we have them!" Elor smiled.

"The worst roadblocks to peace are Christian fundamentalism and Zionism," continued Elor. "Both must be eliminated. Jerusalem is central to our plans. It must be internationalized. The belief that Messiah will rule the world from the throne of King David in Jerusalem must be removed from Jewish consciousness. For that purpose you have been chosen." For one fleeting moment Elor's face revealed beneath the mocking smile a mask of unspeakable evil.

Ari blinked, and Elor was gone. That elusive expression on this mysterious being's face had been terrifying. But it faded from Ari's memory almost immediately, until he was no longer certain of what he had seen.

41

An Irresistible Invitation

The next two years were lonely ones. Miriam seldom came to Jerusalem. She was very friendly when, on rare occasions, she dropped in at Yakov's apartment, but that almost made it more painful. There seemed no hope that any romantic relationship could be reestablished. The one thing Ari had to look forward to was his trip to California—and his impatience to face that challenge only made the months pass more slowly and monotonously.

Not that there were no events of great significance to monitor and analyze for his twice-weekly column. There were many. In spite of rank pessimism on both sides that it could ever actually take place, the Israelis and Arabs came together for historic face-to-face peace talks in Madrid before the end of October. They then moved to Washington, DC in December 1991, for the next phase in their negotiations. It all occurred precisely as Elor had said it would.

That such talks between these sworn enemies had never happened before in the nearly 44 years of Israel's existence, and that they seemed impossible right up to the last moment, with much opposition from both Arabs and Israelis, made Elor's prediction all the more impressive. Ari seemed to have no choice except to believe that the Nine, whoever they might be, were directing human history from behind the scenes.

That these mysterious entities planned to use him to wean Israelis away from the fanatical Zionism that he had always opposed made him feel more comfortable about Elor in spite of Yakov's dire warnings. After all, how could peace ever be achieved unless the "chosen people" delusion were renounced? It all made perfect sense.

Of course, there were the fanatical Muslim fundamentalists who would be satisfied with nothing less than the annihilation of Israel—and Elor had yet to mention how they could become part of the peace process. That bothered Ari, but there was no way to get in touch with Elor to question him on this vital point that had been overlooked in their brief discussions.

At the same time the Madrid peace talks were going on, a veritable Who's Who in international terrorism held its own "peace" conference in Teheran. It was called "The International Conference to Support the Islamic Revolution of Palestine." Drawing upon his Mossad connections and doing original investigation on his own, Ari gathered inside information and devoted two articles to this infamous gathering. The conference was opened by Iranian President Hashemi

Rafsanjani committing Iranian troops to fight Israel. The "peace" that conference hoped to achieve was to result from the utter destruction of Israel.

Ari startled his readers by reporting that there were 400 delegates attending from 60 Islamic countries, including numerous mass murderers. Few Israelis were aware that so many Islamic countries existed. Among the terrorists attending who were based in Damascus and enjoying the protection of peace-loving Syria was Ahmed Jibril. His Progressive Front for the Liberation of Palestine had been responsible for the bombing of Pan-Am 103 over Lockerbie, Scotland. The PLO delegation was headed by its number two man behind Arafat, Sheikh Abdel Hamid el-Saikh, who was also chairman of the Palestine National Council.

Among the resolutions adopted, Resolution 11 was a condemnation of the peace negotiations underway in Madrid. Resolution 3 called for "elimination of the Zionist existence," and Resolution 22 reiterated "the need for an all-out *jihad* against the Zionist regime." Egypt's semiofficial newspaper, *Al-Ahram*, published all of the resolutions in its October 24 edition. Conspicuous by its absence was any condemnation of this conference from Egypt, the nation that had a peace treaty with Israel.

Israeli Ambassador Yoram Aridor lodged a formal complaint concerning the Teheran conference with the UN secretary-general, but it was ignored by that peace-keeping body. Ari pointed out the irony that an Iranian was serving as deputy chairman of the UN Human Rights Committee in Geneva. Those two articles generated more mail and popularity for Ari than anything he had previously written.

— ✦ —

Ari tried to forget the frightening appearance of Elor in his bedroom and to think of him only as he had appeared in human form. Yakov only hinted at the incident now and then, but Ari would immediately change the subject and Yakov would not pursue it. Then in the fall of 1992 the old man's concern seemed to heighten until he could no longer remain silent.

"I'm warning you that the very minions of Satan are trying to use you to their ends," Yakov told him bluntly over supper one evening in February. "What I saw that night in your room left no doubt that Elor is a demon... and you are in grave danger. I pray for you continually—but you have a choice to make."

"But they're for peace," protested Ari. "They predicted and brought about the peace talks."

"What makes you say that?"

"I can't tell you... but surely Israel wants peace! Don't you...?"

Yakov picked up his large Bible and thumbed quickly through its well-worn pages. "Have you read those verses I marked for you... the prophecies about the Messiah and Israel and her land?"

"Yes, I read them twice. Very interesting... but also a bit hard to understand the language sometimes."

"Let me read you some others. Listen to the prophet Daniel." Yakov's voice was edged with urgency. "This is chapter 8, beginning at verse 24: 'And his power shall be mighty, but not by his own power.' Comparing that last phrase, 'not by his own power,' with the New Testament makes it clear that Daniel is referring to the Antichrist. In 2 Thessalonians 2:9 the Antichrist is described as the one 'whose coming is after the working of Satan with all power and signs and lying wonders.' That's what this demon, Elor, is dazzling you with—'lying wonders.' The point is that it's by the power of Satan. John in Revelation 13 also speaks of the Antichrist and he says in verse 2, 'and the dragon'—that's Satan—'gave him his power.' Exactly what Daniel says...."

"But peace!" cut in Ari.

"A false peace!" retorted Yakov. "Daniel goes on to say that the Antichrist will 'destroy the mighty and the holy people.' How? Daniel explains: 'by *peace* shall he destroy many.' It's a trick. 'Peace' built upon compromise and false promises. Trading land for 'peace'—trusting the Antichrist, who will double-cross them, instead of trusting in the God who gave Israel this land. It's the sanctuary of the chosen only for those who trust Him. The Bible warns that Israel will host Armageddon!"

"Chosen people!" protested Ari. "That's so arrogant!"

"It would be if we claimed it for ourselves—but it's not arrogant when God says it. It's arrogant not to believe Him."

"Who says God said it? That's your opinion. But most Israelis that I've talked to don't believe that. With them it's just 'tradition.'"

"It's in God's Word, stated by His prophets from Moses to Malachi, proved by the fulfillment of what they've said...."

"Look, I've read those prophecies... but why don't you lay it out in plain language. Tell me exactly what the Bible says is going to happen."

"Yes, sir!" Yakov's smile brightened again. "In the next chapter, verse 27, Daniel says that the Antichrist 'shall confirm the covenant with many for one week'... actually a week of years. That's his guarantee of a temple in Jerusalem and the peace pact for seven years. Then in the middle of that 'week'—after three-and-a-half years—he'll make the Israelis stop sacrificing in the rebuilt temple, and he'll put his own image there, forcing them and the whole world to worship him as god. Eventually he'll lead all of the world's armies against Israel to finish off the Jews once and for all... and that's when Jesus Christ will intervene from heaven to rescue Israel."

"Did the Hebrew prophets say 'Jesus Christ' in so many words?" countered Ari. "I didn't find that in any of the places you marked."

"Zechariah says they'll recognize their God, Yaweh, as a resurrected man whom they *pierced* to the death. That can only be Jesus... and Zechariah, Isaiah and others who say something similar are Hebrew prophets!"

"That's your interpretation... but I can't just believe it because you say so." He stared out the large picture window at the view of Temple Mount in silence. At last he turned to Yakov and asked, "This 'Antichrist'... what about him?"

"Jesus told the Jews in His day, 'I have come in my Father's name and you receive me not; another will come in his own name and him you will receive.' It pains me that my own people who rejected their true Messiah when He came, and joined with the Romans to crucify Him exactly as their own prophets had warned they would, will receive this false Messiah, this Antichrist, when he comes. And from what Elor has told you, it sounds as though that's who you're supposed to meet in California... the Antichrist himself. And apparently you're to become his ambassador to Israel!"

"What can I do?" demanded Ari helplessly. "They know my every thought. They know we're having this conversation right now. I'm really at their mercy...."

"Elor's deceiving you. Demons don't have that much power. They don't know everything."

"That's easy for you to say... but I've seen his power."

"And you saw me overpower him in the name of Jesus. Believe on the Lord Jesus Christ and put yourself in His hands!" exclaimed Yakov earnestly. "Then you have nothing to fear! Listen to what Daniel goes on to say in chapter 8, verse 25 about the Antichrist: 'He shall stand up against the Prince of princes'—that's Jesus Christ, the true Messiah—'but he shall be broken without hand.' Jesus is the only one who can protect you! He died for your sins so you could be forgiven... and He's coming back to the earth to destroy the Antichrist and all those who follow him. Don't be one of them!"

"Miriam has told me that—and because I can't believe it, she's done with me. Why would her belief in the Messiah—if that's who Jesus really is—lead to something so cruel! We love each other... but she won't see me."

"Don't say she won't see you," corrected Yakov. "She cares. She's concerned about you... and she loves you very much. But she can't continue to see you on your terms. You've asked her to marry you... and she can't do that, not unless...."

"Unless I believe in her 'Jesus'!" interjected Ari bitterly. "That's such obvious, unfair coercion!"

"No. She wouldn't want you to say you're a Jesus believer so she would marry you. That's why she feels it's best not to keep a close relationship... she doesn't want to pressure you."

"Her attitude hasn't helped me to believe!"

"Ari, you need to face the fact that you're a rebel in God's universe, unwilling to admit that you've broken His laws and that you need His forgiveness. He loves you so much that He became a man to die for your sins...."

"We've been through that!" interrupted Ari impatiently. "I may seem stubborn, and I am... but I do appreciate your concern... and Miriam's. It's just that these bizarre beliefs of yours... and then Elor and his plans for me... I feel trapped." Ari stood to his feet and headed for his room.

"I'm praying for you, Ari," Yakov called after him, "and so is Miriam. Very much!"

Those words were strangely annoying. Well, he could be broadminded about it. *Let them pray if they want to—it can't hurt.*

— ✦ —

Under the watchful guidance of the Mossad, Ari kept in touch with Carla by mail. Her letters gradually became less frequent, and Ari, of course, was instructed not to seem to pursue the relationship and to stop asking questions about parapsychology and the secret project with which she was involved.

"Patience, man," David reminded him so often during those trying months that passed so tediously. "She's your ticket to California, and we're as eager as you are. But you've got to play it cool. When she finally invites you, if she ever does—and you can't force that... you've got to pretend you're reluctant to go."

Then in the middle of April 1993, the phone call he had dreamed of for so long came one evening just after he and Yakov had finished supper. It was the old man who answered the phone in the kitchen where he was doing the dishes.

"It's some woman calling from Palo Alto, California," Yakov yelled to Ari, who was in the living room relaxing over that day's edition of *Le Monde* flown in from Paris. Now and then he picked up a copy from a newsstand and perused it eagerly.

Ari was on his feet in an instant and found himself in the kitchen reaching for the phone before he realized that his heart was pounding with excitement. *Calm down* he reminded himself. *Play it cool.*

Ari took a deep breath and let it out slowly. "Yes... Ari here," he said, struggling for control.

"Dr. Thalberg! Great to hear your voice! It's Carla."

"What a pleasant surprise! Please, just call me Ari. Are you here in Israel?"

"Hardly," laughed Carla. "I've been too busy to do any traveling. No, I'm in California. How's everything?"

"Pretty well... but settling into a routine, I'm afraid. How are you doing? Haven't heard from you in quite a while."

"It's getting exciting over here. That's what I called about. You're still enjoying the wonderful world of journalism?"

"I don't know that it's such a wonderful world... but I really do enjoy it, though it gets monotonous at times."

"Well, something's opened up here that will relieve your monotony—and that's putting it mildly."

"You mean... is this the scoop you hinted that you might give me nearly three years ago?"

"You remember that! It's been a long time—but when you find out what's happened you'll agree it has been more than worth the wait."

"Yea? What's going on?"

"I couldn't tell you before, because the project I've been involved in has been top secret. Some aspects still are. But we're about to let the world in on the most fantastic opportunity for peace... not just in the Middle East, but everywhere. And unbelievable prosperity, too. The whole thing is incredible—but true!"

"Like what?"

"We've made a breakthrough in psychic power that's absolutely beyond imagination! The world will be completely transformed. But it's so fantastic that we have to be very careful how the news gets out. So we're inviting top representatives from 120 nations to a world congress. There'll be hundreds of people from the media on hand, but only about 30 will be allowed inside the actual meetings. I'd like you to be one of that select group, Ari, representing *The Jerusalem Post*."

"Psychic power... that sounds a bit far out for *The Post*," responded Ari coolly, trying to control his excitement. "Anyway, I'm one of the junior staff. There are lots of writers who've been there much longer than I have... so I doubt that my editors would let me go."

"Ari, they'll have to. I won't accept anyone else."

"Flattering, but you'll have to convince them. They're very conservative...."

"Don't tell me they're too conservative," insisted Carla. "*The Post* had an article about psychic power... and the possible involvement of ETIs in developing it. You sent it to me... remember? Of course, if you're not interested...."

"Oh, I'm interested," Ari hastened to assure her. "Anything you're involved in is of great interest to me. And I'm interested in the subject. I don't want to give you the wrong impression. It's just that I doubt that my editors...."

"Forget your editors. They'll recognize that this is a news item that comes along once in a lifetime. And I won't let them send anyone else except you, so that's settled."

"So... when is this?"

"June 14."

June 14! Two years and one month from the last time I saw him—exactly as Elor said! Ari's heart skipped a few beats, then began pounding in his chest so loudly that he was sure Carla could hear it. She was talking, and he'd missed some of it.

"... you'll get a formal invitation in the mail in about two weeks. It will include lots of data that you must become familiar with—some of it shocking, much of it unbelievable. Everything is confidential until after the congress—then you can let go with both barrels on the most fantastic story in human history!"

"Sounds too good to be true. You've got me excited."

"Excited is too mild a word. You can't even imagine what you're going to experience and the story you'll be able to give to the world. And I'm sure looking forward to seeing you!"

"Likewise. Thanks for thinking of me...and letting me in on this. I'll be watching for that mailing."

How about that! he told himself when he hung up. *It's happening—just like Elor predicted. Another month...and I'll be in the middle of the greatest challenge I've ever faced. Frightening? Yes—but totally irresistible!*

—✦—

Ari immediately reported Carla's call to David. "Fantastic!" came the enthusiastic response over the phone. "Just the lucky break we needed! And she insists on you. See, we knew you were the man for the job... and I'm sure you can pull it off."

"I played it cool," said Ari. "Made her persuade me. Frankly, that wasn't hard to do. I'm as scared as I am excited."

"So there's going to be some kind of 'world congress' with representatives of 120 nations. That fits with the information we've been getting. Where's it going to be?"

"She didn't say, but I got the impression it will be at that secret CIA lab you've told me about, the one where Carla's been involved."

"From what we understand, the CIA's top psychic is a Jesuit named Antonio Del Sasso...."

"That's the man Elor told me about... the coming world ruler!"

"According to our reports, he's incredible," said David. "He can read minds."

"So can the Nine."

"Just remember the training you've been getting from our psychologists. Nobody can pull out of your mind what you're not thinking of at the time. You've got to control your thoughts so that nothing comes into your mind that would get you in trouble."

"Impossible! I've been practicing hours every day... and I still can't keep that odd thought from popping up involuntarily."

"You'll do it when your life depends on it."

"Thanks a lot!"

"Let me tell you something else," said David somberly. "Several months ago the KGB sent in their top psychic assault team to try to destroy the base. This guy Del Sasso made mincemeat out of them. It was strictly no contest." David paused to let that sink in. "You're going into the dragon's den. I can't emphasize that strongly enough. One slip... and you're finished!"

Ari made no reply. He couldn't let such negative thoughts register. He would make it, come out on top—*Never accept defeat: with enough guts and brains, anything is possible!*

"Then what makes you say that Satan wants my soul? And the Antichrist...why do you mention him?"

"I don't know. It's a concern I have when I pray. I've been praying for you often every day for the past five weeks. Over and over in prayer I've been reminded of what you told me Nicole said when she came to the airport in Paris to say goodbye. That dream of hers that you told me about...it's going to happen to you in California. I just know it!" Tears welled up in Miriam's eyes.

"It means a lot to me...that you care," Ari murmured softly.

"Ari, Satan has a mission for you...and it will be your destruction if you accept it!"

"Yakov has been telling you!" he insisted.

"No, he has said nothing like that. It has come to me in prayer. God reveals things. He has a mission for you also. You will have to make a choice. When it looks like the end has come, Yeshua—Messiah Jesus—will rescue you... if you will let Him. Oh, Ari, do let Him!" The agony in Miriam's voice stirred within him in alternating waves of hope and fear.

Ari could no longer resist. He reached out and pulled her to him and held her tight. Miriam clung to him. "I love you," he whispered. "I'll come back, just for you. And if your Jesus does what you say... if He proves Himself to me... then I'll become a believer, too. But I must have something... some proof."

"I love you, Ari. I'll pray that He will give you what you ask. And I'll be waiting for you...hoping...." She could only cling to him in wordless pain.

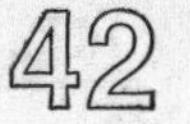

Congress for a New World

It was a long flight from Tel Aviv to London to Los Angeles, where they spent the night, then up to San Francisco the next morning. Due to limited space in the auditorium where the congress would be held, Israel had been allowed only one political delegate, Yetsak Kaufy, and one religious leader, Rabbi Mordechai Margolins, a popular and influential Lubavitcher—and one media representative, which of course was Ari. These three had seats together, and their animated discussion made the otherwise tedious flight pass more quickly.

Ari had been interested in the Lubavitchers ever since he'd researched this esoteric yet powerful group for an article he'd done early in 1991. At that time they had emerged from relative obscurity to international prominence—an inexplicable development that had puzzled Ari. What had led a joint session of the United States Congress and Senate—in spite of the fact that most Americans had never heard of him or his movement—to honor Lubavitcher leader, Rabbi Menachem Schneerson, a resident of Brooklyn, New York, by declaring his birthday to be National Education Day? It was a mystery he hadn't solved. Writing the article had required considerable research. So this was not, by any means, Ari's first personal contact with representatives of Israel's most powerful religious group, though he had never met Rabbi Margolins. Ari found the Rabbi's ideas fascinating, particularly with reference to the Messiah.

"We're absolutely convinced that the Messiah is already here, waiting to reveal himself at the right time," the Rabbi had declared with great enthusiasm at least half a dozen times during the flight. Yetsak Kaufy seemed skeptical, but refrained from expressing his doubts, obviously wary of offending this influential religious leader.

"How will he be recognized?" Ari had asked when the idea had been first presented.

"By his deeds!" had come the instant response.

"But certainly... some special qualifications... credentials of some kind... to make certain he's the right one?"

"Who or what he is has little importance—only what he does," the Rabbi had declared emphatically. "He'll be recognized as the one man able to solve all of the world's pressing problems and bring all nations and peoples together in peace."

"He'll do it that convincingly?" Ari had asked in surprise.

"Absolutely," had come the confident reply. "When the time comes, there will be no doubt in anyone's mind anywhere in the world. Through this one man a new era of universal brotherhood will dawn. The nations of the world will at last live in peace and mutual respect. It will indeed be a New World Order of unity and harmony."

"I hope you're right," had been Kaufy's only comment, and he had sounded sincere.

"So Jesus of Nazareth couldn't have been the Messiah...." Ari had tentatively voiced what seemed to be implied.

"Of course not!" the rabbi had responded emphatically. "No matter what Christians say about him, he failed to bring this universal peace... but the real Messiah will succeed when He comes!"

In spite of his determination to remain open-minded, the conversation made Ari uncomfortable. The Rabbi's statements reminded him of Yakov's dire predictions: "The world will be so obsessed with the desire for peace that anyone who can seemingly pull it off will be hailed as the Savior, be he the Devil himself! In fact, he'll be the Antichrist. This counterfeit Messiah must be accepted by Israel and the world before the return of Yeshua, the real Messiah. He'll come to destroy Antichrist and his New World Order!"

Miriam had repeatedly voiced basically the same warnings independently of Yakov. When Ari had accused them of getting together and agreeing to present him with the same arguments, they had vehemently denied any collusion. "This is simply what the Bible says will happen," Miriam had told him. "It's there for anybody to see for themselves! That the Messiah would be rejected by His own people and crucified the first time He came... to pay the debt for our sins... that's not some recent invention of Christians. The Hebrew prophets said it plainly in the Old Testament... and that only at His Second Coming would He establish His worldwide kingdom of perfect peace."

Ari found himself unable to deny that this book which he had found so difficult to understand without the help of these two followers of Jesus contained statements which seemed to offer convincingly apropos insight. In contrast to Rabbi Margolins's idea of how the Messiah would be recognized, both Yakov and Miriam had quoted the prophet Zechariah: "They will look on me whom they have pierced...." Reading and rereading chapter 12 many times, he'd been deeply troubled, for it *seemed* to be saying that the Messiah would be recognized by marks proving he had been put to death and was now alive again. Nor could Ari erase from his memory the prophecies of Daniel that Yakov had read to him—especially that one phrase that referred to the Antichrist, "by peace shall he destroy many." It haunted him.

Peace! That was what the world congress was all about. And an unnamed man with great psychic power—apparently the Antonio Del Sasso the Mossad had warned him about—was going to demonstrate his incredible capabilities, which he would share with the world as the basis for lasting peace. So the advance information sent to all the delegates and media representatives had explained.

Nor had it helped Ari's peace of mind to learn that the official name of the conference he was to attend was *World Congress 666*. It had been somewhat unnerving to find in the packet he had received the identifying badge he must show to gain entrance—and to see above his name the number 666 in large, bold print. Obviously it was considered important—but why? What did it mean?

Ari had always prided himself on being free of superstition. He considered 666 to be a joke suitable only for class B horror films—which made it all the more puzzling why this number had been chosen for this important congress. The top-secret packet did contain an explanation, but it hadn't relieved Ari's apprehension to read it:

> For many centuries the world has been influenced by the hysterical warning, dishonestly inserted in the Christian Bible by corrupt priests, that a terrifying world dictator known as the Antichrist would arise in the 'last days' and that his secret mark would be the number 666. This absurdity has been accepted as true by so many millions for so long that it has become embedded in the collective unconscious of the entire race—even in cultures where Christianity has not been known. The latter fact may at least in part be traced to a number of Hollywood films which have used this bizarre belief in their sensational plots.
>
> In the opinion of the world's leading psychologists and psychiatrists, this insidious delusion about Antichrist and 666 is *the major barrier to peace*. It must be removed from the collective unconscious. The only way to do so is to destroy this idea by showing the world that it is, in fact, a myth. That is what you will be doing when, together with other world leaders, you wear your badge without fear at this congress, where the foundation for lasting international peace will be solidly laid.

— ✦ —

Ari and his two companions were met when they deplaned by an officious and very vocal man in an impeccably tailored dark silk suit who introduced himself as an Undersecretary of State. "Your baggage will be taken to the Hilton in Palo Alto where you'll be spending the next three nights," he informed them. "You'll find your bags in your rooms tonight." He escorted them outside where they were placed in one of a number of limousines lined up at the curb. Soon they were joined by two political delegates from Poland and two from Holland. At that point the driver and his front seat companion—*they're both CIA*, Ari surmised—were given orders to depart.

"It's about a two-hour drive," Silk-suit informed them. "You'll be taken directly to a secure location in the foothills to the west of Palo Alto where the Congress will meet. Sit back and enjoy."

When they arrived at their destination, Ari was surprised to find the solid steel gate in the tall, thick stone wall surrounding the grounds wide open. Armed guards carefully checked the identification of all those passing through the gate, but that was no more than one would expect at such a gathering. Ari's Mossad briefers had described this property housing the secret CIA lab as a fortress that could withstand an armed assault. On this special day, however, the impression deliberately given was one of complete openness to the world. Outwardly, at least, everything Ari could see seemed to support the pledge in the packet he had received that the psychic powers which had been developed over the past few years would, in the interests of peace, be shared with all mankind.

Limousines continued to arrive in a steady stream, bringing top diplomats from around the world. Once the passengers were deposited in front of the main building, the chauffeurs went on around the circular drive and back out the gate. There they parked their vehicles along the narrow access road that wound its way from the main highway for several miles through the tall pines and redwoods to this secluded location.

Many of the delegates were skeptical and had come only because their governments had sent them and it was an honor to be present at such a high-level gathering. Nevertheless, one could literally feel the charged atmosphere of excitement and anticipation building among this august assembly. Everyone was eagerly looking forward to meeting the great psychic and seeing him display what the advance information had promised would be "godlike powers"—powers that would eventually be made equally available to every person in the world, thus ushering in a New Age of virtually unlimited accomplishment and prosperity. This earth would once more be a paradise. The two Israeli delegates were as eager and optimistic as all the rest, having been given false information by the Mossad as a cover for Ari. He was the lone exception—a spy in the midst, forced to maintain a continual stream of thoughts favorable to the congress in order to prevent his mind from being read and his true motives exposed.

Now that the event Ari had so long anticipated was about to begin, every nerve in his body and brain was on a razor's edge of readiness. *Into the dragon's den!* Those had been David's parting words, and now that he was here Ari sensed the reality of that ominous warning. Nor was it Del Sasso alone whom he had to keep from reading his mind. What about the Nine? In spite of Yakov's open contempt for their powers, did they not know his every thought? That evening, at the hotel in Palo Alto, he was to make his first contact with a Mossad agent to pass on the information he had gleaned. It was a difficult and dangerous assignment.

The day was beautiful and clear, with the temperature in the high seventies and just enough breeze blowing to keep it comfortable. Colorful canopies had been erected to shelter the distinguished visitors from the warm California sun, and there were long tables with every kind of *hors d'oeuvres* and delicious desserts imaginable. United States Marines in dress uniform and side arms circulated among the guests, serving them food and drinks. Ari noticed that the visitors included a number of generals and admirals from the United States, Canada and European NATO nations.

Tours were being offered of the labs in outlying structures, but not of the main building. Ari opted to wander about on his own, noting with interest how accurately the descriptions he'd been given by the Mossad fitted what he was now seeing. He caught a glimpse of Roger, and also of Bourbonnais, in the distance and decided to deliberately avoid any contact with either of them. As the time for the official commencement of the program approached, the delegates began to congregate on the expansive lawn in front of the main building, the level of excitement and volume of conversation heightening together.

— ✦ —

Promptly at 4:00 P.M. a rather frail middle-aged man of medium height walked briskly out of the front door. His high, broad forehead was topped with thinning wisps of gray hair, and he was wearing large, steel-rimmed glasses that gave him a professorially owlish look. Smiling and nodding to the assembled throng, he was followed closely by a tall, powerfully built man with thick, dark hair and matching beard. He was wearing a full-length, black monk's robe with hood thrown back. *Del Sasso!* An imposing figure indeed. Seeming to fix Ari immediately with his deep-set, piercing eyes as though he had been expecting him, Del Sasso suddenly smiled warmly and instantly projected a captivating charm. Next came Carla, stately and radiantly beautiful in a full-skirted, flowered silk dress that complemented the reddish sheen of her long, auburn hair. On her heels came a thinnish man of medium height in his early forties with prematurely graying blond, crew-cut hair and sharp features. He looked unusually pale and obviously nervous. As these four made their way to a small canopy under which they would stand to receive the delegates individually, a thunderous roar of applause greeted them.

Ari became aware that a transformation had instantly taken place. The electrically charismatic presence of Del Sasso, who was smiling in all directions now, had suddenly charged the atmosphere with awe and an almost fearful expectancy. Glancing at the faces around him, Ari could see that the skepticism had been replaced by an almost childlike anticipation of wonders to be seen. It was as though a spiritual power had swept over the crowd. Ari had to fight desperately to prevent himself from being caught up in the sudden wave of frenzied enthusiasm.

A line formed quickly to the left of these four dignitaries. The delegates began to file slowly by, thrilled to meet each one, but especially to be able to converse personally, though briefly, with the head of the experimental laboratory where the breakthrough had taken place and with the world's most renowned psychic. When Ari at last reached the dignitaries, Carla stepped out and gave him a quick hug.

"How wonderful that you could be here!" she exclaimed. Turning to the pale, blond man on her left, she said, "I want you to meet Dr. Ari Thalberg. Ari, this is Dr. Viktor Khorev. Dr. Khorev was the top Soviet scientist involved in psychic research. He defected several years ago—but that's no longer a meaningful term." She put a hand affectionately on Viktor's arm and said, "Viktor, Dr. Thalberg was a professor of mine at the Sorbonne in Paris longer ago than either of us wants to admit. The best teacher I ever had! He now writes for *The Jerusalem Post.*"

"Keep moving," said a courteous but authoritarian voice behind Ari.

"I'm glad to meet you," said Khorev in a thick Russian accent. He seemed preoccupied and not particularly enjoying his place in the limelight.

Carla quickly pulled Ari over to the huge man on her right, who was already looking at Ari closely. "And this is Antonio Del Sasso!" she declared proudly. "He's one of the most remarkable men the world has ever seen—as you will soon discover for yourself!"

"She gets carried away with enthusiasm at times," responded Del Sasso modestly in a deep, melodious voice, enveloping Ari's medium-sized hand in his huge one. It was a warm handshake that lasted for an eternity while Del Sasso's eyes seemed to look into his soul.

"We're so glad you're here. The Nine have told me a great deal about you . . . a chosen vessel for a most important mission!" Again that sudden, warm smile, this time a bit patronizing, as though Ari were a child. "Your dream of a world of justice and peace will be realized. The time is now! Your past accomplishments have played an important role . . . and you will soon taste the victory . . . when each individual will be endued with godlike powers, bringing total freedom from all oppression, inward and outward."

Ari avoided the man's eyes. They made him uncomfortable. He nodded and smiled, then attempted to edge past. Del Sasso grabbed his arm in a powerful grip and searched his face again. "Your attempt to put up a shield of irrelevant thoughts does not prevent me from reading your mind. You have deep conflicts, doubts, important questions, sincere concerns. All will be settled in the next few hours. And then, tomorrow perhaps, you and I must spend some time together—alone."

"A great honor!" whispered Carla. Ari was speechless. He could only nod. This man's presence was as mesmerizing as Elor's.

"He's remarkable, isn't he!" Carla enthused, but Del Sasso was already looking beyond Ari to the next person in line, the delegate from France, who had earlier confided to Ari that he'd been deeply interested in the occult for years—and that the same interest was shared by many of the top leaders in the French government.

"Dr. Ari Thalberg," said a raspy voice, and Ari realized that he had been moved along by Del Sasso's strong arm and was now being greeted by Dr. Frank Leighton, whose badge proclaimed him to be the Founder and Director of the Psychic Research Center. "Carla has told me a great deal about you. We're so glad you could come. I'm sure you'll have a valuable report to carry back to Israel—something that *The Jerusalem Post* will be pleased to print."

"Thank you. I'm honored to be here." *Words, meaningless words... the man is insincere,* Ari instinctively realized, and moved quickly on.

Ari spent the next half hour wandering about in an agony of conflicting convictions. He felt naked. Del Sasso had seen right through him with ease. Yet he had not denounced him as a spy or traitor in their midst. There was something sincere and genuinely charming about the man—yet something sinister at the same time. *A chosen vessel!* The identical words that Elor had used. There was no doubt that this man was in touch with the Nine and that his powers, undisplayed to this gathering as yet, came from them. Godlike powers that Elor had said all mankind would one day possess—exactly what was being offered here. Why not?

The Mossad had badly misjudged the situation. They had sent him on an impossible mission. Neither they nor he was any match for either Del Sasso or the Nine. Conspiring against them was hopelessly ludicrous. Was it possible that the Mossad, as Elor insisted, was also wrong in its appraisal of the Nine's intentions? Perhaps they were not against Israel after all. Elor had almost convinced him. Who could say that their promise to share these incredible powers with the world was not sincere?

On the other hand, Yakov and Miriam—and especially the parts of the Bible they had explained to him—were equally convincing. If the Nine were demons as those two believers in Messiah Jesus insisted, then what? It was a dilemma from which there seemed no escape. Such thoughts, however, had to be put out of his mind if he was to accomplish his mission—which, indeed, he would in spite of the impossible odds. His loyalty lay neither with the Mossad nor the Nine, but must first of all be to himself. His goal was to discover the truth, whatever it might be... then tell it to the world.

Ari's troubled musings were interrupted by the deep, booming voice of Del Sasso calling for attention. Turning around he saw that everyone had gathered in front of a raised platform on which the towering monk was now standing behind a microphone.

"Welcome to 'World Congress 666'!" The words brought Ari back to the present with a vengeance. He hurried over to blend into the crowd so that he wouldn't be so conspicuous, though there was no way to hide from Del Sasso. Was the man looking forever only and directly at *him*?

"You are all aware that the very name and date and substance of this gathering was decreed by higher intelligences who have been watching our progress—or lack of it—for millennia. They have chosen to intervene at this crucial time in order to rescue us from a probable nuclear holocaust and almost certain ecological collapse... and to lay the foundation for a revolutionary new political and economic system that will usher in a New Age of prosperity and peace for all peoples."

Those words brought back to Ari's mind the prophecies that Yakov and Miriam had presented him with and which he had read for himself in the Bible—those verses that Yakov had marked for him. Try as he might, he had been unable to dismiss the words of the Hebrew prophets concerning the Antichrist, nor could he now deny how aptly they seemed to fit this present moment. Distracted by these thoughts, Ari was brought back to the present some moments later when the arresting voice began to explain the significance of the number 666.

"You are each wearing—and with great pride and dignity, I trust—the number 666 on a badge, along with your name, country and office. The significance of doing so has already been communicated to you in the literature you received with your formal invitation. Yet many of you remained skeptical and puzzled. In coming through the reception line, you had questions about this number—though few of you expressed them. Some of you seemed quite confused, in fact. Indulge me, therefore, while I give a brief explanation of the monumental importance of this historic moment.

"Those of you coming from the East may not realize it, but the western world has lived for centuries under the haunting fear of a coming Antichrist taking over this planet and requiring every inhabitant, on pain of death, to wear the number 666. Your courage and conviction in identifying yourselves today with that dread number has broken that powerful taboo in the collective unconscious and has delivered the entire world, from this moment forth, from the debilitating Antichrist superstition that has enslaved so many in the past. The world can now break free from the negative ideas of sin and redemption and the demeaning delusion that man is dependent upon some mythical 'God.'

"Your brave example will be followed by men and women of goodwill everywhere, who will identify themselves with the New Order by wearing a similar badge. So I congratulate you on the vital role you are playing today. Let us all drink a toast to each other and to a new and glorious freedom—freedom from the destructive religious beliefs that have for too long strangled progress and fostered intolerance." It all sounded so reasonable, so noble—and coincided so well with that spiritual aura that now seemed to envelop the gathering.

Applause and cheers were followed by good-natured banter and the clinking of glasses. Everywhere the toast could be heard, "Here's to peace on earth through psychic power!" Ari had neglected to take a glass, but a Marine quickly handed him one filled with champagne. Before he knew it a dozen people had touched their glasses to his, some of them murmuring, "To our own godhood!"

Involuntarily Ari shuddered. Yakov and Miriam had drilled into him that it was the serpent in the Garden of Eden who had introduced this belief to Eve, promising, "You shall become gods," thereby bringing God's judgment upon all mankind. Of course, he had always considered this story in Genesis to be a myth. Yet the fear that it might be true, and that he was seeing the same appealing lie presented again, this time to world leaders and through them eventually to all mankind, brought a sense of dread that he couldn't shake.

The rasping voice of the director, who had taken the microphone from Del Sasso, intruded upon Ari's thoughts. "We will go inside in a few minutes for our first session. There you will all witness for yourselves the awesome capabilities that reside in Antonio Del Sasso. As you already know from the White House report that each of you received, Dr. Del Sasso has powers that no other person, dead or alive—including Krishna, Buddha, Jesus Christ or Muhammad—has ever displayed.

"We're not here to worship him. Nor does he desire our praise. This humble man's only desire is to serve mankind. Antonio continually reminds me that he has been chosen by higher intelligences merely as a prototype of the millions and eventually billions of others who, through his example and guidance, will in due time develop the same godlike capabilities. This is the heart of the Plan and the only hope for a new world of peace, love and genuine brotherhood among all peoples. Only then can we be accepted into the intergalactic community of planetary civilizations that has patiently awaited for centuries our long-overdue coming of age. What a heritage to pass on to our children and grandchildren!

"And now, you may begin to move to your right through the two entrances to the auditorium where you see the Marine guards at attention. Have your badges prominently displayed for admittance. We'll convene inside in about 15 minutes."

Ari headed for the auditorium immediately. It seemed the best way to avoid any further personal contact with Del Sasso, who was moving among the delegates, exuding his great charm, and already heading in Ari's direction.

All Hell Breaks Loose!

The press corps, limited to 30 reporters from the world's most prestigious newspapers and magazines, and handpicked by Carla, had a block of seats in the center of the auditorium. No television coverage was allowed. Ari found his assigned place and sat down. Behind him, the delegates were pouring in. Ari found it strangely ominous to see these sophisticated political leaders jostling their way, seemingly as eager and excited as children at a Saturday movie matinee.

Ari had earlier heard the rumor circulating among the guests that the President of the United States had been deluged with requests from ambassadors, members of parliament, senators and congressmen from around the world who were eager to attend. Thousands had apparently been turned away for lack of space. And now the small, 300-seat auditorium was filling rapidly with those fortunate enough to have been invited. Simultaneous translators were in their booths at the rear, and those delegates who were not proficient enough in English were putting on earphones and dialing their particular native language.

A hush fell over the auditorium as the four celebrities came out from backstage and sat down in a row of chairs facing the audience just behind the rostrum. Leighton was on the right with Del Sasso to his right. Next to him was Carla, then Khorev, the latter looking more grim than ever. Ari wondered how Carla had gotten involved with Del Sasso, and what her fate would be. He was becoming more apprehensive with each passing moment.

"Psychic powers? I'm not easily convinced," muttered the man on Ari's left. His badge identified him as an editor of *Time* magazine. "A lot of hype. I hope this isn't a waste of time. What do you think?"

"Oh, I don't have any doubt that Del Sasso is going to dazzle us," responded Ari. "The question is, who gave him these powers, and why?"

"*Who?*" interjected the man on Ari's right, who had been listening in with great interest. "What do you mean by *who*?"

"You've read the material. Entities from a nonphysical dimension are supposed to be involved," returned Ari. "Who are they and what are they up to? That's my question!"

"Benevolent, highly evolved beings . . . rescuing us from our own destructive tendencies, so it was said. I hope it's true!"

"Remember," added David, "you'll be there for only one reason: to learn all you can. Don't get smart and try to do more than that. We want you back... and not in a body bag!"

"I'll come back... with everything you wanted and more... mission accomplished!"

— ✦ —

The last month before his departure was spent in constant training with special Mossad agents. Mind control was going to be the key. Del Sasso would try to read his mind. Ari had to hide his real thoughts under a cover of memorized stream-of-consciousness that he could keep going automatically every waking minute if need be. His assignment was to see behind the facade that the Mossad was certain would hide the real truth—and then report it in one of the many ways for secretly passing information that he'd been trained in. A dozen Mossad agents would be backing him up in Palo Alto. He had their descriptions and the code by which each could be identified. But none of them would be likely to gain entrance to the congress itself.

The invitation to attend the congress was intercepted and copied by the Mossad before it ever came to Ari, and without his knowledge, so he wouldn't be burdened with keeping that secret. The special Mossad agents to whom it was given for analysis found it to be astonishing beyond their wildest imagination. If the CIA had the capabilities that it promised would be demonstrated, then no power on earth could stand in their way. Yet they claimed that they were going to share these incredible psychic powers with the world in the interests of peace. There had to be more to it than that—and it would be Ari's job to find out the truth.

— ✦ —

Miriam came to the apartment to say goodbye to Ari half an hour before he was to leave for Tel Aviv's Lod Airport. She was obviously sad, but controlled.

"I don't want to sound trite," she said, "but you're in greater danger than you can imagine."

"I know what I'm facing," said Ari, trying to put up a brave front. "I've been well trained... I'll be okay."

"It's not the physical danger I'm so concerned about." There was an arresting solemnity in Miriam's voice. "Oh, I know you don't believe in Satan... but he wants to have your soul. He wants to use you to deceive Israel into following the Antichrist."

"What makes you say that?" Ari had told Miriam nothing about any of Elor's visitations, yet she seemed to know. "Did Yakov tell you about Elor?"

"Elor? No. Who's that?"

"That's what I'm skeptical about," explained Ari. "Not about whether the powers exist. I'm sure they do—but are these entities as altruistic as they claim? That's my concern."

Further conversation was cut off by the sound of Leighton's raspy voice coming over the loudspeaker: "Ladies and gentlemen, distinguished representatives of the world's nations, select members of the press, it is a great honor and joy to welcome each of you here today.

"We are gathered just to the south of San Francisco where, in 1945, hopeful delegates from less than half of the nations we represent met to lay the foundation for the United Nations. Today we lay the foundation for something far more significant...a New World Order that will make all men and all nations truly united and equal. When we earthlings have proven our peaceful intentions, we'll qualify to apply for entrance into an intergalactic community of civilizations that have evolved far beyond us and which stand ready to share their technology and supernatural powers. We will then have undreamed-of access to the vast universe of space and its limitless resources.

"We must crawl before we can walk, take baby steps before we can run and then fly...." To his consternation, Ari realized that Del Sasso was staring at him as though he were reading his mind again. His expression had turned from warmth to malevolence. Quickly averting his eyes, Ari found himself fighting a sudden dizziness. *You're a lying traitor! You won't get out of here alive!* The accusation came full-blown into his thoughts as though Del Sasso had telepathically implanted it there.

Ari struggled to regain control of his mental processes. He seemed to be sinking into an abyss, drawn there inexorably by some terrifying force. With great difficulty he recovered his emotional equilibrium, but in the meantime he had missed almost all of Leighton's speech. He heard only the last few sentences.

"...receiving the power entails submission to the direction of the Nine until they determine that we are well-established in the New Order and capable of carrying on by ourselves. Until there are comparable psychic leaders in each country to form a competent World Council, the Nine's orders will be relayed through Antonio Del Sasso. He is the man whom I now wish to present to you once again—first of all on the giant television screen just behind me, and then, in person, as he gives further live demonstrations of these revolutionary capabilities."

The applause was thunderous. Ari pretended to join in briefly but his heart was not in it. That momentary look of unremitting hatred in Del Sasso's eyes had settled the issue. This was a clever trap. If Del Sasso wasn't the Devil himself, then he was his right-hand man. Ari wanted to stand up and shout a warning, but he knew it would go unheeded. Looking around the audience it was apparent that everyone else was eagerly following like sheep to the slaughter. Even the skeptic from *Time* was applauding enthusiastically.

Should he get up and leave? If they let him go, which was doubtful, he would miss what he came to see. No, he had an obligation both to the Mossad and the *Post*—and to all mankind—to witness what occurred and to bring a warning to the world. Del Sasso had sworn that he would not live to tell the tale. Perhaps. His chance to escape, if it was possible at all, would be better if he stayed until the end and then got lost in the crowd, rather than trying to leave now.

The lights were dimmed and the giant television screen came alive with what seemed to be the most remarkable display of the supernatural that anyone could imagine. Del Sasso was first of all seen holding a thin wire, which he moved slowly over a map. The wire suddenly twisted downward and an assistant hurried over to record the precise latitude and longitude to which the wire was pointing. Several geologists came on to testify that Del Sasso had in this manner pinpointed numerous oil pools around the world in the most unlikely places—pools of high-grade oil that were even larger than those under the Arabian desert. This vast wealth was specifically being located in areas of great poverty. Its development would obviously transform those countries, raising their standard of living to that of the western world and thus contributing to worldwide prosperity.

The next sequence showed Del Sasso imparting some mysterious force through his hands to ordinary plants growing in a pyramid-shaped hothouse. What these plants produced was then displayed: tomatoes the size of volleyballs, cabbage the size of basketballs, apricots the size of baseballs. The video was stopped while an Assistant Secretary of Agriculture joined Leighton on the platform and displayed some of the actual produce. He explained that field tests had demonstrated that seeds from the plants Del Sasso had infused with psychic power would flourish in the most depleted soil and the most arid conditions... and that the resulting fruit and vegetables contained double the normal amount of vitamins and minerals. Apparently Del Sasso had activated some unknown process similar to photosynthesis that allowed the plants to gather much of their sustenance from the atmosphere and sun's rays.

The video then resumed with shots of Dr. Khorev—before his defection—in his secret lab near Moscow, followed by an astonishing series of brief scenes in rapid succession around the world: Soviet leaders plotting the August 1991 failed Soviet coup in a secret meeting inside the Kremlin; generals and their aides conferring at an emergency meeting of NATO to discuss the coup; the president's cabinet meeting in closed session in the White House; drug czars meeting in secret in Colombia; a top level Mafia conclave in Sicily; the Pope in private prayer in his chambers; and officers conferring over a map on the bridge of a Soviet nuclear submarine under the polar icecap. Subtitles in English explained each scene.

The lights went on and Leighton stepped quickly to the microphone amid a buzz of whispered comment erupting throughout the stunned audience. "You were right!" the skeptic to Ari's left confided under his breath. "This is incredible! No doubt about it!"

Ari nodded soberly. "But why Del Sasso? What makes him so special?"

"Well, he's going to share it... teach everyone," came the quick reply. The man had obviously taken the bait.

"You are wondering how we made all of those videos of secret meetings around the world," said Leighton with a self-assured smile. "You'd never guess! They were all shot by Antonio Del Sasso from a laboratory just down the hall to your left—and without a camera of any kind! Actually they were recorded from his brain directly onto videotape just as you saw them." He paused to enjoy the stunned audience's reaction, continuing when quiet had once again been restored.

"You saw Dr. Khorev, for example," Leighton went on, "in his laboratory north of Moscow, and some of his assistants working with him on a secret experiment. That was *before* he came to this country, and he was unaware that the video was being taken at the time. And remember, that was in a top-secret and heavily guarded commando base whose very existence was known to only a handful of Kremlin elite. It was Dr. Del Sasso, in fact, who located that clandestine laboratory for the CIA—with his mind!

"I need not tell you the potential of such capabilities, not only for ending war, but crime as well. That is why we selected the shots of the secret meetings of drug czars in Colombia and of Mafia leaders in Sicily. Those men have not been arrested yet, but you may be certain they will be once the Plan has gone into effect. Ladies and gentlemen of the world community, both war and crime will become as obsolete on this planet as poverty and religious superstition!"

A standing ovation interrupted the speaker. When the applause had simmered down, Leighton introduced, with obsequious superlatives that bordered on worship, the star of the show once again. Del Sasso wasted no time getting into action. "We have among us today, in the very center of the auditorium, 30 representatives of the world's most prestigious newspapers and magazines. Some of these reporters and editors may still be skeptical. After all, they're our watchdogs and need to be careful in what they report. Let me present them to you!"

To the utter astonishment of the audience and to the chagrin and terrified cries of the press, all 30 were suddenly lifted out of their seats and levitated upward until their heads touched the high, vaulted ceiling. Any faint hope of escape that Ari may still have retained was now gone. Del Sasso had no doubt chosen this group because Ari was among them. The monster was toying with him. Obviously, when the time came, the hatred this incredible man had projected would express itself violently, though surely he would not wreak his vengeance publicly. After remaining levitated for a full minute, Ari and the others were gently lowered into their seats once again.

The applause was deafening. There were no skeptics now. Del Sasso needed to do no more. Nevertheless, he proceeded with a rapid series of demonstrations beyond anything Elor had shown to Ari.

There were materializations and dematerializations—but of the most sensational kind. Bullets fired at him from a machine gun at point-blank range left him untouched. A Marine colonel was called out of the audience and given a flamethrower. Strapping it on his back, he turned it on and aimed it at Del Sasso from about 20 feet away. The flame shot out, heading directly for the huge monk, but when it got within a few feet of his chest it disappeared. Del Sasso then started walking toward the colonel. The flames receded as he advanced until suddenly, when he was standing directly in front of it, the flamethrower itself vanished.

Spontaneously the audience, which had been sitting in breathless wonder during this incredible display, came to its feet, cheering wildly. Del Sasso smiled imperceptibly, bowed several times, then returned to his seat on the platform next to Carla. She was beaming proudly, trying to catch Ari's eye, looking for his approval, but he pretended not to notice her.

Leighton was back at the microphone. "It now gives me great pleasure to present to you our keynote speaker of the evening, a man whose presence is a symbol not only of scientific greatness but of the solidarity between the United States of America and the new confederacy of former Soviet Republics—Dr. Viktor Khorev."

Slowly and deliberately the Russian scientist stepped to the rostrum, took his notes out of a plain folder and spread them before him. "Representatives of the world's nations, and honored guests," he began, looking out over the audience. "Since coming here to this remarkable research center, I have been doing what all of you must carefully and courageously do tonight. That is, I have been attempting to understand the evermore incredible happenings in these laboratories and their implications for all humanity.

"What you have seen on videotape is all true, and what you have just witnessed live on this stage is only a small sample of this man's capabilities. His feats are light-years ahead of anything we were able to accomplish or even dreamed of accomplishing during my years of psychic research in the Soviet Union. And the same can be said for the psychic research in any other country.

"There is no way, as both Dr. Leighton and Dr. Del Sasso have already carefully explained, that such power could be developed apart from these entities known as the Archons—or the Nine. I can tell you without fear of contradiction, based upon my many years of research, that no human agency has developed nor can develop such powers. They come exclusively from the Nine—who themselves inhabit a nonphysical dimension of existence, but are capable of entering the physical universe as well. These highly-evolved entities control this power and dispense it as they will and to whom they will. And they have now declared their willingness, through Antonio Del Sasso, to make this power available to the world in order to prevent the destruction of this planet.

"For the world to receive this power, as we have already been told—and you have formal agreements to take back to your governments to be signed when approved—we must of necessity submit ourselves completely to these entities. This must be done through their ambassador, Antonio Del Sasso, of course. I think you are all convinced of the important part he will play in the Plan, and of his unique qualifications to do so. Naturally, if we are to submit totally to the Nine, then we must trust them completely.

"Therein lies the crux of the problem that I have wrestled with over these past few weeks. I want to take you through the process of doubt that I myself have experienced, and then bring you to the happy conclusion I have reached.

"Here is the reasoning process I myself struggled through. First of all, I was raised in an atheistic country and am an atheist myself. Yet I recognize, as every reasonable person must, that only God—if such a being existed—could be trusted totally. This is true because God, by very definition, is loving and kind and above corruption even by His own desires, being self-existent and infinite and thus needing nothing from anyone or anything, being Himself the Creator of all. And because God is, again by very definition, unchangeable, we can on the basis of both His character and His past performance have complete confidence in what He will do in the future. Unfortunately, God doesn't exist, so we are left to our own devices and dare not put ourselves at the mercy of anyone else. And, as I thought it over carefully, that seemed logically to include the Nine as well.

"Being less than God—indeed, they deny the very existence of a supreme deity and claim that each of us is a god in his own right—the Nine could conceivably be corrupted by their own selfish desires. Moreover, they could change. Even if they had been completely benevolent in their dealings with mankind for the past thousand years, we could not have absolute confidence on the basis of that impressive record that they would not turn against or deceive us in the future. That fact left me with a dilemma."

Here Dr. Khorev turned and gestured toward Leighton and Del Sasso, who both wore expressions of concern, but seemed generally pleased with his approach thus far. "Dr. Leighton and Dr. Del Sasso have known of my doubts and have given of themselves most graciously in helping me to work my way through them. It was not easy, because the problem was a most difficult one. The Nine assure us they desire only our good, but how can we be certain?

"One persuasive argument is the fact that the Nine are so far beyond man that they really don't need us. There is nothing we can offer them, it would seem, therefore nothing they would want from us. And so they would have no motive to do us harm in any way. After all, what would be their purpose? For some time I accepted this line of reasoning. I eventually had to face the fact, however, that if they had no interest in harming us, then why would they be interested in helping us? Why would they be interested in us at all? That question left me puzzled, until I realized there was something I had overlooked."

Dr. Khorev paused to draw several quick breaths at this point. A deathlike stillness had settled over the audience. Every eye was fixed in unblinking anticipation upon the speaker. Leighton seemed frozen to his chair and Del Sasso was ominously motionless as though he were going into a trance. The Mossad had indicated that such a state enhanced his powers. Ari's sense of dread was growing. He felt as though a spiritual power were fighting against him, trying to take over his mind. Only with great difficulty and determination was he able to weigh the choices and consequences he now realized that he faced in this awesome moment.

What this Russian atheist had said about God had hit Ari with stunning force. Here was a man who denied God's existence, something Ari had never totally done. Yet he was explaining things about God that Ari had never thought of—especially why He alone could be trusted. His reasoning had been powerfully persuasive. It had loosed a flood of deep and growing convictions that had been forced upon him by his discussions with Yakov and Miriam, yet which he had suppressed because acquiescence meant submission to God.

Time seemed to stand still. The auditorium receded into unreality and Dr. Khorev's voice became a distant drone as conversations he'd had with those two followers of Jesus—the only ones he'd known beside Nicole—came back with new force. He could not honestly deny the truth of their arguments, nor could the words of the Hebrew prophets they had presented to him be disputed. He had known this deep inside for some time, but it had taken the arguments of this atheist to force him to acknowledge it.

Dr. Khorev's voice, now betraying the strain of a growing fear, yet ringing with a courage born of conviction and the urgent desire to warn the world, caught Ari's full attention once again. "There was no need to speculate. The evidence was staring me in the face, but I had been unwilling to accept it. It is a matter of record, if Frank Leighton will be willing to admit it—and if not, there are others here who may have the courage to do so (here he glanced quickly at Carla, who seemed to be listening sympathetically)—that the Nine have been less than forthright in their dealings with those involved in this project even from the very beginning.

"They have promised peace, love and brotherhood. Instead they have produced violence, involving even the death or insanity of those who have believed their promises and submitted to their control. They promised to create millions of psychics in addition to Del Sasso, but have not produced even one in spite of diligent efforts in these laboratories to train others on the Psitron, the same machine on which Del Sasso developed his powers. I now doubt that they ever intended to empower anyone except him. We have obediently given the Nine complete control of this project and of our lives as well, and the results so far—other than the powers Del Sasso displays to seduce us—have not been good!"

It was all coming together for Ari. This Russian was laying out the evil in the Archons which he had sensed in every contact with Elor, but had been unwilling to admit. Now it seemed crystal clear. *What if the Nine are demons? Yakov made an airtight case to that effect by commanding Elor to leave in the Name of Jesus Christ. They're evil. No doubt about it. Bent upon deception, domination—and perhaps even destruction.*

Ari felt an overpowering urge to get up and run for the nearest exit. But it would obviously do no good. Del Sasso could destroy him instantly. And what about this courageous man? Ari had to hear all he could say, and see what happened to him. What would Del Sasso do? Why had he not stopped him already?

From the audience came a restless stirring, a rising murmur. Suddenly Ari palpably sensed a horrifying, primordial, reptilian *Presence* all around him. It was like nothing he had ever imagined. Leighton started to rise from his chair, then sank back, seemingly too stunned to react. An ominous silence—except for the eerie sound of breathing—had settled in the auditorium, like the calm before a storm. The audience was transfixed in paralyzed alarm.

Dr. Khorev's words came in a torrent now, as though he were rushing to get it all out. "It's the complete control they demand that concerns me. I've experienced the terror of totalitarianism. Yes, there are many changes being made in my native country of Russia—a country that I dearly love. However, that land is far from realizing the freedom that all men cherish, a freedom that I sought in the West and which I find is lacking even here."

Ari could not believe his ears. And it seemed even more unbelievable that neither Leighton nor Del Sasso had made a move to stop Khorev. Were they afraid of creating an even worse scene in front of this audience and therefore would simply allow him to finish and then discredit him? And what of the Nine? Why had they not silenced him? Was it possible, as Yakov had declared, that neither they nor Del Sasso was as omniscient as they claimed to be? Otherwise they would have known beforehand Khorev's intentions, and he would not be in this position now.

"This is a crucial gathering. Those of you here today hold the future of the world in your hands. Everything depends upon whether you bow to the will of the Nine or resist them. I warn you now, to submit to their control will be to turn this world into one vast prison—not of bodies confined within cells, but of minds no longer able to think for themselves. The Paradise the Nine offer will in fact be the indescribable hell of a totalitarianism more vicious than anything this world has yet seen. . . ." Khorev's voice had risen to a crescendo of desperation.

At last Leighton seemed to shake himself out of his paralysis. Jumping to his feet, he ran to the rostrum and tried to pull the microphone away from Khorev.

With a last effort the Russian shouted into the mike, "Close your minds to the Nine's influence! Fight back! Don't let them impose their will!" A security guard rushed up and grabbed Khorev, tore the mike from his hands and threw him onto the platform floor.

The unleashing of the Nine's fury came at that moment, and with a violence that swept all rational thought before it. The stillness was broken by a cry of rage from the throat of Del Sasso, seated in meditative yoga position, who appeared now to be in a deep trance. Seats were ripped up from the floor and flew through the air, hurling their occupants like so much flotsam on a stormy sea. The entire auditorium was in a state of massive upheaval. Huge chunks of the roof caved in, crushing scores of delegates to death. And most horrible of all, the laminated wood beams that supported the ceiling splintered off into long spears. They flew through the air like guided missiles and impaled those who were madly scrambling over bodies and debris in an attempt to get to the exits.

Those few who had been seated close enough and managed to reach the exits without being struck down found the doors locked and their escape from the holocaust denied. Pounding with their fists helplessly on the doors and walls, screaming for help, some died of hysteria, while the remainder were crushed under the rain of debris from the collapsing roof that seemed to be aimed at those below by some all-seeing intelligence that was directing the destruction. Clearly, it was the intent of the Nine that there be no survivors to tell the horrible truth.

A special fate seemed to be reserved for the press corps. Whether due to their training to observe events closely and report them, or to some unseen hand that held them, they had all remained seated in frozen fascination, staring around them as though compelled to be witnesses to the unmitigated horror. Ari had tried desperately to get out of his seat but had been unable to move. It was as though some unknown force were holding him down.

Ari could hear Dr. Leighton's rasping voice, in the last spasm of a blasted dream, cursing the Nine. Suddenly he burst into flame and his scream was quickly swallowed up in the intense heat as his body seemed almost simultaneously to melt and to turn to ashes. A uniformed man on the platform, apparently the head of security, whom Ari had seen earlier giving orders to some of the guards, was hit in the middle of the back by a heavy piece of the ceiling that knocked him to the floor. He struggled up on one elbow, pulled his revolver from its holster and in a rage fired several slugs into Leighton's disintegrating body. Then he turned it upon Del Sasso, who was sitting entranced in his chair in yoga position, but the gun was torn from his hand and a heavy beam came crashing down and crushed his skull.

Still unable to rise from his seat, Ari had searched in vain through the terrifying chaos for Carla. Then he saw her reappear from behind a stage curtain, running back onto the platform toward Khorev's motionless form. He was pinned under a section of overhead lighting that had fallen upon him. She and Khorev needed help. There must be a backstage exit. Could that be a way of escape? That thought seemed to break the spell that had bound him.

With great effort Ari struggled to his feet. At that instant, a large portion of the floor opened beneath him. He felt himself, along with the rest of the press section, falling into total darkness. He could see nothing at all, not even his own body. Suddenly he hit what seemed to be a steep, sandy slope.

Still in total darkness, Ari felt himself sliding rapidly down the incline, wondering if it would ever end. He could hear the terrified screams of those falling beyond him, fading into the empty distance without echo, as though there were no bottom to the pit into which they were plunging. At last he crashed savagely against some hard obstruction and lost consciousness.

A Dream Come True

Dead...alive...some state in between? Ari sensed only the searing pain suffusing his body. How long he'd lain there drifting in and out of consciousness, he did not know. When at last he had fully regained his senses, he moved first one limb then another, and decided that, though horribly bruised, he was all in one piece. Had any of the others survived?

"Hello," he called out into the blackness. Nothing but echoes. "Anybody there?" he cried again. The echoes bounced back and forth as they faded into the distance—then absolute silence. Alone! That realization was suddenly terrifying. Where was he?

Reaching out behind him for support in an attempt to sit up, his groping hand found only empty space, causing him to lose his balance and almost fall over the brink and deeper into the abyss. Apparently he was on the edge of a cliff. Cautiously he groped about him. Above him was the slope he'd come bouncing down. It seemed to end in a narrow ledge and then drop off precipitously.

Which way should he crawl? Perhaps it didn't matter. Could he ask God for help? Of course a Creator had to exist somewhere—but he'd never believed He had any interest in His creatures. Yet Khorev, though an atheist, had argued that God, if He did exist, would exemplify the ultimate in morals, justice, love...and Ari had admitted at last what he'd known all his life—that Khorev was right. Perhaps that God, though he had always denied Him, would help him now when there was no other hope.

"God help me!" Ari was startled to hear himself speak the words aloud. He felt foolish as his plea echoed and reechoed and faded into the distance. "Help me, God! Help me!" It was a cry of desperation from the depths of his being—the first time he had admitted needing help from Someone greater than himself. In this dark hole of despair, self-sufficiency and pride were at last revealed as the ultimate folly. Why had he not seen it before?

Groping again, Ari found what seemed to be the rock against which he must have slammed and which had kept him from plunging on further to his death. Supporting himself on that solid object, he managed to get onto his knees, preparing to crawl. Was that a faint diffusion of light straight ahead? He pulled himself up higher on the rock. Yes, from this new position he could make out a tiny pinpoint of light in the stygian darkness.

"God help me!" he said again. This time he *knew* that Someone was listening. Voicing that prayer had changed something deep inside of him. The God that Nicole had believed in, the God that Yakov and Miriam believed in—who they insisted was the God of the Bible, the God of Abraham, Isaac and Jacob—that was the One in whom Ari now knew that he, too, believed.

"I believe in you, God. I believe." A sob caught in his throat. "I believe!" How he now wanted to live to tell Yakov and Miriam of this miracle. Yes, *miracle*.

Groping carefully on hands and knees along the edge of the precipice, he began the precarious journey toward the light. It was slow going. With every move his pain-racked body cried out in protest. He forced himself to keep going in spite of the torture. There was no telling how far it was to that tiny beacon of hope or whether he could even find his way there, but he must not give up—not now.

Ari became aware for the first time that he was cold. Strange that he hadn't noticed it before. That could become an important factor in his survival. When he moved he felt warmth in his body—and move he must, as fast as possible, taking great care not to go over the edge.

As he crawled slowly ahead, the ledge seemed to widen until he could no longer tell whether he was still on the brink of a chasm. After some time he seemed to come around a large obstruction and the distant pinpoint of light brightened noticeably. He had hardly made a few more yards, however, when the light began to fade. A fresh wave of panic swept over him.

Keep calm! It must be getting dark outside. The faint light in the distance was vanishing rapidly. Soon all would be absolute blackness again. It would be folly to continue groping his way. Without the light as a focal point he could take a wrong turn and never find it again. Feeling around until he was certain that he had a secure location, he lay down and fell into a fitful sleep in spite of the bone-chilling cold.

He awakened, shivering violently. How long he had slept or what time it was he had no way of knowing. The ground where he lay was damp. He was almost thirsty enough to lick up any moisture he could find. He groped and crawled a few yards up a slight incline until he found a sandy place a bit higher that seemed to be dry. Burrowing into the sand, he curled up in a fetal position and fell at last into a deep sleep.

Again he awakened shivering, but this time the distant light had reappeared. As he watched, it grew slowly brighter. Daylight at last! Once more he began the painful process of groping and crawling, bumping his head countless times on rocks or huge stalactites protruding down from the cavern ceiling.

All morning, to the best of his estimation of passing time, was spent working his tortuous way through a maze that sometimes ended in a wall of rock and at other times in a sheer drop-off into darkness. Then at last, when he groped his way around a high wall of wet, slippery rock, the light suddenly became strong enough to reveal the ground beneath him for the first time. To his great joy he saw what looked like water just to his right, the new light reflecting on its surface. He had been skirting an underground lake without knowing it. Like a madman he was on his knees, drinking in huge gulps.

On his feet again, Ari began to make much faster progress. Leaving the lake behind, he staggered and stumbled on over the rough terrain for what seemed an eternity. Climbing a steep pile of rocks and rubble in growing light, he came over the top of a rise and there, ill-defined in the distance, he could now make out, through a small opening, trees and sky.

Thank God! I'm going to make it! That thought had no sooner registered than Ari realized to his horror that about 50 feet ahead the terrain disappeared into a chasm that blocked his escape. Another few moments and he found himself standing on the edge of a sheer cliff that dropped off into a fissure no more than 20 feet across but so deep that he couldn't see the bottom. From its depths far below he could hear in thunderous volume the raging torrent whose roaring sound had been growing louder for the last 15 minutes. To his left was a sheer wall of rock rising to the ceiling about 50 feet above him, while to his right the fissure curved around and angled back the way he had come, widening as it went toward the lake. He was cut off completely!

Was this how it would end—coming within sight of a way out, yet unable to reach it? Again he searched the cavern up and down, back and forth as far as he could see. There was no doubt about it. He had come to a dead end.

"Help!" he yelled. "Help! I'm in here! Help!" The words were swallowed up in the river's deafening roar.

Ari sat down on a boulder to think. Was this a cavern that was known to spelunkers? Perhaps, though he had detected no sign that anyone had ever come across the chasm he now faced. Probably there was another entrance and the exploration all took place in another part of the huge cave. The congress had convened on a Monday. Today was Tuesday. The weekend, then, when someone might conceivably be exploring, was four days away.

Famished, his throat parched, the lake at least two hours behind him, Ari felt once more the inevitability of death. Fatigue, pain, hunger, thirst—all could be endured if there were some hope. But with all hope gone, despair swept over him at last.

Ari had never given death much thought. If it happened, at least there was no more consciousness. Best to do it quickly. That would terminate existence—or so he had always thought. Then Yakov had brought up the subject in one of his periodic attempts to convert Ari, and they'd had a heated discussion. Yakov's arguments had been simple but powerful. His words came back to Ari now.

"If life ends in oblivion, then it leads nowhere—and if it leads nowhere, then it has no meaning," the old man had argued. "And that's unbelievable. It would also mean that the universe would be a place of injustice—and that isn't possible, for the God who made it is infinitely just. There must be a continuing existence even after these bodies die in order for life to have meaning and for God's justice to be meted out."

Ari had rejected Yakov's argument because of the consequences it carried. Now he believed. He could thank Khorev for that conviction—a man who didn't believe in God at all.

When he and Miriam had parted company it had been over these same moral issues. "You don't want to believe in a God who is personally interested in you, Ari," she had said, "because that would make you accountable to Him. You couldn't bear that. You've been running your own life without any concern for what your Creator expects from you." Ari could see her face now. She had looked at him with pity when she spoke those words. And he had admitted that he didn't want to believe in such a God for the very reasons she had stated.

Yet within the past 24 hours, through an atheist, he had come to faith in a God who cared for him personally—and he had even asked this God for help. Was it not, however, a two-way street? How could he ask God to help him and remain independent of God's claims upon his life? Was God to be his cosmic bellhop, coming to his rescue, giving him whatever he wanted, yet having nothing to say about the way he lived? That made no sense.

His relationship with Nicole had been shattered over this very issue of whether or not God had some moral standards by which we must live. Certainly if he were to ask God to save his life, then he must be willing to let God decide what that life would be. And had that not always been the case by reason of the fact that God had given him his very existence? Yet he had never allowed God any part in his life. He had lived it by his own whims and will—exactly as both Nicole and Miriam had faithfully told him.

"Sin is against God, Ari," Miriam had said—precisely what Nicole had also explained. Refusal to admit responsibility to God had caused his separation from both of the women he had loved.

He could see the sidewalk cafe, the camera-toting tourists strolling by, the big, orange umbrella sheltering their table, its fringe flapping gently in the breeze, the very spot where they'd been sitting that evening in Paris. And as though it were yesterday, he could hear Nicole once again ask him: "Does it make sense that God, as you admit must be the case, has decreed the laws of physics and chemistry that govern atoms and molecules and the growth and function of our bodies, but has decreed no moral laws, and has no concern for the way we conduct ourselves in relation to Him and others?"

He had known in his heart that she was right but had been too proud to admit it to either Nicole or Miriam. Now, however, with the recognition of his utter inability to help himself, that foolish pride had been stripped away. Yes, he had to admit that he was a rebel in God's universe, that he had lived by his own standards and defied God to do anything about it. It was a horrible admission that pained him deeply as he thought of his utter contempt and disregard for the God who had made him and who loved him infinitely.

"We have gone astray like lost sheep, but God put our sins upon the Messiah, who was Himself God come to earth as a man, and He died for our sins. . . ." Ari couldn't remember the exact words, but Miriam had read to him something like that from the Bible. He had been shocked when she'd told him that she had been reading, not from the New Testament, but from the great Hebrew prophet Isaiah, chapter 53. There could be no doubt that Isaiah was referring to Jesus centuries before His birth in Bethlehem. Ari had known it then. Now he was ready to admit it.

"God, I'm a sinner . . . I've broken your laws . . . lived for myself without regard for . . . for your will for my life." The words came slowly and haltingly at first between sobs of earnest repentance. Then the prayer became a torrent, as though a dam had burst and the pent-up guilt of a lifetime was released in a flood of tears and confession. "I'm sorry . . . I've been a proud fool. . . .

"I don't want to die in this horrible place. But I can't ask you to save my life unless I'm willing to let you determine what that life will be. I'm sorry that I've lived for myself, that I've robbed you of your purpose in creating me . . . that my sins caused you such sorrow and pain. Thank you, Lord Jesus, for loving me so much that you took the judgment I deserved so that I could be forgiven. Thank you for dying for me!

"O Lord, I wish I could get out of here so that you could use me to accomplish something for you in this world. But if that isn't your will . . . then do with me whatever you desire. But I wish you could have some pleasure from my life, to be able to fulfill the purpose for which you created me. God, that's why I want to live. But if I never get out of this place, I want whatever moments of life I have left to bring you joy. . . ."

Ari broke down and wept bitterly. When at last the tears came to an end he felt cleansed, delivered, at peace. Nicole had described it all long ago, in another world it seemed, when he had refused to hear. And now he had experienced the same transformation.

Nicole! She'd had that dream. It had been so real to her that she'd had to tell him at the airport—the last thing she had communicated before she'd been so brutally gunned down. Ari remembered with shame how angry he'd been with her for telling him about it, because in the dream he'd been in grave danger and Jesus had rescued him, bridging a chasm that blocked his way to safety. Now he believed in that Jesus. Could this be the dream coming true?

He had pondered the meaning of her vision many times since Nicole's tragic death—but only in relation to what it had meant concerning her. *I'll be in Jerusalem before you.* The dream had been a premonition of her death. But he had also been in the dream—yet he'd never thought of that. She'd been in a beautiful paradise of peace and safety. He'd been separated from her by a chasm, calling out for help, destruction closing in upon him—and Jesus had bridged that chasm, taking him to safety!

Would the despised and rejected One now appear to take him across the chasm that barred his escape from this cavern?

Certainly he had cried out for help, and Christ had rescued him. Not a physical deliverance, but one of far greater consequence. If he died now, he would go to heaven to join Nicole. Yes, the dream had come true. His escape out of the depths of this cavern was not necessary. He could now die in peace.

Back from the Dead

Take another look! Had he heard a voice, or had the words just emerged from his mind? *Take a closer look!* There it was again, and still he couldn't tell whether it was a voice speaking to him from outside, or words sounding in his head. What did it mean? Take a closer look at what? At the fissure blocking his route? At possible ways to bridge it?

Hesitantly Ari stood up and looked around. Nothing had changed. *Go closer, to the very edge!* Impelled by that command he cautiously approached the brink once again and peered down into the void, then searched either side of that awesome chasm. The roar of the river below was nerve-shattering. Still he saw nothing that he hadn't seen before—nothing to give him any hope.

Wait! Was that a faint trail barely visible in a sandy stretch amidst the gravel and rocks at the base of the sheer bluff rising above him? Impossible. Climbing over the boulders to get a closer look, he noticed that the wall of rock did not go all the way to the edge of the chasm. There was a space about 18 inches wide that seemed to curve around the rampart and out onto the very rim of the fissure. That was where the trail, if that's what it was, seemed to lead. Did he dare to follow it?

Go to the edge! It was a command to be obeyed. Pressing up against the sheer face of rock, he inched his way carefully around the base of the cliff onto a narrow ledge that rimmed the slippery brink of the abyss. That was when he saw it, no more than a dozen steps away, hidden back in a recess—a natural rock bridge that couldn't be seen from any other place! As he looked at it in grateful astonishment he noticed something peculiar about its formation. It looked for all the world like a giant figure, knees resting on this side, torso bending over to bridge the chasm, and extended hands and bowed head just touching the other side. *Nicole's dream!*

As if in a trance, Ari climbed up onto the strange formation and cautiously made his precarious way across it. Jumping down on the other side with a sob of relief, he hurried toward the light. A few more minutes of rugged climbing brought him to the exit where he pulled himself up through the small opening and found himself at last outside. He was standing on a steep, rocky slope looking down on a wooded valley of tall pines and scattered redwoods. *Thank you, Lord! Thank you, Lord!*

There was no trail outside leading away from the small fissure in the rocky mountainside. Apparently the cavern, or at least this end of it, had lain undiscovered throughout its geological history. He would have to pick his own path across the boulders. The sun had already fallen beyond the higher reaches of the coastal range behind him. That would be to the west. Palo Alto and the closest habitation must be straight ahead and below.

Weak from pain as well as hunger and thirst, Ari made his way as rapidly as he could down the hill toward the valley that lay before him. Far above him a passenger jet passed overhead. Hearing the sound, he paused to look up. The plane's vapor trail was turning orange in the diffused rays of sun that must be coming from very low on the horizon. He had perhaps another two hours of adequate light.

Hurrying on, Ari had gone about half a mile when he came to a miniature stream bounding its way down the mountainside. In a shallow pool beneath a small waterfall he drank in convulsive gulps. Then, taking off his coat, he splashed water over his face and neck and cleaned the cuts and abrasions on his hands and arms. He pulled off the tie he still wore, then threw the frayed and filthy rag into the brush. He looked worse than a tramp. Dipping a handkerchief in the water and wringing it out, he used the damp cloth to wipe halfheartedly at the worst of the mud that was caked onto his torn pants and jacket—the expensive suit the Mossad had provided for his attendance at the World Congress. He shuddered at the memory.

Continuing to angle down across the slope, in and out of ravines, wondering how far he'd have to go—how far he *could* go—Ari suddenly heard what sounded like a car engine in the distance. *Thank God!* Another hundred yards and he heard a similar noise, this time much louder. It sounded like a truck engine laboring up a steep grade.

Staggering on eagerly in the direction of the sound, he came out of the trees into a small clearing on the brow of a hill. There it was, a highway, not more than 200 yards below him, discernible here and there where it wound its way through the trees. *Thank you, Lord!* Another ten minutes of beating a laborious path through the thick underbrush and fallen logs and he climbed up a steep embankment and stood upon the asphalt at last.

Which way? Surely Palo Alto would have to be downhill as he had already surmised. He stationed himself on that side of the road and waited. In less than a minute a logging truck came inching down the grade, gears whining. Ari waved and yelled, but the driver went right on. Too heavy a rig to stop. Then came a passenger car, and almost immediately behind it another. The drivers accelerated when he tried to flag them down. Of course—who would risk picking up a disreputable looking bum like him?

Desperately Ari considered his options. How could he get someone to stop?

Just then an old relic of a pickup truck, battered and rusted, came wheezing and backfiring down the steep grade. Ari waved and yelled. With an earsplitting screech of worn-out brakes the vehicle lurched to a halt.

"Hey, buddy, whatch'yer problem?" came the genial query from the driver, a bronzed man of about 50 wearing faded overalls. His long, tangled hair and bushy beard made him look like a hippie left over from the sixties. A strong hand reached out and removed a frayed cord that secured the door. The hand froze. "Saaay, you been in a hurricane or somethin'? Where ya goin', anyway?"

"Palo Alto. Is this the right way?" asked Ari hopefully. He had to yell to make himself heard above the blaring radio.

"Sure is, man. That's where I'm a goin'. Say, where'd ya pick up that foreign accent?"

"Born in Germany. Lived most of my life in France...."

"Sounds like it. Well, getch 'erself in, man, before this baby stalls."

Gratefully Ari climbed in. He sensed momentarily the irony of his situation. Who but this anachronism from a past "give-peace-a-chance" era would dare to pick up a derelict like him.

"Hey, man, what's happened to ya? It ain't rained for weeks 'round here. Where'd ya find the mud?"

"I must look horrible," returned Ari apologetically. "I got lost, fell over a cliff into a river...."

"Ain't no rivers in these parts. You must of come a long ways. Where's your car?"

"I meant a creek. I'm so tired I can hardly think. Forget the car... I just need to get to Palo Alto."

"Don't sweat it, man, I'll take you right to your house."

"I don't live there... I'm staying at a hotel."

"Yeah? Which one?"

"The Hilton."

"Whew! That's not my neighborhood... but I know right where it's at. Now you just settle back and catch some winks. You look like you need it. I'll wake you up when we get there."

As the driver released the brake and resumed his journey down the mountain, the throbbing rock music gave way to a news bulletin:

> Here's another update on that disaster in the foothills of the coastal range above Palo Alto. The dead and missing now stand at 298, most of them delegates from foreign countries. No cause has yet been established for the explosion that destroyed the main building and was witnessed from just outside the property by more than 200 media representatives. The government refuses to identify the kind of work that was being done there. It is rumored to have been a top-secret psychic research center. Officials at Stanford University deny any connection to their institution.
>
> There are two known survivors: Antonio Del Sasso, a Jesuit

> priest, and Carla Bertelli, a journalist specializing in parapsychology. Both were apparently employed at the destroyed installation, though in what capacity is not known. Del Sasso is in the hospital recovering from smoke inhalation and internal injuries, while Ms. Bertelli was apparently unharmed. Neither survivor, however, has been available for comment.

Carla's safe! What happened to Khorev? And Del Sasso, the evil one—what will he do now? Does he know I survived? I've got to get my clothes, get cleaned up…get back to Israel.

The driver reached over and turned off the radio. "Worst disaster ever happened 'round here!" he said. "Ain't been nothin' else on the news all day. What d'ya think…?" He noticed that his passenger was already fast asleep.

— ✦ —

The next thing Ari knew someone was shaking him back to consciousness. He awakened with a start, wondering where he was, then remembered. The cavern…the mountain…the pickup truck….

"You must have been plenty tired! Dropped off and been snorin' all the way down here. Well, there's the Hilton…across the street. I figured…you know …this ain't exackly a limo."

"Thank you! Thank you!" said Ari, still groggy and so stiff he could hardly move. Painfully he reached into his pocket. "Here, let me…."

"No way, man! You don't owe me nothin'!"

Ari climbed out of the truck, slammed the door and waved as the pickup chugged off down the street.

There was no way to avoid the startled glances and whispered comments as Ari limped across the crowded lobby. At the registration counter he hastened to get out his explanation before the startled clerk, mouth hanging open in shock, could object to his presence.

"I've had an unfortunate accident…been lost in the woods. Nearly killed myself…but I'm okay. I've got a room here. Someone else checked me in… name's Thalberg, Ari Thalberg."

The clerk, a meticulously groomed young man in his twenties, punched Ari's name into the computer and after a moment looked up at him in shock. "You were with that delegation at the congress. You're supposed to be dead…."

"I just got out of the mountains and heard the news. Terrible! I was so embarrassed that I got lost and missed the meeting…but now…what luck! I need to get into my room."

"They've put your baggage in storage…but I could have the bellman get it. Your room is still available." The clerk hesitated. "They think you're dead, you know. Shouldn't we notify the police?"

"Look," said Ari, leaning over the counter and lowering his voice to his most confidential tone. "This is so embarrassing... let me tell them... in my own words... after I get cleaned up. Okay? I don't want anyone to see me like this!"

The clerk nodded understandingly. "Here's your key. Room 342. Why not take the fire stairs... just over there. I'll have your baggage brought right up."

— ✦ —

After showering and wolfing down a huge meal delivered to his room, Ari collapsed into the bed. He awakened late the next morning with the sun streaming through the sliding glass door leading out onto the balcony. After shaving and eating breakfast in his room, he called one of a half-dozen memorized numbers.

"Hello," said a deep male voice after several rings.

"I have a valuable export for Syria," said Ari, "in the lobby of the Hilton."

"That's not possible!" came the startled reply. The agent obviously thought that Ari was dead and that he was being contacted by an imposter. There was no code to cover this situation.

"Look, I'm alive," said Ari, "and I really need help—fast."

"We'll take the product... in about fifteen minutes."

Ari packed his bags and went down to the lobby. He had no intention of checking out. Let them think he was still there. He sat in a chair as far from the registration desk as possible and waited. Whoever was meeting him knew what he looked like, though he had no way of visually recognizing any of the Mossad connections.

In about ten minutes two men entered the lobby and sat down near Ari. Casually they glanced around the room, lit cigarettes and looked bored. Finally the taller of the two shifted nervously in his chair and said to his companion in a low voice, "My God, I don't believe it. It's the package."

"I've got to get back to Israel fast!" said Ari softly.

The second man stood up. "I'll bring the car around. Give me two minutes." He turned and walked back out the main entrance.

— ✦ —

Safely in the car and on his way to San Francisco's International Airport, Ari was reluctant to explain what had happened. "I've got tons to report... but I don't know the classification on this information... it's that incredible," he told the two agents. "I'm only going to give it to my *katsa* back in Israel. That's David Kauly. Let him know that I'm coming."

"We'll do that," said the taller man, who had introduced himself as Sam and his companion as Mike—obviously not their real names. Sam looked at his watch. "We're in good time. You'll easily make the next El Al flight."

"You can at least tell us how you survived," said Mike, who was driving, "and where you've been all this time."

"You couldn't believe what happened if I told you," replied Ari. "I find it difficult to believe it myself. The floor literally opened up and the entire press corps was dropped deep into some underground cavern. I don't think any of the others survived. It was a miracle that I'm still alive... and that I managed to find my way out in the late afternoon of the next day."

"So you weren't in the auditorium when the actual explosion took place?" asked Sam.

"I don't know anything about an explosion, though I saw pictures of it on the news last night. I was gone by then... and I doubt that anyone inside was still alive when it happened. They'd already been killed by other means. I witnessed that. The explosion, I suspect, was to cover up what had happened and to destroy all evidence."

— ✦ —

Seventeen hours later David met Ari at Tel Aviv's Lod Airport and eased him quickly through customs. To Ari's joyful surprise, when they came out into the waiting area, there were Yakov and Miriam. Their smiles of relief and pleasure were like a healing balm to Ari's spirit. David had told the good news to Yakov, who had called Miriam. The three of them had come together in David's car.

"The *Post* announced that you were dead!" exclaimed Miriam, throwing her arms around Ari. "I didn't believe it." She held him at arm's length, looking into his eyes searchingly. "You have something wonderful to tell me. I know it. Oh, Ari, darling...!"

Ari pulled her to him. "Your prayers have been answered," he whispered as he held her tightly.

Releasing Miriam, Ari embraced Yakov, sobbing as he clung to the old man, "You were right, Yakov... you were right. I'm sorry I gave you such a hard time!"

"I knew you'd come through," said Yakov. "The Lord told me—just like he told Miriam."

David had stood to one side looking uncomfortable, but waiting patiently. Now he led them to his car. Yakov sat beside him in the front, while Ari and Miriam sat in the back. For the moment it seemed enough just to hold Miriam close to him. The explanations, the details, the recounting of the incredible spiritual journey that had found its culmination in the amazing events of the past few days would come in due time. But for this glorious few moments he would give himself over to joy.

"I'll hold off the debriefing at headquarters until tomorrow," said David, "let you spend the night at the apartment... on the condition that you put everything on a tape recorder immediately. *Everything*. Yakov will stay up with you until you're finished. Miriam, you'll have to keep out of it . . . go to your cousin's right away. Ari has to be able to think. . . ."

Neither Miriam nor Ari heard a word David said. At that moment Ari was asking her, "Will you marry me?" This time he was sure of the answer.

Under Suspicion

Early the next morning David came by the apartment, picked up Ari and the tape he and Yakov had made the night before, and drove him to Mossad headquarters in Tel Aviv. Wondering why it was required, Ari brought along the suitcase with two weeks' change of clothing that he'd been told to pack. David looked grim, but seemed unwilling or unable to explain his somber mood.

"Don't say anything about being allowed to stay at your apartment last night," David began as soon as they were in the car.

"Why not?" asked Ari in surprise.

"It was an unauthorized favor I did for you," David responded cryptically. "If you're asked, of course you tell the truth. Just don't bring it up."

"I don't get it."

"You may not be back in that apartment for a long time. I certainly wouldn't make any wedding plans.'

"What is this . . . a new assignment already? I just got back. Miriam and I were going to get together tomorrow and set the date. . . ." Ari's voice trailed off in disappointment.

"No, it's not a new assignment. You're going to be kept under protective custody."

"If you think Del Sasso—or Elor—might try to come after me . . . well, you know the Mossad can't fight them. But Messiah Jesus can . . . and I'm under His protection now."

"Don't mention *him* at headquarters!" warned David. "You're in enough trouble."

"Trouble? I thought I'd be a hero! I got out of there alive, with information no one else knows . . . except Del Sasso and Carla. And they're not going to tell the truth."

"You think Carla's on Del Sasso's side?"

"Why wouldn't she be? They worked together."

"You really believe that?"

"Why wouldn't I? I don't know what you're getting at. She's the one who invited me. . . ."

"That's the problem."

For the first time Ari realized that David seemed to be regarding him with suspicion. "Look, you really have me mystified. What's going on?"

"You'll find out. I've already said more than I'm supposed to." He lapsed into silence and concentrated on his driving.

Ari couldn't let the subject drop on that note. "David, we've been friends for three years. If something's wrong, then tell me. Sure, I told you last night that I became a follower of Jesus two days ago. I'm convinced He's alive. But Yakov—he's a believer, and everyone seems to respect him. I don't see how my new faith could be such a big problem."

"You know this Jesus thing doesn't go over in Israel. Yakov's a special case... a war hero. You're not."

"But Jesus was a Jew," protested Ari, "born right here in Bethlehem... so why the prejudice? I don't think most Jewish people know what our own Hebrew prophets said about the Messiah, and how Jesus fulfilled everything. You can't deny it! Have you ever...?"

David cut him off. "Forget the Jesus stuff! You don't need that on top of your other problems."

"What problems?"

"I've already said too much. I won't be in charge of your debriefing... the Chief's taking over."

"I don't mind that. I think he ought to hear for himself what I have to say. Israel's in great danger. It's incredible what went on at that congress!"

"That's the problem—incredibility."

"You're talking in riddles. David, we're friends. We trust each other...."

"Should I still trust you?" There was sorrow in David's voice, as though he'd been betrayed. The anguished look he gave Ari said more than words.

"What do you mean by that?" Ari demanded.

"What do you think I mean?"

"As God is my witness, David, I don't know. I risked my life for Israel. I thought that you, and the Chief especially, would be pleased. I just don't understand. You've got to spell it out. I've brought back the information...."

"They're not going to believe you," David interjected.

"Come on! You're kidding me!"

"We have other reports.... Now, I'm not saying any more!"

Ari was stunned. *Other data that contradicts me?* He thought about that for some time before it came to him. *Del Sasso and Carla, of course—but the Mossad wouldn't believe them!*

"You mean information from Del Sasso and Carla?" asked Ari incredulously. "They're the only other survivors, according to the news reports. Of course they'll say I'm lying." He paused for a moment in disbelief. "You're not suggesting... that the office is going to believe them instead of me!"

"You're still linking Del Sasso and Carla?" asked David, giving Ari another suspicious look.

"Of course. They worked together...."

"You really think so?"

"Think so... I know so! Carla never made it a secret that she was working there."

"You almost convince me you're sincere...."

"David... what are you saying?"

"Take my advice and change your story."

Ari exploded indignantly. "I can't just make something up! I'm giving the facts... and the Chief had better pay attention."

There was a long, awkward silence. As David drove he kept glancing over at his onetime friend beside him, whenever the winding road allowed, as though he were trying to analyze his expression and posture and somehow deduce whether he was really telling the truth.

"You don't believe me," said Ari at last with great disappointment. "I don't understand why."

"I didn't—but now I'm not sure...."

"I don't know what lies they're going to come up with... but even if it's two against one, you ought to believe me... we've been friends. And the office... well, I'm an Israeli!"

"You really think it's the two of them against you?"

"They both survived, didn't they? I can't imagine either one of them admitting what really happened!"

"You're either an incredible liar—or you're telling the truth," said David and lapsed into a troubled silence once more.

Ari was stunned. After thinking their conversation over for several minutes, he blurted out, "I can't believe this! Why have you turned against me?"

"Look, in case you didn't know it—and no one's going to believe you didn't—Carla was a Soviet plant, a co-conspirator with Khorev. That's the finding of the FBI and CIA. You were her longtime friend, and she brought you into the picture... which doesn't make it look good for you."

"She's no Soviet plant! I'd stake my life on that!"

"What's she to you? Why defend her? That makes you look bad. And to make it worse... she's become a religious fanatic just like you. Claims she survived the holocaust because 'Jesus' rescued her. The 'coincidence' becomes too much...."

"She does?" exclaimed Ari in surprise. *Then she would know that the Nine are demons! That changes everything!*

David's expression reflected a deep inner conflict. "Look... if we hadn't been such close friends I wouldn't be telling you this. I'm not supposed to... but take my advice and change your story. Right now it agrees with hers. That's damning."

"*Damning?* Why would you believe del Sasso when you've got two eyewitnesses who contradict him?"

David gave Ari another puzzled look and said no more.

— ✦ —

When they arrived at the gray, stark-exteriored headquarters on King Saul Boulevard, David was taken directly into the head of Mossad's large office and the door was shut. Four other top Mossad officers were already in there: Yosi Maidan, Moshe Yshai, Shimone Hofi, and Eiten Yaar. David greeted them and sat down in one of two chairs still empty in the semicircle facing the Chief's desk. The Mossad head, who was talking when David entered, nodded in his direction and carried on.

"He's lying. We have a copy of the full statement Del Sasso gave to the FBI—and they're positive he's telling the truth."

"No question about it," added Eiten Yaar.

"There's no way Thalberg could have been inside that auditorium at the meeting and survived," continued the chief. "No way at all!"

"That 'cavern' he fell into is the biggest cock-and-bull story I ever heard," added Shimone Hofi. "Did he really think we'd believe it?"

"And his story agrees with hers...the journalist's," declared Yosi Maidan. "She's the one who invited him. She was Khorev's accomplice. It's airtight."

"We can't have him spreading his story around. And we can't have a public trial," mused the chief. "He knows too much. Our whole operation over there would be in jeopardy. We've got to break him, destroy his memory...." Nodding of heads indicated agreement all around.

"Any problem with that, Kauly?" asked the chief. "He was your man."

"If that's the consensus," said David after a moment's hesitation, "I'll go along with it."

"This whole Archon thing—entities without bodies from another dimension—is so fantastic that nobody would believe it," suggested Moshe Ishai. "Of course, the CIA and FBI are officially denying that Archons ever had anything to do with the operation...or that they even exist. We have to go along with that...or it would jeopardize our operation. We can use Thalberg's insistence upon extradimensionals to prove he's insane."

"Good idea," agreed Yosi and Shimone. The others nodded.

"So we all agree," declared the chief, "that we're going to...uh...use this approach, right?" Heads nodded. "Now, let's discuss the best way to go about it."

47

In "Protective Custody"

After about an hour of waiting, Ari was at last escorted in by a secretary. As soon as he entered the room, he could sense the animosity. He was no longer one of them, but had already been written off as the enemy.

Besides the Chief and David, the other four were strangers to Ari. He knew of them by reputation, but had never met any of them, nor was he properly introduced now. The Chief simply recited their names and positions as a matter of formality. No one made a move to reach out and shake the hand Ari offered, then withdrew in embarrassment.

As soon as Ari was seated, the Chief turned on a tape to record the proceedings. "You're a very clever man, Thalberg," he began, "and we had hoped to use your considerable talents on other assignments around the world. But now we've got a problem... and I'm going to level with you right up front. Your story—and admittedly we haven't heard all the details yet—is completely contradicted by other impeccable testimony that's been made available to us."

"If you mean Antonio Del Sasso's version of what happened," responded Ari, "then I'm not surprised. Nor should you be. He's Israel's enemy."

"What proof do you have of that?" demanded the Chief.

"David knows that I'd been contacted several times by an entity... he calls himself Elor of the Nine. That's the group of extradimensionals who gave Del Sasso his powers and who work with the CIA. They wanted to use me to destroy Zionism and internationalize Jerusalem... which at that time I thought would further the cause of peace...."

"That whole Extradimensional Intelligence thing is a bunch of garbage ...not worthy of sane conversation!" interrupted Shimone derisively.

"Shimone's the one who did the investigation on that," added the Chief, backing up his man.

"Garbage? That's odd," returned Ari. "I was told by someone present in this room that the CIA was in touch with ETIs who possibly didn't have physical bodies—which would make them EDIs." He turned to David for corroboration.

"I was misinformed," muttered David apologetically, "which I only found out a few minutes ago."

"Hold on!" insisted Ari. "Some of your men... when you had me under surveillance... saw Elor and the incredible things he did!"

"That was the preliminary report, but now there's some dispute about what they really saw... some confusion...," said David lamely.

"You can't change your tune so easily!" protested Ari. He turned to the Chief. "One of your own people did an article in the *Post* about the involvement of ETIs in psychic research—and the scientifically acceptable possibility that they might have evolved beyond the need of bodies. What about that?"

"There's a big difference between ETIs and EDIs," declared Shimone. "That whole EDI hoax was perpetrated by Carla Bertelli—and we fell for it until we learned the facts. It was a diversion that was invented to explain the destruction Khorev and Bertelli planned. But I'm not telling you anything you didn't know...."

"I resent that!" responded Ari hotly. "You're accusing me."

"Let's get down to the facts," said the Chief. "You told two of our men on the way to the San Francisco airport that the floor of the auditorium opened up and dropped you into an underground cavern...."

"That's right," nodded Ari.

"Investigators have carefully sifted through the ruins—searching for bodies, trying to make identification of remains and to find the cause of the explosion—and although the floor is buckled and torn up in places, there's absolutely no sign of any opening such as you describe. Furthermore, geologists over a period of many years have mapped that area thoroughly, looking for oil and minerals, and there has never been any indication of an underground cavern of any kind, much less of the proportions you report."

"Geologists have been wrong thousands of times," retorted Ari. "They don't know everything. I'm telling you the cavern's there. I think I could find the place where I got out. Let's go over there and I'll prove it!"

"You *think* you could."

"I'm sure I could. It's not very large, but...."

"We're not flying off to California on hopes and dreams. This big hole in the floor that you fell through... it just sealed itself?" asked the Chief sarcastically.

"I can't explain that—but do you think I could make up such a story?" countered Ari.

"You're clever enough to make up anything... that's why it's so puzzling that you'd come up with such an unlikely fiction. Did you really think we'd believe that wild tale?"

"It's not fiction or a wild tale. I'm telling you the truth. It's not the kind of tale I'd come up with if I were lying... I'd invent something more believable."

"You've been watching too much TV... lost touch with reality. I think you need some psychiatric help."

Ari took a deep breath. "If I'm as clever as you suggest, then surely if I were fabricating a story I wouldn't come up with something as bizarre as falling into an underground cavern, would I? I'd simply say that I stepped out of the auditorium to go to the men's room... or to get a breath of fresh air, or something like that. Right?"

"I think you're clever enough," suggested Moshe Yshai, "to come up with a wild tale just so you could use that argument... a genius out of touch with the real world."

"What I went through in that hell hole," protested Ari, "my imagination couldn't concoct anything like that! It's a miracle that I got out alive! It's all on the tape. Listen to it... or I'd be happy to go through it again."

The men around him shook their heads and looked at one another as though they felt sorry that such a brilliant person had lost his mind. Their performance was almost enough to cause Ari to wonder whether he had lost touch with reality. No, he wouldn't succumb to their game, if that's what it was. Yes, what he had just lived through was fantastic, beyond belief, but it had really happened.

"Okay," said Ari with a shrug, "I don't know what I can do to convince you of that part. Forget it for the moment. What we need to get down to—and it's all on the audiotape I gave David—are the incredible things that happened in the auditorium before the whole thing blew up. That's what's important. I'm telling you, Israel's in danger. This guy Del Sasso...."

"Exactly where were you when the explosion took place?" cut in Yosi Maidan, the Mossad explosive specialist.

"As I told Mike and Sam—and you'll find all the facts on the tape in great detail—I wasn't aware of any explosion until I saw it on the news when I got to the hotel the next night. That must have happened after 30 of us went through the floor...."

"Back to fantasyland again!" interrupted Shimone with disgust. "So what happened to the other 29 who all supposedly fell into the same place you did?"

"You tell me what happened to them! I'll bet my life that none of the remains have been identified—or ever will be—as belonging to any of the media people who were present!"

"We don't have a report on that," cut in the Chief, "but I'm sure they'll be found."

"If they are, you can take me out and shoot me!" declared Ari confidently.

"Well, back to your story," persisted the Chief. "You say they fell into the same hole you did. Why didn't any of them survive and get out?"

"I don't know. After falling what seemed like hundreds of feet, I happened to hit a steep, sandy slope and slid into a big rock that kept me from going on over a cliff. That's what saved my life. The others must not have been so lucky. I heard screams of people falling beyond me... but after I regained consciousness I yelled for them but got no answer. It was dead silence and total blackness in there."

"Del Sasso, in a sworn statement to the FBI, says you were never there," interjected Eiten Yaar, who'd been closely watching Ari in silence.

"That lying devil!" Ari had turned red with anger.

"He says," persisted Eiten, "that he specifically asked Ms. Bertelli where the *Jerusalem Post* reporter was and that she seemed embarrassed and said something about your being delayed, but you'd be there soon. . . ."

"That's a lie! She introduced me to Del Sasso and we had a conversation that left me very uncomfortable. I wasn't dreaming. I was there—and talked to him."

"Did someone give you a ride into town in a pickup?" asked the Chief.

"Yeah—fiftyish, long hair and beard, tanned, hillbilly English . . . a refugee from the hippie era."

"A news report of the destruction and loss of life came on his radio. You heard it, but said nothing to him about being there. Doesn't that seem like an unnatural reaction . . . if you'd gone through that holocaust and escaped . . . not to say anything about it?"

"Not at all! I was on a secret mission. I had information that I wanted to bring back to Israel . . . and I didn't want to be held up by the local police, the FBI or whoever might have taken me into custody for lengthy questioning if I'd let anyone know that I was a survivor. I wanted to tell *you* the facts, not them. Doesn't that make sense?"

"You told him . . . and the hotel clerk . . . the same story about being lost in the woods, falling over a cliff. . . ."

"I had to tell them something. That seemed the most likely explanation of my battered and bruised and bloodied and muddied appearance."

The Chief nodded to Yosi. "Read him the pertinent part of the FBI report."

Yosi pulled some papers out of his briefcase and began to read: "Del Sasso, unconscious from smoke inhalation and internal injuries, was found by firemen next to the corpse of Khorev. This is consistent with his story that he saw Ms. Bertelli and Khorev suddenly leave, suspected something and ran after them. Bertelli had disappeared, but he caught Khorev. They argued. Khorev seemed anxious to get out of the building. There was a huge explosion and that's the last he remembered until he came to in the hospital.

"Bertelli didn't have a scratch. Yet she claims that when she made her escape by a stage exit everyone else—except Khorev and Del Sasso, who were both battered—was already dead. And how did they die? According to Bertelli, they were hit by falling chunks of ceiling . . . and many were impaled by splinters of the laminated overhead beams that pursued people like guided missiles. . . ."

"That's right!" interjected Ari. "I saw it happen!"

"We know your stories agree," said Yosi sarcastically. "She even says, like you, that the floor opened up and the entire press section fell through. Her description of what happened inside the auditorium before the explosion sounds like a horror movie. It's beyond belief for the real world. But let me go back to the FBI report verbatim.

"Bertelli also claims that Del Sasso was already in the lobby waiting for her when she got there. Not only does this conflict with his testimony, but with the location where he was found. If he'd been in the lobby, why would he have gone back toward the auditorium after the explosion? And how could he have gotten to the lobby ahead of both Bertelli and Khorev if he left the auditorium after they did? As for Ari Thalberg...."

"That's enough," interrupted the Chief. He turned to Ari. "We think you're lying, Thalberg. You were never in that auditorium."

"They checked my name off at the gate when I entered!"

"That's the first thing the FBI thought of—and your name is one of three that were not checked off. The other two became ill at the last minute and didn't make the trip."

"Somebody's doctored the records. I saw the guard put the check by my name—with a pen!"

"I believe the FBI," insisted the Chief. "Not always, but in this case. There were about 200 other media persons around the gate, all have been contacted, and none remembers seeing you."

"That's a joke. How would they know what I looked like? I hadn't been outside of Israel...."

"There were reporters from Paris, and Berlin—and other cities—who knew you in the past as Professor Hans Mueller. They didn't see you go in."

"I was in a car when we went through the gate. They weren't peering in the windows...."

"None of the drivers taking delegates from the San Francisco airport remembered you."

"The FBI is covering up!" protested Ari. "I'll take a polygraph test right here in Israel from your best experts! Go into the minutest details of what I saw happen...then compare it with what Bertelli says. Check the phone records. I've talked to her once since I last saw her four years ago in Paris. You've seen all my letters to her and hers to me. When could we possibly have rehearsed...."

The Chief cut him off. "We're going to investigate this in detail...just as the CIA is also doing. I don't know all of the answers yet—but at the moment the evidence points to a conspiracy between Khorev, Bertelli and you. She 'rescued' Khorev from the KGB in Paris. Now the KGB says it was staged by Khorev and a rogue agent named Chernov who later attacked that same CIA installation. Khorev and Bertelli were working together, there's no doubt. You knew her in Paris years ago, had contact with her there just before you came to Israel, and she brought you into the project to provide an alibi. It was a setup from the start..."

"Absolutely preposterous!" interjected Ari, beside himself with anger and frustration. "What motive could either Bertelli or I have for wanting to destroy...."

"You both believe that Jesus was the Messiah and that he's coming back to rule the world. Right?"

Ari nodded. "If you take what the Hebrew prophets had to say, you can't come to any other conclusion. . . ."

The Chief held up his hand in protest. "Don't try to convert me! The fact is that what you both believe about this supposedly resurrected Jesus coming back to rule the world is in irreconcilable conflict with the New World Order that we're all working for. There's your motive. It springs from religious paranoia."

Ari opened his mouth to respond, but the Chief cut him off again. "This is still under investigation. You haven't been charged with any crime—yet. But until it's resolved, I'm placing you under protective custody. Get your suitcase and go with Yosi and Moshe. They'll take you to a safe house. You'll be under 24-hour guard. Don't make it difficult for us."

48

The Warsaw Ghetto Syndrome

Confined to a small apartment on one of Tel Aviv's back streets, and under constant guard, Ari found the next few months to be the most difficult period of his entire life. Miriam had promised to marry him as soon as possible—and now he was unable even to see her. In an earlier time, Ari would have made his escape and given the Mossad a run for their money. Now, however, instead of taking things into his own hands as he had always done in the past, he waited patiently for God to give him the direction he so urgently needed.

The one visitor Ari was allowed was Yakov, and that only because of the old man's illustrious military career and his insistence upon seeing his "good friend" two or three times a week "whether the Mossad likes it or not." Those visits were like manna from heaven—not only because of the letters brought from Miriam (Ari was otherwise forbidden to send or receive mail), but because of the spiritual sustenance that came from the times of prayer and Bible study he and Yakov enjoyed together.

Yakov had brought Ari a Bible on his first visit. It was a book that Ari had been deeply prejudiced against, though he had never owned or even read more than a few pages of it in his life. Now he found himself absorbed in the study of Scripture. He was like a starving man who had stumbled upon life-giving food. Unable to get enough of the book that he was now convinced was God's Word to mankind, and with little else demanding his time, Ari determined to read it through carefully from Genesis to Revelation.

"It's so awesome that the Creator of the universe has actually communicated to us—told us His will for our lives," Ari gratefully reminded Yakov nearly every time he visited. "I can't get over it! And to think that I completely ignored God's Word all my life... and so do most people. What a tragedy!"

"There are some verses in Deuteronomy 8 that I want to point out to you," Yakov had said when he'd handed Ari the Bible on that first visit. "That's the fifth book in the Bible—the last of the books Moses wrote."

Two armed guards sitting in the same room listened contemptuously at first, then with growing interest. "After God brought our ancestors out of Egypt to take them to this promised land, they were so rebellious that He kept them in the wilderness 40 years before bringing them across the Jordan. And in this brief passage God explained why He kept Israel in the wilderness for so long, and that He wanted them and their descendants—which includes even us today—never to forget that experience and the lessons it taught.

After showing Ari where the verses were in the Bible he'd just given to him, Yakov read from his worn and marked copy in a loud, firm voice:

> "And you shall remember all the way which the Lord your God has led you in the wilderness these forty years, that He might humble you, testing you, to know what was in your heart, whether you would keep His commandments or not.
>
> "And He humbled you and let you be hungry, and fed you with manna which you did not know... that He might make you understand that man does not live by bread alone, but man lives by everything that proceeds out of the mouth of the Lord."

"Those are the verses," continued Yakov, "that Jesus quoted to Satan when the head of the Archons came to harass Him in the wilderness, probably not too far from here. You'll read about it when you get to the New Testament. Jesus had been fasting for 40 days and Satan tried to persuade Him to take matters into His own hands and satisfy His hunger... but He declared that knowing God and doing His will was the first priority."

Yakov put a hand warmly upon Ari's arm. How he wanted to see him grow strong in his newfound faith! "You're going through a wilderness experience, too, Ari. Look upon it as a gift, an opportunity from God—a time when you can prove your trust and obedience by submitting to whatever He allows in your life. He won't abandon you. It might seem so at times, but he'll bring you through in victory!

"It's like the tests Mossad gives you after your training to be sure you've learned your lessons and are ready for the mission they want you to accomplish. God has a mission for you, Ari. When the time has come, He'll set you free to do it. But first, you have to realize that you have no strength or wisdom in yourself—nothing at all that God needs. You're totally dependent upon Him for everything. It's a humbling experience, but absolutely essential if God is to be able to use you for His purposes in this world."

"Six months ago I would have been out of here like a shot," Ari confided in a low voice to Yakov. "These guys couldn't have kept me in here! But now—everything's different. I'm learning to trust God. I'm at peace, even in this place—happier than I've ever been in my life. I don't recognize myself," he added with a fleeting smile.

"Praise God for that!" said Yakov fervently.

"It hasn't been easy," Ari admitted honestly, "but I know it's for the best. I think of Miriam day and night. I love her so much more now! It's a new dimension of love—which makes it all the more frustrating. Now that the past barriers to our marriage no longer exist... here I sit like a caged animal." He shook his head ruefully, but without the old rebellion and anger.

"Wait and see the salvation of the Lord, my friend," beamed Yakov. "As it says in the Psalms, 'Wait patiently on the Lord.'" The words of David from so long ago fell like a healing balm on Ari's soul.

—✦—

"Your friend, Carla Bertelli," Yakov told Ari one day after he'd been confined for about three months, "married Ken Inman. That's the man she'd been engaged to years ago. She walked out on him when he became a Christian...even though he was in the hospital recovering from a bizarre auto accident that should have killed him. Amazing that she finally became a follower of Jesus, just like you did, through that same holocaust."

"I read about it in the paper," replied Ari. "It happened two weeks ago, but they just reported it. I wish I could talk with her, now that she's a believer. At least she's not under house arrest and she and Ken can share their lives. But the news reports sound as though she's getting the same treatment in the U.S. that I'm getting over here. She's accused of sabotage while Del Sasso has become a hero. I get really angry about that sometimes—and then the Lord reminds me that He will take care of Del Sasso when and how it suits Him best. That calms me down in a hurry."

"You got a letter from Carla yesterday," confided Yakov in a low voice, though the guards were paying no attention to them. "I knew you'd want to know what she said, so I opened it...."

"Well, tell me!" said Ari eagerly.

Yakov leaned closer and spoke in a whisper. "She has a friend in the FBI—a Christian. Didn't give his name, of course. He got her entire story on tape, and she wanted to be able to give him your story...so I sent her a copy of the tapes we made that night. She doubts it will do any good, but she wants him to have it for his files. She says there are too many people high up in Washington involved with the Nine for the truth ever to get out. She wonders what their next step will be."

"I still don't get the picture," said Ari. "Why did Del Sasso—or the Nine—let Khorev keep talking at the congress? If they'd shut him up right away, that slaughter wouldn't have been necessary."

"Like I told you long ago," mused Yakov, "demons aren't all-knowing. Their knowledge and power, though far greater than ours in many ways, are definitely limited. As brilliant as Satan is, even he makes mistakes. I think he believes his own lies and is the prisoner of his ego."

"How do you know he makes mistakes?" asked Ari, eager to learn all he could. "Is it in the Bible?"

"I wouldn't know it if the Bible hadn't told me...and I certainly wouldn't speculate about Satan or any other spiritual matter. Of course, his first and biggest mistake was to rebel against God. He's made lots of blunders, but I'll just mention two that show his confusion. At one time he inspired Peter to tell Jesus not to go to the cross—and later he inspired Judas to betray him to be killed."

"Very interesting! I just read about both of those incidents the other day, but didn't put them together."

"I'm sure the Nine didn't know what Khorev was going to say... and when it happened they couldn't decide what to do."

"But why such destruction? Why kill everyone?"

"From what you said on the tape, Khorev laid it out so clearly that it wouldn't have been easy to refute. He was presenting the facts and challenging Del Sasso and Leighton to admit it. I think the Nine became enraged at Khorev and exposed themselves. They try to pose as loving and benevolent beings, but they're really hatred and evil personified... and sometimes the mask slips. They lost control—and from your description of even the first few moments of their reaction, it quickly had gone so far that they couldn't afford to have any witnesses."

"And Del Sasso... why didn't he react sooner?"

"He's apparently been so demonized in order to be a channel of such incredible power that he's pretty much under their control. He couldn't do anything until they did it through him. After that debacle they've had to change their tactics. I understand that Del Sasso has founded a success/motivation company called Shamans Unlimited—to 'empower' people to control their own destiny—and it's literally exploding internationally. This may be more effective in demonizing the world than the first approach...."

"Yeah," cut in Ari, "from what I've read, he's a household name now—a big hero. They call him 'the lone survivor.' Carla doesn't count, because she's supposedly the enemy that caused it. And I'm never mentioned, because the official line is that I wasn't even there. I know my name was checked off at the gate. There would be other ways to verify that I was there. The FBI's covering up..."

"I think the Mossad's doing some of that, too," whispered Yakov. "You're a dangerous man. They can't let you out. I don't know what they're going to do... but they'll have to do something soon."

"Why? They can just let me rot here. I'm a nonperson—even in Israel. Nobody knows I'm in this place... or that I even exist. And who cares? It's maddening!"

"I scarcely see David anymore," reflected Yakov. "Thought he'd intervene. He must know you're telling the truth. But things have changed. You remember how he said the Nine were anti-Israel and the CIA was working against us? Well, I think Mossad's been compromised in order to pacify the United States and to keep the Arabs from walking out on the peace conference. Israel thinks that its hope is in a partnership with other nations. But the Bible warns that they'll all turn against her. Israel's only hope is in the God of Abraham, Isaac and Jacob. He'd protect her—and He's the only one who can—if she'd only turn to Him!"

"It's like the Warsaw Ghetto," suggested Ari. "You remember. When that woman who survived the massacre returned to tell everyone that those who were being taken away were being slaughtered, no one would believe her. The truth was too horrible to accept. And the truth I'm trying to tell the Mossad is apparently too shocking for them to believe. They *have* to prove I'm wrong in order to keep their own sanity."

— ✦ —

In the United States, though Carla Inman had not been put under house arrest, she was forbidden to tell her side of the story publicly until the Senate Committee had concluded its hearing and arrived at a decision. Ari's testimony was granted even less of an airing. No one heard it except the Mossad. When it became apparent that the U.S. Senate was going to vote in favor of Del Sasso and against Carla, the Mossad held an in-house hearing of its own. The conclusion it reached was inevitable.

To prove their willingness to get at the truth, the Mossad gave Ari a battery of lie detector tests. "There's no doubt that he really believes he's telling the truth," the polygraph experts testified at the Mossad hearing. "Whether he actually is or not... that's another question."

The committee had already arrived at its conclusions, but needed further justification "for the record" in order to prevent possible criticism if the case should be reviewed in the future. Of course the in-house psychiatrists had their explanation all planned. But it looked good to be meticulous, so they went through the motions.

Ari was given a series of in-depth psychological examinations. Dr. Mordechai Margolins, Israel's most eminent psychiatrist and the current president of the World Association of Psychiatrists, presented the findings of the psychological examination team to the committee. He did so in a detached, clinical tone of voice that made it sound as though he were unbiased and infallible:

"The subject, Ari Thalberg, is clearly in a state of classical psychotic breakdown. In fact, he's a textbook case. He's lost the ability to distinguish between the real world and a fantasy world—a world of unreality in which he spends most of his time. He's had severe hallucinations and has heard 'voices' which he thought came from some 'god.' Though he's apparently not experiencing the full range of psychosis at the present, it could return at any time. It may well be that the stress of having to lie about his experience in California was too great, causing him to retreat into fantasy in order to maintain his own self-perceived integrity.

"His religious delusions—that 'Jesus' saved him from the underground cavern he concocted, then later imagined he fell into—led to the belief that this mythical 'Jesus' must therefore be alive...and further, that this delusional figment had also 'saved' him from his 'sins' by dying on the cross and resurrecting the third day. It's a common fantasy embraced by hundreds of millions of so-called Christians around the world, and which, tragically, many of our own people are falling for right here in Israel.

"Dr. Thalberg is a danger to himself as well as to others. We recommend confinement to a psychiatric hospital with administration of bilateral electroconvulsive therapy. For those on the committee who may not be familiar with ECT, let me assure you that it has come a long way from the early days when electric shock was administered that would send the patient into convulsive seizures. It is now done with the latest anesthetic pharmacology (thiopental, thiamylal and methohexital) and in conjunction with the most advanced psychopharmacology, using drugs such as succinylcholine as a muscle relaxant and chlorpromazine for diminishing the psychotic symptomatology.

"Of course, one of the major benefits of this therapy will be permanent memory loss. One must distinguish between brain damage, which will only be temporary, and memory loss, which will be permanent. The patient will be delivered from the delusions that now cloud his thinking. Once those encumbering symptoms have been removed, standard psychotherapy will be able to proceed more effectively. We owe Dr. Thalberg this opportunity for recovery."

Dr. Margolins' decision fell like a death sentence upon Ari. He rose to make a final plea on his own behalf, but was pulled back into his chair by the guard on either side of him.

"Of course," the chief hearing officer added, addressing Ari in a more sinister tone, "we recognize the possibility that, in spite of the polygraph results, you have deliberately deceived this committee. If so, why not confess this now and at least save yourself from treatment in a psychiatric hospital. We might offer some leniency...."

"What I have told you is absolutely true," replied Ari resolutely. "I cannot lie to save my skin. I am in God's hands and accept whatever is His will. Do your worst. You can do no more than what He allows."

The members of the committee exchanged knowing glances. If there had been any doubts, that statement by Ari was more than enough to demonstrate the validity of the clinical diagnosis of obsessional religious psychosis.

— ✦ —

Ari was taken in chains to a psychiatric hospital, where he was confined to the heavily guarded wing for dangerous criminals undergoing treatment. He was given a bed in a large room with five other inmates. All had been ruled criminally insane. One of them, Ari became convinced, was an informant placed there to report to the authorities. It was not long, however, until he had great difficult retaining such analytical thoughts.

If he'd thought he might find some sympathy or understanding from anyone in this appalling place, Ari soon realized that he'd been tragically mistaken. The inmates were human guinea pigs—and the staff treated them as such. Ari found himself shattered and near insanity after each so-called treatment, with symptoms ranging from total despair to detached unreality. It was a desperate struggle just to remember his own identity.

Day followed night in a blur of near insanity. Time soon lost all meaning. The drugs and shock treatments were taking deadly effect, eroding Ari's memory. Recollection would return in part when the effects of the last "treatment" began to wear off, but there was a growing cumulative effect that was devastating. Unknown to Yakov or even David, Ari had become the subject of brainwashing experiments fashioned after those that the CIA had funded and employed upon some of its own citizens for years. So long as one was involved in a "scientific experiment" in pursuit of "expanded knowledge" of how the brain functions—as Nazi doctors had long ago demonstrated—almost anything could be easily justified in a bureaucracy that no longer recognized God's laws but was making its own rules based upon convenience and expediency.

Aided by the neurotoxic chemicals they were using to dysfunctionalize his brain processes, the psychiatrists were steadily convincing Ari that he was insane and that his experiences in California had never occurred; they were but the fantasies of a diseased mind. On a deeper level, however, Ari continued to fight a desperate battle to retain his personal identity. It was a battle that he didn't understand and in which the odds were stacked so heavily against him that the ultimate surrender of his will, the goal which the psychiatrists sought, was only a matter of days, perhaps a few weeks at most.

Each time Yakov visited Ari he could see the progressive deterioration. He complained vigorously to David and to the Chief, but to no avail. Their arguments were unassailable.

"It's a medical matter," the Chief insisted, "completely out of my hands. The psychiatrists made their diagnosis and they're following that up with the best treatment available. Ari's in excellent hands—Israel's top specialists, highly respected internationally."

"It was never a medical matter!" retorted Yakov. "He was declared insane because he stuck to his story... because he wouldn't say what you wanted him to."

"He has delusions," insisted the Chief. "The things he claims to have witnessed and experienced in California never happened—but he really believes they did. He passed all the polygraph tests, so we know he's not deliberately lying. *Something* flipped him into another world—a fantasy world of EDIs and psychic miracles... unbelievable events that happen only in science fiction thrillers. That's the problem they're trying to cure. They think he'll come out of it in another four weeks at the most."

"They're making him insane with the drugs they're giving him!" insisted Yakov. "I've been doing some research. Do you realize that *every* psychiatric drug is highly neurotoxic? They work by destroying the normal function of the brain cells."

"This is a very specialized field," said the Chief, trying not to sound too patronizing. "You can't do a little reading at the library and then tell the experts they don't know what they're doing! You've got to trust the doctors. They tell me they're making progress... that he's forgetting those fantasies."

"He's forgetting *everything*. He was brilliant—mind like a computer—but now he can hardly carry on a conversation! How can this be happening in Israel? It's like the experiments the Nazi doctors performed on Jews!"

"I think you're too emotionally involved," suggested David, trying to back up the Chief without offending Yakov. "It's no reflection on Ari. The brain is a complex organism. Maybe he did fall over a cliff and hit his head...."

"God help us!" exclaimed Yakov. "Don't you see what's happening? Society's becoming a pool of experimental animals for a bunch of power-mad egomaniacs. These so-called experts will soon have the authority to declare all of us insane if we don't think the way they want us to... and to prescribe drugs to make our behavior conform to their standards. It's coming to that. If they can do it to Ari, they can do it to any one of us!"

Yakov's protests and pleas were in vain. As the Chief argued so reasonably, the psychiatrists had made their diagnosis. And since they were the experts, with specialized knowledge that couldn't be challenged by anyone else, there was no way to prevent them from carrying out the full treatment program.

"The stonewalling I'm getting from the Mossad," a distraught Yakov confided in Miriam, "only proves the point I'm trying to make about psychiatric abuse. There's nothing we can do now—but pray."

49

A Surprising Confirmation

"Haven't I seen you somewhere?" asked Ari. With great effort he directed the question to the new orderly who stood before him balancing a medicine tray. "What's your name?"

In one of his more lucid moments, Ari was sitting on his bed in his large, shared room. Having difficulty knowing where he was, and remembering almost nothing since he had returned to Israel, he was, nevertheless, getting disjointed memory flashes of more distant events. The medic, who had just been assigned to this wing in the psychiatric hospital, had come into the room with two guards to administer medication.

"I'm Dmitri Petrekov," came the reply in thickly accented and faltering Hebrew. The round face, pug-nosed and accented by broad Russian cheek bones, lit up in a hearty, transparent smile. "No, you've never seen me." The stranger corrected the patient gently, then added almost apologetically, "It's time for your medication." He held out some pills and a paper cup of water.

Shaking his head in helpless protest, Ari pushed the outstretched hand away. "No... please. Those things destroy my memory... that's what they're trying to do." Ari looked up at Dmitri more closely. "Your face... I know I've seen you... somewhere."

Again that pleasant, patient smile. "That's impossible. I just arrived three weeks ago from Russia, and this is my first day on the job... and if you don't take the pills I'll have to give you a shot."

"Lord Jesus, help me!" whispered Ari.

"You believe in Jesus?" asked Dmitri, lowering his voice so the others in the room couldn't hear.

Ari nodded weakly. "Do you?"

"Yes!" whispered Dmitri. "Praise God! Are there any other believers in here...?"

Ari shrugged. He was trying desperately to concentrate. "I didn't see you here...," he continued quietly, searching Dmitri's face and struggling to focus his memory. "You were in a lab... psychic research... near Moscow. Yes,... you worked with... with... Khorev... Viktor Khorev."

Dmitri's eyes opened wide in astonishment. "How could you know? It was a secret commando base. You were never there...."

Clutching his throbbing head with his hands, Ari tried to sort through images that were surfacing in kaleidoscopic confusion. "You were leaning over a psychic... big, heavy man, strapped into a large chair. Khorev was in kind of an observation booth above looking down on you... and some others...."

"That's the lab I worked in with Viktor!" exclaimed Dmitri. "How is it possible...?"

"A video...," continued Ari haltingly, "I saw you on a video... a giant screen in an auditorium... lots of important people."

"There was no video," countered Dmitri, becoming all the more mystified. "It was top secret."

"A monk... big man... hooded robe... Del Sasso, made the video with his mind... and Khorev was making a speech... then... all hell broke loose...."

Ari fell back on his bed in utter exhaustion.

Covertly Dmitri slipped the pills into his pocket and leaned closer to whisper, "I'm not giving you anything." Then aloud he said, "Now take your pills like a good patient." He pretended to push something into Ari's mouth, then gave him a drink from the paper cup.

Ari looked at Dmitri with gratitude. "You don't think I'm crazy?" he whispered. "I really saw you?"

"You described where I worked... and there was a hooded man... I remember that. This is remarkable!"

"I want my pills!" demanded Mousa, a tall, thin, compulsive man who occupied the bed next to Ari's. "My head's hurting!" Mousa had been a top *katsa* who'd accidentally been given too large a dose of LSD in an experiment ten years before. His behavior was so unpredictable that it was too dangerous for him to live in the outside world, so he'd become one of several permanent guinea pigs. Somehow he'd picked up the conviction that he held a privileged position among the ward's experimental derelicts.

"Yes, you're next," Dmitri assured him. With a pat on Ari's shoulder, he moved on.

It was at that moment that another medic ushered Yakov into the room. He stood at the foot of Ari's bed and observed him sadly for a few moments before Ari realized he was there.

"Yakov!" exclaimed Ari when he'd seen him at last.

"How's it going?" asked Yakov, trying to sound cheerful in spite of his fears for Ari's sanity. He sat down beside his friend on the bed and put an arm around his drooping shoulders.

"I'm okay." Ari straightened up and smiled. "I'm going to make it." Then he remembered something. "The new attendant... over there," he whispered to Yakov. "He's a believer!"

"Really?" Yakov hurried over to catch Dmitri just as he was about to leave the room. "When do you get off?" he said in a low voice. The two guards were already out of the room, holding the door open, waiting impatiently.

"At three."

"I must talk to you!"

"How do we meet?"

"When you leave the hospital, exit out front and go to your right, then turn right on the first cross street and just keep walking until I come along in my car. Okay?"

Dmitri nodded. "I think he's doing fine," he said in a reassuring tone loud enough for the guards to hear. "He's a good patient." He waved at Ari and the other inmates, then left the room.

— ✦ —

Yakov waited in his parked car two blocks from the hospital. He let the orderly go on past, followed him for another 200 yards until he was certain that no one was observing, then picked him up.

"I appreciate this very much," said Yakov as soon as the man had entered his car and they were driving away. "I'm Yakov Kimchy."

"Dmitri Petrekov." Warmly he shook Yakov's outstretched hand. "Sorry that my Hebrew isn't very good."

"You're doing great. Now about Ari Thalberg. You remember him... the believer...?"

"Yes, yes, remarkable man...."

"He lived with me until he was put in there," continued the old man. "He tells me you know Jesus...."

Dmitri's face lit up with that brilliant smile. "Yes. Praise God for that. Otherwise I couldn't have survived the Gulag. They were determined to break me."

"You've been in a labor camp?" asked Yakov sympathetically.

"Three of them. But with the new openness they let me out... and I just immigrated here three weeks ago. Today was my first day on the job. I'm grateful for the work, but it's criminal what they do to those pitiful creatures...."

"I'm glad you see that!" exclaimed Yakov, sensing that he'd found a sympathetic ear. "The shock treatments and drugs are destroying Ari's mind!"

"I realized that... and held back his medication on my shift. They'd fire me, if they knew...."

"Thank God!" exclaimed Yakov. "The Lord will protect you. If we could only find a way to keep them from giving him anything on the other shifts!"

"That would be difficult. Why's he in there, anyway?"

"It's a long story. He was on an assignment for the Mossad and came back with some information they didn't want to believe—so they declared him insane. They're now trying to wipe out his memory. That's basically it. Criminal is right! He was a brilliant man... but the 'therapy' is destroying his brain."

"I'd say he's very remarkable," returned Dmitri thoughtfully. "Said some things about me that it was impossible for him to know."

"Really. Like what?"

"Said he'd seen a video of me in the lab where I worked in Russia, which he couldn't have, because it was on a secret base. But he described it and even named the head scientist there that I worked with, Viktor Khorev. That was...."

"Khorev?" interrupted Yakov, excited now. "The Soviet parapsychologist who defected to the U.S. several years ago?"

"Yes. I knew he planned to defect, and kept it a secret. That got me put in the Gulag."

"Oh, God, thank you! Thank you!" exclaimed Yakov gratefully. "God has sent you to save Ari's life. Thank you, Lord!"

"I don't understand."

"Are you certain that Khorev defected?"

"That was his plan when he left Moscow for Paris."

"He wasn't involved in some plot with a Colonel Chernov?"

"Chernov?" laughed Dmitri. "How do you know about him? You must be joking. Alexei Chernov was the most vicious man I've ever known. He hated Khorev with a passion, and put me in the Gulag!"

"This is fantastic! A miracle that you should come to Israel at this time... and to the very ward where Ari's being kept! Thank you, Father. Thank you! Thank you!"

Yakov wiped the tears of gratitude from his eyes. "Tell me how to get to your apartment. I'll drop you off there...but I want to come back as soon as I can with a friend. Would you be willing to tell him what you've just told me?"

"Of course. Especially if it will help this poor man to get out of that madhouse!"

—✦—

Yakov returned to Dmitri's apartment early that evening with David. The Russian immigrant's host family had gone to a movie, so it was possible to talk freely.

After introductions, the three men sat down together in the small living room, and David turned on the tape recorder he'd brought. "Now start at the beginning and tell me what you told Yakov this afternoon."

"Today was my first day on the job. When the patient, Ari Thalberg, whom I was seeing for the first time, saw me, he insisted that he'd seen me before. I told him that was impossible, but then he started telling me about the laboratory where I had worked near Moscow... and where he claimed he'd seen me. It was on a secret commando base that I know he had never visited. No outsiders were ever allowed on that base. In the lab we were involved in top-secret psychic research. His description of the interior of the lab was accurate. He said we were doing psychic experiments... and he even named the head of the lab, Dr. Viktor Khorev."

At the name of Khorev, Yakov and David exchanged knowing glances, and David became obviously excited.

"You knew Viktor?" Dmitri asked.

Yakov shook his head. "I suppose you know he's dead."

Dmitri nodded sadly. "It was big news in my country several months ago ...some congress that met near San Francisco to discuss a world government... and all the delegates from around the world were killed when someone set off a bomb. I saw Viktor's name on the list of victims...."

"It's now being said that he set the bomb," said David.

"I knew Viktor very well. He would never do anything like that!" declared Dmitri firmly. "It was hinted in the papers that the installation that was destroyed had been involved in psychic research. That was Viktor's life. He would never destroy anything... but certainly not a facility involved in psychic research!"

"We don't believe he did it, either," continued David, "and you may have the information that could clear your friend's name. So keep going. How did the patient know about you and the lab where you worked?"

"Claimed he'd seen it all on a large screen in an auditorium... projected from a video. He said a certain Del Sasso, a monk who wore a hooded robe—and that was very significant to me—had made the video with his mind...."

Again Yakov and David glanced knowingly at one another in elation.

"I'll never forget an experiment," continued Dmitri, "where we saw this hooded man... it must be the same one... projected onto a screen in our lab. The image came from the mind of one of our psychics, who was supposedly out of his body probing a CIA installation in Washington. In fact, the patient, Thalberg, seemed to be describing that very psychic and that exact experiment...."

"This is incredible!" broke in David. "You can't imagine what this means. But keep going. The psychic was out of his body, you say, probing a CIA installation?"

"That's what we thought. I've since become convinced that he wasn't out of his body at all, but that a demon was projecting the images into his brain. I think the whole thing was demonic... and this monk seemed to be the focus of incredible Satanic powers. Khorev was convinced that this hooded figure was the one who killed several of our psychics."

Yakov poked David good-naturedly and gave him an I-told-you-so look. To Dmitri he said, "My friend's skeptical about demons... but he'll come around." Then on a more serious note he added, "I'm afraid your friend Viktor fell victim to 'the hooded one' as well."

"I pleaded with him... and warned him before he left for Paris that he needed God's protection... but it has haunted me that I didn't tell him about Jesus. I was a new believer and hardly knew how...."

"Now about the defection," interjected David uncomfortably. "Could you tell us about that?"

"Well, Viktor—that's Dr. Khorev—was convinced that some ETIs without bodies were providing the American psychics with power that our psychics weren't able to tap into. In those days, before Marxism got thrown out of the former Soviet Union, you couldn't even suggest anything that might challenge what was proudly called 'scientific materialism.' But Viktor was determined to pursue that line of research... so he decided to defect to the West at a conference in Paris."

"That's where Carla Inman says she rescued him from Chernov, on the streets of Paris, and got him to safety at the U.S. embassy," David told Yakov. "And Del Sasso says it was a setup!"

Turning to Dmitri, David asked, "You're sure Colonel Chernov didn't help him defect? I want to be absolutely certain about that."

Dmitri looked puzzled. "I already told Yakov... Chernov was Khorev's bitterest enemy. So where you got the idea that Chernov would help Khorev, I don't know, but it's insane."

"So Del Sasso's the liar!" declared Yakov triumphantly. David nodded grimly.

"There's no doubt that Thalberg saw me in my lab," continued Dmitri in a puzzled tone. "But how that was possible is a mystery to me. The video... I don't understand that. He says he saw it on a giant screen in an auditorium just before—and these are his exact words—'All hell broke loose.'"

"That was the congress Ari attended!" exclaimed Yakov.

"Exactly," said David, turning off the tape recorder.

"Thank you *very* much!" he told Dmitri gratefully. "You may have saved a man's life... at least his sanity. Not a word of this, now, to anyone. Can we count on you for that?"

"Absolutely. Keeping a secret for my friend Viktor got me thrown in the Gulag... but I'd do it again."

Once outside and back in Yakov's car, David confided to the old man, "I can tell you for certain that the Chief—and Margolins and the other psychiatrists—won't want to hear this, even if we could prove it. Our only chance to do that would be to involve Dmitri. I still don't think they'd accept it... and that kind man might end up an inmate, too."

"I agree. So what do we do?"

"How we handle this situation from now on," replied David thoughtfully, "... that's the real problem. But I may have some ideas."

50

Out of the Night

"Can you be in the lobby of the King David in 30 minutes?" The urgency was apparent as soon as Yakov heard the voice on the other end of the line.

"Ah, David... I was just getting ready to go out to visit Ari. What's up?"

"This is related. I'll see you at the King David!" There was no hiding the suppressed excitement in his friend's voice.

When Yakov arrived, he saw David standing in a far corner of the crowded lobby engaged in close conversation with a sandy-haired American in his late forties. Rather tall and of muscular build, the man's military bearing seemed obvious, in spite of the tennis shorts and flowered sportshirt he was wearing.

"Meet my friend, Don Jordan," said David as Yakov approached. "Don, this is Yakov Kimchy. He shared his apartment with Thalberg... until this incredible scandal that makes me ashamed of my colleagues at the office."

"So good to meet you, Yakov," said Jordan warmly, reaching out to shake his hand. "I've heard a lot about you from David."

"And I've never heard a word about you...." Yakov gave David a sharp look of reproof. Why would he be speaking so freely in front of this stranger!

"Relax, you old war horse," said David. "I've known Don for at least 25 years. Goes back to Vietnam. We were a couple of young bucks then. I was military attaché at our embassy in Saigon—and he was at U.S. Military Intelligence headquarters. We had a close relationship... learned to trust one another. He's with the FBI now and a good friend of Ken and Carla Inman. And—how about this—they attend the same prayer meeting."

Yakov's face lit up with a sheepish grin. "Sorry, brother." He reached out and shook Jordan's hand again, this time with great enthusiasm.

"Can't even find a place to sit down in here," complained David apologetically. "So we'll just stand. Now down to business. Don just 'happens' to be here with a group of Christians on a tour of Israel. We're old friends, so it doesn't matter who sees me with him. We had dinner together last night, went over the whole thing. I told him about Dmitri and gave him a copy of the tape. He agrees we've got to get Ari out—fast."

"Thank God!" exclaimed Yakov. "What can I do?"

"Plenty. But first, why don't you give us your end of it," said David, turning to Jordan.

"It's doubtful that we'll ever stop Del Sasso—but we've at least got to try. The first consideration is Thalberg's safety. He's a key witness. Both our governments have been compromised, so for the moment at least we have to work outside the law. There's a whole network inside both the CIA and FBI that knows the truth and will sacrifice everything for it. And I understand there's a faction within the Mossad. . . ." He turned to David for confirmation.

David nodded. "No problem. I'm not the only one. . . ."

"Now what I'm responsible for," Jordan continued, "is to provide Ari—and Miriam, of course—with new identities and protection at a safe location in the United States. Unfortunately, if she didn't change her identity, Ari could be traced through her—so they could never get together. Within a week . . . I don't think I can do it any faster than that . . . David will have from me, for each of them, two sets of U.S. passports, driver's licenses, social security and credit cards, and airline tickets, with detailed instructions and disguises to match their doctored photos. Ari and Miriam will use set number three for their flight from Frankfurt to Chicago. They'll use set number four from Chicago to . . . well, at this moment I don't know what that destination will be, but it will be identified when you get the documents."

"I'll also provide two similar sets of Israeli passports and papers and disguises," added David. "Ari and Miriam will fly under one set of names from Tel Aviv to Rome, and under different identities from Rome to Frankfurt. Then, of course, under their American identities from there on. Four different identities on four different airlines should make it impossible to pick up the trail."

"And my job?" asked Yakov.

"From now on, you won't talk to Dmitri inside the hospital even if you happen to come into contact when you're visiting Ari. Watch for him this afternoon when he gets off work and pick him up in your car. Make certain you're not observed. Explain that you won't be talking to him any more in the hospital, but you'll be picking him up every afternoon—and that tomorrow he must make a complete list of the medications they're giving Ari and an exact description of the containers of each kind . . . and give you a sample of each pill. The next day you'll pass on duplicate containers of sugar pills, which Dmitri will substitute the following day. That's three days from now. On the fourth day, when you visit Ari, his head should be starting to clear. You'll explain what's happening and that he must continue to act disoriented and drugged. We'll have something in the placebos to keep his eyes dilated. You've got that?"

"Got it."

"We've already made the ECT equipment break down twice. It's in for repairs now—and I'll make sure it isn't fixed until Ari's gone," continued David. "That takes care of the easy part. Getting him out of there without anyone sounding an alarm for at least five hours is not going to be so simple. Now here's what we're going to do. . . ."

—✦—

True to his word, one week later Jordan delivered the American passports and other identification documents and airline tickets. They came by diplomatic pouch to the U.S. embassy in Tel Aviv in the name of a senior staff member who was part of Jordan's network. He, in turn, passed them on secretly to a *katsa*, Yehuda Cohen, to whom David had already delivered the phony Israeli passports and Alitalia tickets to Rome and the Lufthansa tickets on to Frankfurt. Yehuda would be the driver who would take Ari and Miriam to the airport, provided everything went according to plan.

Dmitri had performed like a professional snoop. His last task was completed without a hitch: replacing the placebos with the original medications. David had insisted upon that additional move as a safeguard for Dmitri. The crucial drug substitutions would be one phase of the operation that the ensuing investigation would never uncover.

For a number of reasons, not the least of which were the airline schedules, it had been decided to pull off Ari's escape during the day rather than under cover of darkness—but not during Dmitri's shift. That dictated the means to be used. Dmitri left the hospital at about 3:10 P.M. At 3:30 two *katsas* in disguise and with fake Mossad IDs—Yehuda Cohen and Josef Burg—entered the hospital. They presented the nurse in charge with orders signed by Dr. Margolins, the chief psychiatrist. Ari was to be taken to his office for a special battery of tests that were estimated to take about five hours. Margolins had already called an hour earlier for the patient to be dressed in his street clothes. Cohen and Burg handcuffed Ari and left with him immediately.

When Ari was shoved into the back seat of the waiting car, there, to his great joy, were David on the far side, with a key to unlock his handcuffs, and Miriam between them laughing and crying at the same time. Their embrace, after six months of separation, had to be brief. David saw to that. There was no time to waste.

"How are you feeling, Ari?" asked David brusquely.

"Not back to normal by a long shot, but much better," came the reply. He looked eagerly from Miriam to the passing street scene as the car sped away. "What a relief when those shock treatments ended! You can't imagine what it's like in there. And then—the drugs! What a change when I started getting placebos!"

"Great! Now both of you pay close attention. Your passports and other IDs have your own photos, but doctored up to change your appearance. You each have four different identities—one for each time you board a new plane—and each set is in a packet numbered from one to four and also labeled with the cities of flight origin and destination. On your last flight from Chicago to Denver there's no passport control or customs, so you can relax—but just be sure you remember your latest names."

Yehuda, who was driving, pulled over to the curb. Josef jumped out and walked into an office building as Yehuda drove on. "Dr. Margolins' office is in there on the third floor," explained David. "Ari may remember him...he's the chief psychiatrist...."

"Do I ever!" exclaimed Ari. "He's the fiend who put me in that torture chamber!"

"He and a few others," said David dryly. "Well, he was 'persuaded'—with a gun at his head—to call the hospital and then to sign a release for Ari to come to his office for some tests. Josef's going up to help the other two make sure everything stays under control for the next six hours until you're safely in Rome. It was a bit complicated. Two appointments and a dinner engagement had to be cancelled...explanation to his wife...receptionist and nurse replaced with our people for the afternoon...but that's routine stuff.

"He'll be released about 10:00 P.M.—with the threat that Ari is only the first, and that unless he reviews some of the other cases under his care there will be more vigilante action. Our people are identifying themselves as members of the Citizens Committee to End Psychiatric Abuse. We've had a few flyers and brochures printed up with that name on them and dropped around town the last few days. That will give them something to worry about...and hopefully sidetrack them from thinking that the people behind this operation are interested primarily in you, Ari."

David put a briefcase on Ari's lap and showed him how to open the two false compartments, one on top and one on the bottom. From the bottom compartment he pulled out a flat plastic container marked #1. "Now, here's packet number one. As you can see from the photos in the passports, Ari, you'll have to put on this mustache and these heavy eyebrows, put these four marbles into your mouth, two on each side, to fatten your cheeks, and wear these plain glasses with heavy, black rims at all times. Miriam, false eyebrows and eyelashes for you as well, a red wig, makeup and these large glasses. Look at your names. You're Ygal and Aerni Yaar on this phase, which is the toughest one.

"I'm not going into the terminal with you," continued David. "Yehuda's disguised so he'll help you in with your baggage and point you out to our man in customs, who'll take you through. Hopefully without problems. Then you're on your own. The flight leaves in one hour."

"Where's Yakov?" asked Ari.

"He wanted to be here to say goodbye, but that would have made it too complicated. Every additional element raises the danger of detection ten times. He wanted me to give you this as a wedding present. He apologized for not having time to wrap it. Anyway, he wanted you to use it right away."

David held out a Bible and Ari took it gratefully. "Thank him for me!" said Ari. "I hated to leave the first Bible I ever owned—Yakov gave me that one too. I'd underlined it...made notes in the margin...was getting familiar with it, but of course I couldn't bring it."

Ari noticed something sticking out of the pages and opened it there. The marker was an American $100 bill. Underlined on the page in red were these words:

> And you shall remember all the way which the Lord your God has led you in the wilderness these forty years, that He might humble you, testing you, to know what was in your heart, whether you would keep His commandments or not.
>
> And He humbled you and let you be hungry, and fed you with manna which you did not know... that He might make you understand that man does not live by bread alone, but man lives by everything that proceeds out of the mouth of the Lord.

Ari gave Miriam another hug. There were tears in his eyes. "I'll explain why those verses later," he said in a choked voice. "They mean a lot to me."

The remainder of the brief ride to the airport was spent donning the disguises, getting used to the new feel and look, and addressing one another by their new names. Saying farewell to David was not easy. "You look after Yakov," both Ari and Miriam repeated. "We want him to come to the U.S. as soon as it's safe."

"I'll take good care of him... and hopefully that can be arranged some day."

"And you take care, too," said Ari as he reached over and gripped David's hand in both of his. "I owe you more than I can ever repay. If I had one wish, it would be that you would believe in Messiah Jesus... then I'd know we'd meet again."

"I didn't believe your story—but I do now. My apologies," returned David, holding on to Ari's hands. "Who knows... about this Jesus... maybe...." He was afraid to say any more, but Ari and Miriam understood.

— ✦ —

At Lod Airport, Ari and Miriam, alias Ygal and Aerni Yaar, got the full treatment of the world's most intense scrutiny of passengers and baggage. If they attracted any extra attention at all it was because of the affection they obviously had for each other. The practiced eyes of the hardened officials who saw all kinds and could spot a phony at a glance had no doubt that this pair was genuinely in love—and probably on their honeymoon.

The thoroughness of airport security was reassuring in one sense, but they both knew they could not relax—in spite of their disguises and the Mossad agent carefully shepherding them through—until they were aloft. "Thank you, Lord!" Ari breathed inwardly as they boarded.

Once the plane was airborne, Ari and Miriam held each other tightly in a long embrace. Then they settled back in their seats, Miriam's head on Ari's shoulder. *Honeymooners, obviously*—was the verdict written in the eyes of more than one sympathetic passenger seated nearby.

"Isn't God good!" Miriam whispered. Ari could only nod and squeeze her hands. "I think Yakov protected me by not saying how bad it really was at the hospital... but I suspected the worst, and prayed for your deliverance day and night. I really believed that God was going to do it... and here we are!" She snuggled up closer.

It took Ari some time to get control of his voice. "They came within a hair of breaking me," he said quietly. "But you know, I believe even that horrifying experience was part of God's plan. The first time I read the Bible through I came to the words of Jesus, 'Except you deny yourself and take up the cross and follow me, you can't be my disciple,' and it was like a revelation. I *knew* that my real problem wasn't the many enemies I'd faced in my life. I was my own worst enemy—always looking out for myself. And I said, 'Lord, right now I give up my own plans, my ambitions... even Miriam'—darling, I really said that—'I give myself to you to do with me what you will.' And since that moment I've had a peace and joy that I wouldn't trade for anything this world could offer!"

"I loved you with a passion before," said Miriam softly, "but I love you even more now. I made the same vow many years ago, and I've been waiting for God to give me the man He had chosen—a man who wanted nothing but His will. Oh, how He's answered that prayer, Ari, my dearest love!"

With a heart too full for words, Ari pressed her hands to his lips. Now at last he could relax, fall asleep from the overpowering weariness he felt, beside the woman he loved. They were in God's hands—together.

51

Rendezvous

"What happens if the police are waiting for us?" asked Miriam. Looking down from clear skies at the menacing smog bank shrouding Rome's Leonardo da Vinci Airport, she was reminded of the perils facing the two fugitives as soon as they landed. "Tel Aviv could have called by now."

"Relax," Ari admonished, putting a protective arm around her. "If we look nervous... they might take us for drug smugglers. Have a dog sniffing our bags and find that kosher sausage," he added with a laugh.

"I'll just hang on to your arm and look like I'm in love. How's that?"

"Great. Just try to make it convincing."

"Ari! I'm serious. Suppose the Mossad is down there waiting for this flight?"

"A month ago my primary resource would have been my martial arts expertise, quick wit and whatever," confessed Ari, "but now we're in God's hands. If we're arrested... well, we'll trust Him to work it out. But I don't think the Mossad has a clue where to look... and they can't watch every arriving flight in every airport in the world. David's planned this thing too well...."

Indeed, there was no sign of either the police or the Mossad when they entered the terminal. "Aren't we in transit?" asked Miriam with concern. "Why are we heading for baggage and customs?"

"You and I are continuing on to Frankfurt and Chicago," Ari reminded her in a low voice, "but Ygal and Aerni Yaar are stopping over in Rome... forever. We become someone else here—remember?"

The records would show that Ygal and Aerni Yaar picked up their suitcases at the baggage claim and were cleared through customs. "You didn't fill in your address in Rome," observed the rather officious middle-aged woman whom they found themselves facing in passport control.

"Thought we might rent a car," replied Ari casually. "Head up to Florence and Venice first—maybe Switzerland, the Italian lakes—then back to Rome later."

"Better get reservations right away," suggested the matron as she stamped their passports after verifying their pictures. "Everything's crowded this time of year."

"Thanks. We probably should," said "Ygal."

Following the markers to "Ground Transportation," Ygal and Aerni exited the terminal, approached a taxi, seemed to remember they'd forgotten something, and reentered by another door.

"So much for that charade," said Ari, looking at his watch. "We've got almost three hours to wander through the duty-free shops, relax, change, and destroy everything belonging to Ygal and Aerni. We're Yetsak and Deborah Vanunu now—until we get to Frankfurt."

Seating themselves in an isolated corner of the main terminal, Ari and Miriam familiarized themselves with their new identities. Addressing one another by their new names, they rehearsed the brief written history of Yetsak and Deborah as to date and place of birth and other general information that was included with the passports, driver's licenses and credit cards. These were all found neatly arranged in packet two when Ari took it from the false bottom in the briefcase.

While occupied with this transformation, Miriam tore up the receipts for their Alitalia tickets and bent and twisted Ygal and Aerni's credit cards until each was in four pieces. With a razor blade provided for that purpose, Ari shredded the passports and driver's licenses they were abandoning. Then while he deposited the fragments in three different trash containers, Miriam took the plastic bag containing everything involved in the disguises they'd worn, walked to a far section of the terminal and scattered the contents of the plastic bag among three trash containers there.

The half-hour rental of shower cubicles provided the privacy for their second change of identity. Like those being abandoned, their new disguises, prepared by a Mossad specialist, were minimal, yet transformed their appearances remarkably. Those provided through Don Jordan by an FBI makeup expert for the last two legs of their journey would prove to be equally creative.

It was a grueling trip, with two otherwise unnecessary stops on the way to Chicago, with yet another flight from there. David and Jordan, however, had wanted to be certain that their trail couldn't be followed. It was better to go to some extra trouble and be safe. That the Mossad, FBI and CIA would mount an intensive worldwide search for them was beyond question.

"This is like a dream," whispered Miriam, putting her head on Ari's shoulder as their jet lifted off on its way to Frankfurt's International Airport. "I still can't believe it's happening!"

"*You* can't? Imagine how I feel... after a lifetime of demons playing their games with my mind! That psychiatric ward was just the climax. It's like waking up from a nightmare. I don't recognize myself. I really *am* a new person!"

Miriam was silent for a few moments. At last she sat upright and half-turned in her seat to look squarely at Ari. "Does it bother you at all that we're outlaws now... fugitives, with false identities that we'll have to keep up, maybe for the rest of our lives?"

"It bothers *you*, doesn't it."

She nodded. "It seems so dishonest."

"I'm not happy about it... but what other choice was there? I had to get out of Israel. And it's the only way for us to be together. You know that."

"Yes, I know. But I pray God we don't have to hide from the police forever. How can we raise a family?"

"Hear comes the bride...," he intoned rather loudly.

"Hush!" exclaimed Miriam. "You're embarrassing me."

Ari smiled contentedly. "I don't know how it's going to be arranged, but I'm insisting on wedding bells as soon as we get where we're going... wherever that is."

"I thought we were going to Denver."

"That's right. But I think we go on by car... somewhere in the mountains, maybe."

"They didn't tell us?" Miriam's voice betrayed her fear of the unknown. "What do we do?"

"Relax, love. They've brought us this far. They won't abandon us now."

After another pause in the conversation, Miriam said, "Speaking of starting a family... what about your son?"

"You heard me give David all the details," said Ari wistfully. "He'll try to find him and see what can be done. His foster parents are real Christians. When they hear that I'm a believer... I'll just have to trust God for all that," he finished with a sigh.

— ✦ —

Again a change of disguises, destruction and disposal of past identifying documents, and substitution of airlines. It was all accomplished smoothly at Frankfurt's International Airport and then once more at Chicago's O'Hare.

"I'm so tired and confused at this point," commented Miriam after they were safely aboard their United Airlines flight from Chicago to Denver, "that if someone asked my name there's no telling what I might say. I don't know who I am anymore."

"We're naturalized American citizens now," returned Ari with a yawn. "That means we've got lots of rights. Just tell them you're taking the Fifth Amendment...."

"You still have to give your name, silly!" She looked at him and couldn't believe her eyes. He had dropped off to sleep.

— ✦ —

It was a weary pair, now alias Marty and Sara Berg, that found themselves at last, more than 30 hours after leaving Tel Aviv, lugging their carry-ons up the jetway into Denver's Stapleton International Airport. "We made it!" exclaimed Miriam under her breath as they came out into the terminal and turned doggedly toward the baggage carousels to retrieve their suitcases. "I hope it's not a long drive on top of all this!"

"Whatever... it will be worth it to finally get to a safe place and stop running."

They had walked scarcely 50 feet from their arrival gate when a tall, broad-shouldered man seemed to appear from nowhere at Ari's side. His deep voice quietly intoned the dread words, "Ari Thalberg and Miriam Zeira... you're under arrest!"

Miriam stiffened, gasped and clutched Ari's instantly tense arm more tightly.

"Keep walking and act natural," the voice continued.

Miriam felt Ari relax. With an audible sigh of relief he whispered, "We're okay. It's the code phrase that identifies our contact."

"You...! Why didn't you tell me?"

"I forgot. Sorry."

"When you exit with your baggage," continued the low voice beside them, speaking rapidly, "you'll find a new, dark gray, 4-door Buick Century just outside, license number MGJ 148. The keys in packet four will fit. A map with instructions is in the glove compartment." With those welcome words, the man was gone.

They found the car without incident. It was parked at the curb about 100 feet from where they exited the baggage area. Just as the voice beside them had promised, the dark gray sedan was brand new and the keys in packet four, which Ari had wondered about, did indeed fit.

"Map... instructions... it's all here," said Miriam happily, having opened the glove compartment while Ari started the engine. "And there's a key to a house... on Clover Lane in Boulder! Doesn't look too far... less than two hours, I'd think."

"You're going to have to keep me awake," warned Ari, peering intently into the rearview mirror as he pulled slowly out into the traffic. "Looks good. No one's following. Which way do I go?"

"Just follow the traffic around, then straight ahead until you're outside the airport. Take the first right at the main intersection. That's going to be Quebec Street. Stay on that to I-70 going west... and I'll guide you from there onto the Denver-Boulder Turnpike... that's Highway 36."

It was a crystal clear, sunny afternoon with none of the smog that increasingly plagued the Denver area. The visibility was almost unlimited. Once away from the city and on the Turnpike, the view opened up to the west.

"Get your nose out of the map and take a look at those snowcapped peaks straight ahead!" exclaimed Ari. "That could almost be the French or Swiss Alps... or maybe Southern Germany. Magnificent! Is that where we're heading?"

"It is *beautiful*," responded Miriam, looking up from the map. "Nothing like this in Israel! No, we're not going up into the mountains. Boulder seems to lie just this side at the base of the Rockies... that's what they're called. It's not as far as I thought. Another 40 minutes, maybe."

—✦—

"There's the number, on the mailbox!" exclaimed Miriam with suppressed excitement when at last Ari had turned the car onto Clover Lane and they were driving slowly along the semirural street. The houses were on large lots and surrounded by open fields. The view, looking down upon the city of Boulder a few miles in the distance with the Rockies towering above, was magnificent. The dashboard clock indicated a few minutes past 4:30 P.M.

"That's an automatic door opener," said Miriam as Ari pulled into the driveway and the car rolled toward the two-car garage that was attached to the beautifully landscaped, rambling, ranch-style house that spread out to the right. She pointed to the device clipped to the visor over his head. "There. Push the button."

"There's a car in there!" muttered Ari in surprise as the garage door slowly opened. "What does that mean?"

"Maybe there's a car for each of us," suggested Miriam.

"I don't think so. Somebody's here. I don't like the looks of this! The instructions say the house isn't occupied." He backed the car away from the garage toward the street. "Wouldn't that be something if we've come all this way...."

"Now you're the one who's paranoid," suggested Miriam. "Maybe it's an extra car left by the owners. The house must belong to somebody."

"You stay here," cautioned Ari. "I'll go check it out."

Cautiously Ari went up the walk that led from the driveway and climbed the steps onto the broad, covered porch. He walked noiselessly past a large window, apparently of the living room, to reach the front door on the other side. The drapes were drawn, preventing him from seeing inside. Silently he put the key into the lock and turned it.

The door was wrenched open from within and in the ensuing confusion Ari was aware of strong arms gripping his shoulders and of two voices, both vaguely familiar, shouting meaningless phrases. Was it after all to end like this in bitter failure?

"Ari, man, it's me—Ken Inman!"

"You're here! Oh, glory!" exclaimed another voice. It was Carla!

Reeling with the emotional impact, Ari gave way to the hugs and exclamations of joy. "Is this your house?" he asked. "I thought you lived in California ...near Stanford University."

"We do," explained Ken. "We're just the welcoming committee."

"Where's Miriam?" demanded Carla.

"In the car," returned Ari happily. "We saw your car in the garage... and I was a bit concerned. Am I glad to see you!"

"Well, we can't leave her out there!" Carla was already out the door.

"What a wonderful surprise!" exclaimed Ari. "I hoped we'd somehow get to see you and Carla...but I had no idea it would be so soon."

"You can't imagine how we've been looking forward to this. Wouldn't have missed it for anything. From what we've heard, it's a miracle you made it after what you've been through! Anyway...God has answered our prayers."

Carla burst through the doo· with Miriam in tow. "Miriam, this is my husband, Ken."

Wiping tears of joy from her eyes, Miriam looked dazed. "I'm having trouble believing this is really happening." She clung to Ari. "Darling, we made it!"

"You two must be absolutely wiped out!" said Ken sympathetically. "How did it go?"

"Perfect," replied Ari gratefully. "A smooth operation all the way. And the car, and this house...who set that up...your friend Jordan?"

Ken nodded. "Some wealthy Christian is covering the rent on both of them ...and any other expenses...as long as necessary. And even he doesn't know where this house is located."

"Jordan did a fabulous job. I sure hope we can thank him personally someday."

"You will...he plans to be here for the wedding."

Ari gave Miriam another hug. "Did you hear that, darling? There's going to be a wedding! I wonder whose it could be?"

"Okay, practical matters," interrupted Carla. "While you men bring in the suitcases, I'll show Miriam her room...and the rest of the house."

"We want to hear all about everything...tomorrow after you've had a good night's rest," said Ken as together they went outside and headed for the car.

"It's so incredible to be here!" As he spoke, Ari was quickly searching the neighborhood with practiced eyes. In spite of his euphoria, his years of experience wouldn't let him forget security concerns. "Sure you weren't followed here?" he asked Ken.

"Absolutely. Some of Jordan's men escorted us for the first 100 miles to make sure no one was on our tail...and they were satisfied. Nobody's been watching us since the Senate gave its verdict two weeks ago."

"I never heard about that."

"Branded us both as liars...but won't prosecute us. They're afraid of what we'd say in open court. But with the way the powers that be fooled the media...and the way it's been reported...we've been thoroughly discredited. The enemy doesn't think we're a threat anymore. Of course, they would have had us under surveillance the moment it was known you were missing," added Ken. "That's why Jordan told us to come over here two days ago. And we're not going to show ourselves anywhere until we're ready to go home. Then Jordan's men will cover us again."

"I can hardly wait to hear Carla's story...and yours, too. I understand you confronted Del Sasso a few times and shut down his demonic powers. I'd like to hear about that!"

"I didn't...God did it. We've got a ton of things to talk about...."

Back in the house with the suitcases deposited on the living room floor, Ari put an arm around Miriam. "When's the wedding, darling?"

"How about tomorrow?" she replied ecstatically.

"That's a bit soon," laughed Ken. "Lots of details....Tomorrow you get your marriage license...as Marty and Sara Berg, unfortunately, but one day that'll get straightened out. We planned the wedding for Saturday...if that's okay. That's four days from now. Gives time for some other guests to fly in...."

"Other guests?" said Ari and Miriam in unison, looking at each other questioningly. "Who did you invite?" Ari asked his bride-to-be. She shrugged and looked questioningly at Ken and Carla.

"There'll be a few," said Ken cryptically, "maybe even a surprise or two...."

"Now," said Carla firmly, taking charge, "while Ken helps get your bags into your rooms, I'll fix a quick supper. We can talk a bit...and then I know you two must be wiped out and want to get to bed early. You could probably sleep around the clock, so try to stay awake until I've put something on the table, okay?"

Epilogue

The days before the wedding passed quickly. Much that had been puzzling was clarified as the four friends spent long hours talking—sometimes in quiet sorrow for things past or regretted, sometimes in exuberant and joyous laughter as they rehearsed the ways in which God had led them to this hour. The tragic death of Viktor at the hands of an Archon after Carla had half-carried him out of the disintegrating auditorium and pleaded with him to accept Christ was discussed with great sorrow.

Carla's account of her surrender to Christ and how He rescued her from the Nine brought great joy. The diabolically clever rehabilitation of Del Sasso and the probable increasing persecution of Christ's followers in the near future as the New World Order was established was discussed with concern.

The discovery by an FBI-led geological search team, following Ari's description of key landmarks, of the underground cavern honeycombing the mountain beneath the ruins of the research complex (thus corroborating Ari's story) laid to rest some of the nagging questions which had plagued them. For the rest, they must trust the One who had proven Himself, as of old, the God of Abraham, Isaac and Jacob, and whose promises would not fail.

Still to come would be the hearing before a newly formed Senate committee at which two surprise witnesses would appear. The first would be Dmitri Petrekov, on leave from his job at the psychiatric hospital in Tel Aviv and flown in from Israel. He would testify that he had known Viktor Khorev intimately, that Viktor had indeed planned to defect in Paris, that Colonel Chernov had attempted to prevent it and, upon his return from Paris, had arrested him, Dmitri, for not revealing his knowledge of Viktor's plans. It would be firmly established that Chernov was Khorev's bitterest enemy, and the idea that they could have been working together for the destruction of the CIA lab was preposterous.

But the witness who turned the tide would be retired Red Army General Nikolai Gorky, former chairman of the Kremlin's Committee Overseeing Psychic Warfare Research. Working as a taxi driver in Moscow, he would be located by Jordan on a tip from Dmitri. Gorky would testify that as Colonel Chernov's superior he had sent him to bring Khorev under arrest back to the Soviet Union and to destroy the secret CIA lab where Khorev worked.

The Senate committee would have no choice but to exonerate Carla from the previous charge that she and Khorev had conspired to destroy the installation. That would still leave unanswered the question as to the cause of the astonishing destruction. Of course it could not be attributed to the Nine, whose existence was officially denied, and who, secretly, were still in contact with a number of very powerful leaders in Washington through Del Sasso. The latter, untarnished even by the new testimony, would remain a hero. His newly formed Shamans Unlimited would literally explode internationally, and its "success-motivation" seminars would demonize increasing millions under the guise of leading them into "personal empowerment."

With the discovery of the cavern, the Mossad would be forced to admit the truthfulness of at least that much of Ari's testimony. That he was a follower of Jesus, however, and not yet an Israeli citizen, would bar him from a return to Israel. That land, a sanctuary for the chosen people flooding into it from around the world, was now closed to him because he was a believer in the most famous and influential Israeli who had ever lived. The contradiction was incomprehensible.

After years of preparation, the Nine had brought Ari to Israel to fulfill their own diabolical end—a purpose for which he'd been chosen by them at birth. But there was Another who had His own plans and had turned evil into good. Looking back with gratitude now, Ari could see where, in spite of his own rebellion, God's hand had intervened repeatedly in his life and had patiently drawn him to Himself. In that promised land, he had finally acknowledged himself to be a son of Israel—and had become a son of God. There, too, he had met Miriam. Surely they had a destiny to fulfill together.

— ✦ —

On October 20, Ari and Miriam, alias Marty and Sara Berg, were married by Don Jordan in a quiet ceremony in the living room of the house in Boulder that had become their new sanctuary. In addition to Ken and Carla, there were three other guests—Dr. and Mrs. Pierre Duclos and little Ari Paul, now almost five years old. True to his word, David had located them in a Paris suburb and they had made immediate arrangements to come. Shyly, the little boy had held his father's hand during the brief ceremony.

It was agreed at the wedding that as soon as Ari's legal status was established, Pierre and Francoise Duclos would bring the child back to take his place as Ari's son.

At the close of the ceremony, Jordan had read aloud a special wedding telegram sent through him by Yakov. It said simply:

The Lord hear thee in the day of trouble;
the name of the God of Jacob defend thee;
Send thee help from the sanctuary, and
strengthen thee out of Zion;
Now know I that the Lord saveth his anointed;
he will hear him from his holy heaven with
with the saving strength of his right hand.

—Psalm 20:1,2,6